Susan Meier is the author of over fifty books for Mills & Boon. *The Tycoon's Secret Daughter* was a Romance Writers of America RITA® Award finalist, and *Nanny for the Millionaire's Twins* won the Book Buyers' Best award and was a finalist in the National Readers' Choice awards. She is married and has three children. One of eleven children herself, she loves to write about the complexity of families and totally believes in the power of love.

Melissa Senate has written many novels for Mills & Boon and other publishers, including her debut, *See Jane Date*, which was made into a TV movie. She also wrote seven books for Mills & Boon under the pen name Meg Maxwell. Her novels have been published in over twenty-five countries. Melissa lives on the coast of Maine with her teenage son, their rescue shepherd mix, Flash, and a lap cat named Cleo. For more information, please visit her website, melissasenate.com.

Also by Susan Meier

A Mistletoe Kiss with the Boss
The Boss's Fake Fiancée
The Spanish Millionaire's Runaway Bride

The Princes of Xaviera miniseries
Pregnant with a Royal Baby!
Wedded for His Royal Duty

Manhattan Babies miniseries
Carrying the Billionaire's Baby

And look out for the next book
Coming soon

Also by Melissa Senate

Detective Barelli's Legendary Triplets
The Baby Switch!

As Meg Maxwell
Santa's Seven-Day Baby Tutorial
Charm School for Cowboy
The Cook's Secret Ingredient
The Cowboy's Big Family Tree
The Detective's 8 lb, 10 oz Surprise
A Cowboy in the Kitchen
Mommy and the Maverick
Whose Wedding Is It Anyway?

Discover more at millsandboon.co.uk

CARRYING
THE BILLIONAIRE'S
BABY

SUSAN MEIER

THE MAVERICK'S
BABY-IN-WAITING

MELISSA SENATE

MIX
Paper from
responsible sources
FSC
FSC® C007454

This book is produced from independently certified FSC™
paper to ensure responsible forest management.

For more information visit: www.harpercollins.co.uk/green

Printed and bound in Spain
by CPI, Barcelona

MILLS & BOON

First Published in Great Britain 2018
by Mills & Boon, an imprint of HarperCollinsPublishers,
1 London Bridge Street, London, SE1 9GF

Carrying the Billionaire's Baby © 2018 Linda Susan Meier
The Maverick's Baby-in-Waiting © 2018 Harlequin Books S.A.

Special thanks and acknowledgement to Melissa Senate for her contribution
to the Montana Mavericks: The Lonelyhearts Ranch continuity.

ISBN: 978-0-263-26516-3

0818

CARRYING
THE BILLIONAIRE'S
BABY

SUSAN MEIER

For my friend, Di.
My partner in crime on the golf course.

CHAPTER ONE

JACOB MCCALLAN STRODE down the quiet hall of Waters, Waters and Mont–gomery—the law firm employed by his family—with tall, lanky Pete Waters, senior partner.

"So, how's your mother holding up?"

Jake glanced at Pete, not surprised he'd asked. His father had died five months before and everyone was worried about his mom. "She's working to pull herself together. Some days are better than others."

"Rumor has it she headed the last board of directors meeting."

Jake grimaced. Nobody was supposed to know about that, but Pete had sources everywhere. Jake chose his words carefully. "She tried."

"Tried?"

"It was no big deal. She walked into the meeting saying she wasn't ready to be put out to pasture and would assume Dad's role as chairman of the board. I took her out of the conference room and privately told her that the corporate bylaws name the CEO as acting chairman."

"You."

He nodded. "Me. I told her that if we went against the bylaws, we risked being sued by shareholders."

"How'd she take it?"

"She was a bit confused. A bit hurt. I think she believed taking over as chairman would give her something to do now that Dad's gone."

Pete took a long, slow breath and blew it out in a gust. "That's rough."

Painter's scaffolding crowded the end of the private corridor to Pete's office. He pointed to the right. "We'll go the long way."

The "long way" took them past cubicles filled with workers on the phone or frantically typing on computer keyboards, then a file room. A wall of windows exposed rows of files—thinner than they had been before most things were stored on computers—and five copy machines.

Jake frowned and slowed his steps. *Was that Avery Novak standing in front of one of those copy machines?*

He couldn't really tell because the tall redhead's back was to him. But a man didn't forget silky hair long enough to tickle his chest when she straddled him.

He told himself to keep walking. He and Avery had had a short fling, which she'd mercifully broken off after three weeks. They'd been dynamite in bed. But out of bed? They would have done nothing but argue about politics and principles if Jake had ever risen to any of her bait. The woman was ridiculously headstrong, and she didn't like rich people.

No matter how hot they were together, he had looked down the board and seen a future filled with her being critical of his privileged lifestyle, and in general acting as if he were Marie Antoinette and she was a beleaguered peasant. His only regret was that *he* hadn't been the one to break it off.

Jake and Pete were just about at the end of the long glass wall, when she turned. Her huge green eyes widened. Her mouth fell open and she quickly lowered the file she held to her stomach. But it was too late. He'd seen the baby bump.

Baby bump!

She had to be at least five months pregnant. Maybe six. *Oh, God... Six?*

That took them back to February—when they were dating.

That could be his baby. *His child.*

He glanced at Avery again. Her figure hadn't changed much except for the baby bump, yet she'd looked more womanly, more attractive. He remembered her soapy and sexy in the shower, added the baby bump to the naked body he knew so well, and something raw and emotional ripped through him. Stronger than lust, more profound than awe that they'd created a child, the feeling rendered him speechless. The reality that that "bump" could be *his child* slammed into him like an eighteen-wheeler, mostly because his father had been a terrible parent. He had no idea how a good dad behaved. What a good dad did—

But, no. It couldn't be his child. Avery would have told him. Wouldn't she?

He and Pete finally walked past the file room. Pete still chatted on about Jake's mother. "I understand that she's on shaky emotional ground. But you really have to hold the line with her coming into the business and trying to do things."

"Actually, I'm thinking of giving her a job."

"What?" Pete stopped walking.

Jake stopped too. "She lost her husband." A movement from the file room caught his eye and he glanced up in time to see Avery racing away. His throat constricted. His gut clenched. Why run away from him if that wasn't his child?

Embarrassment?
Maybe.
Had to be.
She was probably embarrassed she'd found another man and gotten pregnant so soon after him. Because it couldn't be his baby...
Otherwise she would have told him.

He faced Pete. "Mom's grieving. She's searching for meaning in her life. Trying to be chairman of the board proves she wants something to do. Why not give her something?"

"Because she's been a socialite for forty years and doesn't have any skills?" Pete sighed. "Jake, giving her a job is only going to make your life difficult. There are better ways to handle her grief than having her underfoot."

"I'm not sure I agree. Maybe she has skills we don't know about? Or maybe she won't even want a job? At least if I ask, she'll feel wanted."

"I think you'll be sorry."

"Perhaps. But I think I should ask. She's leaving today for a week in Paris. I thought if I offered her something, it would perk her up enough that her friends could snap her out of her depression."

"You're sure she's going?"

"She and her girlfriends have been spending the first week of September in Paris for decades." He took a brief glance up the hall, but Avery was gone. "She'll recognize she needs to be with her friends and go. Besides, there's a charity ball over the weekend that I'm attending this year. She won't miss my first time there and a chance to introduce me to her friends."

"What if she jumps on your job offer and doesn't care about going to the event?"

"A condition of her coming to work for us will be that she takes the week in Paris first."

Pete shrugged as if grudgingly agreeing with Jake's decision.

They reached Pete's office and Jake took one final glance up the hall. He didn't see Avery, but his chest tightened anyway.

As Pete droned on about fulfilling the bequests in his dad's will, Jake realized three things. First, Avery was independent enough that she could consider it her right not to tell him about his own child. Second, if that baby really was his, he was in trouble. He had no idea how to be a parent and he would need all the time he could get to figure it out before the baby was born. Which meant, number three, he was going to have to confront her.

Today.

Avery didn't get home until after nine that night. Law firm associates did all the paperwork and the bulk of the legwork on most cases. Before she'd gotten pregnant, she'd fought for the extra work. She sat in on every meeting they'd permit her to attend, and campaigned to be a part of every important case. She had a plan, with big goals, and had only allowed herself five years to get the experience she would need to start her own law firm back home in Pennsylvania. She'd had to cram in everything she could.

Then she'd started hooking up with Jake. It was wrong. From day one, she'd known it was wrong. Her dad had gone to jail for something he hadn't done because a rich employer had used his money and influence to ride roughshod over the system, and her dad couldn't afford high-priced counsel to fight him. That was why she'd become a lawyer—to be a voice for people who couldn't pay five-hundred dollars an hour to defend themselves from something they hadn't done. She couldn't date someone just like the guy who'd sent her dad to prison.

No matter how sexy Jake was, an undercurrent of privilege ran through his life. Riding in his limos, taking his helicopter to Maine for lobster, sleeping in a penthouse monitored by security guards only reminded her that people like Jake didn't know a damned thing about real life, about suffering and struggle...about being normal.

She didn't want her baby getting lost in the shuffle of drivers, maids and nannies, any more than she wanted her little girl or boy growing up thinking money somehow made her better, even as he or she stayed behind a wall of bodyguards, rode in bulletproof limos and lived with the threat of being kidnapped.

She also didn't want to risk the consequences if Jake found out her dad was an ex-con. He could demand that she stay in New York—away from her dad—or even try to take the baby. Then she'd have no way of shielding her child from the craziness of the McCallan life.

So, she'd made the decision not to tell Jake she was pregnant to protect her child. Immediately, relief had coursed through her. Joy at becoming a mom had blossomed. With Jake out of the picture, she was ready to become a parent. Sure, it changed her plans a bit. She'd be returning to Pennsylvania two years sooner than she'd thought, and without sufficient experience, but she'd adapt. She wanted this baby enough that she'd change her life any way necessary.

She kicked off her subway shoes, tossed her briefcase on a chair and headed to her bedroom, but her doorbell rang.

Closing her eyes in misery, she muttered, "Damn it."

She could ignore the bell, but she had a sneaking suspicion Jake McCallan had been sitting in a limo somewhere down the street from her building, waiting for her to come home. He'd seen her that morning. Seen the baby bump. Stickler for detail that he was, he'd undoubtedly done the math.

The bell rang again.

She headed for the door, shaking off her fears. Lawyers planned for all contingencies. Her first choice might have been not to tell him, but that didn't mean she didn't have a backup plan, a Plan B. He was a super-stuffy aristocrat, who wouldn't want a crying child in his world. All she had to do was remind him that a baby didn't fit into his well-ordered life and he'd back off.

Wondering how such a serious, stuffy guy could be so good in bed, she walked to the door and opened it. "Jake. How nice to see you."

It *was* nice to *see* him. He had black hair cut short to be neat, but strands poked out, making him look sexy and interesting. His solemn blue eyes always made her want to tell him a joke. But his body was a work of art. He could be an advertisement for the gym. Going three days a week had virtually turned him into a god. And the sex? Amazing. Just thinking about it made her weak-kneed and breathless.

He pointed at her stomach. "That's my baby, isn't it?"

She opened the door a little wider, urging him inside. "Nothing like a little small talk to warm up a room."

He stayed right where he stood. "There's no point to small talk. We have nothing to say to each other, except to discuss whether you're keeping my child from me."

"I'm not. Technically, I'm keeping a pregnancy from you."

He cursed.

"See? This is exactly why I didn't tell you!" She caught his arm and dragged him inside, leading him to one of the two teal-and-white trellis-print club chairs in front of her marble tile fireplace. Though the legs that carried her across the dark hardwood floors were extremely tired, she walked into the kitchen and took a glass from the first white cabinet then filled it at the sink in the center island. Bringing it into her living room, she said, "I knew you'd freak."

He took the water. "I'm not freaking. I'm in shock. You've known about this for months. I just found out today—and only because I ran into you. Not because you told me."

"Okay," she soothed, sitting on the white sofa across from him, keeping control of the conversation. She had to be calm, rational and appeal to his love of order in his life.

"What do you want to know?"

He looked up at her, his gorgeous blue eyes serious, direct. "How?"

She laughed. "I think you pretty much know the basics of how babies are made."

"No. How did you get pregnant? You told me you were on the pill."

The insinuation that the pregnancy was her fault rattled through her like an angry wind, but she gave him a little leeway because he was still processing all this.

"My doctor blamed the antibiotic she gave me for bronchitis. You and I met—" At a coffee shop on Valentine's Day, both dateless and treating themselves to a latte. They recognized each other from the law firm and had an impromptu dinner where he was just so charming and sexy they'd ended up in bed. "—when the bronchitis was all but gone from my lungs." She shrugged. "But while I was celebrating feeling better, I was also finishing up the meds and forgot the antibiotic's effect on birth control."

He set his untouched water on one of the coasters she had on the glass coffee table by the club chair. "I never thought to ask about antibiotics."

Her heart did a crazy little flip. Every time she was ready to write him off as sanctimonious, he'd do something like that. Something that would make her wonder if deep down he was fair. But she knew better. A man with enough money to buy his way into or out of anything had no reason to look at the other side of a situation.

Still, he hadn't blamed her for the pregnancy, so she could go back to Plan B, remind him of how much trouble a baby could be and let him bow out gracefully.

"My goal had always been to get a job at a big law firm and buy a nice condo that would go up in value as I paid down the mortgage."

His earnest blue eyes stayed on her face, as he waited for her to explain why she was rehashing things he already knew.

She cleared her throat. "What I didn't tell you was, I'd made that plan so that I could get tons of experience and learn from some of the best lawyers in the world before I sold the condo for a profit and returned to Pennsylvania to start my own law firm."

"Oh."

She wasn't surprised that she'd stunned him. Every damned time they'd gone out she'd said or done something that raised his eyebrows or caused him to frown.

Their problem wasn't merely a case of a middle-class woman with an upper-class man. They were opposites in just about every way.

"I didn't really keep that from you."

"Like you didn't really keep the pregnancy from me?"

She sighed. "We dated for three weeks. There's no law that says I had to tell you my plans for the future."

"So, you weren't seriously dating me. What was I? Beefcake?"

The way he said it, with his calm, poised tone, as if he didn't realize how funny he sounded, made her laugh.

He glared at her. "No. Come on. I'm curious. Did you just go out with me because we were good in bed?"

"You were pretty good."

He cursed and rose from the teal chair to pace. "Seriously!"

"You do realize another man would be so damned complimented by that he'd probably glow in the dark."

"I'm not like most men."

No kidding. "Okay. Why did you continue to ask me out when we both realized on our third date that we weren't compatible?"

He took a patient breath, but ran the fingers of both hands through his hair. A gesture she'd never seen. She pulled back a bit. The last thing she wanted to do was anger one of the richest men in New York City when she didn't have a leg to stand on to keep their baby from him. Her moving to Pennsylvania without telling him would have been the easiest thing for both of them. But now that he knew, convincing him he didn't want to be part of this baby's life was her best option. She'd never do that if they continued to argue over pointless things.

"Anyway," Avery said, bringing them back to the real

discussion. "My life plan has been altered a bit. With my down payment on this place and the extra I've put on the mortgage every month, not to mention the increase in real estate values, I can sell the condo early and still make a profit. Then once I pass the Pennsylvania bar, I can start my own firm there."

"If you wanted your own law firm or even to jump the ranks of Waters, Waters and Montgomery, all you had to do was say the word."

She gaped at him. "Really? You think it would be okay for me to jump over the heads of lawyers who know ten times what I know? To be made partner before them because my ex is their biggest client?"

He drew a breath and expelled it quickly. "So, you're really leaving?"

Another thing he had a habit of doing was not answering her questions, but changing the subject so they wouldn't argue. This time she appreciated his stopping them from going down another useless road, so she let that slide too.

"Well, I'm not packing up and heading out tomorrow. My doctor is here in New York. I plan to have the baby here. Plus, I have to sell the condo. And I do need the experience I'm getting at Waters, Waters and Montgomery. But eventually I have to go."

"And you expect me to be okay with that?" When he faced her, his sapphire eyes had gone from serious to furious. "You think I don't have rights, options?"

Fear raced through her, but she calmed it. This was the most rational man on the planet. If she stayed neutral, he'd stay neutral. If she set out her plan logically, especially highlighting how he benefited from it, he would follow it.

"Okay, let's start this over again. I am pregnant. The

baby is yours. I've had the goal since high school to earn a law degree, get some experience in New York City and then return to Pennsylvania to start my own law firm. The baby doesn't stop that plan. Yes, I have to take the Pennsylvania bar exam and, yes, I will have to get a job at another law firm in Pennsylvania while I study for it. But the goal hasn't changed. Isn't going to change. That's nonnegotiable."

He paced in front of the fireplace. "And, realistically, Pennsylvania isn't that far away. I can drive there to visit or send a limo to bring the baby to me."

She winced. There were a billion things wrong with his idea. Especially considering she didn't want her child sucked into "McCallanville," a world of pampered rich people who didn't understand reality.

She argued the easiest point. "I'm not putting my baby into a limo alone."

"There will be times he should be with me."

"With you? Don't you mean with a nanny? Even when you're home you're on the phone or computer." Just thinking about it filled her with anger. "Why should my baby spend his time with a driver and a nanny when he or she could be with me? I won't let my child be raised by a nanny, Jake. Not ever."

He closed his eyes and shook his head, obviously controlling his temper. Finally, he said, "How much?"

"How much what?"

"How much do you want to make you more agreeable?"

She gaped at him. "Are you trying to bribe me?"

"I'm trying to make you more agreeable."

"And you think if you give me a few hundred or even a few thousand dollars, I'll give you what you want in a visitation agreement?"

"I was thinking more like a few million."

Her eyes widened. "You're insane! I have a plan. I don't need your money! I don't *want* your money. I want to do what's best for the baby. So should you."

He studied her. She could all but see the wheels turning in his head as he came to terms with the fact that this situation wasn't about money. In his world, everything came down to money. She couldn't even fault him for trying to find her price—though she did want to deck him. The truth was, she didn't even want child support. But she figured it was a little too early in the game to tell him that. His brain would have to work so hard to process it that he'd probably have a stroke.

"We're going to need a written agreement."

For ten seconds, she wished he hadn't seen her that morning at the law office. But while her dad had been in prison for something he hadn't done, she learned wishing for things to be different didn't change them. Plus, she hadn't given up on Plan B, convincing him he didn't want a crying, pooping, spitting-up baby destroying the peace of his life. And that would take more tact and diplomacy than she could muster tonight.

"Okay. But we should have a few more conversations to see what we both want before we even try to get anything on paper."

He considered that. "Agreed."

He headed for the door. Though Avery gave him a pleasant smile as she saw him out and said goodbye, another alternative jumped into her brain.

If she couldn't make him see a baby didn't fit into his life, there was a risky Plan C. She could tell him that her dad had been in prison and remind him of the can of worms that would be opened once the press started digging into the life of the woman pregnant with his child.

They both knew he wouldn't want that kind of media attention any more than she did. If anything would send him scurrying away from her, it would be the horror of that much negative attention from the press.

There was just one little problem with Plan C—

When she told him about her dad, she'd also be handing him the ammunition to take her child, or to at least keep her and her little one in New York City. All he would have to do would be tell the court he wanted to keep his child away from Avery's ex-con dad.

Then even if she kept custody, she'd be stuck in New York, away from the people she wanted to help.

Away from the dream she had nurtured and worked for since she was fifteen.

If Plan C went south, it could ruin her life.

CHAPTER TWO

THE NEXT MORNING, a quick knock on Jake's office door brought his gaze up from the documents on his ornate mahogany desk, the desk that had once belonged to his dad. Because the list of people his secretary would let down the corridor to his office was slim, mostly family, he automatically said, "Come in."

His brother Seth opened the door and poked his head inside. As tall as Jake and with the same dark hair, Seth hadn't gotten their mom's blue eyes, and had irises so brown they were almost black. Especially when he got angry.

"I won't ask you if you're busy. I know you are, but can I have five minutes?"

Jake sat back on his soft leather office chair. "Sure. What's up?"

Seth walked to the seat in front of the desk. "Just curious if you're really going to offer Mom a job. I mean, it would be kind of fun to watch, but there are twelve people on the board who don't want us giving an office and a paycheck to family members who aren't actually coming into work."

"Since when did you start caring about what the directors think?"

Seth winced. "Since they began calling me because

they don't want to insult you by questioning your judgment."

"The way they used to call me when they wanted to complain about Dad—"

He left the sentence open, giving Seth the opportunity to mention if the directors had told him anything about their father, a man whose business practices had been so sketchy they'd teetered on the edge of illegal. Ten years had given Jake a chance to fix most of their dad's messes, to argue him into working fairly or to quietly go behind the scenes and make amends with contractors their dad had threatened to ruin. But Jake didn't want his brother, his sister and especially not their mother to know what a cheat and a thief Tom McCallan had been. Not to preserve their dad's reputation, but to finally shake it off. He didn't want to remember that his dad had emotionally abused him and Seth until his brother had all but dropped out of their family. He didn't want to remember the times his father had publicly humiliated him. He just wanted to get on with his life.

Seth didn't say anything, and his facial expression remained casual.

Jake breathed a silent sigh of relief. Obviously, with Tom McCallan gone the directors believed as he did: the past was the past. It was time to move on.

He caught Seth's gaze. "Pete Waters doesn't like the idea of me hiring Mom either. He thinks she'll be underfoot and that she doesn't have any real skills. But I had a talk with her this morning. I told her there might be a possibility of a job, but she really had to work."

Seth winced. "How did she take that?"

"I think she felt becoming chairman of the board was her due, and a job, though interesting, is a step down." He shook his head. "I'm hoping that going to Paris will make her see she doesn't want any of it. That she's useful enough working with her charities."

"That'll make the board *and* Pete happy."

Jake sighed and sat forward on his chair again. "Speaking of Pete, there's something else I have to tell you."

"About Pete?"

"No. About the lawyer I was dating from his office."

Seth grinned. "The hot redhead."

Jake grimaced. It was typical of Seth to judge a woman by looks alone. Though he had to admit Seth had hit the nail on the head with his description of Avery. She *was* hot, and talking to her the night before had made his head spin. Especially, looking at her stomach and knowing that baby was his. Feelings he'd never before felt had grabbed his chest and squeezed until he couldn't ask the things he should have asked. Like for a DNA test and a good explanation about why she'd kept her pregnancy from him.

"Yes. She's pregnant."

Seth's mouth fell open. "Holy hell. And the baby's yours?"

"She says it is."

"No DNA test?"

He wasn't about to tell his brother he'd turned into a ball of confusion the night before just looking at Avery's belly. He wasn't that kind of guy. He might have had a moment of pure emotion but that was only because he'd been surprised. He was back to his usual controlled self now.

"We ran into each other at a coffee shop on Valentine's Day because neither one of us had a date. She works eighty hours a week. Most of our time together started after nine. It's very clear she doesn't go out with many men. Besides, I trust this woman. She wouldn't lie about something like this."

And that was the bottom line. He did trust her. Not because she was honest, but because the last thing she'd want was more involvement with him or his life. She'd made that abundantly clear. If this baby wasn't his, it would have been her joy to tell him that.

"What are you going to do?"

"First, we need a halfway decent custody agreement."

"What do you think that's going to cost?"

"She doesn't want money."

Seth burst out laughing. "Seriously?"

"She's a lawyer. She can earn her own. Plus, she made a smart choice when she bought her condo. Her plan is to move back to Pennsylvania where the cost of living is a lot lower than what we have here." He shrugged. "There's no price for her. She doesn't need our money."

"Mom's going to have a fit."

"No kidding. Especially since Avery's got to be six months along." He remembered her swollen with his child, and suddenly imagined a little boy that was his. Not just an heir, but someone to teach everything from throwing a spiral to getting what you want in a negotiation. He never thought he'd have a child. Never thought he *wanted* a child. But he needed an heir, and he *wanted* to be a dad. If nothing else, he wanted to do better than his father had done with him and Seth. And come hell or high water he intended to be part of this baby's life.

Seth laughed. "Six months and she only told you now? This just keeps getting better. You should rent an arena and sell tickets for when you tell Mom."

"Very funny."

Seth sat back. "I'm going to be an uncle."

Jake met his brother's gaze. "I'm going to be a dad."

Confusion swam through him again, tightening his chest with a combination of elation and fear. For as much as he longed to right things with this child, he also realized he could screw up worse than their dad had.

Seth sighed. "It's official. We're adults. I got word today on Clark Hargrave buying my share of the investment firm we started. He's pulled the money together. Once it comes through, I'm out of the investment business."

"Really?" Jake sat back. "Does that mean you can permanently take over the CEO position I left to become chairman of the board?"

"Do I have a choice?"

"You've been doing the job since Dad died, but if you want to leave I could appoint Sabrina." Both Seth and their baby sister Sabrina had MBAs, but while Seth had started his own company, refusing to work for their dad, Sabrina currently ran a consulting firm for start-ups.

"And ruin her life too?" Seth rose. "I'll do it, but I'm hiring two assistants and a vice president, so I'm not chained to my desk the way you are."

"It's a deal." Jake rose too, extending his hand to his brother.

Seth shook it. "I think we're both crazy."

Considering workload alone, Jake would have agreed with him, except he liked who he was. He had been grateful for the chance to fix the reputation of McCallan, Inc. Now that he had a baby on the way, getting it right was a thousand times more important. He would make his child a part of everything he had—

Unless Avery Novak disappeared. And she just might. They hadn't gotten anywhere close to agreement the night before, and she was just offbeat enough to think running was the answer.

He couldn't bribe her.

He didn't think he could outwit her. They were an even match.

The only thing left was sweet-talking her.

Almost at the door, Seth turned. "If you don't mind, I think I'll run this pregnancy by George Green."

Jake's brow furrowed. "The private investigator?"

"You dated Avery Novak for only three weeks, but you don't think you need a DNA test. You don't seem to care that she's moving to Pennsylvania. Either you're still half in love with her—"

"I'm not."

"Or you're so happy to be having a child you're not thinking clearly."

He sighed. "I'm thinking perfectly fine."

"Let me call George anyway, have him do a bit of research into her past to make sure everything's okay."

"I don't know."

"It's just a precaution. Plus, you never know what he'll find. Maybe there's something in her past that could help you."

Jake ran his hand across his mouth. Calling a private investigator to make sure Avery was on the up-and-up was one thing. But digging up dirt, ruining someone's life to extort them into compliance sounded so much like something his father would do after one of his fits of rage that he hesitated.

"Look, Jake, Mom's already at odds. If this blows up in your face, she's going to go over the edge. You know it. I know it. This isn't just about you."

Jake tossed his pencil to his desk. "All right. Call George. But I want to be the one to talk to him."

"Great. I'll set a meeting for this afternoon."

"Not at the office."

"Your place?"

He hesitated again. A horrible feeling washed through him. Was he pulling one of his dad's tricks? Looking for something in Avery's past? His intention was to make sure Avery could be trusted, but what if he found something that might make her seem unfit? Would he take her baby?

He stopped himself. There was no reason to get ahead of himself. A woman he barely knew, albeit that she'd been vetted by Waters, Waters and Montgomery when they'd hired her, was having his child. There was nothing wrong with checking up on her. Plus, he couldn't dismiss what Seth was saying. Their mom was fragile. Their father might have been dead five months, but she wasn't bouncing back from the loss. They didn't need a scandal, or worse yet, a thief in their lives right now.

"Have him meet me at my house at about six."

The feeling rolled through him again. The awful fear that he was becoming his dad. This time, he ignored it.

As Avery arrived at her office, she closed the door and hit the Contacts button on her phone to call her mom.

She hadn't been able to sleep the night before. After hours of tossing and turning, she'd realized she'd been lulled into a false sense that she was in control of this situation with Jake because she had a Plan A, Plan B and even Plan C.

But Jake McCallan was much too careful, too smart. Sleeping with her ten times had been one thing. Having her as the mother of his child was quite another. If he hadn't checked into her past before this, he would be checking now.

And once he did, Plan C would be as dead in the water as Plan A, and Plan B wouldn't stand a chance.

Still, right now, her priority was to warn her mom. When she answered, Avery said, "Hey, Mom."

"Avery! What a nice surprise. What's up? You never call on a weekday."

She winced. She didn't like reopening old wounds, but she wouldn't let her mom be blindsided. "I have a feeling some people are going to be coming around asking questions about me."

"You mean like the private investigators who checked into your life when you were hired by the big law firm?"

Avery said, "Yes," but her heart stuttered. Pregnancy hormones must be making her slow and dull. Jake wouldn't have to hire a private investigator to check out her past. All he had to do was ask her boss. Pete Waters had investigated her before he hired her. But where Waters, Waters and Montgomery considered it an advantage to employ a woman whose dad had been unjustly convicted—because it motivated her to work hard for their clients—all Jake would see was that her dad had been in jail.

And he could use that.

She ran her hand through her hair and walked to the filing cabinet. There were no windows in her office. Associates didn't get offices with windows. That was her place. A very small person in a very big world. A world that was quickly spinning out of control.

She squeezed her eyes shut. There was absolutely no way to fight this. "This is a mess, Mom. It's going to bring up all Dad's troubles again for you guys."

"Avery," her mom said softly. "We live it every day. The whole town knows your dad was in jail but got out when Project Freedom proved he'd been framed. Let someone come and ask questions. We're fine."

"Okay."

"But that doesn't mean we don't want you starting your law firm. Your dad went through hell for six years and we don't want to see that happen to anybody else."

"Neither do I."

"And we're proud of you."

"Thanks." She sucked in a breath, blew it out slowly. Her parents being okay with an investigator coming to town solved one problem. But there were thirty others nipping at her heels, things she wouldn't burden her mom with.

"So…this guy who's coming to ask us questions… does this have anything to do with the baby?"

She swallowed. She should have known her mom would figure this out. Who else from New York would care about her dad's past?

"The baby's father and I ran into each other. He saw I was pregnant and pretty much did the math."

"And you think he's going to look into your past hoping to find something he can use to get custody of the baby?"

"He might. Or he might just use it to keep me in New York."

"Oh."

Her mother's hopeless tone caused all of Avery's fears to rush to the surface. "He could ruin all my plans."

"Or maybe the two of you could work this out?"

The more she thought about it, the more she doubted it. But to placate her mom she said, "Sure."

"I mean it." Her mother's voice brightened. "All you need is a little trust. In fact, if you told him about your dad so he didn't have to send a private investigator to

Wilton, then he might see you're an honest person and negotiate a little more fairly."

Avery laughed. "That is the most optimistic thing I've ever heard."

"Sweetie, he's going to find out anyway. And if you don't tell him, it might make him suspicious and maybe even angry that you held such important information back. But if you tell him, it could be your door of opportunity to start some trust between you."

Her mother sounded so sure that for a second Avery waivered. "I don't know."

"Your dad and I aren't running. You shouldn't either. Face this head-on."

If it was anybody else but Jake McCallan, she might be able to cobble together enough optimism to give it a shot. Knowing her mother would keep trying to persuade her if she didn't at least say she'd consider it, Avery said, "I'll think about it."

After some gossip about the flower shop owner, Avery hung up the phone and squeezed her eyes shut. If Jake discovered her father's past and confronted her, she could come out swinging, quote bits and pieces from the hearings that freed him and defend him.

But to tell Jake herself? To explain that her dad had been framed by a coworker with a sick wife, who could have freed him the day his wife died but waited until his own death to admit to his crime? To tell Jake about weeks and months of waiting for hearings, about having her dad's old boss oppose a new trial, about the worry that Paul Barnes had bribed the judge? It would be one of the most vulnerable moments of her life. She was a fighter, not a beggar.

But her mother was right. Jake was going to find out.

And soon. If she could humble herself to explain this to him, it *might* be the beginning of trust between them.

Then maybe she could use Plan C. Once she told him about her dad, reminding him of the field day the media would have could show him how difficult having her baby in his life would be.

It was risky. But as her mom had said, he was going to find out anyway.

She got to work to take her mind off everything. An hour later, her private cell phone rang. She glanced down, saw the caller was Jake and squeezed her eyes shut before she answered.

"Good morning, Jake."

"I'd like to finish our discussion from last night. How about dinner tonight at 4 Charles Prime Rib?"

She blew her breath out in a quiet stream. She didn't want to cause an argument, but if she was going to tell him about her dad, she didn't want to go to a restaurant. Especially not some place where anyone could see them and where paparazzi hung out at the entry, waiting for celebrities. One look at the pregnant belly on Jake's date and the photographers would go nuts taking pictures.

"Maybe a coffee shop would be better? Someplace low-key."

A few seconds passed in silence. He clearly wasn't thrilled to have her change his plan.

"I just don't want to run into the photographers who hang out in front of those ritzy restaurants you like."

He sighed. "Okay. How about that small coffee shop up the street from your condo?"

"Great. That would be great."

She hung up the phone equal parts grateful for the opportunity to talk to him and terrified at the thousands of ways this discussion could go wrong.

At nine o'clock, she strode up the still busy street to the brick building housing the coffee shop where she was meeting Jake. Large windows fronted the well-lit establishment. The place was crowded with chatting people hovering at the bar on the left, or lounging at one of the curved booths with cushioned seats.

She stepped inside, glanced around and found Jake in the back, at one of the compact wooden tables for two. Disciplined Jake wouldn't waste the space of one of the big comfy booths, no matter how much she would have loved to sink her tired body into those cushions right now.

Convinced her mother was right—with the addition of Plan C—and ready to have the discussion, she walked up to the table. "Hi."

He rose. Nice-fitting trousers and a pale blue dress shirt outlined muscles created in the gym. Her mouth all but watered. But she told herself to settle down. Not to salivate over how good-looking he was, or to realize how easily she could unbutton that shirt and feel all the fabulous muscles of his chest.

Her breath shivered and she took a quiet drink of air to steady herself. "I see you went home to change."

"I had some time."

Something about the way he said that set her warning signals to high alert. But before she could say anything, he asked, "Can I get you a coffee?"

She shook her head. "I'll have a bottle of water. I can't drink coffee. Another unfortunate side effect of pregnancy."

"Another?"

She sure as hell wasn't going to tell him that pregnant women were easily aroused or that just looking at him had made her want to rip his shirt off. "You'd be surprised what happens to a body when a woman is pregnant."

He walked away and she settled herself on the seat across from his while he went for her water.

Setting it on the table in front of her, he asked, "So did you have morning sickness?"

She opened the bottle. "Horribly."

"But that only lasts the first trimester, right?"

He'd done some homework. More proof that if he didn't already know about her dad, he would soon.

"Yes. But some things bring it back."

"Like what things?"

"You're going to laugh, but certain toothpastes just about kill me."

He caught her gaze as he sat across from her. "Really?"

"I went through four brands before I found something I could brush my teeth with."

He laughed.

She rolled her eyes. "Consider yourself very, very lucky that your part in creating this baby was a lot more pleasant."

He laughed again and Avery said a silent prayer for strength. She'd never seen him this comfortable or relaxed. There might never be another chance as perfect as this to tell him her father's story.

She sat up straighter, pulling together all her confidence—

"Why if it isn't the lovely and talented Jake McCallan."

Avery's head snapped to the right and she saw the pretty blonde who'd walked up to their table.

Jake groaned. "What do you want, Sabrina?"

The blonde smiled at Jake. "Nothing." She slid a

glance at Avery. "I just rarely see you anywhere but the office and dinner once a week at Mom's. And with company too."

Jake shook his head. "Avery, this is my sister, Sabrina. Sabrina, this is Avery Novak. She works at Waters, Waters and Montgomery."

Sabrina extended her hand.

Avery froze. *His sister* just happened to be in the same coffee shop where they'd planned to meet twelve hours ago?

Shell-shocked and confused, she took the hand Sabrina extended. Social convention dictated that she rise, but then she'd expose the baby bump. And it wouldn't be long before everyone in his family would know she was pregnant. And once the news was out, it would really be "out." They'd tell their friends. Everyone would know. There'd be no way to ease him out of the picture. No way for him to quietly disassociate himself from her.

Damn. She had no idea why she thought she could trust him. The minute he was out of her sight, he'd probably told his entire family. Worse, he hadn't warned her that he'd told them. How could she explain her dad's situation to him and think he'd listen? Think he'd keep it to himself and give her what she wanted? He wouldn't. Let it come out in court, at a custody battle, where the evidence could speak for itself.

Or maybe it wouldn't.

Maybe his lawyers would twist it the way Paul Barnes had gotten the DA to twist the evidence of her father's innocence into a story of a coworker who'd only confessed after he was dead to get his friend out of prison.

Damn it! Damn it! Damn it!

She couldn't deal with this right now. Especially not in front of his sister.

She popped out of her seat, grabbed her purse and turned away from the table. "We'll talk another time, Jake."

Her pulse pounding, she raced out the door and into the hot first-day-of-September evening. She couldn't believe how this situation kept spiraling. Anger poured through her in waves. If she couldn't trust Jake not to say anything to anyone until they had their situation resolved, how could she trust him with anything?

A hand caught her arm, slowed her down, then stopped her.

It had to be Jake.

She spun to face him. "Now what? Would you like me to sit with a reporter from the *New Yorker* and give an interview? Maybe we can get ABC to put us on *Good Morning America*?"

"Will you stop? I didn't tell her to come here!"

"You expect me to believe it was a coincidence?"

"It *was*! And you're being stupid. It was my sister for God's sake. Not a girlfriend."

"I would have much rather that she'd been a girl-friend!"

He stepped close. "Really?"

He smelled spicy and male and all her pregnancy hormones popped. She ignored them. "You can date anybody you want."

"I'm about to be a father. I want to settle one life crisis at a time. I don't want to date anybody."

"Well, you might as well, because you and I are oil and water. Our lives clash. Even when we try to get along, we fight. We'll never get a custody agreement hammered out. We're going to end up in court."

"Because you intend to be stubborn?"

"Because I had a *plan*!" Three plans, actually. And all three had failed. "You don't believe this about me, but I love plans. I love order. Just because I don't say it with a calm, rational voice, doesn't mean I—"

He caught her by the upper arms and hauled her against him, and for twenty seconds they stared into each other's eyes. Warmth coursed through her. Her breasts met his chest. Their baby bumped against his stomach.

A million emotions flashed through his blue eyes. She was pretty sure his intention had been to stop her tirade by kissing her. Then he'd felt the baby bump and frozen.

Except for those eyes. Every emotion from confusion to fear to happy surprise and anger raced through them.

CHAPTER THREE

JAKE DROPPED HER ARMS then stepped back, away from the temptation of Avery's mouth.

He couldn't believe how desperately he wanted to kiss her. He'd caught her arms to shut her up, but staring into her eyes he'd remembered her fire and wanted to taste it again. Then he'd felt the baby—*his baby*—and his brain had scattered in a million directions.

"Well, that was interesting."

"Not really." She shrugged. "You said yourself we both prolonged our relationship because we were so hot in bed. We're accustomed to touching each other. And when we touch, sparks fly."

"That's about the size of it." He took another step back. Not wanting to talk about the myriad feelings racing through him when he'd felt the baby bump, he said, "It really was a coincidence that we ran into Sabrina."

She took a breath, then looked away as if thinking it through. Her long red hair shimmered when her head moved, and he struggled not to reach out and touch it. Not to reach out and touch *her*, if only in amazement that she carried his child. But that was wrong. A weakness he couldn't afford with her.

When she caught his gaze, the anger was gone from her eyes too.

"We're both just a little too edgy right now. Not sure of each other or how to handle this situation. We're going to have to be more careful about where we meet next time."

"Should we meet in one of our apartments?"

"No. We should meet in *mine*. We never know who's lurking in the bushes outside yours. And—" She held his gaze with an intensity that might have scared another man but almost made him laugh. He had no doubt why Pete Waters considered her his top associate. That stare could terrify any witness and probably some judges.

"No more touching on public streets." She looked around then glanced back at him again. "We don't know who could have seen that."

He said, "Sure," as she turned and walked away. The way she could so easily leave, snatching control out of his hands again, sent a wave of annoyance through him. "I notice you didn't say anything about touching on private streets. Maybe alleyways. The lobby of your building."

She didn't turn around, didn't acknowledge anything he'd said, just kept striding up the street.

A laugh escaped. She might not have turned, but she'd heard him. He'd seen the way her spine straightened. God help him, but he'd needed the validation that he still got to her, still had a little bit of control. Even if it was only teasing her.

When he pivoted to return to the coffee shop, he almost plowed into his sister.

"Mom is going to have a cow."

All the fun of teasing Avery instantly evaporated.

Sabrina's face fell. "You are going to tell her, aren't you?"

"Eventually."

"Eventually? That woman has got to be at least six months pregnant! What are you going to do? Call Mom from the hospital and say, *It's a boy*?"

"I'd like a boy." He really would. Someone to teach everything he knew. Someone to inherit everything he'd worked for. Now that he was adjusting to being a dad, the thought filled him with a pleasure that was almost indescribable. If he and Avery weren't the worst possible match, he might think this was fate. Destiny. A sign they were meant to be together.

Of course, though it might not be romantic fate, it still could be fate. Not a way to bring him and Avery together, but a way for him to have an heir.

"Are you even listening to anything I said!"

Forcing himself back to reality, he sighed. "Yes. I heard you. You think I should tell Mom."

"Soon."

"All right. Soon."

But the more he thought about fate and heirs, the more he realized that he'd have to see Pete Waters again—at the corporate headquarters. Not Pete's office. Avery Novak wasn't just smart. She was sexy and unpredictable. And he'd already slipped and almost kissed her. He had to get the facts about his parental rights before he tangled with her again.

But he didn't get the chance to summon Pete to his office. The first thing the next morning, his phone blew up with calls from his lawyer. There were thirteen messages that started at five, while Jake was in the shower, and kept going until Jake finally walked into his room and saw his phone blinking hysterically, as if Pete had continually hit Redial.

When the phone rang again, he answered. Pete didn't even bother with hello. "Are you crazy?"

"I think we both know I'm not."

"Then why is there a picture of you with Avery Novak in the society pages?" Pete's voice rose. "Are you the father of Avery's baby?"

Jake squeezed his eyes shut. "Yes."

"Hell. When she told me she was pregnant, she said she had no intention of marrying her baby's father. And she's returning to Pennsylvania after the baby's born."

"Her leaving New York doesn't have to be a big deal."

"It will be to your mother!"

He knew that. But right now, he was more concerned with the picture of himself and pregnant Avery in the newspaper. He didn't want his mom to see it and have a meltdown, especially when this was an easy fix.

"Okay. I'll fly to Paris today instead of tomorrow and tell her." He paused for a second to consider, but only a second. Avery was responsible for most of this mess. He wasn't flying to Paris alone. "And consider this Avery's official call that she's taking the rest of the week off."

"She can take the next month off because there's no way in hell I can let her touch anything that even remotely relates to any of your cases. You do realize at some point you'll be on opposite ends of a custody battle? The conflict of interest is off the charts if she even touches a file that relates to you or your family or your company."

"I know that. But you have to give me a minute to catch my breath, Pete. She only told me on Monday. I'm just starting to wrap my head around the ramifications of all this. What I need from you right now is a summary of my rights and choices."

"This is something I'd usually hand off to Avery." He sighed deeply. "This is a mess."

"It doesn't have to be. We all just have to keep our heads and handle it."

Pete sighed again. "I'll assign someone to write your summary."

"Good."

"It'll be waiting when you get back."

"Email it to me."

Jake hung up and phoned his driver then dressed quickly, but not in a suit. He pulled on casual pants and a sports shirt and covered them with a navy blue blazer. When he reached the street, the limo awaited him. Twenty minutes later, he was knocking on Avery's door.

Wearing black slacks and a pretty peach-colored blouse that highlighted her long red hair, she opened the door.

When she saw him, she groaned. "If whatever you want takes more than two minutes, I'm going to be late for work."

As she stepped back, he walked into her condo. "You don't have to go to work today. Remember how you worried someone would see us yesterday?"

She crossed her arms on her chest.

"You were right. A reporter for the *Gazette* took a picture. We made the society pages. Baby bump and all."

"Oh, no." She sank onto one of her club chairs.

"My mother's in Paris and I had planned on flying there for the weekend, but I told Pete we'd go today and tell my mom before she sees it online."

She gaped at him. "You told my boss my baby is yours?"

"No. *My lawyer* saw the picture in the paper. He figured it out and called me."

"And he's sending me to Paris with you?"

"No. Having you go was my idea."

She bounced out of the chair and grabbed her briefcase. "Then I'm not going! I have a job."

He winced. "Well, you do but you're off anything that has to do with McCallan, Inc."

Her face fell. The briefcase slid to the floor.

"Pete says it's conflict of interest since we could be on opposing sides of a custody battle."

"There are still plenty of other things for me to work on. The firm has defense cases that don't even nip the edge of any of your corporate work. Those are the ones I want anyway."

"That's for you and Pete to settle when we get back. Right now, we have to tell my mother about the baby. And before you argue, I'm not doing this alone. *You* kept this from me for six months. I'm sure you had your reasons. But the bottom line is, we are both this baby's parents. If we want to make fair, equitable decisions for our child, that starts with us presenting a unified front right from the beginning."

Avery stared at him for a few seconds. Though she wanted to argue, she saw his point. They did need to start being parents to their child. And she suddenly saw what her mom was talking about when she said they needed a step to begin trusting each other. If she did this for him now, that could begin a trend of cooperation.

Or maybe this could be the first step of their negotiations?

"I want to strike a deal."

His eyes narrowed. "A deal?"

"I'll go to Paris with you, if you agree not to use

something in my dad's past against me when we start talking custody."

"Something your *father* did?"

"Do we have a deal or not?"

"Was he a serial killer?"

"Actually, he didn't do anything wrong." She winced. "That's kind of the point."

"He didn't do anything wrong, but people thought he did."

"Yes."

"So, he was unjustly accused of something."

"He was actually tried and convicted. He spent six years in prison. Then one of his coworkers confessed that he'd framed my dad. He also produced sufficient evidence that my father was innocent and eventually he was released."

"Oh."

She pointed at her watch. "Time is ticking away. If you don't want the deal I need to go to work. My father is as innocent as a newborn baby. One of the nicest guys you would ever meet. It wouldn't be fair for you to dredge it all up again. Worse, if you did, it would reflect poorly on you."

"Yes. It would." His head tilted. An odd expression flitted across his face. "So, the deal is you'll go to Paris with me if I don't bring up what happened to your dad."

"Yes."

"Okay."

Relief washed through her. It wasn't exactly the culmination of any of her plans, but she'd won a significant victory.

"Good. Let me pack a few things and we can be on our way."

She tossed a dress and enough jeans and T-shirts, un-

dies and toiletries for a day or two into her scuffed-up
duffel bag. As she slid the wide strap to her shoulder,
she caught a glimpse of her reflection and grimaced.
The thing looked as if it had gone through a war. Just
like most of her personal possessions. She might live
in a beautiful home in a great part of the city, but only
because her condo had been an investment. When she
returned to Pennsylvania, she would live in a small
house in a small town. Most of her money would go
toward her practice.

She'd always have enough to take good care of her
child but he or she certainly wouldn't live in the lap of
luxury. Her condo and nice work clothes might have
fooled Jake into thinking she had more than she did,
but she wouldn't be able to hide the truth forever. She
was squarely in the middle class.

Her relief at her deal with Jake faded into nothing.
Getting him to agree not to use her dad was a victory,
but there were so many other things he could use. So
many other ways he could keep her in New York, destroying the goal she'd been working toward since she
was a teenager. Especially since she'd planned on her
child going to public school, taking a bag lunch and
riding the bus. None of this would sit well with the
clan McCallan.

Jake had tons of things he could use about her life,
about what she wanted to do with her life, to give him
leverage.

She and Jake took the elevator to the lobby and
walked onto the street. At six thirty, the city was beginning to show signs of life. Car tires made soft swish-
ing noises as they drove through puddles left behind by
the storm the night before. Streetlights flickered as the
sky shifted to whitish gray.

Jake directed her to a black limo. The driver opened the door and she slid inside onto white leather seats. Jake slid in behind her.

The driver closed the door and Avery heard another door open and shut. The engine started. The limo began to move.

Jake smiled ruefully. "I rushed you so much. I'm not even sure you've had coffee yet."

"Can't have coffee, remember?" She glanced around, her tension mounting. A family accustomed to limos would not let their first grandchild ride a big yellow school bus.

He winced. "Sorry. I've got some juice stocked if you'd like that."

She nodded. "Yes. Apple if you have it."

He opened the door of what looked like a console table exposing three bottles of juice. All of them orange.

"You sure you don't want orange juice?"

"It gives me heartburn."

"Sorry. We can stop somewhere."

"No. I'm fine. Let's just get to the airport."

Pulling his phone from his pants pocket, he said, "We're not going to the airport. We use a private airstrip." He hit a speed dial number. "And everything you need will be on the plane."

The person he'd called must have answered because he said, "Andre? I need you to make sure there's apple juice on the plane. And…" He caught her gaze. "Eggs for breakfast? Oatmeal? Box cereal? Bacon?"

Bacon? Her stomach growled. There was no sense in pretending she wasn't hungry. "Bacon and eggs and rye toast would be great."

"With apple juice?"

"With apple juice."

They reached the airstrip in just a bit over an hour, and climbed onto the McCallan family's private jet. She'd expected something compact and simple. Instead, she entered luxury so intense it magnified all her fears. The setup of the front space was more like a den than an airplane cabin.

Jake pointed to a door in the back of that section. "The kitchen is behind the first door and behind that are two small bedrooms." He pressed a button and the cabinet doors eased apart to reveal a large-screen TV. "And that's the TV."

She swallowed. They hadn't dated long enough for her to meet his mother or fly in his jet. His apartment and assortment of limos and drivers had been enough to scare her. Seeing the rest of his lifestyle sent another shock wave of reality through her.

If she thought she could control this situation with Jake, get him to visit their child in Pennsylvania, never bring her to his own home, in his jet or to the family's three-story penthouse across from Central Park, she'd only been kidding herself.

And she was in way over her head.

CHAPTER FOUR

FOG PREVENTED THEM from leaving until nine. The cook made good use of the time by preparing breakfast and some sandwiches for lunch before he headed back to the city.

Jake watched in amusement as Avery ate like a starving woman. But he didn't say anything. He was getting smarter about dealing with her. Negotiating had worked to get her to go to Paris with him to tell his mother about the baby. Though there was no way he'd have used her dad's conviction against her—particularly since her father had been exonerated—finally having her tell him something personal was a significant first step.

So maybe they could use the eight-hour flight to talk some more, open some doors, make some more deals?

He settled in on the comfortable sofa, close enough to Avery that they could talk but not so close that he'd spook her. He'd be light, congenial, maybe get her to chat a little more about her dad so he could tell her he didn't want to ride roughshod over her, just see his child. And they could figure this out.

But as soon as the fasten seatbelts light went out, Avery opened her briefcase.

"What are you doing?"

She glanced over at him, her stunning green eyes

cautious. "Taking a few days off means I'll fall behind. I can't afford to fall behind."

"If what I'm guessing about conflict of interest is true, your caseload just got a lot smaller. A few days off won't matter. Why don't you relax?"

"Because I need this job for another three months. I want to be able to show Pete he can still count on me. I'll rest after the baby's born."

"I think you're crazy. You should take advantage of the unexpected free time."

She set her file on her lap. "Are you telling me you aren't going to work at all in this very long flight?"

"I'm not." But he should. Except he hadn't thought to bring his briefcase. Even panicked about his mother, he should have remembered this nearly eight-hour flight and been prepared. But adrenaline over seeing Avery and coaxing her to go to Paris with him had pushed his job out of his head.

He couldn't recall ever forgetting something so important because of a woman and peeked over at her. She'd removed her black blazer. The peachy color of her blouse enhanced the red of her hair. Her complexion glowed. She *was* gorgeous. And soft. Her pale, pale skin was probably the softest he'd ever touched.

The memory of it stirred his blood, scrambled his pulse.

So maybe he wasn't in the best frame of mind to negotiate visitation?

He cleared his throat. "What are you working on?"

She didn't even look up. "Haven't you ever heard of client confidentiality?"

He shrugged. "I am your client."

"You're not *this* client."

She fixed her attention on the papers in the file.

Bored and deciding that watching the news was better than staring at the top of Avery's head, Jake turned on the TV.

She glared at him. "Seriously. I'm trying to focus here. I'm sure there's a television in one of those bedrooms of yours back there."

There was. But he didn't really want to watch anything. He wanted to talk to her. Even if he was a bit confused by her right now, he needed to figure this out. He didn't like things hanging in the air. He wanted this solved.

An antsy sensation snaked along his skin. A memory of something his dad used to say. *Desperate people make mistakes. Never go into a negotiation desperate.*

He sucked in a breath. If there was anything he hated worse than fearing he was like his father, it was realizing something his father said was actually true. The pregnancy *had* rattled him. Becoming a dad was equal parts frightening and exciting. The mother of his child was too different to second-guess her motives or plans. She was also gorgeous. And thinking about all that wasn't helping.

He glanced at her briefcase and saw her silent laptop. He pointed at it. "Can I use that?"

She peered up again. "My laptop?"

"Yes."

"You didn't bring anything to do, did you?"

He sighed. "No. Foolishly, I thought we'd talk, remember?"

"I'm working."

"So you've said."

She took the laptop from her briefcase, opened it and started typing.

"Don't pretend you need it just because I want to use it."

She didn't even look up. "I'm not pretending I need it. I'm creating a screen name for you, so you don't have to use mine and won't be able to see any of my documents."

"I'm not interested in your documents."

"You already asked about the case I'm working on. I don't want to take a chance that your curiosity will get the better of you."

"I'm not curious."

Her fingers click, click, clicked across the keyboard. "I think you are."

He gaped at her. How did she do that? Twist what he said and did into a completely wrong meaning? He swore sometimes she did it on purpose.

Or maybe she didn't have any other frame of reference?

He knew very little about her background. She knew very little about his. Because they hadn't really talked when they met up those ten times. They'd had better things to do.

She handed him the laptop.

"Thank you."

"You're welcome." She turned her attention to her file again. "I'm guessing you have off-site storage and you can get into your files."

"Yes."

"Good."

Her tone said she was already out of the conversation, but he still studied her. Realizing they fought because they didn't understand each other wasn't a great leap. The question was, did he want to do anything about it? He'd planned to negotiate with her, but if she refused to talk, the courts—and his superstar lawyers—would get him a good deal.

Maybe he should just let it all alone? Let her work and ignore him. While he worked and ignored her. Stop trying to be friends?

That suddenly seemed like a very good idea.

He accessed his files and got lost in the financials for a project that was going sour, relaxing in the world he knew. Money. How to make it work for him. How to make sure his family never ran out. How to assure the McCallan legacy stood forever. The family name lived forever. Because that's what he did. He made plans. He took control. And sometimes that control came in the form of letting his lawyers handle things.

Four hours later, they ate the sandwiches that had been prepared by the cook. Then Avery took a nap that lasted until an hour before they landed. When she woke, she spent the rest of the flight finishing up the work she'd been doing that morning. When the pilot turned on the fasten seatbelts sign, she tucked her files and notepads into her briefcase, then collected the laptop she'd lent him.

While she all but ignored him, he focused on deciding what he would say to his mom, introducing Avery to her and—hopefully—avoiding a meltdown.

Because at this point, that's where his priority lay. With fixing that part of this problem.

Their descent into Paris was silent. Avery knew Jake was a bit miffed at her for not talking, but she was fine with that. She wasn't sticking her foot in her mouth or saying something she'd regret by speaking before she was ready. Especially since the consequences of his finding out about their baby were finally sinking in.

Number one, she would lose her job. Conflict of interest wasn't simply a matter of her not working on any of his cases. She couldn't work for the law firm representing Jake in their custody battle. Not just for Jake's protection, but for hers.

Number two, they would go to court over visitation. Jake was accustomed to getting his own way and would make demands she could never agree to. A judge would have to decide.

Number three, she needed an attorney. Hearings were no problem for Jake. He had a battery of lawyers, while she had…herself. She could probably do a credible job on her own, but someone once said a man who acts as his own attorney has a fool for a client. She wasn't losing her dream of starting her law firm in Pennsylvania, or losing control of her child's life because she didn't spend the money for good counsel. As soon as she got back to New York, she would hire a lawyer.

Figuring all that out restored her confidence. The jet landed at eleven o'clock at night Paris time, though it was only five o'clock in New York. Walking to a waiting limo, Avery watched workers scurry to get their bags from the belly of the plane. In ten minutes, they were on the road.

"So how long until we get to the hotel?"

"Forty minutes."

Still gruff. Still miffed.

Which was fine, except his gruffness reminded her of dating him, and that reminded her of stealing time at his penthouse, making love in his shower, grabbing a bagel on the way out the door because they didn't stop to talk.

Neither of them had wanted to.

She ended those thoughts by looking out the window, at the countryside rolling by. It was too dark to see anything except open fields that gave way to clusters of houses and eventually the city.

Avery's senses perked up. She'd never been to Europe before, let alone Paris. *The* Paris. Not just city of love, but city of culture and history. And, oh, dear God, the architecture. Streetlights showcased aged brick-and-stone buildings that lined the avenues like society matrons in the receiving line of an ambassador's ball. The Eiffel Tower was lit like a beacon. Moonlight sparkled off the Seine.

By the time they reached their hotel, she was breathless. The limo pulled up in front of the entry of a building that looked to be five or six stories. White columns and white shutters accented weathered red brick. Brass lamps sat on either side of a revolving door trimmed in the same shiny metal.

The rotating door guided them into the lobby, as Jake walked with her, his hand on her elbow guiding her.

Which was probably more necessary than she wanted to admit. Her head swiveled from side to side, as she took in the luxurious black, gold and white lobby. She would have run into the bellman, two other hotel patrons and a coffee table if he hadn't steered her away.

The man behind the reservation desk nodded to him. In perfect English, he said, "Good evening, Mr. McCallan." He nodded at Avery. "Mademoiselle."

"Good evening."

"Your room, of course, is ready." He handed a key card to Jake. "It's your favorite."

"Thank you." He pocketed the key. "Have the concierge call the Bristol. Let my mother know we've arrived safely."

"Very good."

Avery's happy bubble burst. She'd forgotten they were in Paris to talk to his mom. Working during the flight, thinking through her ever-changing situation with Jake and ogling the architecture on the drive here, she hadn't given herself twenty seconds to prepare.

She glanced around the lush, expensive lobby, which suddenly seemed like a symbol for Jake's mom. Fancy, elegant, rich.

She was so out of her element that hiring an attorney now looked like the smartest conclusion she'd ever drawn. She could not handle this family, fight their money, on her own, any more than her dad could fight Paul Barnes with a public defender.

They rode up in the elevator in silence and walked down an equally quiet corridor. White-wood-trimmed walls were painted a soothing gray. When Jake opened the door on the last room on the right, she realized she was following him to *one* room. *His* room.

"Are we sharing a room?"

"It's a suite."

It was a gorgeous suite. The original features of wide wood trim and carved crown molding paired with thick throw rugs and a comfortable sofa and chair to create a sitting room that was both sophisticated and comfortable.

"I'm not sleeping with you."

"I never asked you to."

"Why not just get me my own room?"

"Because I don't want you to be alone."

"What you really mean is you're afraid I'll bolt and you'll be on your own with your mother."

"No. Because if you bolt our deal is off. And that's not good for you." He sighed. "Look, you're a pregnant woman in a strange city. Do you speak French?"

Her chin lifted. "Do you?"

He rattled off a line as smooth as silk and deliciously sexy.

"Point taken."

"So, we settle in, have dinner and get a good night's sleep before we talk to my mom in the morning. If we're lucky, you'll be back on the jet noon tomorrow."

Disappointment sneaked up on her before she could stop it. She probably didn't have a job to go back to. And she was in Paris. *Paris.* They were going to eat in a hotel, sleep, see his mom, then fly out? It hardly seemed fair.

The bellman discreetly entered. Jake pointed to the right. "Ms. Novak will take that room." He turned and pointed at the second door. "I'll take that room."

As the bellman distributed their bags, Jake shrugged out of his jacket. "Before I shower, I'll order room service. By the time I'm out, our dinner should be here."

She sighed. "All neat and tidy, huh?"

"I'm tired, I'm hungry and tomorrow I have to tell my mom she's going to be a grandmother in a few months, but we never told her. I'll have to explain why she missed the joy of knowing, of seeing your belly grow, of buying gifts and telling her friends. If I want to relax in the shower I don't think that's too much to ask."

Unexpected guilt shimmied through her. She'd never thought of his mother missing out. Mostly because she'd just plain never thought of his mother, never added her into the equation of the pregnancy.

She remembered her own mother's elation when Avery had told her. And her dad's—

Jake's dad died without knowing he would be a grandfather.

Sorrow swooped through her heart, leaving a trail of gut-wrenching regret in its wake. "I'm so sorry."

Halfway to his room, he faced her. "You're sorry?"

"Yes."

His expression shifted, softened. "I think that's the first time I've ever heard you say that." Then he turned and walked into his room.

She fell to the sofa. Guilt sat on her shoulders like one of the gargoyles she'd seen on a nearby building. She squeezed her eyes shut, then rose from the sofa and headed to her room.

Trying not to think about any of that, she showered. But as she stood in front of the mirror drying, she saw her pregnant belly.

She put her hands on either side just as the baby kicked. She hadn't merely deprived Jake's parents of the gift of knowing they were to be grandparents. She'd deprived Jake of so much more.

She slid the shower cap off her long, unruly red hair and combed it out before slipping into panties, a bra and an oversize T-shirt, getting ready for bed. She added the thick white robe provided by the hotel because the room had a slight chill. Then she padded to the door and opened it.

He was right about the food. A table had been set in the middle of the room, complete with a white linen cloth and a lovely bouquet of flowers as a centerpiece.

Jake stood by the window, looking out at the stunning display of lights woven through the city. When her door closed with a soft click, he turned from the window.

He wore sweatpants and a T-shirt, something similar to what he'd worn in the mornings when she'd stayed over at his penthouse. A memory tiptoed through her again. Him giving her a sexy kiss goodbye before she raced away to catch an elevator.

"I never thought to ask if you were hungry."

The aroma of beef hit her, bringing her back to the present. She closed her eyes to savor it. "Starved."

"I took the liberty of ordering a steak for both of us, but there's also a bowl of steamed vegetables, and macaroni and cheese."

"Macaroni and cheese and steak'?"

"If it's too fattening, eat one or the other."

She approached the table. "Are you kidding? It's my dream meal."

He headed for the table, too. "Good."

Before she could pull out her chair, he reached for it.

"Thank you."

"You're welcome."

He sat across from her and lifted the silver warmer from his plate. "Both steaks are medium."

She lifted her warmer, too, and let the scent drift out to her. "Smells perfect."

"Bread?"

He handed the basket to her and she winced. "I think steak and macaroni are enough calories for one night."

He laughed. Sort of. He clearly thought what she'd said was funny, but he wasn't ready to fully laugh with her yet. She supposed she didn't blame him.

"So, have you figured out what to say to your mother?"

He shrugged. "Yes and no. I have a few ideas of how to soften the blow because I know how surprised she'll be, and the loss she'll feel when she realizes how much she missed."

Because he'd felt it too. He didn't have to say the

words, she could hear the regret in his voice. Guilt rippled through her again at the same time the baby kicked.

She set down her fork and rose from her seat. She couldn't make up for what he'd missed before—mostly morning sickness and exhaustion so she couldn't feel too much remorse—but she could bring him up to speed right now.

Walking to his side of the table, she undid the belt of the fluffy white robe. "Baby's kicking. Want to feel?"

CHAPTER FIVE

HIS GAZE FLEW to hers, his eyes wide with surprise. "Really?"

"Sure."

Her T-shirt was so long she didn't worry about the fact that she wore only bra and panties beneath it. The robe fell open.

He looked at her belly.

"Go ahead. Lay your hands on either side."

He gingerly laid one hand on her T-shirt-covered baby bump.

She reached down and took his other hand and brought it to her stomach too. "We may have to wait a few seconds…oops. No. There he is." She laughed. "Or she."

Jake laughed nervously. "Oh, my goodness."

"Feeling that makes it real, doesn't it?"

"Yes."

His voice was hoarse, so soft that she barely heard him. They had a mere three weeks of dating, but she knew that tone. His voice had gotten that way only one other time—the first time he'd seen her naked.

Something inside her cracked just a little bit. Her pride. He might be a stuffy aristocrat, but there was a part of him that was a normal man. And though she had her reasons for not wanting him to be involved with her child, she had to play fair.

The baby kicked again, and she stayed right where she was. "Ask me anything. I can see you're dying to know."

He smoothed his hands along her T-shirt as if memorizing the shape of her belly. "I'm not even sure what to ask."

"There's not a lot to tell. You already know I had morning sickness. At the end of a long day, I'm usually exhausted. But as far as the baby is concerned, this—" she motioned to her tummy "—feeling him move—is as good as it gets."

The baby stopped. She waited a few seconds to see if he'd start up again, but he didn't.

She stepped back. "Food's getting cold."

"Yes. Of course. Please eat."

She smiled slightly and retied the belt of her robe as she walked back to her seat.

After spooning some macaroni and cheese into one of the small bowls provided, she dug in with gusto.

"I care about all of it, you know."

She peeked up at him, over her macaroni. "All of what?"

"Not just the baby. You. I know you want to stay sharp in your profession, so you don't want to quit your job, but…really… Avery. If you'd let me, you'd never have to work another day in your life."

She studied him. This time the offer of money wasn't condescending or out of place. It was his reaction to touching his child, albeit through her skin. And it was equal parts of moving and silly.

"Don't let him or her wrap you around their little finger already."

"What?"

"Oh, Jake. The first time he kicked I about fainted

from the wonder of it. You're drunk on happiness, awe, the joy of feeling your child for the first time."

"It's pretty awe-inspiring."

"Yes. But at the end of the day, he or she is going to poop and spit up, cry all night, get skinned knees, ask for a car before he's ready, be a moody teen and probably get into trouble somewhere along the way. Maybe even big trouble."

He laughed. "Well, that certainly sucks all the mystery out of it."

"I'm just trying to show you that this is real, not fantasy."

"I get it." He ate a bite of steak, then quietly cleared his throat. "But if you wouldn't mind, I'd like to hang on to the joy a bit."

"Are you telling me I'm too much of a realist?"

"You're too much of an arguer...too much of a lawyer. Always looking for something wrong or something to defend. Do you know that Pete spends most of his time spelling out what could go wrong with all my projects, all my deals, all my interactions?"

"That's a lawyer's job."

He leaned back and laughed. "My point exactly."

She'd never thought about it like that before, but what he'd said was true. She did look for trouble. Maybe because her teenage years had been so full of it with her dad's arrest and conviction.

"Huh."

Jake watched Avery's pretty face contort as she seemed to think that through. "What? No argument? You're actually considering it?"

"Sort of."

She spooned more macaroni into her mouth and his heart took a flip. As ridiculously antiquated as it was, he felt a powerful pride at feeding her, providing for her, and he suddenly knew that if he pushed this and demanded she recognize she always argued with him, no matter what he said, she'd shut down again.

Somehow a window or door of cooperation had opened and he did not want to see it close. In fact, if it killed him, he intended to keep it open.

The wonder of having felt his child move rolled through him again in a warm wave. He owed that to her. He'd have never thought to ask to feel the baby move. He had no experience with pregnancy. But she'd given him the opportunity. He wanted this cooperation to continue.

They finished their dinner and he tried to think of small talk, but none came. How did a couple top sharing the experience of feeling their child moving? A soft glow filled him, mellowed him. They couldn't talk about it any more than they already had. But he still wanted to savor it.

So, he rose from the table. "If you'll excuse me, I'm going to my room."

"It's only seven thirty, our time."

"I know. I'll watch a little television and hope to fall asleep because morning is going to be here really quickly."

She gave him a polite smile. "Sure. I'll watch some TV too. It'll be fun trying to figure out what they're saying since everything's probably going to be in French."

He could have suggested they watch together so he could translate for her, but he didn't want to risk his good mood—or *hers*. He *liked* getting along with her and maybe he wanted to savor that, too.

"Good night."

"Good night."

He turned to walk to his room but before he was halfway there, she said, "By the way, what should I wear to meet your mother?"

He faced her, catching the gaze of her stunning emerald eyes. He'd seen her dressed up, dressed down, naked. With hair up, hair down, hair a mess. She always stole his breath. That was what had gotten him into trouble with her. They hadn't needed to talk, hadn't needed to be friends. He just loved looking at her, touching her. And now they had no common ground, except their baby.

"You could dress up if you like. But really, just take off that robe and put on a pair of pants and you'd be fine."

She winced. "You noticed I didn't have pants on?"

"Hard not to when you showed me your belly. I didn't question it, just figured you wanted to be comfortable." He shrugged as if it was no big deal, but if the awe at feeling his child move hadn't overwhelmed him, he would have been annihilated by her bare legs.

She rose from the table too. "Okay." She turned and headed to her room then spun around again. "Is your mom expecting us?"

"Before we left New York, I had one of my assistants let her know I'd be meeting her tomorrow morning after breakfast, and I told the front desk here to call her to let her know we'd arrived. She's in a nearby hotel. I wanted to put a little space between us to give us some breathing room."

She nodded. "Okay. Good night."

He smiled and watched as she walked away, then raced to his room. They'd had an hour of normal conversation. She'd shown him the baby, let him feel his child move. And tomorrow morning, he was going to lead her into his mother's suite, like a lamb to the slaughter?

That would ruin every good thing that had happened between them. Control freak that he was, he refused to lose the good will she was showing him, and there was only one way to soften that awkward meeting.

He pulled out his cell phone and video called his mom.

When she answered, her face appeared on his screen. "Jake? Don't tell me you're phoning to cancel tomorrow morning. I bowed out of a spa trip with my friends to see you. You said it was urgent."

"It is. Look, Mom, I'm going to tell you something and I don't want you to go bananas."

She lifted her aristocratic nose as she fluffed out her perfectly coiffed yellow hair. "I don't go bananas."

"You're going to when you hear this… I just found out I'm going to be a dad."

Her eyes widened. "What?"

"An old girlfriend is pregnant."

Her mouth fell open, then closed, then fell open again. "You're going to be a grandmother."

"Oh, my God!"

"I came here to tell you that, with Avery, but I suddenly realized it wasn't fair to either of you to have that kind of awkward meeting. I'm telling you now so that when we come to your suite tomorrow morning, you can be nice to her."

Her head rose as her spine stiffened. "I'm always nice."

"You're always proper."

"I'm thrilled at becoming a grandmother."

"Yes. Well, you don't know the whole story. Avery is six months pregnant."

Her mouth fell open again. "And you're only telling me now!"

"I just found out myself."

"Oh." She blinked long lashes over her perfect sky-blue eyes. "You know what? It doesn't matter." She pulled in a shivery breath. "I'm going to be a grandmother."

He laughed. "Yes."

"We'll have a baby to spoil."

"Maybe not spoil. Avery's very down-to-earth."

"Is she pretty? Is our grandchild going to be beautiful because their mother is beautiful?"

"Hey, I had a hand in this too."

"I know that, dear, but take your good genes and add a beautiful mother and we could end up with a stunning child."

He laughed. "You're okay with this?"

"Okay? For Pete's sake, Mr. Worry Wart, I'm over the moon. Since your father's death I've been so out of sorts." She stopped, sucked in a breath and totally changed the subject, obviously not wanting to talk about her husband dying. "I'd planned on having only coffee for our visit tomorrow. I'll need to get something else. What does she drink? Soda? Water?"

"She seems to like apple juice."

"Then that's what I'll get. I'll see you tomorrow."

He hung up the phone surprised at how well that had gone, then he groaned. His mother might be thrilled, but there was no way in hell she'd let Avery off the hook for keeping the pregnancy from them. She'd say something—

Well, if she did he would be in the room with them and he would smooth it over.

He groaned. Really? In the plane, he'd insulted her over using her laptop. He really didn't know enough about her to know what smoothed things over or riled her even more. In fact, he was pretty good at riling her. And in spite of his attempt to fix things with his mom, seeing her tomorrow morning could still be a disaster.

For Avery, meeting Jake's mom was like getting an audience with the queen.

When Jake knocked on the door of his mother's suite

at the plush Le Bristol hotel, a maid answered. She led them from the entryway into a sitting room with a view of the city. Maureen McCallan sat on a Queen Anne chair to the right of a sofa. Her yellow hair had been styled in a perfect chignon. Her black dress and pearls screamed high society. *Old-school* high society.

Avery gave a silent prayer of thanks that she'd put on the dress she'd packed. The pretty royal blue sheath brought out the best in her coloring and though it didn't exactly hide her stomach, it didn't accent it either.

Mrs. McCallan waited for Jake to walk over and lean down to kiss her perfectly powdered cheek.

"Mom. You look great."

"Even one day in Paris works wonders." She looked at Avery. "And who is this?"

"I'm Avery Novak, Mrs. McCallan," Avery said, stepping in to shake her hand.

His mom took the hand Avery offered, but she smiled coolly as she glanced at Avery's belly. "It looks like you have something to tell me."

Jake said, "Mom!"

His mom took a long, deep breath. "So... I'm going to be a grandmother?"

"Yes."

Her lips twisted as she tried to hold back a smile. "Really? Have you done a DNA test?"

Jake shook his head, clearly annoyed, but said, "Avery would sometimes rather wrestle a bear than be in the same room with me. If this wasn't my baby, we wouldn't be here right now."

Maureen laughed. "So what is it you don't like, Avery? Our money, our lifestyle, our name?"

"All of them, ma'am, except the name. Nothing wrong with the name McCallan."

"At least you have the decency to be honest."

"Oh, she'll be decent like that more than any of us really wants."

"Good. I like knowing what or whom I'm dealing with." She rose from the chair. "Now, we were supposed to have coffee, but you can't drink coffee," she said to Avery as she walked to a discreet bar in the corner where a silver tea service sat on a silver tray. "I do however have an assortment of juices. What would you like?"

"Apple if you have it."

"Apple it is."

She brought coffee and juice over to Jake and Avery who had settled on a comfortable blue sofa, then returned to her Queen Anne chair.

"Tell me everything."

Avery held back a wince. "There's not much to tell."

"Did you have morning sickness?"

"Horribly."

Maureen clapped her hands. "Oh, that's great. Legend in our family is that morning sickness means your child will have a head full of hair."

Avery fingered her own thick hair. "If he's anything like me, he won't have to worry about that."

Maureen gasped. "He? You know it's a boy?"

"No. It's just easier to say *he* rather than *he or she* all the time."

"Too bad. I'd like a boy." Maureen stopped and smiled. "But a little girl would be so much fun. Imagine the clothes we could buy for her!"

"Mom, Avery may not want us to overindulge her."

"I'm returning to my home in Pennsylvania," Avery said. "It's a small town. She might not want to be wearing party dresses and tiaras."

Maureen laughed. "I was thinking more along the line of tights and long tops. Saw the cutest outfit the other day in the park. A baby had on caramel-colored tights with a giraffe-print top. So cute."

Avery smiled. "It sounds cute." It really did and it also didn't seem over-the-top or off-the-wall. "I've always been a sucker for black patent leather Mary Janes."

"Oh, I love those." Maureen smiled at Avery then said, "You really have to move to Pennsylvania?"

Jake said, "She's starting a law practice in her hometown."

"Oh."

"I wouldn't ever deprive you the chance of seeing your grandchild though." The words spilled out, a combination of Avery's guilt over keeping the pregnancy a secret and the realization that she'd deprived Jake's family. "Pennsylvania's not that far away."

"No. It isn't," Maureen said congenially.

Avery almost relaxed, but the memory of meeting her dad's boss at company picnics rose in her brain. Paul Barnes had been the epitome of politeness. He'd played softball, made ice cream sundaes for the kids and doled out the mashed potatoes for the evening buffet.

But he hadn't had an ounce of compassion for her father. He hadn't even considered that her dad had been telling the truth when he said he hadn't stolen the money missing from their accounts. When evidence came up that proved he was innocent, Barnes hadn't believed it. He'd contested her father getting a new trial.

She told herself to stop being suspicious and tried to push the memory of six poverty-stricken years out of her head, as she smiled at Jake's mom. She relayed the baby's due date, her doctor's name and the hospital where she planned to give birth.

"Would it be too much to ask for me to be there?"

Avery laughed. "The labor room is fine, but I don't want anybody in the delivery room."

Maureen laughed. "I'll take what I can get." She rose from her chair. "I hate to push you out but I'm having lunch with friends and need to change."

Jake rose too and turned to offer Avery a hand to stand. "That's fine. We were planning on heading home anyway."

"Heading home? We barely had a chance to talk! Besides, you have a ball on Saturday."

"I decided to skip it, so I can get Avery home."

Maureen said, "You'll do no such thing." She pulled in a breath and faced Avery. "Avery, have you ever seen Paris?"

"No."

"Fabulous. Jake can show you around today. We can have dinner tonight at eight and tomorrow we'll all go to the ball together."

Jake said, "Mom, Avery has things to attend to—"

But Avery interrupted him. She knew his mom would probably come up with a million questions today and she'd want to talk again tonight. She owed the woman that much. Plus, she really, really wanted to see Paris.

"I'd actually like to tour the city."

Jake caught her gaze. "Really?"

She laughed. "I'm starting a law firm that helps people who fall between the cracks of public defenders and high-priced counsel. I'm not going to have money for travel. This will probably be the only time I'm in Paris. I'd like to see at least some of it."

Maureen clapped her hands together. "That's fabulous! Meet me here around seven-thirty for drinks."

CHAPTER SIX

THEY STEPPED OUT of Le Bristol, onto the quiet street. Jake sucked in a long breath. "Thank you."

She faced him, her smile lighting her eyes. He could have stared into those green orbs forever, but she said, "For what?"

He broke the spell by looking away. "For agreeing to stay."

She laughed. "I meant what I said about wanting to see Paris."

He supposed that could be true, but there was more behind what she'd done than a desire to see the city. She hadn't merely been kind to his mother; she'd been respectful. And so open about everything that his mother had been like her old self. He hadn't seen that happiness on his mother's face since before his father's death.

He'd never realized a grandchild would turn her mood around, then wondered why he hadn't. She needed something in her life right now. Someone to love. And what better than a baby?

His appreciation for Avery's kindness multiplied exponentially.

"I'll be happy to show you Paris. I'm at your disposal for the whole day."

They reached the corner of the hotel. With their view unobstructed, they could see the Eiffel Tower.

She gasped. "That's what I want to see."

He said, "Okay," and pulled out his phone to call for a car, but she stopped him.

"Why don't we walk?"

He gaped at her. "Walk?" He switched screens on his phone and began searching for the distance from the Bristol to the Eiffel Tower. "I know it looks like it's just right over there." The answer popped up and he displayed the phone to her. "But it's almost two miles."

She shrugged. "So? I want to see Paris, but I don't just want to see things like the Eiffel Tower. I want to see *Paris*. Walk the streets." She pulled in a long drink of air. "Breathe in the smells." She sniffed again. "What *is* that?"

He laughed. "Any one of a number of restaurants." The temptation to take her hand rose in him. The impulse was so natural it would have made him caution himself about appreciating Avery so much that he did something stupid, except they'd dated. Three weeks might not seem like a long time, but it had set precedents, habits that were slowly seeping into their association again.

Especially since they were getting along. All he'd remembered from their time together was sex and arguments over politics. But now that they were getting along, the arguments faded into nothing and memories of how soft she was rolled through him.

Morning sun poured down on them. The scents, sights and sounds of Paris flowed around them. Resisting the urge to hold her hand, he motioned for her to start walking.

They bumped along with other tourists, glancing

around, took a side street or two, bobbed in and out of shops along the way, not really saying anything. When they came to the Gagosian Gallery, she stopped.

"This is what I'm talking about. Walking, we'll find things like this and can pop in and have a look around."

It wasn't what he'd usually do. He liked plans. He didn't just "pop into" art galleries or museums any more than he'd think he could pop into the ballet. But he was resisting their attraction and they weren't arguing, so why spoil it?

In fact, he was beginning to wonder if he shouldn't try to use it. Rather than walk silently through the streets, they could be talking. Learning about each other. She'd already told him about her dad. He knew about her job from Pete Waters. But she knew virtually nothing about him.

Which might be why she constantly drew all the wrong conclusions.

He opened the door for her and they entered. He knew the exhibits changed regularly, so he wasn't sure what they would find. Today, bright paintings stood out in stark contrast against white walls. She gazed around with a look of such wonder that he laughed.

"You like?"

She glanced at him. "You don't?"

And here was his first chance to tell her something about himself. "When it comes to art, I'm a take-it-or-leave-it kind of guy."

She ducked into the first exhibit. "You're telling me you don't like art?"

"I prefer practical things over showy. Things like sofas and cabinets. A cleverly arranged kitchen. That's art to me."

She paused in front of a painting, but looked at him. "I get that you're practical, but a kitchen as art? Really?"

"I cook."

She laughed. "You make bagels."

He shook his head. "Nope. Learned to cook when I was at university, so I wouldn't starve."

She scoffed. "Right." Her gaze took a trip down his proper navy blue blazer and gray trousers. "Like a Mc-Callan would ever starve."

It wasn't the first time one of her digs had gotten to him. But it was the first time he realized sidestepping her insults had kept them from getting to know each other. She thought the rich had it so easy? Well, she hadn't lived with his father.

"While I was at university, my father made me live on an allowance that was just barely enough to get by for a month. I quickly discovered how much cheaper it was to cook for myself than eat out, and started making my own breakfast, lunch and dinner. I also started saving chunks of each month's deposit."

She stopped walking and genuinely seemed interested. "I get the cooking but why save some of your allowance?"

"Because my dad had a tendency to do odd things at the drop of a hat. I went to the house for dinner on Friday nights and one Friday he got it in his head that I was pampered. The next month he withheld my allowance to teach me coping skills."

She stared at him. "He held back the money you depended on to live?"

He sniffed a laugh. "More than once. And he didn't just do that to me. When my brother Seth entered university, Dad did it to him too. It sounds crazy—" It was crazy and cruel and arbitrary, and just thinking about it filled his veins with the fire of anger, but this was his life. Probably the most important thing he could tell her so she could get to know him. "But in my father's mind, he was teaching us discipline and street smarts."

"It sounds like a mind game to me."

Surprised that she hadn't sided with his dad and agreed that pampered sons needed to be taught lessons, he said, "What he did was capricious and bordered on cruel. My brother Seth didn't catch on as quickly as I did and spent a month homeless."

This time she gaped at him. "What?"

"You heard me."

"I can't believe your mom would allow that!"

"She didn't know. It was sort of a point of pride for us not to tell her." They ambled to another painting. In this one reds, yellows and oranges mixed and mingled in such a way that it reminded him of the fire of hell. Or maybe it was talking about his father, remembering the difficulties of his and Seth's childhood.

"He broke Seth."

"Broke him?"

"My dad pushed us too hard and too far. Berating us for an A that he thought should have been an A-plus. Refusing to pay tuition. And when we got jobs—realizing the only way to have any security was to earn our own money—he'd raid our bank accounts, taking money we'd earned. There was no such thing as security in our lives. I learned not to put my check in the bank, to pay cash for things like rent and to hide any extra money under my mattress. I learned to combat my father's impulses with plans and logic.

"Seth's senior year he couldn't handle it anymore. The fact that our father had friends in places that allowed him to steal from our accounts broke him. He dropped out of university, disappeared for the longest time. When he finally got in touch with me two years later, he was working for a brokerage firm during the day and going to school at night, living with two room-mates, incredibly happy."

She held his gaze. Her green eyes soft with sympathy. "Oh."

He shook his head; the last thing he wanted was her pity. "I don't want you to feel sorry for me. I just thought if we knew a thing or two about each other, maybe we'd get along."

She nodded, but he still saw the sympathy in her eyes.

"Seth is very successful now. He works for McCallan, Inc., but he just sold half of a brokerage firm he started with another friend. He's very happy."

She only continued to stare at him.

He frowned. "It shocks you to hear how Seth made his own way? Or to hear that our lives weren't exactly easy?"

"No. I'm standing here wondering if Seth gave up, how much guts did it take for you to stay?"

"Guts?"

"No matter how difficult leaving seemed, staying was probably a hundred times harder."

His chest softened with something he could neither define nor describe. He'd never told his mother about the things his father had done to him and Seth. He'd never told her about the double dealings and deceit he'd found at McCallan, Inc. when he'd gone to work for the company. And really, he hadn't told Avery either, not the whole of it, not the worry or the strength it took to be one step ahead of his dad, yet she understood.

He didn't think anyone would ever understand.

"I couldn't leave. I always knew I'd be the one to

take over the family business. I had no idea my father would die this soon and that I'd barely be in my thirties before I was running it all, but I had a responsibility."

She continued to hold his gaze. "Yes, you did."

"And Seth is back. Willing to do his fair share."

"But the responsibility rests on your shoulders."

"Someone has to lead. Besides, I like who I am. I like that when I went to work for my dad, I saw Seth and I weren't the only ones he bullied. He hurt lots of people with his quick temper and snap judgments."

"It's why you're so logical."

He sniffed a laugh. "Yes. But the bottom line is I forced him to clean up his act and basically restored the family name. Still, if you look in our closet, you're going to find plenty of skeletons."

"Is that why you agreed not to use my father's conviction against me?"

"No." Because they'd reached the end of the exhibits, he put his hand on her arm and ushered her toward the door. "I agreed to that because I don't believe what your dad did or didn't do has any bearing on our child."

"He's innocent."

"Exactly. And he's still our baby's grandfather. Just as I want my mother to be a part of our child's life, your parents need to be a part of it too."

He opened the door for her and they walked outside into the sunshine, stepping around a gaggle of happy tourists who looked at brochures, studied maps and laughed together.

As Jake and Avery headed up the street, he said, "Good or bad, every child needs to know his full heritage."

She stopped and took a quiet breath. "I'm not sure

how that's going to happen with me living in Pennsylvania."

Her honesty hit him right in the heart. "We'll work it out." He met her gaze. For the first time in their history, they'd held a conversation that hadn't ended in an argument. "See how we're talking now? Open-mindedly and realistically. That's how we'll figure it out."

She nodded.

"But for now—" He looked around. "It is an absolutely beautiful day in Paris." His good mood restored, as thoughts of his father flitted away and spontaneously seeing the city seemed like a great idea. "We'll stroll up to the Eiffel Tower, find a nice bistro for lunch and then stroll some more."

"You do realize you just planned our entire afternoon."

Disappointment that he'd totally misread spontaneity filled him. "Really?"

"It's okay. Except…" She raised her foot enough to show him her high heels. "These are fine now, but in another hour or so I'm going to want to toss them in the Seine."

He laughed. "So we need to go back to the hotel?"

Avery said, "Yes. Thank you." But her head still spun over what he'd told her and how she didn't know him at all.

Though she now understood why he was so stuffy, so careful about everything he did, she'd never even considered how strong he was. She hated that his father had been cruel to him, but loved that he seemed to have found his way—and was happy. She was also glad that he'd trusted her enough to confide in her. Because she suspected this story wasn't something he told everyone.

Uneasiness unexpectedly tightened her chest. She

liked having his trust, but it suddenly made her feel close to him. He wasn't just a stuffy guy she'd dated six months ago. He was someone she was getting to know.

But wasn't that good? After all, they had a lot to iron out about the baby.

"What do you say we change now?"

Pulled out of her thoughts, she said, "What?"

"Change now. Not wait until after lunch. Let's be comfortable. Let's enjoy this."

She smiled at him and he smiled back. For ten seconds she didn't hear the sounds of the tourists and buses. She didn't hear the birds or the traffic. She simply looked into his eyes. He was such a good-looking guy that she wasn't surprised by the sizzle of attraction that raced from her chest to her toes and back up again. But this time, she felt a connection form. A real one. Because it was smart to get to know each other, to be reasonable with each other, she decided that was good too.

"Okay."

They returned to their hotel to put on comfortable shoes and jeans and T-shirts. Avery immediately felt more like herself. And, Jake? Well, he looked totally different. But having heard his story it seemed appropriate that he look different. Carefree, even though she knew he wasn't. But maybe for today he could be?

"Now, weren't we planning to walk to the Eiffel Tower?"

"Yes. I'd love to see the Eiffel Tower." She'd also love to see him relax. Completely. And enjoy the day.

"Let's go then."

They rode down in the elevator and walked outside, this time looking like two ordinary tourists. He reached for her hand, then tucked it into the crook of his elbow. The gesture was so casual, yet so intimate, that it threw her.

As easily as possible, she pulled her hand away. "You don't have to hold on to me. I'm fine."

"I don't want to lose you. Not that I think you'll get lost." He winced. "Honestly, I just don't want you to fall."

She shook her head, but had to admit it was cute that he was so concerned about her. Except it gave her an odd feeling. The sense that the real Jake was hovering just under the surface of the man she knew. And with the right word or situation, his facade would crack and she'd be face to face with—what? A nice guy?

That could be stretching things. He might have had a totally different childhood than she'd believed, but that childhood had made him who he was. Too cautious. Too careful. Very guarded.

Getting to know him didn't mean she'd like him.

She brushed her hair out of her eyes. "I'm pregnant not sick."

He held up his hands in surrender. "Okay, I get it." He glanced down at her tennis shoes. "And you look ready to walk. Let's go."

They meandered to the Eiffel Tower, enjoying the sunny afternoon. The sight of the city from the tower took her breath away. After a little more walking, followed by a boat ride on the Seine, they had a late lunch in a bistro. Through their meal, they listened to the sounds of the city, breathed in the scents swirling in the air and filled themselves with sandwiches with crusty bread and salads that made her groan in ecstasy.

But after that she was tired. They returned to the hotel and she immediately fell asleep. When she woke, she realized the only thing she had to wear to dinner was the dress she'd worn that morning.

All the fun they'd had together melted away into reality. They might have spent a great day, but there was no worry that something would happen between them—no matter how sweet he was when his guard was down. When it came to things like dressing for dinner, they were on two different pages.

For a second she felt awkward having to wear the same clothes, but she lifted her chin. There was nothing wrong with the sheath. It was pretty, and sufficiently fancy. Sure, she'd worn it that morning, but it didn't smell. If Jake or his mother didn't like her wearing the same dress, they would simply have to get over it.

Still, she pulled her hair to the top of her head, fixing it in a loose knot with tendrils trailing down her neck and near her ears to at least make the dress look a little more elegant. Then she slipped into the only jacket she'd brought, the black blazer she'd worn on the flight over.

When she stepped out of her bedroom, Jake was already in the sitting room wearing a black suit and red tie, about the same level of formal as her dress, but not the same clothes he'd had on that morning.

"You look wonderful."

Heat rose to her cheeks. "Thanks."

"I like your hair like that."

She sucked in a breath. Even if he was only saying that to be nice, she appreciated it. "Yeah, me too."

He directed her to the door and opened it for her. When they stepped out of the lobby, onto the street, he waggled his eyebrows at her. "Want to walk?"

"To the Bristol?" She laughed and displayed her high heels again. "Shoes."

"Got it."

He nodded at a driver standing in front of a black limo and the man jumped to attention, opening the back door for them. The limo was obviously Jake's, in spite of his suggestion that they walk—

Which meant he'd *teased* her?

She shouldn't have been pleased, but she was. Not because it broke the ice, but because he'd made a joke.

A joke.

From the stuffiest man she'd ever met.

A man who had been emotionally abused by his dad.

A man who worried about her.

As the connections piled up, she ignored the nagging sense of menace that accompanied them. They *needed* to get along to raise a baby together. Hell, they needed to get along to figure out visitation. Getting comfortable with each other was good.

They arrived at his mother's suite and while Maureen sipped a cocktail and Jake drank a beer, Avery sat on the sofa talking about the pregnancy, the baby, her plans.

Maureen listened, nodding, laughing in all the right places and not once mentioning Avery's dress.

They went to the restaurant his mom had chosen only to find she'd invited two of her girlfriends to join them. They hugged Avery and clucked over her, and through the first two courses made her feel like the only woman to ever have a baby.

Over beef Wellington, they started talking about their own pregnancies. Somehow that shifted into a discussion of maternity clothes and how styles had changed and how a woman now at least had a shot at getting a decent gown for a ball.

"You are coming to tomorrow night's charity event, aren't you?"

Annalise Jones asked the question innocently, and

Jake casually said, "No. We're going back to New York tomorrow."

But his mother gasped. "Back? Tomorrow? Jake, you promised me you would attend this year!"

"And Avery needs to get home."

Avery looked at Jake. "You're not going because of me?"

"I don't want to impose any more than we have."

"But you'd like to go?"

He shrugged. "The hospitals and homes being funded do good work." He shrugged again. "It might be interesting to meet the people who run them."

"You should go."

"I'm not leaving you alone at the hotel while I attend a ball."

She'd thought he'd offer her the use of the family jet to return to New York the next day, but before she could say anything, Julianna, Maureen's short round friend, spoke up.

"Bring her to the ball. You buy two tickets every year. You should use them."

Avery said, "I don't have anything to wear," at the same time Jake said, "She'll be tired."

"Oh, nonsense," Maureen said. She faced Avery, "We can get you a dress." Then she looked at Jake. "And you can take her home early. It's not like you have to stay at the ball all night. I just have some people I want you to meet."

CHAPTER SEVEN

IN THE END, they agreed to go. In the limo ride back to their hotel, Jake politely turned to Avery.

"You can bow out if you want. You can even take the McCallan jet home tomorrow." He didn't want her to go. He wanted her to stay. Maybe a little more than he should. "I know you're eager to get back to your job."

She shook her head. "I don't think I have a job anymore."

"If I gave you that impression, I'm sorry. Pete never said you were fired, just that you couldn't work on McCallan cases."

She shook her head again. "Conflict of interest stretches beyond me staying away from your cases. When I go to work on Monday morning, I'm going to get a speech on—" She lowered her voice to sound like Pete. "Even the appearance of impropriety." She brought her voice back to normal. "And he'll be right."

"So, you're unemployed?"

"Probably. And I might as well go to the ball." She glanced over at him. "Just how fancy does this thing get?"

"I've never been. You'll have to talk to my mom." He winced. "She'll probably be happy to take you shopping."

"Another hit to my savings."

"No. This one is on me. You wouldn't be going if we weren't in Paris. And you wouldn't be in Paris if I hadn't brought you here."

"I can pay for it."

"So can I."

The limo stopped in front of their hotel. Jake exited and helped Avery slide out. The night air was cool as they walked to the hotel door.

Hands in his trouser pockets, beside her but with two feet separating them, he felt the strangest sensation. Not quite that he needed to help her walk. More like he wanted to be close to her. She was the mother of his child. She'd been incredibly sweet to his mother. And when she smiled at him, his stomach plummeted, his breath shimmied in his chest.

He'd never felt this kind of connection before. But it was like a mirage. One second it was there and the next it wasn't. It never hung around long enough for him to figure out what it was.

Telling himself he was all kinds of crazy, he walked her through the quiet lobby. They rode up in the elevator in silence and parted ways in the sitting room.

But he barely slept. Not only had he told her his biggest secret in the name of getting to know each other, but the way she'd treated his mom proved she was a good person, a kind person. Somehow, he'd missed that when they'd been dating. But now that he was seeing it, everything he thought he knew about her shifted, changed—nagged at him.

He didn't fall asleep until almost five. By the time he woke up around eleven, she was gone. A note on the breakfast cart left by room service told him that his mother had sent a car to pick her up to go shopping.

He yanked his phone off his bedside table and hit

the contact key for his mother. When she answered, he said, "Do not let her pay for her gown."

His mother laughed. "Are you kidding? I would buy the mother of my grandchild the sun, the moon and all the stars if she'd let me. She's in good hands."

"I take it she's not with you."

"She's in the fitting room, trying on the lovely white dress. Reminds me of a wedding dress."

"Mom!"

The hair on the back of his neck stood on end. And he knew why he'd been feeling so odd that he couldn't sleep. When he first discovered Avery was pregnant, there was no chance in hell anything would happen between them. Now, everything felt different. The sexy woman of his dreams was merging with real Avery... and he liked her.

And it meant something.

Or it didn't. They needed to figure that out.

"I'm just describing the gown, dear. Oh, there she is now. I'll talk to you later."

Avery stepped out of the fitting room and onto the platform in front of the three mirrors designed to show her how the dress flowed from every angle.

She frowned, then glanced back at Jake's mom. "It looks like a wedding dress."

Maureen smiled. "It does. Isn't it lovely? And aren't you lovely?"

Avery laughed. She wouldn't call out Maureen, but she saw what was going on. "I'm attending a ball, not my wedding." She turned to the sales clerk. "Do you have something in a creamy, peach or coral color?"

"Of course."

The sales girl scampered away, and Maureen clapped

her hands together. "I'll bet peach looks absolutely gorgeous on you with your red hair."

Avery stepped down off the platform. "If we get the right shade, it's my best color."

Maureen rose. "Do you need help getting out of that?"

"No. I'm fine." She turned to go into the dressing room, but paused and looked at herself in the mirror one more time. "It is pretty, though, isn't it?"

"You're going to make somebody a beautiful bride."

"Maybe." She took in the elegant white gown one more time. "But probably not."

"Oh, sweetie! Don't say that!"

"I'm committed to my work, Maureen. And the baby." She laid her hand on her stomach. "Not sure there's going to be enough time left for a man or a marriage."

Maureen picked up the back of the white gown and followed Avery into the fitting room. "I've found that in life people make time for the things that are important."

"You sound like my mom."

"That's because older ladies are very smart. We have a handbook."

Avery burst out laughing.

Maureen tugged down the zipper of the dress, then slipped out of the small room.

After the door closed behind her, Avery took off the gown. She was wrestling it back onto the hanger when the sales clerk returned with two wonderful peach-colored dresses.

She looked at the first and said, "Let's try this one." The off-the-shoulder style and crisscross beading on the bodice would draw everyone's eye to her top, not her belly. Plus, the skirt of the gown was loose enough that it wouldn't hug her baby bump, but not so loose that it belled out. The chiffon fabric simply flowed from her waist to the floor.

The sales clerk helped her into the dress. When Avery saw herself in the mirror, she knew there was no need to try on the second one. Maureen agreed. A few minor alterations were required to the top, and the sales clerk arranged to have the gown nipped and tucked and shipped to Avery's hotel that afternoon.

When they stepped out into the sunshine, Maureen breathed deeply. "That was fun. We should do it again. Maybe shop for baby clothes together."

Avery said, "Sure." Mostly because she'd be unemployed in New York until the baby was born. It was an easy way for Maureen to be involved and a great way for Avery to supervise what she bought.

They headed to the waiting limo, but Maureen stopped abruptly. "You said you don't know the baby's sex, but I think we should find out. It'll make everything easier. Especially for people who want to buy gifts." She gasped. "And the nursery."

The driver opened the limo door. As she climbed in, Avery said, "I don't want to know the baby's sex until it's born. I want the surprise. I'd planned on making the nursery navy blue and gray, then adding a splash of pink or light blue depending on the sex of the baby."

Maureen nodded. "I like it."

"You're not upset about not knowing the sex of the baby before it's born?"

She considered that. "It would make things easier, but I'm trying to decide if I like being able to buy the right clothes or if the excitement of finding out the baby's sex at the hospital will be more fun."

The driver got into the limo and pulled out into the street.

Avery said, "I like the old-fashioned way."

"Really? You seem like such a modern girl."

"I am. Sometimes I even get a little too far out with my thinking. But my parents are very down-to-earth. They keep me grounded."

"Interesting. Jake's down-to-earth too. I remember something my dad used to say about opposites being good for each other. Something about balance. Anyway, Tom and I were opposites. He kept me from flying off to the moon and I kept him from being too hard on the kids."

Avery had to fight to stop a gasp. Her husband had been extremely hard on his sons. He'd hidden that from Maureen, but it wasn't Avery's place to tell her. She hadn't made a commitment to Jake not to tell his mom—or anyone—any of the things he'd told her about his father. He hadn't asked her to keep a secret, but in her heart, she suddenly realized that he'd trusted that she would.

He'd trusted her with probably the biggest secret of his life.

Maureen walked her into the lobby of her hotel and after a quick kiss on the cheek, Avery rode up the elevator and ambled back the hall to their suite.

When she opened the door, Jake spun away from the window to face her. His cheeks bore the black stubble of a day's growth of beard. His hair was a mess. If his room hadn't been dead silent that morning as she'd eaten breakfast, she'd think he hadn't slept.

Their gazes caught. The warmth of familiarity washed through her. She'd learned more about this guy, the father of her child, in the past twenty-four hours than she had in three weeks of dating—three weeks of sex without intimacy.

Awkwardness filled the room. He'd shown her Paris. Made her laugh. Told her a secret that she'd vowed not to share without once ever saying a word. Now he looked like he'd been through a war.

"I found my dress."

"Good."

She pointed at her bedroom, a room of safety where she could think some of this through. "If you don't mind, I'm getting used to having a nap every day."

He laughed. "Go ahead. I've got some work I need to do." He paused. "If I can use your laptop again?"

Grateful that he'd be busy, she said, "Sure," ran into her bedroom, retrieved the laptop and handed it to him.

"Not going to set it to my screen name?"

"No." She caught his gaze. "I trust you."

That was the whole hell of it. She did.

He trusted her. She trusted him.

What had Paris done to them?

CHAPTER EIGHT

AVERY DIDN'T COME out of her bedroom all afternoon. Around six o'clock, Jake walked over to knock on her door to make sure she was okay, but a bad feeling swirled through him when he raised his hand to the white wood. He was concerned about her, but she was clearly avoiding him.

Did he really want to interrupt her when she didn't want to see him? Since they'd arrived in Paris, he'd been sensing a connection forming, but what if she hadn't?

What if he'd told her his biggest secret, relaxed with her, made jokes with her, when she'd been cringing inside, wishing she was home?

Chastising himself for making a big deal out of her avoiding him when not talking was their normal routine, he returned to his room, showered and dressed in the tux he'd brought for the ball. They weren't friends or lovers or *anything* anymore. He'd thought getting to know each other would make things easier. It appeared she didn't. It wouldn't be the first time he'd misinterpreted her. So, he would let her alone.

He exited his quarters to find her standing in the sitting room, staring out the large window with a fabulous view of the city.

Turning to face him, she quietly said, "I'm sorry I needed a little time this afternoon. I don't want you to think I didn't appreciate your generosity. I have never enjoyed two days as much as I have these past two. Thank you for giving me a chance to see the city."

He tried to say, *You're welcome*, but nothing came out. She'd shocked him. He might have opened up to her, but the only time she'd told him anything personal was when she'd negotiated about her dad. But more than that, she looked amazing, so striking, his tongue stuck to the roof of his mouth.

When he found his voice, he said, "You're welcome." He waited a beat, then couldn't hold it in any longer. "You are so beautiful."

She glanced away and began fussing with the wrap she'd brought out, unfolding it so she could slide it over her shoulders. "Thank you." She met his gaze. "Your mother paid for this, but I intend to send her a check."

He could have argued. He could have laughed at her thinking his mother would actually cash a check when she'd meant the gown as a gift. Instead, he realized Avery was diverting his attention away from the compliment.

Something primal and male rose up in him. If he wanted to tell her she was beautiful, if he wanted to dwell on that all evening, there was nothing she could do to stop him.

"You *are* beautiful, you know."

She shook her head. "You've told me that a million times."

"In bed," he agreed. "This is different."

"So, before this, you didn't think I was beautiful with clothes on?"

He laughed. "Deflect all you want." She'd never been

uncomfortable with him telling her she was beautiful. Their association back then had been light, careless. Today's compliment was personal. And whether she wanted to admit it or not, it pleased her.

"You're not going to stop my good mood tonight. I'm about to attend a party with probably the most attractive woman in the city. I intend to have fun." He motioned to the door. "Limo's waiting."

They walked down the hall without saying a word. Rode the elevator in silence. Traversed the lobby like two strangers, but when they got outside, into the music of the city, he took her hand.

As the driver opened the limo door, she wiggled her hand away before sliding onto the seat. He slid in beside her.

"So, you don't have any idea what to expect tonight."

He said no, and for once that didn't set his nerve endings on fire. He wasn't worried about his mom, thinking about the people he would meet—

He felt like dancing. The day had been a constant series of ups and downs, but having told her about his dad and having her tell him she'd enjoyed the day, he felt lighter. It was confusing and weird, but he liked it. He liked this strange feeling that for once in his life he could completely relax.

"We're just going to wing it?"

"Yes." He paused to glance at her. "I thought you would like that?"

"It'll be fine."

They didn't say anything else on the way to the hotel. He guided her toward the ballroom with one hand on her elbow and she didn't yank herself away. He considered that a win.

His mother met them two steps before they entered

and walked with them through the receiving line, introducing him to heads of charities that benefited from his donation and he accepted their thanks.

Attempting to find their table, he was stopped by friends of his parents and more people on the boards of the charities who wanted to meet him.

By the time they got dinner, he was starving. He ate with gusto, then eyed the food on Avery's plate.

"Going to eat those potatoes?"

She turned to gape at him. "Who are you and what have you done with Jake McCallan?"

He laughed. "I'm just in a weird mood."

"Well, it's freaking me out."

"Why? We're in a city that's thousands of miles away from our home. You think you lost your job. I'm still reeling from discovering I'm about to be a dad." He almost told her that he'd been getting warm, fuzzy feelings about her all day, and decided that would make things weirder. "Why don't we just let go tonight?"

"You mean for once? Because I can't imagine you've ever let go before this."

"How do you know?"

"You're really bad at it."

"How can a person be bad at letting go?"

"You have tells. For most people spontaneity happens..." She paused and finally said, "Well, spontaneously. I can see you thinking things through."

He almost pondered that but suddenly saw that was her point. "I'll get this."

She rolled her eyes. "I doubt it."

"You're also not eating your potatoes." He took her plate and exchanged it for his. "If I'm dancing, I'll need the carbs."

She laughed.

* * *

Damn it! He'd made her laugh again.

He finished her potatoes with lightning speed, then had two glasses of champagne while the directors of the boards of the charities made speeches thanking employees, volunteers and most of all, donors.

There was a ten-minute pause that felt like an intermission while waiters discreetly cleared tables and guests mingled. Then the band started to play.

He held out his hand. "Shall we?"

She almost told him no, but he looked so eager, she couldn't resist. "Sure. Why not?"

The song was a waltz. Calm. Normal. No worries about his exuberance causing a scene. In fact, he was a flawless dancer. But with his hand on her waist and her hand on his shoulder, familiar longings trickled through her. His scent brought back memories of being together. She yearned to inhale deeply, stand on her tiptoes and kiss him until he ran his hands up and down her spine—

She shook her head to clear it of that thought. Knowing she had to put her mind elsewhere, she said, "I see somebody took dance lessons."

"Yes."

He twirled them around the floor and the romance of the move almost had her swooning. He was tall, dark, handsome and she'd touched him, tasted him—

Oh, Lord. She had to get her mind off that.

"Sorry about thinking you were crazy back at the table."

"That's all right. I understand."

"You understand why I'd think you were a bit nutty or you understand why I'd feel that way?"

"There's a difference?"

"There's always a difference."

"And the lawyer is back."

The music stopped. Eager to get away from him, to stop touching him, remembering things best left alone, she stepped away. "There's nothing wrong with being precise."

"And you call me stuffy."

"Usually you are stuffy."

"But tonight, *you're* stuffy."

She wasn't about to tell him she was fighting an attraction that was driving her crazy. She'd blame pregnancy hormones except this feeling was more about remembering. And maybe making a connection. The nice guy, the *fun* guy she'd spent the day with had also been her wonderful lover.

Obviously in deference to the older crowd, the band began to play the music for a jitterbug, something she only knew because of her grandparents.

Jake caught her hands and swung them to the left, then the right, and spun her around so fast she blinked.

"What are you doing!"

"We're dancing, remember?"

"Again?" She suddenly got it. Their bodies were brushing, causing memories of making love with stuffy Jake to mingle with the reality of dancing with fun Jake. And drive her to distraction. Which meant the easy answer was to stop touching. Stop dancing. "This is a grandpa song."

"I had lessons, remember?"

"And I only know as much about this dance as I can recall from dancing with my grandfather when I was five!"

"Piece of cake for you. I'm the one who leads. You just follow."

Despite her protests, they danced a jitterbug lively

enough to get a round of applause and a few kudos from their fellow dancers.

When they returned to their table, Maureen bounced out of her chair and helped Avery to sit.

"What is wrong with you? You're the one who said she'd be tired, and instead of taking her home you dance her to death!"

Jake laughed. "I know. I'm sorry. I'm just..." He paused. "...in a weird mood."

Maureen produced a glass of apple juice. "Well, no more dancing."

Avery glanced at Jake. She was glad to be away from the memories touching him evoked, but he looked happy. Totally relaxed. For the first time ever.

She suddenly felt guilty for letting her hormones get the better of her. The guy had had a miserable childhood. She'd had a blissful one, even if her teen years had gone bad. But in spite of that, she'd always had the love of family. His father had tortured him. Surely, she could stop her reactions and let him enjoy the evening.

"It's okay. I could probably dance to another song or two."

Annalise grinned. "Or I could dance with you, Jake."

The woman had to be thirty years older than Jake if she was a day. Though Avery wasn't jealous, per se, she didn't want him dancing with Annalise. If he was going to be happy, relaxed, it was going to be because of her—

Her heart stuttered.

Hormones and chemistry were one thing. This feeling was quite another.

She took a sip of her apple juice, fanned herself.

Jake snapped to attention. "Are you okay?"

"Yeah. Yeah. I'm fine." She wasn't. The feeling of familiarity that had scared her so much that afternoon had joined with their sexual chemistry and morphed into joy at being with him.

But only because he was behaving differently. Silly. Funny. Maybe he was happy to be with her too?

Oh, Lord. She couldn't think that way. She couldn't like him. Well, she already did like him. But she couldn't *like* him.

That would only cause complications over custody and visits after the baby was born.

So no. No liking him. No romance.

Jake knew the second Avery changed. The air around them grew strained again.

Well, that wouldn't do. Not when he was having fun. *They* were having fun.

He rose from his seat. "You know what? Maybe it is time to head back to the hotel." He wasn't a hundred percent sure what he was doing, but he did know Avery was probably tired. If he wanted to extend this night, it wouldn't be on the dance floor—or with his mother and her friends watching.

She looked up at him, her green eyes confused. "I'm fine."

"Yeah, well, we'll probably want an early start in the morning. The time difference works in our favor, but we still need to get some sleep." He pulled out her chair for her. "Annalise and Julianna, always lovely to see you." He helped Avery stand. "Mom, I'll be in touch when you get back to New York."

He didn't give his mother a chance to argue, just ushered Avery out to the coat room. As she slid into her wrap, he texted his driver and they stepped out into the unusually warm night.

"Typically, it's colder than this in Paris in September."

She smiled slightly. "Global warming."

He shoved his hands into his trouser pockets. "Probably."

The limo pulled up. Avery got inside and he followed her. They made the trip in silence but when they were a few blocks away from the hotel, he leaned forward and said, "Can you let us out here?"

The driver slowed the limo, then pulled up to the curb. As he walked around to open the door, Avery faced Jake. "What are we doing?"

"You've never walked in Paris at night."

Her brow wrinkled in confusion. "No. I guess I haven't." Her eyes clouded as she considered that, but there'd be no need to think about it, if she wasn't tempted.

He coaxed her. "It's a beautiful night. Our last night here."

The driver opened the door.

She sighed. "Okay."

They got out, and the limo pulled away. The street still bustled with tourists. It wasn't crowded, just busy enough to give the sense that they were part of something bigger than themselves.

He slid her hand beneath his arm and tucked it into the crook of his elbow. He expected her to argue, but she was too busy looking around.

"It's so beautiful here."

"And, as I mentioned, the night's warmer than usual. Seemed a shame to waste it."

"Yes." Her soft voice tiptoed into the night, as the moon tossed silvery light across the Seine like glitter. Subtle noise from the other tourists surrounded them.

He tried to think of something to say, but nothing came to him. Right now, in this minute, making her happy, making sure she didn't regret this trip, was the only thing he wanted—even if she was back to being the woman who argued with nearly everything he said.

They stayed silent, as she glanced around. "You know, when I was a little girl, before all the craziness of my dad being arrested and going to prison, I used to dream about becoming a high-powered business person in New York City and coming to Paris anytime I wanted. Maybe having my own apartment here." She laughed. "A second home."

He almost stopped walking. Was that a secret? From her? The woman who neither wanted nor needed anybody's help?

"Then I'm glad I twisted your arm to come with me."

"You didn't have to twist my arm. We made a deal, remember?"

He remembered. She'd already told him her biggest secret, but as part of a negotiation. Admitting childhood dreams was different. It was like telling him that before her father's troubles she'd wanted all the things everybody wants. What had happened to her dad had shaped her world, her goals, her dreams.

Part of him rebelled against that, if only because it wasn't fair that an event in someone else's life would form her dreams as it stole a bit of her childhood and most of her innocence.

"Even without you coming here with me, I wouldn't have used what happened to your dad against you. It's the past."

"I know that now."

Ridiculous pride filled him. His honesty had made her feel better, but she'd made him feel honest, trustworthy, good just as he was—a feeling he'd never had before.

The hotel came into view. They walked the rest of the way without speaking. He didn't want to break the mood, or think too hard about what all this might mean. He just wanted to enjoy Paris. When they stepped into the bright lights of the lobby, he was almost sorry.

Riding in the elevator, he remembered how the evening had begun, with him teasing her. Walking down the corridor to their suite, thoughts of dancing with her almost made him laugh out loud. Then she'd confided in him. For real this time. Not as part of a deal.

It had been one of the happiest nights of his life.

He opened the door and she stepped inside, immediately turning to the right to go to her room.

He didn't even think about it. He caught her hand and twirled her around to face him, then pulled her into his arms. His lips met hers softly at first, then when she didn't protest, he deepened the kiss, opening her mouth, tasting her. His hands ran down her bare back, then smoothed up again, enjoying the feel of her luxurious skin.

She slid her arms around his neck. The kiss went on and on, as if they'd done this a million times, and in a way they had. But never like this. Never a kiss of happiness. Or joy. Or a whole jumble of confusing emotions that culminated in one thought.

What if this was love?

Real love? Not the feeling a person had when they were dating somebody with whom they were compatible. But real, honest-to-God love.

The idea was so foreign he almost stopped kissing her, but her warm lips lured him back. Tempted him to go further, faster, indulge his cravings—

And that's when the real debate began.

Did he want to fall in love with somebody he usually

argued with? Someone who wanted a life totally different than the one he had planned? He'd already lost control with her. No, he'd *given up* control to please her. And that was dangerous. Not that he thought she'd use him, but they were about to negotiate the most important thing in his life: the fate of his child.

If dealing with his father had taught him anything, it was that opponents were opponents. It didn't matter if it was his father or a total stranger. One never gave up control. Never trusted someone so much that he put important things in jeopardy—

No matter how well his opponent kissed.

He pulled back, watched her eyes open, held her gaze long enough to hope that something in her pretty green orbs would ease his fears, but all he saw were her fears.

He released her. "Thank you for a lovely evening."

Her gaze clung to his. "Thank you too."

He turned and walked into his room, deciding the kiss had been the perfect way to end anything between them except parenting their child.

CHAPTER NINE

THEY RETURNED ON SUNDAY to seventy-degree temperatures in New York City. Jake had missed four days of work and was eager to get to his apartment, his computer and the forty-two messages in his phone. Avery was told via email to report directly to Pete Waters's office the next morning.

Vacation was over. And, from Jake's cool behavior on the plane, so was anything that might have been budding between them in Paris. It could have confused her, could have hurt her, except she knew Jake McCallan. The fun Jake she'd danced with was an aberration— thank goodness. She did not want to fall in love with the guy who'd probably be taking her to court.

When she arrived at Waters, Waters and Montgomery on Monday morning, Pete explained exactly what she'd expected, including reminding her of the firm's stance on "even the appearance of impropriety."

She resigned, so he didn't have to let her go, and, grateful that she had, Pete volunteered to write a glowing letter of recommendation and provide three months' severance pay—her salary right up to her due date.

Given that that was all she'd anticipated earning, it wasn't a financial hardship to leave. She returned to her condo, changed out of her work clothes and slid into sweatpants and a big T-shirt.

With a pint of ice cream in one hand and the television remote in the other, she sat on her sofa, preparing to channel surf.

She'd never had this much time off in her life. Part of her wished she'd stayed in Paris—but being that far away from home or her doctor wasn't a good idea. Just like that kiss hadn't been a good idea.

But, oh. It definitely had been a Paris kiss. Filled with passion and emotion but with an underlying—something. Maybe regret. With the way he'd pulled away and then barely spoken to her on the plane home, it was clear even he knew they couldn't get involved. Not when they hadn't resolved all their issues about the baby.

She took a bite of the chocolate, vanilla and strawberry ice cream, as the unvarnished truth poured down on her. She was pregnant, had no job and had kissed a man who would be on the opposite end of her custody battle.

But, oh, that kiss. So surprisingly romantic from such a by-the-book guy—

Was she crazy? Did she really want to be pining over someone so different than she was? Someone who had to be told how to be spontaneous? Someone who would never move to her small town—which meant she'd have to stay in New York City and give up her dream? Which would mean losing herself. Losing the person she'd worked to become since high school. Or, the more likely scenario, getting her heart broken when she left him.

Because she would leave him. She could not give up her dreams.

She spooned another bite of the ice cream, this time just chocolate and strawberry together. As the smooth flavor rolled across her taste buds, she closed her eyes in ecstasy. But that kiss wouldn't leave her brain. It had been so romantic. A kiss like they'd never shared before, if only because it had been filled with emotion.

Real emotion.

From the stuffiest guy on the planet.

She stopped that thought. Squelched it before it could take root.

That kiss played fast and loose with her heart when she needed to be stable. Getting involved with Jake was just plain foolish. Stupid. And she was neither foolish nor stupid.

The adrenaline of drawing that conclusion filled her with energy. Instead of kicking back, she should be doing something. And Lord knew, she had enough to do. She might not be working, but she had to take the Pennsylvania bar exam. She had to sell her condo. She had to move to Pennsylvania.

Well, actually, she couldn't move to Pennsylvania until after the baby was born. She wasn't switching doctors this late in the game. Still, it would take time to sell her condo and probably time for the purchaser to get a mortgage.

So maybe it was good she didn't have a job? She could call a Realtor, get the condo on the market and spend her time making sure it was spotless for showings—as she studied for the bar. It would be good to do that exclusively for three months. No job taking up her study time. No making notes, reading law, into the wee hours of the morning.

She took one last bite of vanilla mixed with chocolate, and strode to the kitchen. After returning the ice cream to the freezer, she picked up the phone and dialed the number for her Realtor. The sooner she put her condo on the market the better.

Her agent eagerly agreed to meet her that night to get the required information and take pictures to get the condo up for sale.

Short, blonde Eileen Naugle arrived around eight, all smiles and happiness. "This place is gorgeous!" She spun away from the kitchen and grinned broadly at Avery. "I can't imagine why you'd want to sell it."

As Eileen snapped a few pictures, Avery said, "Moving back to Pennsylvania."

The agent grimaced and said, "Pennsylvania?" as if Avery was nuts.

She shrugged and pointed at her belly. "I want to raise the baby with my family."

Eileen clasped Avery's hand. "Yes. That's a good idea. You are so lucky." She glanced around the condo. "And so am I. This place is fantastic. Nicely designed." She winked at Avery. "It'll sell in a heartbeat. Did you just redo it?"

"The remodel was finished last year. But I work a lot." She walked Eileen back through the hall and motioned for her to look into the half bath. "I don't think this bathroom or the full bath for the guestroom have ever been used."

Eileen peered in and gasped. "Oh, it's lovely." She took two pictures.

Leading her to the master, Avery said, "This room is the one room of the house that got the most use. I ate out. I worked late. The only thing I really did was sleep here." *And fool around with Jake.* But there was no reason for Eileen to know that. No reason for it to pop into her head either. Anything between her and Jake was over...

Still, they were fun memories.

They arrived at the decent-sized master with the

same wide-plank hardwood floors that were through-out the home. A queen bed with tufted gray headboard sat on top of a white shag area rug.

She snapped three pictures. "This is perfect."

"And, of course, the bathroom." She and Jake had had some fun times in that shower too. But instead of seeing the scene as it had happened, she pictured it with the emotional, happy Jake who'd kissed her in Paris and her chest tightened.

She had to stop thinking about it…

About him.

But dancing with him and then sharing that kiss had stirred up memories. Or maybe longings.

Which was wrong. Totally, totally wrong.

Walking inside the master bath, Eileen glanced around nodding. "This is good. You might have used it but you're a very neat person."

After Eileen took a few pictures, Avery led her back to the living room. As the Realtor removed the agency agreement from her briefcase, Avery made her a cup of coffee in her single-serve coffee maker.

She read the agreement while Eileen sipped her coffee.

"The price is based mostly on square footage and location," Eileen said. "The condition of the unit is a bonus. We can advertise as move-in ready. Though I'm not going to put it on the market yet. I have a few private clients who will want to see it first."

"That's fine," Avery said, signing the agreement. "Since I'm no longer working, just give me a call before you show it and I'll disappear for a few hours."

She rose and Eileen rose too. "This will be so much fun!"

Avery glanced around her perfect condo. The first slice of sadness hit her. Suddenly, she wasn't sure she would call it fun to be moving out, leaving the job she'd loved and the city that had somehow gotten in her blood—or the guy who was the father of her child.

As they walked to the door, she said, "Thank you for your help."

Eileen smiled. "My pleasure."

Avery opened the door and there stood Jake, hand raised as if he was about to knock. The bedroom and shower memories tumbled back, heating her face and scrambling her pulse.

Eileen smiled. "Well, hello."

Lowering his arm, Jake said, "Hello."

Avery said, "Eileen was just leaving."

But Eileen's smile grew. "You're Jake McCallan, aren't you?"

Jake held out his hand to shake hers. "Yes."

"I'm Eileen Naugle." She reached into her pocket and presented her card to him. "If you ever need assistance buying or selling, I'd be happy to help you."

Jake looked at Avery. "She's a real estate agent?" His eyes narrowed. "You're putting your condo on the market?"

"I told you I was." Avery quickly turned to Eileen. Stuffy Jake was back with a vengeance. "Thank you very much. Call me if you need anything."

Eileen said, "Sure."

Avery caught Jake's arm and yanked him into the entryway as Eileen walked to the elevator.

Closing the door, Avery sighed. "She probably feels like she just won the lottery."

"The lottery?"

"Connections are everything to real estate agents. Expect a fruit basket and a nice-to-meet-you card in your office tomorrow morning."

He didn't laugh. He didn't even smile. "I'd gotten the impression you weren't moving until after the baby was born."

"I'm not. It'll probably take a few weeks to sell the condo and then even more time for the buyer to get a mortgage."

She wanted to invite him to sit, ask him if he wanted some coffee, maybe tell him about her day, but she stifled that urge. Stuffy Jake wasn't the kind to want to hear about her day. The man who'd kissed her so eloquently in Paris hadn't flown home to New York. No matter how much she'd thought about him that afternoon, no matter how easily she superimposed fun Jake into her memories, she and the real Jake McCallan weren't a good match.

"So you'll be around?"

"If by *around* you mean will I still be living in New York, then the answer is yes."

"Good because my mother's talking about going shopping with you. She got in this afternoon." He pulled his phone from his jacket pocket. "I'm texting her number to you. She feels it would be imposing for her to be the first one to call."

Avery laughed. "That's very sweet."

"She also wants to be part of the pregnancy but she's concerned about being a nuisance."

"I'm out of a job. I resigned this morning to save Pete the trouble of letting me go. I'm getting a decent severance package, but I'm left with three months of nothing but studying for the Pennsylvania bar exam. She won't be a nuisance. She'll be a welcome break."

He frowned. "You'd welcome the chance to spend time with my mother?"

She casually said, "All my friends will be working

from nine in the morning till nine at night," but she suddenly missed the man who'd danced with her at the ball. The man who'd taken her for a moonlight stroll along the Seine and kissed her in the dark, quiet sitting room between their two bedrooms.

"You'll need company?"

She nodded, wishing the company she'd be getting could be that guy from Paris.

"Great. I'll text your number to her and tell her she can call anytime."

"Yes. Breakfast, lunch, dinner, shopping. I'll need breaks between long bouts of studying. Tell her I'm open to just about anything." She paused. "Except having her pay for everything. Sometimes she's got to let me pick up a check."

"She can do that."

"Okay then."

"Okay."

She walked him to the door, opened it for him. "Good night."

"Good night."

The air between them stilled. She remembered how he'd caught her hand, twirled her around, pulled her into his arms and kissed her. She almost closed her eyes waiting for it.

But he smiled briefly, turned and walked down the hall.

She closed the door with a sad sigh. She shouldn't miss the guy who'd been with her in Paris. She hadn't even wanted that kiss. She'd been halfway to her bedroom before he twirled her back. Now she missed him. Missed open, honest, happy Jake.

And she wasn't even entirely sure he existed.

Not wanting to watch more TV, she took out her laptop and searched for *studying for the Pennsylvania bar exam.* Fourteen courses popped up. And that was just the first page.

After twenty minutes of sorting through the entries, her phone rang and, still staring at the computer screen, she answered, "Hello."

"Avery. It's Eileen. I have two people who want to look at the condo tomorrow."

"Really? Already?"

"I told you I had a few clients I knew would be interested. It's not just location. It's that your place is move-in ready. Both of these guys are foreign businessmen who do a lot of work in the city. Both want something simple, no muss, no fuss. I'm bringing one at nine and the other at noon."

"Okay."

She disconnected the call and shifted screens to Jake's text to get his mother's number. After a few pleasantries, she told Maureen that her Realtor had two people coming to look at her condo and asked if she wanted to go shopping the next morning then have lunch.

Maureen said, "Yes! Fantastic! Where would you like to go?"

"You pick," Avery said. After they decided, she hung up the phone and laughed to herself, shaking her head as she walked down the hall. If nothing else had come of the trip to Paris, she had someone she could have lunch with once or twice a week for the next three months.

Unless being with Maureen reminded her of Paris?

She frowned. Thinking about that made her heart skip a beat and swell with longing.

But she could control that...

Couldn't she?

CHAPTER TEN

Two days later, Jake rose from the big chair behind his desk, as his brother and sister entered his office. His secretary had called to announce them, so he wasn't surprised by their arrival. The reason for their visit—as a team—sort of puzzled him though.

As pretty, petite Sabrina sat on the first chair in front of his desk and Seth sat on the other, Jake said, "What's up?"

Sabrina said, "Have you seen Mom lately?"

"Spent three days with her in Paris last week."

"It's all she talks about," Seth said. "How wonderful Avery is and the baby."

"I know. I went to Avery's house Monday night and asked permission for Mom to call her."

"And she said—"

"She said sure. She can't work at Waters, Waters and Montgomery anymore because of conflict of interest. And she doesn't seem predisposed to find another job at six months pregnant. Especially since she needs to study for the Pennsylvania bar exam. I think they'll probably go shopping." He shrugged. "She likes Mom. And Mom adores her." He looked at Seth then Sabrina. "So, what's the problem?"

"Mom's emotionally fragile right now."

"And being with Avery lifts her spirts."

Seth winced. "Yes, but for how long?"

Jake spread his hands in supplication. "About three months. Her doctor is here. She's not moving to Pennsylvania until after the baby is born."

Sabrina's pretty face fell. "She's moving to Pennsylvania?"

"It's where her family lives. That's what studying for the PA bar is all about."

"So, after Mom spends three months doing lunch and shopping with the mother of her first grandchild, Avery's going to Pennsylvania, leaving her alone again?"

Jake scrubbed his hand across his mouth. When Sabrina put it like that, he saw their concerns. "What do you want me to do? Forbid them from seeing each other? Limit the time they spend together?"

Seth quietly said, "How about figuring out a way to keep her—and Mom's grandchild—*your child*—in New York?"

He squeezed his eyes shut. Seeing Avery on Monday night had been the hardest thing he'd ever done. He'd wanted to chitchat. Make small talk, for God's sake. Hear about her day. He might have made up his mind in Paris that they were a bad match, but on Monday night, the only thing that had kept him from tumbling into the easy familiarity they'd started in Paris was the knowledge that she was his opponent. But even then it was hard. They'd shared too much. Gotten too close. And now he was vulnerable.

He didn't want to convince her to stay. He needed her to go.

"I can't. But even if I could, what if you guys are panicking prematurely? What if three months is enough to bring Mom around? And what if she and Avery form a good enough relationship in that time that Mom's comfortable going to Pennsylvania to visit her grandchild and Avery's comfortable enough to spend weekends with her, here in New York?"

Sabrina sat back in her chair. "It takes a whole year of mourning to get someone through her grief. Mom's only through five months."

"And she'll have three months with Avery to build the friendship that could take her through the rest of the year and beyond. Avery's a good person." He hadn't realized just how good until they'd spent those days in Paris together. "She and Mom will have a child in common. Enough to form a permanent friendship." He leaned back, fully convinced this was the right thing. "This baby could be just what Mom needs."

Seth drew in a breath and rose. "If Avery stays in New York long enough."

Jake rose too. "The bond may already have formed. The next three months will simply cement it."

Sabrina stood more slowly. "I hope you're right because this works both ways. Getting Mom involved with this woman could break her heart. I saw how Avery ran out of that coffee shop."

Jake winced, remembering that day. Especially how he'd wanted to kiss Avery. But also, how much she'd hated his life, his family's lifestyle. Too big of a dose of that lifestyle could send her packing sooner than she needed to go.

"I'll warn Mom to tread lightly."

When his mother called later that day to gush about lunch with Avery on Tuesday afternoon, he told her not to overwhelm her, but he also realized he had to make sure Avery understood his mom was fragile. After hanging up, he called Avery, but she didn't answer. After two more tries, he left a message on her voice mail that he'd be visiting that night. Though he didn't think it was a good idea for him to see her, his mom was the bigger worry.

At the end of his work day, when every other person employed by McCallan, Inc. had left the floor hours before, he had his driver take him to Avery's apartment building, rode up on the elevator and knocked on her door.

She opened it with a wide smile. "Hey, what are you doing here?"

Her hair was a mess, but her eyes were bright and happy. Memories of their kiss in Paris sizzled through him. He wanted to take her into his arms and kiss her senseless.

"I guess you didn't get my message."

She grinned. "Haven't looked at my phone all day."

Her extreme good mood brought everything back again. Dancing. Laughing. Walking along the Seine in the moonlight.

He should turn. He should run. But he needed to talk to her about his mom. "Can I come in?"

She stepped back so he could enter. "Sure."

The condo smelled like heaven. "Is that spaghetti sauce?"

"My mother's homemade," she said with pride. "And the spaghetti's boiling. I have a big bowl of salad and rolls are in the oven." She smiled at him. "Care to stay for dinner?"

His common sense told him to talk to her about being careful with his mom, maybe limiting their visits, and then race away before his buzzing hormones caused him to cross a line. But his stomach rumbled.

"You can't tell me you're not hungry," she said with

a laugh. "And I made way too much." She headed to her kitchen, her steps light, her tone airy. "I now understand why I always ate takeout. Cooking for one is impossible."

He followed her to the bright space with white cabinets, marble countertops and the big, big island made for cooking. Needing the distraction, he ambled around, taking in the perfect kitchen, and almost walked into her when she spun away from the stove.

She caught his shoulders to steady herself. His hands went to her waist to make sure she didn't fall. Their gazes met. Try as he might, he couldn't seem to get his hands to lift off her waist.

His voice was barely a whisper when he said, "I didn't mean to bump into you."

Her eyes darkened with desire that echoed the need billowing through him, making him long to kiss her, to run his hands down her back and maybe through her silky hair.

"It's okay. You were preoccupied with looking around."

Yes. He had been. *Preoccupied.* Not longing to touch her, but studying the room.

The return of rational thought helped him step away from her. "I like your kitchen."

He was glad when she turned and began stirring her sauce. "Meaning you could cook here?"

"Yes."

"I knew I wanted the kitchen to be functional. People notice that when they're searching for a new home. But it also had to be bright and happy." She faced him with a smile. "I think I captured that."

While his entire body was still strung as tight as a violin string, her expression had gone back to normal, as if she wasn't being driven crazy with wanting.

The temptation to kiss her, to remind her of just how good they were together, ripped through him, but common sense and sanity roared back. Paris might have been fun, but it had also been confusing. So many things had happened in those few days, things he normally didn't do, like confide in someone he barely knew. He hadn't thought that through. Though it had felt good to unburden himself, and the outcome hadn't been bad, he didn't fully understand why he'd gotten so comfortable with her when she could potentially use what he'd told her against him.

He didn't think she would, but the lapse had been perplexing and reminded him that the way they'd been in Paris had been wrong.

Since it was too late to get out of eating with her, he decided light conversation would save him until he could politely race away. "Maybe you should have been a decorator."

"Instead of an attorney?" She laughed. "Remodeling this place was fun. But being a lawyer is more fun. I don't mind going for a jugular now and again. It's good for the soul. Cleansing."

He laughed, but he knew that going for the jugular was her true nature. Not the soft, sweet woman he kept seeing. Not the woman he'd danced with in Paris.

He had to remember that.

"Can I set the table or something?"

She pointed at a cabinet. "Dishes and glasses are up there." She motioned to a drawer above the lower cupboards. "Silverware is there."

He grabbed two plates and the silverware. Paper napkins sat on the table, so he used those.

When he returned to the kitchen area, the rolls were in a basket and she was straining the spaghetti.

"The wine's there." She directed him to a wine rack beside bookshelves full of cookbooks.

As he pulled out a bottle, he said, "You must cook a lot more than you admit."

She shook her head. "Nope. All those are my mother's attempt to domesticate me." She brought the spaghetti to the counter. "It'll probably be easier if we bring our dishes out here instead of taking the spaghetti and sauce to the table."

He plucked up the plates and brought both to the big center island. "Ladies first."

"Good. I'm starving."

"I thought you had a big lunch with my mother."

"That was yesterday." She patted her stomach. "But even if it had been today, this child of ours loves to eat."

She filled her plate and walked into the dining area. He filled his, set it on the table then returned to the kitchen for the wine. As he poured himself a glass, he said, "Can I get you some juice?"

"No, but I'd love a bottle of water."

He got her water. Before he took his seat at the table again, he shrugged out of his suit coat, plopped it on the back of his chair and rolled up his sleeves.

When he finally sat, he dug into his spaghetti. Then groaned. "Oh, Lord, that's good. You make me ashamed that I told you I could cook. I don't make anything this delicious."

"It's all about the recipe."

"And timing. And instinct." He glanced over at her. "Don't forget. I might not cook this well, but I cook. I know what goes into it."

Avery held back a sigh. Though what he'd said was complimentary, he delivered it the way a boss talks to an employee. With team spirit that revved up the happy employee being praised, but really didn't touch her.

Her head tilted as she studied him. Same face, same hair, same crystal-blue eyes, but somehow she couldn't see this guy dancing.

She turned her attention to her spaghetti. She missed Paris, but she knew this was for the best. They needed to get along and she didn't "get along" with fun Jake. She wanted to kiss him. She wanted to fall for him. She wanted him to sweep her off her feet—

She experienced a longing so intense she almost sighed again. This was ridiculous. Yearning for something she couldn't have, something that she wasn't even sure existed, was senseless.

Except, he had to exist. She had not imagined what had happened between them in Paris. Several times while walking the streets, dancing, laughing, talking about his father, she'd felt she was dealing with the real Jake.

That's what bothered her. What if *this* guy was the aberration, and Paris Jake was the real one?

Her phone rang, bringing her out of her thoughts. She bounced off her chair. "I have to get this. There were two showings of my house yesterday and both parties were interested. I'm dying to hear if anyone made an offer."

She lifted the phone from the counter, tapped the screen to answer it. "Eileen?"

"Oh, sweetie, do I have good news for you!"

"I got an offer?"

"You got two competing offers. I've been on the phone since three, going back and forth between them. In the end, I got you two hundred thousand more than list price."

She swayed. "What? That's amazing."

"There's just one catch. You have to move out by next week. Both offers were all cash. Both wanted to take possession on Monday."

"Monday! I can't be out on Monday."

"Sure, you can. Let me negotiate the sale of your furniture with the condo. You hire a mover and pack all your personal items, which will be only a small box truck full of stuff and you're out of there in four days."

The thought of two hundred thousand dollars over asking was too good to pass up. It wasn't as if she was working. She had time to get organized and moved.

"Okay, yes. If the buyer also takes the furniture, I can be out on Monday."

Jake scowled and mouthed, "Monday?"

Eileen said, "Congratulations."

"Thanks." She hung up the phone totally dazed.

"Do not tell me you just agreed to be out of here on Monday."

Still stunned, she fell to the seat across from his. "I had to. Both offers are all cash. Both want the apartment on Monday." She looked over at him. "I should have told her I had nowhere to go. But the offer she wants me to take is two hundred grand over list price." She sucked in a breath. "I thought the asking price was fantastic. I'd have been happy with that…but two hundred thousand dollars more than list?" She shook her head. "I can't turn this down."

"You also can't live on the street."

"I guess I could move to Pennsylvania. Live with my parents until I find a place in Wilton."

"But your doctor is here. You said you were staying for the whole three months."

"I can't if I don't have anywhere to live."

"You can live with me."

She laughed.

When he didn't, she frowned. "Oh. You're serious?"

She pictured a hundred things like eating breakfast together and waiting for him to come home at night and the intimacy of it overwhelmed her. For as much as she'd like the chance to lure Paris Jake back across the Atlantic, she wasn't ready to live with him.

She shook her head. "I don't think so."

He drew a breath, blew it out in a huff. "Okay. So not at my house. How about the family's beach house? It's September. The weather is still warm. And you're not working. Why not enjoy these last few months?"

"If I moved to Pennsylvania I could get a jump on job hunting. I have to take the bar exam, but I'll also need some experience at a firm there."

"Get it after the baby is born. Your doctor is here. My mother loves being part of the pregnancy. You just said yourself you're getting two hundred thousand dollars more than you expected. Take the time off. Relax a bit."

"I shouldn't." But the thought of having three months of nothing to do but study was very, very tempting. And at a beach house, where she could get some sun, smell the fresh air...

"Okay, if you won't do it for yourself, then do it for me. My mom's been a mess since my dad passed. She came home from Paris talking about you and the baby, just like her old self. You know she's not a stalker or anything. She's looking for something to occupy her."

The way he campaigned for his mom hit her right in the heart. Not because he was kind to his mom but because she suddenly realized how heavy his burden to his family was, and she couldn't say no. It benefitted her, but it also helped him. She'd learned enough about him in Paris to know his life wasn't easy and something inside her couldn't make it more difficult when she could ease his burden by doing something wonderful like live in a beach house.

"Okay."

His eyes widened in disbelief. "Okay?"

She shrugged. "I don't want to leave my doctor and I can study for the bar at a beach house as easily as I can here."

"More easily."

"So, it makes sense."

"Thank you."

Seeing the relief in his eyes, she felt a zing of rightness. Not that she'd done something good. Her decision to stay at his beach house was as much for herself as for him. The sense was more that they'd made a decision together...like a team.

She pulled that thought back, reminding herself that it was dangerous to start liking stiff and formal Jake. He wasn't really a likable guy. He could be. Only a fool would have missed the way his eyes had darkened with desire when he'd bumped into her at the stove. But he'd yanked himself back, because he didn't want to be the guy who melted when they were together.

That was the real bottom line.

He might like her. But he didn't want to. Otherwise, he wouldn't be able to pull back so easily.

Paris Jake was gone. Stuffy Jake was back. It would be dangerous to her heart if she somehow forgot that.

CHAPTER ELEVEN

THE NEXT DAYS passed in a whirl for Avery. The only moving company available on short notice couldn't start until Saturday. But they arrived Saturday morning and immediately began working. Because adding the condo's furnishings into the sale meant she only had to pack personal items, when Maureen surprised her with lunch on Sunday the packing was done and the boxes were already in a truck, waiting to be delivered.

Maureen said, "Well, that's wonderful. We'll drive out to the house right now. We'll eat lunch while your crew unloads the truck, then we can unpack the things you need."

Suspicion tiptoed through Avery's brain. A few weeks ago, the McCallans didn't even know about the pregnancy. Now they were all but running her life. Not only had Jake convinced her to stay and provided a place, but now Maureen was here watching over her.

It had taken the visit from stuffy Jake to remind her the McCallans were accustomed to getting their own way. But she remembered now, and she intended to be very, very careful in dealing not just with Jake, but also with his mother.

"I'm not going to need much help. Jake says there's

a room in the back where I can keep all my boxes so I don't have to rent a storage unit."

Maureen slid her arm across Avery's shoulder and directed her to the door. "Considering time for a mortgage, you might want to start looking for your Pennsylvania house now. That way the papers will be signed and it will be yours when you're ready to move."

Taken aback, Avery said, "That's a good idea."

"After I call Jake and tell him to meet us at the beach house with the keys, we can look at listings online on the drive out to the house."

"Okay." Her spirits rose and the little nagging fear that the McCallans were taking over her life began to recede.

Of course, she was paranoid. Stuffy Jake put himself and his family first. Plus, her dad had been bulldozed by people with less money than the McCallans. But as long as they were talking about her moving to Pennsylvania as if it was a done deal, she didn't have anything to worry about…

But she'd keep her guard up.

The drive to Montauk was spent using their phones to look at houses in her small town of Wilton. Maureen seemed to favor Cape Cods, but to Avery the floor plans were too closed off.

When they pulled into the driveway of the beach house, Avery looked up and saw the enormous home and she blinked, wondering how Maureen could have seen good in any of the houses they'd researched online. Compared to this beast even the big Colonial they'd considered had been tiny.

They got out of the limo and Avery stared at the monstrosity before her. Three stories of stone with huge windows and brown shutters, the house could have been a castle for Britain's royal family.

She said, "Wow."

Jake strode toward them, bouncing a set of keys in his hand. Dressed in jeans and a T-shirt, with his hair sexily tumbled and a day's growth of beard on his chin and cheeks, he looked like Paris Jake. Memories came back swift and sure, first Jake standing by the window, unshaven with his hair wild, looking like he hadn't slept; then the kiss, the way he'd taken possession, emotionally, sexily.

She blinked, trying to force the images away but they wouldn't leave.

"I thought the plan was to move tomorrow?"

"Everything was packed," Avery said, working not to stutter over how good he looked or the wonderful memories. "No point in waiting."

"We've brought lunch," Maureen said, displaying her bags of Chinese food. "Eat with us then you can show Avery everything she needs to know about the house."

She'd rather he left. She liked Paris Jake a little too much and she didn't want to start superimposing his characteristics on real Jake the way she had when she showed the condo to Eileen.

He unlocked the door to a foyer so big and so empty, their footsteps echoed around them as they walked through to the kitchen in the back. Three French doors stood side by side, providing a heart-stopping view of the ocean.

"Oh, my God."

Maureen walked up behind her. "I know. It's lovely, isn't it?"

"It's spectacular," Jake agreed. "Wait until you see it from the third floor. I'll take you around after we eat."

She didn't want to go any farther into the house than she had to. She didn't want to see Jake looking like he did in Paris and acting like a stranger, but more than that she only needed a bathroom, bedroom and kitchen.

She glanced around. The size of the place was simply overwhelming. Not comfortable, not cozy. She didn't want to insult Jake or his mom but she had no idea how someone relaxed here.

In the airy white kitchen with three ovens and two refrigerators, they heated the Chinese food Maureen had brought and ate at a table with an ocean view. Then they took a quick tour of the downstairs, through a formal dining room, a library, an entertainment room and three sitting rooms, one of which faced the ocean. Jake opened the wall-sized door that folded until the space blended into the enormous patio behind it.

The heat of the day raced into the room, bringing with it the salty scent of the water, reminding her of vacations before her dad was arrested. The beach had been her favorite place back then.

"It's amazing."

For the first time ever, she could see her child fitting into the McCallans' life. Not the limos, penthouses and mansions part, but the big yard and the beach. She could see a little girl in a pink ruffled-rump bathing suit making a sandcastle on the private stretch of ocean beyond the big grassy back yard, or a little boy running up to the waves, dangling his toes in the water and giggling as he ran out again.

Maureen sighed dreamily. "It's the perfect summer retreat."

Looking past the long stretch of grass at the blue water, Avery could see that.

Maureen brushed her hands off as if she'd done her work for the day then turned to Avery. "I'm going to let you alone. Give you some time to get settled." She leaned in and kissed her cheek. "I'll call you Tuesday. No pressure if you're busy studying."

When the front door closed behind Maureen, the room filled with awkward silence. Except this time, with the thoughts of her child vacationing in this house running through her head, Avery's heart squeezed. All this time she'd been thinking about her feelings for Jake and the way he treated her and she'd missed the obvious. This stiff, formal man was her child's father. Avery might move on, but her child had to deal with this Jake forever.

"Are you ready to see the upstairs?"

She looked at him, remembered him funny and silly in Paris and knew *that* Jake would make a much better dad.

"Sure."

With Jake leading, they climbed the circular stairway in the foyer. It twisted in such a way that they passed the second-floor windows at the same time his mom's limo drove off.

He stopped and faced her. "I totally forgot about your car. Driving out with my mom means you left your car behind in the city."

"I don't own a car."

"How do you get to work?" He frowned. "You take the subway?"

He said *subway* as if her using it was a crime. "It's not poison and it's really convenient. And cheap." Once again, she worried for their child. Not that he'd be hurt or kidnapped because of the McCallans, but that he'd get a skewed perspective of life. "It costs a small fortune for parking downtown, and renting a parking space in my building would kill my monthly budget."

"Sorry." He shook his head. "Got it."

He walked by the first bedroom and the second, but

stopped at the third and opened the door on a room large enough to have two reading chairs by a bay window, a king bed and two dressers.

"We can bring up a box or two of your clothes and unpack if you like."

Seeing the room, she relaxed, but only a bit. All of her worst visions about her child's time with Jake ran through her head and she wanted some time alone to think this through. "No. I'm fine. I can get them myself."

Jake sighed, not wanting to offend her, but wondering if her lifting boxes and carrying them up a flight of stairs was a good idea. "You're sure."

"If I have to take the clothes out of the box one shirt at a time, that's what I'll do."

"Okay." Now she was the beleaguered peasant and he was Marie Antoinette again. She'd taken his comment about the subway all wrong and suddenly she hated him.

They might not become best friends, but after her doing him the favor of staying in New York, he didn't like the idea that they had to be enemies either.

But could people be opponents without being enemies?

His father would argue they couldn't, but it didn't seem right to be enemies when she was helping him. Plus, he'd spent his life working not to be like his dad. Maybe this was one of those things he should consider changing?

As they walked down the stairs, he got a call from one of his vice presidents. Scuttlebutt had it that a bid they'd submitted was millions of dollars higher than the closest competitor.

At the bottom of the steps, he motioned to Avery that he would be going into the library to talk to Bill

Cummings. She nodded and headed for the back of the house, where the movers had stashed her boxes.

Immersed in the discussion, he sank into a thick leather chair behind a French provincial desk and for two hours debated the wisdom and feasibility of changing their bid.

His call completed, he spent five minutes looking for Avery, then realized she was probably in her room, maybe showering or napping after the long day.

He didn't want to leave without saying goodbye, and making peace, but he also didn't want to go up to her room.

He returned to the library, turned on the computer and located the bid to go over the numbers one more time.

She ambled into the library over an hour later, looking as she had when she awoke from her naps in Paris. Hair tousled. Eyes sleepy and sexy.

His breath caught. His heart softened. She was the sexiest woman he'd ever met and recently he'd been realizing she was also the kindest. He refused to let his dad's antiquated ideas hurt her anymore. He just wasn't sure how to change things. "You were sleeping."

"I thought you'd left, but when I went into the kitchen to make a sandwich, I saw your car."

He rose from behind the desk. "I didn't want to leave without saying goodbye." And making peace, but what would he say? *I'm sorry I'm rich? I'm sorry I want to see my child a little more than I think you're going to let me?*

She smiled. "Thanks."

That smile did things to him he would never understand. He longed to run his fingers through her rumpled hair, maybe tilt her chin up for a kiss.

And that was another problem.

He had to work out how they'd handle their attraction if they were to remain friends. He'd seen what had happened in Paris. When they mixed getting along with their attraction, he'd kissed her, confided things he should have kept to himself.

Maybe it would be better to leave and think this through before he offered an olive branch.

He motioned for her to walk out with him. "Since you're fine and set up, I'll be going."

She yawned. "I'll probably get a shower and go back to bed."

"Sounds great."

A strange feeling settled over him, the way it had when they'd walked side by side in Paris and she wouldn't let him hold her hand or put his arm across her shoulders. Awkward didn't describe it. Neither did uncomfortable. It was more like melancholy. But it wasn't coming from him. It was coming from her.

She stayed at the front door as he walked to his car. Once he was inside, she inched backward into the house, closing the door behind her.

He put the car in gear and headed along the circular driveway, but his thoughts stayed on Avery. She was a normally happy woman. But today she'd been off. He'd thought she was angry, but what if she'd been sad?

He wished he was the kind of guy who could go back and ask her. But what would he say? "You looked sad. It made me feel awful."

That was going beyond offering an olive branch and making peace.

Besides, she'd think he was crazy.

He was an hour into the drive when their conversation about her taking the subway replayed in his head and he realized she didn't have a car. Not only had he taken her to a huge house that made her uneasy, he'd stranded her there.

Now *that* was a reason to go back.

He turned around at the first opportunity and headed to the beach house. By the time he arrived, it was dark. Not one light shone in the rows of windows in the three-story stone giant. He blew his breath out then ambled up the sidewalk to the front door.

He opened it into darkness, recognizing he wasn't going to get a chance to talk to her. He tossed his keys on an available table, then decided Avery probably wouldn't find them there. Even if he left a note explaining that he was giving her the use of his car, it would do her no good if she didn't find the note or the keys.

Walking into the kitchen, he turned on the light, found a pen and paper and wrote a note explaining that he was leaving the house key and the keys to his car, which was parked in the driveway.

When he was done, he shook his head. He should have called his driver first. Actually, he should have called his driver on the way back to Montauk. But he hadn't.

Now it was late.

Texting Gerry, he headed up the hidden stairway in the back of the butler's pantry.

Pick me up at the beach house tomorrow morning around nine.

It looked like he'd get a chance to talk to her after all.

The next morning, Avery awakened with a start, her heart pounding, her breath coming in shaky gasps. She looked around, remembered she was staying at the Mc-Callan beach house and rolled out of bed.

She'd get accustomed to the emptiness of the huge, cavernous house. She would. She had to.

She brushed her teeth, washed her face and tiptoed into the silent hallway. It was like being alone in a hotel. The vacant corridor echoed with her footsteps. So why did she have the ungodly feeling she wasn't alone? That someone was following her?

She swore she heard a noise. A faint sound. Like somebody dropping something.

She picked up the pace, racing down the big circular stairway to the foyer, her thin robe billowing behind her, telling herself not to jump to conclusions. If there was somebody else in the house it was undoubtedly a maid. Or gardener. Or somebody else employed by the McCallans.

She should calm down.

Just because she was in a huge mansion she didn't know, stuck here unless she called a taxi, that didn't mean something sinister would happen. As for that feeling that she wasn't alone—she'd already figured out it was probably a maid.

She pushed open the door to the kitchen and stopped dead in her tracks. She was not imagining the scent of toast. She sniffed the air…or was that bagels?

"Good morning."

Her heart tumbled. *Jake.*

"What are you doing here?"

He motioned her to the table with the view of the ocean. "I made bagels."

Confused, she walked over and took a seat, her traitorous heart knocking against her ribs. Had he realized how uncomfortable she was and come back the night before to protect her? If he had, it was about the sweetest thing he'd ever done. "Thanks."

Setting two bagels on the table, he sat across from her. "You're welcome."

He was dressed in the same clothes he'd worn the day before, though the scruffy beard was gone...*because it was Monday*. "Shouldn't you be at work?"

"I'm getting there. My driver will be here at nine."

Maybe he hadn't come back for her, but because his car had broken down? "What happened to your car?"

"Nothing. I was an hour into the drive home last night before I realized we'd left you here without transportation." He shrugged. "You could have called one of our drivers, but I figured you'd rather have access to a car. So I'm leaving the Porsche."

He had come back because he'd recognized she was uncomfortable.

Her heart warmed. Her pulse fluttered.

"Anyway, when I realized we'd stranded you, I drove back. You were already asleep, and I didn't bother you." He shrugged again. "Or my driver. Nobody wants a Sunday night call, telling them to drive out to the beach to pick up their boss. Especially when it was just as easy for me to stay."

She stared at him. This was Paris Jake coming out and he didn't even realize it. She wondered if he knew he was thinking about her, putting her first, then the baby kicked.

She grabbed her stomach. "Oh, ouch! That was a good one."

His face lit up. "The baby?"

"Yes."

He wanted to touch the baby. She could see it in his expression. But he wouldn't ask.

She laughed. "Come here. I know you want to feel him."

He eased out of his chair and walked over cautiously.

When he reached her, he stooped down to be eye level with her belly and put his hands on either side of the baby bump the way she'd taught him in Paris.

The baby didn't kick this time. It did a full-on stretch and roll.

His gaze jumped to hers. "He totally changed positions."

She should have been uncomfortable with his hands on her so intimately, but the shine in his eyes stopped that in its tracks. This was the guy she wanted to be her baby's father. The unguarded man who simply reacted, didn't think everything through.

"He probably gets tired of being in one spot all the time."

The baby tumbled again and Jake laughed. "Cramped quarters."

The happiness in his voice made her heart swell. He loved this baby. It was weird to think she'd ever believed he'd be happier not knowing he was a father. But her fears from the day before weren't unfounded. This guy would make a great dad. The stuffy guy? Not so much. And come hell or high water, she had to teach him to be himself with their baby.

She tried a joke. "Too bad I can't give him one of the ten bedrooms upstairs."

He winced. "You took a tour?"

"No. I just counted doors in the hall and figured there had to be at least two more bedrooms on the third floor."

"We usually have a lot of guests here. Especially after our Christmas ball."

She rolled her eyes. "I'll bet it's a blast."

"It is." His words weren't sharp, but they were defensive.

Hating the way she'd ruined what could have been

a very nice moment, she batted her hand. "Don't mind me. I've got to get studying today and I don't really feel like it."

The baby stopped moving and Jake rose. "Then don't study. Take a walk on the beach."

She gaped at him. "Have you seen the walk *to* the beach?"

"It's just beyond the yard."

"The yard is the size of a football field. Someday when I'm in the mood for serious exercise I'll tackle that."

His phone pinged and Jake grabbed it from the table. "It's my driver." He glanced around uneasily. "Are you going to be okay here?"

"Sure. Yes." She smiled, forcing herself not to look ungrateful. She loved when he behaved informally, kind, ready to be a father. She wished she could figure out a way to have him act that way all the time.

He tucked his phone in his pocket and turned to her. For thirty seconds, Avery thought he was going to kiss her. Not a heart-stirring, heart-stopping kiss like they'd shared in Paris, but a goodbye kiss. The way he once would have kissed her when she was racing out the door of his penthouse.

Their gazes met before he quickly turned away.

But that almost kiss cemented her feelings. Jake was changing. That guy she met in Paris? That was the real Jake. And not only would he make a great dad, but Avery wasn't just crazy about him. She could trust him.

And that was a problem.

Was it smart to trust him when she wasn't really sure the changes would last?

CHAPTER TWELVE

SHE HATED THE HOUSE.

Jake wasn't letting his mind go there to get his thoughts off the way he'd almost slipped and brushed a quick kiss across her lips before he left. The almost kiss had been an aberration. The way she didn't like the house was a fact.

If they were going to get along, he had to do something about the house.

He arrived at the office, still antsy about Avery being unhappy, but when he bumped into Seth in the hall on his way to his office, the answer hit him.

"Do you and your friends still have that little beach house in Montauk?"

Seth said, "You mean the one down the road from the family house?"

"Yes."

"We have it, but we don't use it as much now that Clark married Harper and Oz and Tina live together."

"Good. I need it."

Seth laughed. "You need it?"

"Avery's condo sold. I invited her to live in the family house and she hates it."

Seth's eyes narrowed. "Hates it? How can she hate it?"

"It's big and she's alone. I know she'd be happier in your bungalow if you don't mind."

"Sure. It's better to have someone staying there than leaving the place empty."

"She'll be there until the baby's born... If that's okay."

"I told you. We don't use it as much as when we could leave work early on Fridays, drive up and drink beer for three days." He sighed. "I miss that."

Jake remembered having to drive to Montauk to bail him, Clark and Oz out of jail. "I don't."

Seth only laughed. "I'll get you the keys to the place when I go to lunch."

Seth started down the hall but Jake called after him, "It's clean, isn't it?"

Without turning around Seth called, "We have a service come in after anyone uses it."

Jake's spirits lifted. He pulled out his phone to call Avery but decided he liked surprising her. When Seth brought the keys to him after lunch, Jake told his administrative assistant he would be working in the car the rest of the day and took the limo back to his apartment to change into jeans and a T-shirt, then told Gerry to drive him to the Montauk house.

He didn't question why he'd changed clothes. Avery seemed to be more comfortable with him when he wasn't in a suit. And he, well, he liked being comfortable. They were going to a bungalow beach house, something that virtually sat in the sand. Being in jeans and a T-shirt and tennis shoes was simply smarter.

Opening the door of the family house, he called, "Anybody home?"

"In the kitchen."

He followed the sound of Avery's voice and found

her making a peanut-butter-and-jelly sandwich. "I hope that's not your dinner."

She stared at him for a few seconds. Her gaze took a stroll down his T-shirt and jeans and she smiled. "Why? Peanut butter has lots of protein and raspberry jelly's just plain good."

His body reacted the way it always did when she looked at him. His heart rate picked up. His muscles tightened. It took every ounce of discipline he could muster not to walk over and kiss her.

"Because it's almost four and you need a vegetable."

She laughed. "I get plenty of those. This is a snack." She took her sandwich from the counter and dropped it on a little plate. "So, what's up? Why are you here?"

"I have a surprise."

She smiled again, as if totally thrilled. "You do?"

This smile washed through him like much-needed summer rain. The attraction was a complication but her liking things he did for her was right. Good.

"Yes. My brother owns a beach house with two friends. It was something they bought to spend week-ends out of the city when their investment firm took off. Anyway, they barely use it anymore since his two friends have settled down, and I asked if you could stay there a few months."

"You're moving me?"

He held out his hand. "Come with me to see it and if you don't like it, you can stay here."

She displayed her plate with the peanut-butter-and-jelly sandwich on it. "Can I bring this?"

He laughed. "Sure."

He snagged the Porsche keys from the center island and led her outside to his car. "I'll tell Gerry to wait for us."

Her head tilted. "Won't he be bored?"

"He's taking classes a few nights a week. When I'm gone for stretches like this he studies. Trust me, I'm not abusing him."

She winced. "Sorry."

"That's okay. I'd rather you bring up things like this than hate me in silence."

She muttered, "I don't hate you," as she rounded the car hood to the passenger seat.

Warm relief filled him, until he realized he knew that. It wasn't him she disliked but his lifestyle. Moving her to a comfortable home fixed that. He was so proud of himself he tossed the keys in the air before he opened the Porsche door and slid inside.

The drive to Seth's beach house took ten minutes. The second Avery saw the bungalow, her eyes lit.

"Oh, my gosh."

Aqua with white shutters and a white stone walkway to the navy blue front door, the little house all but said peace and tranquility.

She shoved open her car door and raced up the walkway, Jake on her heels.

She couldn't get in fast enough after he opened the door. A tan sofa and two chairs sat on a fluffy beige rug that covered hardwood floors. Multicolored throw pillows and bright orange curtains broke up the monotony of all the browns. Beyond the living area was a white kitchen that had two sets of French doors that showcased the ocean that wasn't even as far away as the walk across the backyard at the family house.

"It's perfect."

He bounced the keys in his hand, enjoying his pride at pleasing her. "There are three bedrooms and three baths." He pointed out the French doors. "And as you can see, the deck is huge."

She nodded eagerly, motioning to the big white dining table beside the kitchen. "And I can study there." She turned to him with a smile. "You didn't have to do this."

"I know." He drew in a quick breath. "I hated seeing you uncomfortable."

"Thanks." She laughed and impulsively hugged him.

He squeezed his eyes shut as happiness filled him. The kind he rarely felt. Their baby brushed his stomach and the rightness of the moment about swept him away.

He did hate seeing her uneasy, but there was more to it than that. More to it than responsibility. He had this odd feeling that this was his place. With her. And the more she liked the things he did for her, the more he wanted to do.

They were no longer enemies.

But they were still opponents.

His thoughts from Paris came tumbling back. That getting along meant losing control.

You can't be an equal. Always negotiate from a position of strength.

His heart stilled as his dad's words echoed in his brain. He'd always believed that was one of the things his father had gotten right. And he still believed negotiating from a position of strength was good for business. But what if it was the wrong thing for him personally?

And what if that was his real problem? The way his dad had treated him had turned him into a crafty businessman. Someone even able to take down his father when the time was right. But it hadn't taught him a damn thing about being a dad or having any sort of personal relationship at all.

That's what really had been troubling him since

Avery told him she was pregnant. He didn't know how to be a parent, let alone a good father, but the truth went deeper. He didn't know how to have a personal life.

The conclusion was so striking he almost needed to sit. She'd called him stuffy. But he wasn't stuffy. He just always held himself at a distance. It made life easier. Less complicated.

He'd learned that from dealing with his dad. Keep him at arm's distance, while keeping the relationship equitable. Get comfortable and he'd snatch the rug out from under you.

But Avery wasn't his dad.

She was smart, beautiful, the mother of his child and their encounters had gone from sexual to adversarial to…personal. She was picking her way along the same way he was. Adjusting to having him in her life. But she was doing it a hell of a lot more honestly than he was.

All this time he'd thought he was protecting himself, when maybe he simply didn't know how to let go.

He pulled himself out of Avery's hug. "We should go get your stuff."

She headed to the door. "Great."

He drove them back to the mansion and she bounced out of the car like an eager kid at Christmas.

"I only took one suitcase of clothes upstairs to my room. Let me repack that and I'll be good to go."

"You don't want the other things?"

"Not for right now. I'd like to leave most of the boxes stored in your back room, if you don't mind."

"Okay. You're the one who'll be living with next to nothing."

"I'm fine with that. Jeans, a few shirts, some pajamas and I'm good."

They walked into the foyer and she raced up the

stairs to pack. Ten minutes later, she arrived at the top of the steps with a duffel bag big enough to hold a body.

"Don't you carry that!"

He ran up the stairs and caught the handle of the duffel, so he could take it down the stairs. "No wonder you said you only needed one suitcase."

"Hey, there's a hair dryer and curling iron and cosmetics in there too."

"Oh, well, that explains it."

He managed to get the thing in the trunk of his Porsche, though just barely. They drove to Seth's beach house and once again she hurried out. As they headed up the sidewalk, with him carrying her duffel bag, she took the keys from his hand and opened the door for him.

She made a small production number out of choosing her room, then he tossed the duffel bag onto the bed. He expected her to dismiss him so she could unpack; instead she turned to him.

"Let's take a walk on the beach."

He hadn't intended to—

Or had he? He glanced down at his T-shirt, jeans and tennis shoes and wondered if his subconscious hadn't planned this all along.

If he was going to be fair and honest, the way she was, maybe it was time to go with his feelings.

"A walk on the beach sounds great."

They stepped out onto the back deck and she locked the French doors then pocketed the keys.

This time, he didn't debate holding her hand and she didn't fight it. They strolled down to the water. When they reached it, she took in a long drink of air and sighed.

"Now, this is a beach house."

She turned them to the left and began walking along

the shore, a few feet from the wet mark left by the last high wave. Warm sun beat down on them. The sound of the surf became background music.

"My family and I used to go to Virginia Beach."

The stiffness of his chest loosened a bit. Now that he wasn't fighting his feelings, he saw the comment for what it was. She was telling him things about her life again, continuing the process of getting to know each other.

"Oh, yeah?"

"I have a brother. He's a year older than I am." She peeked at him. "He's a firefighter."

"No kidding."

"He's not a thrill seeker. He likes helping people."

"Must run in the family." He wanted to ask why her brother hadn't been the one to go to school, to sacrifice his life to make up for the fact that there had been no one to help her dad, but he stayed quiet.

"We're not nuts."

"I know."

"In a way, we're sort of like you. You give money to help people. We use our careers."

"Makes sense." He supposed it did, except it rubbed him all the wrong ways that she'd had a dream of working and living in New York and she'd abandoned it.

Still, when they returned to the bungalow an hour later and he stepped into the cozy house, he supposed there were different kinds of comforts in the world. This was a house a person could relax in. He could see himself cooking in the kitchen, watching a football game on the big screen in the living room, as Avery studied at the long dining table.

And for the first time since he'd met her, he wondered if they didn't actually belong together.

* * *

Avery had never had such a good time. Jake really was becoming a different person, and she and the baby were part of it.

But they needed more time. God knew when he'd visit again. She had to make the best use of every minute she had with him.

As she closed the door, she said, "I'd cook you supper, but we don't have any food here."

He winced. "Sorry, I should have thought of that."

"There's a market up the street."

"You've been there?"

"I took a spin in your pretty black Porsche." She grinned at him. "It's not every day a girl gets a sports car left at her disposal."

He laughed and pulled the car keys from his pocket. "Let's go."

Settling behind the steering wheel as she buckled her seat belt, he asked, "What do you want to eat?"

"A big juicy steak." She rubbed her hands together. "I saw the grill on the deck. We can get some veggies and makings for a salad and have a feast."

"Sounds like a good idea." Before he shifted into Reverse to get them on the road, he pulled out his phone. He clicked a few buttons then said, "Hey, it looks like I'm going to be here at least another three hours. If there's anything you want to do, go. I'll call you when I'm ready."

He hung up the phone and glanced at her. "See? I take care of my people."

She wished she hadn't been so critical of him, then realized this might be a good time to show him she could change too. "I know. I've seen it before. I'm sorry for being judgmental."

He grinned. "Well, what do you know? Another apology."

She laughed. "Just drive."

It took them twenty minutes to find the store. Coming at it from a different direction, Avery lost her way twice. Jake laughed at her, then used his phone app to find the store the easy way.

They picked up steaks, veggies, things for salad, pickles, peanut butter and jelly, and Avery had a good time laughing at the way he gasped at the prices. He'd shopped, of course, while at the university, but not recently. He also seemed to love her strange cravings.

At the checkout he let her pay half. Another sign that he'd been paying attention when she talked. She teased him that he was paying for that night's dinner and she took care of the milk, juice, four different kinds of cookies, bread, eggs, peanut butter, jelly, hamburger meat and pickles.

"That'll keep me until tomorrow."

Sliding into the driver's seat, he cut her a sideways glance. "Seriously."

"I'm kidding."

He gave her a doubtful look and appeared to be about to tease her, but his phone rang. He slid it from his pants pocket and tossed it to Avery. "Answer that."

She glanced down at the caller ID. "It's your mom."

"Put it on speaker."

When she pressed the button, he said, "Hey, Mom."

"Jake, oh, Jake. I can't find Seth!"

Wincing at his mom's melodrama, he said, "Is he lost?"

"Clark was killed in an automobile accident this afternoon."

Jake instantly pulled the Porsche into a convenience

store parking lot to give his mother his full attention. "Say that again?"

"Seth's partner Clark was killed today." Maureen burst into tears. "I'm reeling. And if I am this upset I can only imagine how bad Seth is. Sabrina went to his apartment. He's not there."

Avery watched fear race across Jake's face. "I have an idea or two of where he could be. I'll find him."

"Let me know the minute you do."

Avery disconnected the call as Jake shoved the gearshift into Reverse and laid rubber pulling out of the convenience store. "I'll take you home. We'll get the food inside," he said as he sent the car screaming down the quiet street of the lovely beach town. But when he looked over at her, his gaze dipped to her stomach and he slowed his pace.

He drove carefully down the streets to Seth's bungalow. When they got there, he helped her carry her groceries inside and even put the perishables in her fridge.

Then he headed for the door and she followed him.

"Where do you think you're going?"

"With you." He was so upset his driving couldn't be trusted. But he seemed to restrain himself when she was in the car. Maybe to protect his child? Maybe to protect her? Whatever the reason, she wouldn't let him go alone. Not now. Not when their feelings for each other were growing and changing and potentially becoming something wonderful.

"I'm not letting you drive by yourself like this."

"I'm fine."

"Good, then we'll just have a nice trip into the city together."

"It's late and you're tired."

She pushed him toward the door. "Oh, crazy, crazy

man. I've told you. I'm pregnant. Not sick. Now get a move on or I'll grab the keys and drive."

That threat was enough to get him walking again. Inside the car, he started the engine and headed to the city.

She kept him talking, first just small talk, then when he seemed calm, she segued into asking about Seth's friend.

"They just found out Clark's wife Harper is pregnant."

"Oh." *Oh, Lord.* She began to understand his anxiety. He knew Clark's child wouldn't have a dad and it affected him differently than it would have before he'd learned he was going to become a father himself.

The almost three-hour drive seemed never ending, but eventually they made it into the city. After trying Seth's cell phone again and again, they stopped at his apartment. Jake had a key. He didn't knock. He opened the door and walked inside, but Seth wasn't there.

Sitting on the sofa, he pulled out his phone. Avery sat beside him.

"I have the number for Clark's parents. I didn't want to have to bother them, but if he's there with them—"

He broke off as he hit the Contacts button. After a few seconds he said, "Hello, this is Jake McCallan, there's no need to disturb the Hargraves." Avery assumed he was either talking to a maid or someone who'd gone to their house to comfort Clark's parents. "I'm just calling to see if my brother Seth is there." A pause. "He isn't? You're sure?" He closed his eyes. "Thank you."

He disconnected the call. "Okay, so next is the apartment of an old girlfriend."

"You can't call?"

"I don't have her number. I only know her address because they had a party there once." He combed his fingers through his hair. "Seth believes Clark saved him. He was this blue-collar kid, scraping by, but he took Seth in when Seth dropped off the grid because of our dad. Clark didn't expect any money—not even rent—he just took him in."

The unexpected confidence filled her heart with both joy and sorrow. It was wonderful that he knew he could turn to her. Heartrending that he had to.

"People who don't have money can be very generous."

"Seth paid him back by giving him half of the investment firm without any up-front capital." He shook his head again. "They lived in their dodgy apartment for the next five years, long after each could have afforded his own place." His eyes closed. "This will have hit Seth too hard to comprehend. I know he considers Clark more of a brother than he does me."

Avery rubbed her hand across his shoulders. "Hey. When you needed him, Seth left his investment firm to take a place in your company. You're brothers."

He blew his breath out on a sigh. "Yes. We are." He rose and extended his hand to help Avery stand. "Let's go find him."

Seth wasn't at his last girlfriend's. He wasn't at any of the hangouts he frequented. Desperate, Jake drove to the neighborhood where Seth had lived with Clark and Oz.

Avery's heart nearly exploded with relief when Jake said, "There's his car."

They parked on the street five cars behind Seth's. As they approached the Cadillac SUV, they could see Seth behind the wheel, leaning back on the seat as if he was sleeping.

Jake knocked on the window and Seth's head snapped up. "Open the window."

Seth opened the door. "What? What do you want?" He looked around. "What time is it?"

"It's after midnight."

Avery hugged her arms around herself, warding off the chilly night air. "We're here to take you home."

Seth rubbed his hand down his face. "You heard about Clark?"

"Mom called."

Seth closed his eyes, obviously struggling to control his emotions.

Avery's heart broke for Seth, but she saw Jake's strength. He wouldn't let Seth go through this alone. He wasn't just the leader of his family; he loved his brother. Made allowances. Didn't cast aspersions or point fingers.

Jake said, "Avery will drive your car back to your place and I'll drive you."

Avery noticed the empty liquor bottle beside Seth in the passenger seat. Understanding why Jake wanted her to drive, she held back a wince, and as playfully as possible said, "I've always wanted to drive a Caddy."

Seth sucked in a long breath. "This is wrong."

Jake reached in and undid his seatbelt. "Yeah, I know."

"He wasn't even thirty."

Sliding the shoulder harness down his arms, Jake helped him out of the SUV. "You told me he was a year or two younger."

"And Harper's pregnant."

"I know. We talked about it last week."

Avery helped Jake walk Seth to the Porsche then quickly opened the door. They got him into the passenger's seat and buckled in, then Jake reminded her of the address to Seth's apartment. She put it into her phone GPS just in case she lost Jake as they were returning to Seth's.

After a twenty-minute drive, it took ten minutes to find a parking space on the street and another ten to get Seth upstairs and onto his bed, face-first, in his clothes.

When they walked into the sitting area, Jake said, "I'm not sure if he's passed out or sleeping."

"It probably doesn't matter."

"I called my mom while we were driving here to let her know Seth was safe." He dug into his pocket and produced the Porsche keys. "Here, take these. I'm staying." As soon as the words were out of his mouth, he shook his head. "Actually, it's awfully late for you to be making an almost three-hour drive back to the beach house."

She yawned.

"You're staying too." He pointed back to the hall. "Seth has a spare bedroom. I'll sleep on the sofa."

That seemed absolutely stupid, considering their past.

And their present.

They were having a baby. He'd kissed her in Paris and almost kissed her at least three times since they'd returned. She liked him—might even love him. She'd never stopped her merry-go-round of work long enough to really get to know anyone to love them. Yet, it seemed fate had set things up with Jake so she'd not only have time, she'd have ways to get to know him. Not just as a boyfriend or lover but as a wonderful human being.

She caught his hand. "Are you daft? Not only have we slept together often enough that it's ridiculous to be splitting hairs, but I like you." She caught his gaze. "And you like me."

His eyes stayed locked with hers. "I do."

Light burst inside her. He liked her, but more than

that, two weeks ago he never would have been able to make the admission.

But neither would she.

She turned him in the direction of the hall. "Go."

They walked to the bedroom and found extra toothbrushes in the guest bathroom. After stripping down to T-shirts and underwear, they climbed into bed.

Instinct and need rattled through her. The urge to nestle against him trembled along her skin. But it was late and she was tired. She would bet he was too.

Still, she didn't roll away. She lay unmoving beside him, half hoping he would turn and kiss her. For some reason, she couldn't kiss him. Probably because she'd been the one to break the ice and admit she liked him, and force him to admit he liked her too.

He had to make the next move.

She yawned. The warmth of his body spread into the covers and over to her. She closed her eyes and let it take away the chill that had seeped into her bones while they stood on the street with Seth.

CHAPTER THIRTEEN

AVERY FELL ASLEEP almost instantly and Jake closed his eyes, savoring her nearness and the fact that they'd said what they'd both been thinking.

They liked each other.

He'd thought they were opposites, but the more he got to know her the more he realized they shared work ethic, love of family, a desire to do something good in the world.

A few weeks in each other's company had shown them the obvious. They were more alike than they were different.

He'd always believed it would be frightening to be so vulnerable, but every time he thought of having her in his life there was a tightness in his chest that was more anticipation of joy than fear.

The thought kept him awake for another hour. Things might not work out and she could leave him. They could still fight. They hadn't settled the logistics of their lives…a million things could happen.

But he didn't give in to fear. Never had. Never would. He took action. He could control so many of the things that might bedevil them. He would focus on those.

Confident, he drifted off.

Hours later, he woke with a start. He would have

bounced up in bed, except something held him in place. He glanced down and found Avery nestled into his side. Her head on his shoulder like a pillow.

His heart expanded as the events of the day before came back to him. They'd walked on the beach, shopped, found Seth together. But all those were quickly overshadowed by how damned wonderful she felt snuggled against him.

He enjoyed the feeling for a minute or two, then slid out of bed to use the bathroom and brush his teeth. When he returned she was awake, sitting up on the bed with all her glorious red hair a tumbled mess flowing around her.

"Good morning."

It took a second before he found his voice. They weren't just a hookup anymore. They liked each other. She was beautiful, smart, kind. And his for the taking.

"Good morning."

She got out of bed before he had a chance to get back in. Disappointment roared through him. "Where are you going?"

"There's a little person on my bladder. Never question a pregnant woman on her way to the bathroom." She rose to her tiptoes and brushed a quick kiss across his lips. Her eyes filled with promise. "Get back in bed."

He laughed lightly as she scampered past him, though his heart thudded in his chest. Everything was so different between them now. Better.

She returned a few minutes later, slid under the covers and nestled against him.

"I wonder if Seth is up."

Her voice was soft, a low, quiet whisper, because if Seth was still sleeping, she wouldn't want to wake him. Now that they had spent time together, real time, doing normal things, he knew that about her. He knew she was good. She knew he wasn't stuffy as much as responsible.

She was the first person ever to really know him. The first person to ever really care to know him. And she'd come back to bed, because this was right.

"I doubt he's awake yet."

"I don't hear anything beyond the door."

Jake shrugged, feeling her silky hair move against his skin, waking all his nerve endings.

"He's going to need fluids, aspirin and something to eat."

"If he drank that whole bottle of whiskey, the something to eat might have to wait until about noon or so."

She shifted against him. "I wonder what time it is."

He leaned over and got his phone from the bedside table. "A little after seven."

"We should get up. Check on Seth."

He realized she was stalling. Maybe waiting for him to make the first move. "Or we could stay here."

She laughed, low and throaty. "Why, Mr. McCallan. Are you propositioning me?"

She knew damned well he was, but he liked the flirting. He liked being reminded of how they had been when they met, as much as he liked how their relationship had morphed into something more.

He pulled back, smoothed his hand along her tummy, feeling the child that would bring them together before he let it skim down her hips, along her thighs and back up again.

She sighed with contentment, and he bent down, pressed his mouth to hers, starting slowly, enjoying her plump lips, then he deepened the kiss as she rolled to her side.

He could have ravaged her. That's what his hormones ached to do. It's also what he would have done six months ago. But this was no longer about having sex. This was about emotion.

He liked her.

And she liked him.

The sheer joy of it filled him as a horrible retching noise rent the air.

Avery's eyes popped open. "Oh-oh."

Jake sighed.

"We should go and help him."

He nuzzled her neck. "He's a grown man. He'll be fine."

"Um, Jake. If we can hear him, that means he'll be able to hear us."

He thought about that then cursed.

"All right." He tossed the covers back and got out of bed. "You get the aspirin and some bottled water and I'll check on my brother."

He walked to the master bedroom wearing only his T-shirt and underwear, but Avery took the time to step into her jeans. Her sexy, butt-hugging jeans.

If Seth hadn't interrupted them, they would have made love. And if they'd dated like two normal people instead of just falling into bed, he was sure they'd *be in love* right now. Because he was absolutely positive that was what was happening between them.

Even the fact that they'd found a house they both liked, albeit that it was Seth's, proved they were finding common ground. They were going to build a life together.

And he wasn't letting any of it to chance.

Avery drove the Porsche back to Seth's beach house and had to admit it was an amazing car. She put the top down and the air that spilled inside wreaked havoc with her hair, but she didn't care. For the first time since she got pregnant, she wasn't worried about Jake. Wasn't worried he'd find out about the baby and try to take it. Wasn't worried that he'd discover her dad's troubles. They were falling in love. For real.

Her life felt good. Wonderful.

She wasn't in the door of Seth's cozy bungalow two minutes before her phone rang.

Seeing it was Jake, she smiled as she answered, "Hey, you."

"How was the drive out?"

"Effortless. That car is fabulous. And now that I know I can handle it on the highway, I was thinking I should take a day and visit my parents."

Jake didn't say anything for a few seconds. When he did speak, his voice had changed to cautiously optimistic. "If you're going to visit your parents, maybe it would be a good thing for me to go too."

Her heart caught. He wanted to meet her family and she wanted him to meet them. But she didn't want him to cut her visit short. She had things to do. She might be falling in love, but her life plan hadn't changed. She would be starting a law firm in Wilton. But she and Jake weren't at the place where they could talk about things like moving in together, let alone where they would live. And she couldn't take anything for granted. She had to go forward.

"Did you forget or not hear that I said I wanted to take a day? A *whole* day?"

"I can take a day."

She laughed. "Really?"

"Yes. You came to Paris with me to tell my mom about the pregnancy. I can take a day and introduce myself to your parents so they don't think the father of their grandchild is an unmitigated snob."

She winced. "I never told them you were a snob. I told them you were stuffy."

"So? I can be stuffy with them and meet or exceed their expectations."

She laughed again. "Stop. I just want you to be you."

His voice softened. "I can do that too."

He could. She knew that now. She also knew that he could surprise her and be funny, or kind, or understanding the way he was with Seth.

"We'll plan on tomorrow?"

"Sounds good."

She hesitated. It was on the tip of her tongue to ask him to stay at the beach house with her that night so they could get an early start, but she knew what would happen, and, honestly, there was a part of her that wasn't ready. She might have thrown caution to the wind at Seth's apartment, but now that things were really happening, her fears had reawakened.

He was still a rich guy, someone accustomed to getting everything he wanted. Her family had learned a huge lesson with Paul Barnes. Wealthy people didn't think the way average people did. They also used their power and influence to make sure they got what they wanted.

The overflowing emotions she had for Jake didn't mitigate or change the fact that they lived two different kinds of lives and wanted two different things out of life. They could laugh and play all they wanted. But at the end of the day, he was responsible not just for the family business but for his family.

And she wanted to change the world. Or at least her little corner of it. No matter how funny or friendly or downright happy they were, their lives would not easily mesh. One of them was going to have to make a huge compromise.

And she didn't think it could be her.

But maybe this trip would show them if it could be him?

"Okay, I'll see you tomorrow morning."

"You will."

"Bring doughnuts."

She disconnected the call to the sound of his laughter. But she also realized their trip to Wilton just might prove that he couldn't compromise any more than she could.

They were on the road the next morning by eight. He'd left his penthouse at four, with Gerry driving so he could work, and he arrived at the bungalow on time to eat two of the doughnuts he'd brought for breakfast. Then they headed for Pennsylvania.

Avery liked the Porsche so much that he kept the top down and they drove in the warm sunshine. She prompted him to take an exit a few miles past Allentown then directed him another couple of miles to the small town of Wilton. They glided along streets filled with quaint buildings and shops until they stopped at a ranch house.

After pulling up to the closed garage door, he turned to Avery. "That's not as far as I thought it would be."

She brightened. "I know!"

Thinking out loud, he added, "I bet it would be under an hour by helicopter."

An older woman raced from the front door before they could open their car doors. When Avery got out, she grabbed her and hugged her.

Jake exited the Porsche more slowly, examining the house and understanding why Avery loved Seth's bungalow so much, then looking at the short red-haired woman and taller bald man.

The man stepped forward, "I'm Dennis, Avery's dad. Everybody calls me Denny." He pointed to the woman who had her arm around Avery's waist. "That's Avery's mom, Andrea."

He said, "Hello," and shook both of their hands. As they walked into the small uncluttered home, he watched Denny in awe. This man had spent six years in prison for something he hadn't done, but you would never know it. In his jeans and sweatshirt, he was quiet and unassuming, but he had an easy laugh and a sparkle in his eye. He didn't appear bitter or angry. Just normal.

Avery's mom took her into the kitchen to get coffee and cake, but Jake could hear her grilling Avery about her pregnancy, whether she was taking care of herself. She seemed pleased to hear Avery had lost her job, then not so pleased to hear she was living in a beach house owned by Jake's brother.

"Why don't you come home?"

"My doctor's in the city," Avery casually replied. "Besides, I have a whole house to myself. I've got my Pennsylvania bar exam things scattered all over the dining room table. When I get hungry, I eat. When I get tired of studying, I go for a walk on the beach. Remember our beach trips, Mom?"

Andrea let out a long sigh. "Of course, I do."

"Seth's house is like one of the ones we used to rent. Except it has a big screen TV and a patio the size of Ohio."

Her mother laughed. "You always were one for exaggeration."

"And the beach is semiprivate so I'm not running into weirdos."

"That's always good."

Jake chuckled and Denny cleared his throat. "They could gab like that for hours."

Jake faced him. "Does Avery visit often?"

Denny shrugged. "In spurts. She loves it here in the summer, so when she doesn't have a lot of work to do, she's here on the weekends."

"It's not really a long drive."

"Depends on what you consider long."

"I've been traveling almost three hours to get to the beach house where Avery's living."

"You've been going there?"

"I don't exactly check up on her, but I do like to make sure she has everything she needs."

Denny laughed. "Good man."

The warmth of Denny's approval filled him. So, he pushed just a little bit more. "Have you and your wife ever been to the city?"

"Avery's dragged us there a time or two."

"You don't like it?"

He leaned close and whispered, "It's amazing. I love the restaurants. I could do without the shopping though."

Jake chuckled, fully understanding. "Have you ever been to a Knicks game?"

"Wanted to, but there never seems to be time."

"Maybe I could arrange for you to get tickets."

Denny seemed surprised. "That would be great."

"You tell me the next time you'll be in New York and I'll make sure there are tickets at the door for you."

Avery and her mom walked in. Avery held a tray

with four pieces of cake on it. Andrea held the tray with coffee and mugs.

"Hope you don't mind simple."

He glanced at her. "Simple?"

"Just plain plates for cake and mugs for coffee."

He laughed. "If the cake is good, I'd eat it with my fingers."

Andrea beamed.

The cake was delicious. So was lunch at the diner. As he expected, his choice of T-shirt and jeans got him through the town with minimal notice. Everyone noticed Avery, though. They stopped. Talked. Hugged her. And then shook his hand when she introduced him.

It was all easy and nice. There were a few residents who gave them sideways glances, but he suspected that had more to do with the fact that there were those in the town who didn't believe her dad was innocent.

But Avery didn't seem to care. She focused on the people she liked, the ones who liked her.

He glanced around as she chatted. This would make an exceptional place to bring a child for long visits, to give him or her the opportunity not merely to see, but also to experience the other side of life.

It wouldn't only be good for their child. It would be good for him too. He wanted to understand everything about Avery, and to enjoy a little peace and quiet himself a few times a year. Week-long visits to her parents would benefit all of them. And if there was an emergency in the city, a helicopter could get him there quickly.

Everything was working out perfectly.

It was time to call Pete Waters.

CHAPTER FOURTEEN

THEY RETURNED TO the beach house a little before dark. The Porsche roared onto the driveway in front of the two-car garage. Jake pressed the button that opened the doors and once the Porsche was parked, he closed them again.

She didn't think that strange until he followed her into the kitchen and tossed the keys onto the center island.

"Where's Gerry?"

"Probably at home with his family." He caught her gaze. "I thought I'd stay tonight."

The day before that suggestion would have made her think of all the things they still had to work out. But after the way he'd gotten along with her parents, made small talk with her friends and obviously liked her hometown, everything seemed right. She fit into his world. But more important, he fit into hers.

She walked over to him, slid her arms around his neck and kissed him. "I'll need a shower first."

He tightened his arms around her waist. "How about if we shower together?"

She laughed. "That sounds like a great idea."

He kissed her deeply, wonderfully, and she melted into him. The kiss went on and on, an expression of pure emotion. Then he picked her up and carried her to the bedroom.

* * *

An hour later, sated and happy, clean and dry, she snuggled close to Jake in the big king-size bed of the bungalow's master bedroom, unable to believe how lucky she was.

Pressed against his side, she felt him take a long breath. She sat up. "Are you okay?"

"Yeah. Probably more okay than I've ever been in my life."

"But?"

"I'm wondering how much I missed."

"Missed?"

"With you—" He glanced at her. "With *us*, things just happen. Even the way we found each other on Valentine's Day. Most of what we've done hasn't been planned and it's been remarkable."

"This really is the first time something like this has happened to you?"

"When I was a kid, I was too afraid to just let things happen. I was also constantly trying to stay one step ahead of my dad. Then, when I went to work for him I had to watch him like a hawk."

"You had good reason."

"I totally changed the company's reputation."

She lay back down and nestled against him. "So now you can relax."

"Part of me is afraid I won't be a good father because I didn't have a good father."

"Are you kidding? I'm guessing you've been more of a dad to Seth than your father ever was."

He stayed quiet.

"Jake, a lot of it comes naturally. We're going to see our little boy or little girl and just melt like two sticks of butter."

He laughed. "You have the best ways of phrasing things."

She tapped his chest. "And you have a whole lot of love in that heart beating in there. All a child wants is to be loved."

"The way your parents loved you?" He took another breath. "I had a short chat with your dad. He had no complaints about you. Nothing he'd change."

She thought about that. Though she had no doubt Maureen loved her children, she loved them a little differently than the way Avery's parents loved her. Easily. Naturally. No strings attached. No work required.

"That's sort of the key to parenting. Just to love your child exactly as he is and guide him through the tough stuff."

"I really liked your parents."

"They liked you too."

"And your small town."

Her heart skipped a beat. She'd seen the way he'd looked around. But more than that, she'd seen how easily he'd gotten comfortable. He might not be ready to say the words, but he could live there. She could already picture it.

"It's a beautiful place. I can understand why you love it so much."

"It was a great place to grow up."

"I'll bet. That park was amazing."

Part of her wanted to say, *So that's why I think we should live there.* But it was still too soon. They'd dated three weeks in the winter but had only gotten to know each other in the past two weeks.

She couldn't ask him to move for her any more than he could ask her to move for him.

"I'm not sure if this is good timing or bad but I have

another charity ball on Saturday." He shifted so he could see her face. "I want you to go with me."

"To announce to the world that this is your baby?"

"I think the world got that point when the tabloid printed our picture, remember? It's why we had to race to France."

She smiled at the memories. "If I'm going, I'm wearing the same dress I wore to the ball in Paris."

He shrugged. "I don't care. You looked stunning in that dress."

"I did." She laughed. "I'm not vain. It's just not easy to find a dress that looks that good when you're six months pregnant."

"Getting close to seven," he agreed, his voice filled with something that sounded like awe.

She knew exactly what he felt. Her skin virtually sparkled from the light of happiness glowing inside her. It wasn't all from the baby. It was from him. He'd gone from being stuffy and bossy to easygoing and happy. And now he talked. Not only about little things. About everything.

Though she knew the pregnancy had begun his metamorphosis, she'd like to think she'd been the one to make him happy, that a little bit of compromise had taken them a long way. Sure, they needed more time to cement what they felt. And after that there were tons more compromises to make. But from the way he'd reacted to her parents and to Wilton, she knew everything would work out.

The ball on Saturday night at the Waldorf turned out to be nearly a carbon copy of the one in Paris. The attendees and the language they spoke might be different, but the protocol was the same. Maureen walked with Avery and Jake through the receiving line, proud to have her son beside her and eager to introduce Avery as the mother of her soon-to-be-born grandchild. Like Jake, she didn't seem to mind Avery wore the same gown.

Of course, that could be because—with the exception of Annalise and Julianna—the people who saw her wear it the first time were across an ocean.

Still, everything was perfect, wonderful.

They danced the entire first set of songs without even once returning to the table. They had just finished a dance and were laughing when the band announced their break. As they walked to their seats, Jake slid his arm around her waist and she leaned into him.

Annalise sighed. "You're such a lovely couple."

Maureen sniffed. "They are, but it looks like one half of that couple is getting tired."

She was, but she didn't want to leave. She couldn't believe how easily she'd gotten adjusted to his life, his mother, attending parties littered with the rich and famous. But it was more proof that with a little compromise they fit.

"Let's stay for another couple of dances."

"Okay by me."

They danced the night away, then went back to his penthouse and made love. Jake fell into a sound sleep almost immediately but it didn't bother her. When they were dating he had been the lightest sleeper on the planet. It was as if he had been so bogged down by worry that he never totally relaxed. Now he slept. Peacefully. Easily.

She wanted to take the credit for that too.

The baby moved and she waited for him to stop, but he didn't. Not only did he roll around as if doing somersaults, but he kept her wide awake. Not wanting to disturb Jake she eased out of bed.

Chilled, she shrugged into a huge robe she found in his dressing room and padded toward the kitchen. She poured herself a glass of milk and made a peanut-butter-and-jelly sandwich and headed to his office.

He'd used her computer on the flight to Paris so she decided it was okay to use his. Like his documents, her notes for the bar exam were available through off-site storage, and rather than waste this whole night, she would use it to study.

She slipped into the office where his laptop sat open on a polished oak desk. She knew he'd worked on it that afternoon but was surprised he hadn't turned it off. She hit the Enter key to wake it up, only to discover an email from Pete Waters was up on the screen. She raised her hand to minimize the email, but as she did, she saw her name.

Oh, now she really couldn't look at it.

If this was about their custody battle or even about the fact that they might not need one, she couldn't see this.

Except the words *pro bono* caught her eye.

This email was not about their custody battle.

But it was about her and…

The pro bono arm of Waters, Waters, and Montgomery?

She sat down, swallowing hard as she read the short email. A deal between Jake and Pete Waters. His family would sign a ten-year contract to retain Waters, Waters and Montgomery and the firm would agree to expand their pro bono arm any way *Avery* wanted.

So she would stay in New York City.

CHAPTER FIFTEEN

JAKE AWAKENED THE NEXT morning and rolled over to hug Avery, but she was gone. He got out of bed, slipped into the pajama bottoms he'd carelessly flung halfway across the room the night before and walked out to the kitchen.

She wasn't there.

"Avery?"

He strolled through the hall, into the empty living room and finally headed for the office. He found her sitting at the desk, but facing the view of the skyline outside the huge penthouse window.

"Why would you be making a deal for me to work with Waters, Waters and Montgomery?"

His heart sank. Not because he didn't want her to know, but because all of this was happening the wrong way. The most unromantic way. And he'd wanted his proposal to be something she remembered for the rest of her life.

He took a few steps into the room. "It was all part of a marriage proposal."

She swiveled the chair around, her expression horrified. "Getting me a job was part of your marriage proposal?"

He laughed. "No. Well, sort of. After I'd asked you to marry me—" He walked over to a bookcase, removed three fat volumes and revealed a wall safe. With a few twists of a dial, he had the door open. He took out the jeweler's box.

She bounced out of the chair. "Don't even ask!" Her eyes filled with tears that quickly spilled over. "I've spent the biggest part of my life preparing to take my place in the world, as an advocate for people who fall through the cracks."

"And you can do that at Waters, Waters and Montgomery." He stopped, his heart simultaneously crashing and filling with fear. "Sweetheart." He struggled to keep his voice from sounding desperate. He'd genuinely figured out the best compromise position, yet she didn't see it. "I have to stay in New York. You can be more flexible. This works for us."

"More flexible?" She should have looked small and helpless in his huge robe. Instead, she looked regal, strong. "I thought after our visit to Pennsylvania, you saw another compromise. One that actually required you to bend a little."

His face scrunched in confusion. "You thought I was considering moving to Pennsylvania?"

Her chin lifted. "It's not such a stretch. An hour helicopter ride to the city, remember? But really, that's not the issue." She reached across the desk, turned his laptop toward him. "This is a finalization memo. There had to have been discussions. Meetings. Other emails. Planning." She caught his gaze. "You did all this without ever once consulting me."

His heart did a silly thing, like a rumba that combined his fear that her anger was too great to pacify and a horrible, horrible feeling that he was like his dad, had done something his father would have done. Easily. Without thought that it was wrong. Because he didn't think it was wrong. He saw it as right. Just as his dad always did.

"I…" He swallowed.

Why hadn't he told her?

Because he wasn't accustomed to consulting anyone.

Why wasn't he accustomed to consulting anyone?

Because he was the boss.

Like his dad.

No! He'd fought that and won. This was just the overplanner in him coming out again.

"I know this is going to sound like an excuse but, honestly, I'm accustomed to doing things that I see need to be done. You've gotten me to stop planning, but I can't completely stop thinking ahead. I run a conglomerate. If I never planned, the companies would fall apart. Thinking ahead is what I do."

"Even if you're wrong?"

"This isn't wrong! You said yourself your original dream had been to get an education, find a high-powered job in New York and get an apartment in Paris. A second home."

She gaped at him. "That was the dream of a child. As I grew up, that dream changed into something more meaningful."

"And working for the pro bono arm of Waters, Waters and Montgomery, you'll have the more meaningful job. If you would take a few minutes and think it through, you would see this is right. This is the right answer."

"And if you would take a few minutes to think it through, you would see that if you think that's right, you don't know me at all. You don't know my heart. You don't know that I've worked all these years with a very specific goal in mind. To help my friends. My neighborhood. Not some equally worthy group of people that I don't know. But my friends." She walked up to him, caught his gaze. "Because I don't think you understand loyalty." Her eyes filled with tears again and she swallowed. "I don't think you understand friendship or community." She swallowed again. "Or love. All you see is what you want. What you need."

With that she brushed past him.

He let her go. He had to. What she said was the truth. He thought he loved her. But she was right. He couldn't love her if he didn't know her. If he'd truly known her, he would have realized a job in New York might appease her but it wouldn't satisfy her.

He was so casually selfish that he didn't even see it in himself anymore.

His heart cracked as pain pummeled him. He'd lost the best thing he'd ever had because he was selfish.

Avery didn't pack, only changed clothes. Wearing jeans and a T-shirt, she stormed out of Jake's penthouse and was on the street in what felt like seconds.

She was glad he hadn't followed her. Her heart absolutely ached with grief. And not even for herself. But for him.

She'd seen from the look on his face that even after their conversation about how to love their baby, everything she'd told him about loving her had surprised him. He'd been born confident, privileged, believing everything he said and did was right because he only ever came at problems with one need in mind. His. Or his family's. Most often his family's.

She stood on the sidewalk, seven months pregnant, broken, with a hundred dollars in her wallet, two credit cards and a three-hour cab ride to Seth's beach house, and then she'd have to get herself and her belongings to Wilton.

She took a long breath to steady herself and called her dad. "Any chance you feel like a drive to the city?" She could leave her clothes behind, but eventually she'd have to go back to the beach house for her books and laptop. Today, however, was not that day.

Her dad answered sleepily, as if she'd awakened him. "Where are you?"

She hailed a cab. "I'm on my way to Broadway. Remember the hotel you and Mom loved."

"Yes."

"That's where I'll be. In front of that hotel."

Her dad's voice dipped. "Are you okay?"

"I'm fine." She struggled with a sob that wanted to erupt and grief that cut the whole way to her soul, but she said, "Really. I'm just not staying at the beach house anymore."

A taxi finally stopped. She glanced back at Jake's building, realizing she'd given him at least five minutes to put on pants and come after her. But he hadn't. He was up in his ivory tower. Warm. Safe. Coddled.

If she'd accepted the form of love he wanted to give her, she'd be compromising for the rest of her life.

Compromising everything she wanted.

Because the rich didn't compromise. They took what they wanted.

So why did her heart hurt? Why did her chest feel anchored down with grief?

She drew a shaky breath as she reached for the door. "Gotta go, Dad. See you in front of the hotel."

"It's gonna be a couple of hours."

"It's Sunday. Traffic will be light. But even if it isn't, I'm fine. I'll get breakfast. Watch tourists. I'll be okay."

She thought that until the taxi left her off and she began looking for somewhere to eat. Then her knees began to shake and her heart shattered into a million pieces.

She could call Jake a snob all she wanted. She could recognize that he liked things his own way, that he pushed and manipulated, but deep down she knew he was a prisoner of his life.

And maybe he was right. Maybe he really didn't have choices.

Jake spent Sunday sitting in the chair where he'd found Avery that morning, staring out the office window the way she had been. Sunlight sparkled off the windows of high-rises. The sky was so clear and blue, he could see for miles.

The sun set. The moon rose. At one point, he told himself to get up off the chair and take a shower, but he didn't listen. He just sat there.

Monday morning, he called Seth and told him he wouldn't be in to work that day. Then he hung up the phone so Seth couldn't ask why.

Tuesday, he actually showered but didn't dress beyond sweats and a T-shirt. What had happened with Avery, everything she'd said, became an endless loop in his brain, taunting him one minute, tormenting him the next.

Wednesday, he drove to the beach house but she wasn't there. Neither were her things. Seth phoned that afternoon to tell him that she'd returned the keys, and though Jake said, "Thanks for letting me know," a shockwave went through him.

What if she'd come to the office hoping to see him?

When his heart rate picked up and his hope restored at just the possibility, he ran his hand across his mouth.

Loving her wasn't helping him. It was ruining him. He hadn't been to work in days. He'd abandoned Seth in his time of grief. And God only knew what his mother was up to.

He called Gerry.

As Gerry drove him to the office, he called his mom. She chatted on about things that should change in the city, projects she wanted him to take on, and he saw his calendar fill up with meetings he'd need to hold. It rattled through him that his life always seemed to be dictated by somebody else. It rattled through him that all his free time was now gone. It rattled through him that he'd probably never find real love again.

But lots of people in life were given worse destinies. He would step into his.

When he arrived at work, his office quickly filled with assistants and vice presidents. He didn't blink. He handled everything.

The mess cleared around six, when everyone either had their question answered or had an appointment to see him the next day. A half hour later, Seth poked his head in the door.

"I see the thundering herd is gone."

He nodded, eager to talk to his brother and help him too. "Come in." He motioned for him to take a seat. "How are you feeling?"

Seth's eyes filled with sadness. "The shock wore off and the grief that followed was brutal."

"I can only imagine."

"How are *you* feeling?"

He shook his head as if he didn't understand the question. "I'm fine."

"Avery looks like hell."

His head snapped up. "Does she look sick?"

"More like worn and tired."

Hearing that, he pulled himself together again. "It's part of pregnancy. Her mother will make sure she gets sufficient rest."

"*You* should be making sure she gets sufficient rest. I saw you two that morning at my apartment."

"You were so hungover you were probably also seeing unicorns and rainbows."

"You couldn't hide the looks that passed between you or the way you just sort of meshed."

He laughed. "Seriously? Meshed? The woman wants to live in Pennsylvania."

"What's wrong with Pennsylvania?"

"I belong here."

"Who says?"

"My job for one. Plus, Mom." He thought of the eight million things she wanted him to accomplish in the firm's name, took a breath and sighed. "It doesn't matter anyway. Avery accused me of manipulating her, but the truth is she was manipulating me too. Not overtly."

It made him feel odd to say that. Avery hadn't said one word about their situation. Adding himself to her trip to Pennsylvania had been his idea. And when he even thought something negative about her his heart hurt. So he stopped himself.

"You're really upset because she thinks you're controlling."

He raised his gaze to look at Seth. "I am controlling. I see the way a thing should go and move heaven and earth to get it there."

"It's why the company is successful. You made us honest again."

"Apparently, I wasn't honest with Avery. I just went to Pete Waters and made a deal for her to head his pro bono department."

"Without asking her?"

"I wanted to surprise her." He shook his head and closed his eyes. "I liked surprising her. Surprises made her happy. I thought the job with Pete would make her happy."

"You are really new at this love stuff."

Offended, he stiffened. "I've had girlfriends."

"We've all had girlfriends, but we don't always fall in love." His head tilted as he studied his brother. "It really did surprise you, didn't it?"

"I thought it was perfect."

"Nothing is perfect."

"Right."

"I'm serious." Seth studied him for a few seconds. "You don't miss her?"

"I'm happier when I'm angry with her, when I'm not thinking about how much fun we had. But you just disabused me of my perfectly acceptable excuse of thinking she manipulated me. And now all I can remember are the good times. So, I miss her again." He squeezed his eyes shut and let the hurt roll through him.

Seth laughed. "Jake, go after her. Compromise. Figure this out."

Jake gaped at his younger brother. "Look who's giving me advice. You haven't had a steady girlfriend in four years."

"Because I made a mistake. I let the woman I wanted get away."

Jake's face scrunched in confusion. "There was someone you were serious about?"

"I didn't even know it until it was too late." He

glanced up at Jake. "And even then I think I could have fixed it. But I did the same thing as Dad. I sucked it up, told myself I was a McCallan and it was her loss."

"The way he used to when a negotiation went bad."

"Exactly. I did that and I lost. Don't lose. Go after her."

He shook his head. "I can't. She didn't accept my proposal. She wouldn't even let me propose. Part of me knows she's right and the other part realizes that if she didn't like the deal I made with Pete Waters, then maybe she doesn't know me well enough to love me."

Seth sat back. "You really think that?"

"I don't know what to think."

"What do you want?"

He wanted to feel forever what Avery made him feel. He wanted fun dinners, relaxed afternoons, hot sex that was still warm and intimate. He wouldn't tell even one of those to his brother.

"I don't know."

"Have you ever really thought about it? I mean, being brought up as the guy to replace Dad never gave you a chance to figure out who you wanted to be."

He'd never looked at it that way, but he supposed that was true.

Seth rose. "Do me a favor. Before you write off the woman Mom thinks is absolutely perfect for you and I thought was cute and funny enough to give you a real run for your money…think about it. If you didn't have the shackles of this job, what would you be doing right now?"

CHAPTER SIXTEEN

AVERY GOT UP every morning at six, cried, then took a shower. The first day after she'd left New York, she'd quickly realized living with her parents in a three-bedroom ranch with one bathroom wasn't an option.

The next day, she'd busied herself with finding an apartment or rental house she could move into immediately and found a vacated Cape Cod that was for sale. It made her think of Maureen and she cried when she signed the purchase agreement, but she told the listing agent it was pregnancy hormones then spent an hour listening to Alice Johnson's pregnancy stories.

Because that's what life was about in a small town. And being a part of her community again would probably save her. She went to the post office, the diner and shopped at the grocery store for her mom, listening to stories, talking about the law firm she intended to start.

Though not many people needed a criminal lawyer, everybody had a tale about an estate settlement gone wrong, sexual harassment, a lease, a brother-in-law who'd borrowed money and hadn't paid it back... and suddenly she felt like Judge Judy.

She walked to the ranch house and told her parents she'd paid cash for the Cape Cod and would be moving in within a week. Though they were concerned about her living out the last months of her pregnancy alone, at the end of the week, once the deed had been recorded and her check had cleared, they helped her cart her boxes over.

Maureen called. Pretending to be chipper, Avery was glad to have the Cape Cod to talk about because it prevented awkward silences. She even gave her the address so she could send housewarming flowers.

Two days later, sitting on the floor of the empty living room—the purchaser of her condo now owned her living room furniture, dining room table and bedroom set—she looked around at the rest of her life.

Eventually, she would paint the dark woodwork white, install hardwood floors bleached and stained a pale gray and furnish the room with a white burlap sofa and chair with a bright print area rug and flowers on the mantel of the stone fireplace.

She'd remodel the kitchen and knock out a wall, so she could see her daughter or son playing in front of the fireplace on cold winter nights as she made soup.

The picture that formed brought tears to her eyes again. Jake should be in that picture too. Leaning over his laptop at the kitchen table, while he talked on the phone.

When the soup was ready, he'd say, "Sorry, gotta go. Dinner's on the table." Then he'd eat a real meal with her and their child. They'd do homework together, get the kid's bath together and read stories as a family. Because that's what he needed. A slice of real life. The chance to be himself.

But he'd never get it because controlling things until they were perfect, flawless, no chance of spilled milk or actual human contact had been ingrained in him.

She got up from the floor, stretched and let the baby move around, repositioning itself to be comfortable.

When the old-fashioned doorbell sent a loud buzz through the house, she winced, realizing that was another thing she'd have to change. And the sooner the better.

She wobbled to the door. A dark wood frame housed beveled glass that had been pieced together like art. Two long rectangular pieces stood like sentries on the right and left side, while smaller pieces mixed and mingled to make something that looked like a crystal sunrise.

She was definitely keeping that.

She opened the door without thinking and when she saw Jake standing on her wide front porch with huge white columns, her mind went blank.

"Hey."

He wore a black leather jacket over a T-shirt and jeans and with a few days' growth of beard he looked disreputable and sexy. Just normal enough to be a good dad and just sexy enough to be...*hers*.

Her hormones kicked in and she almost started to cry, but she caught herself. This guy was smart and savvy. And he was her child's father. They'd never gotten around to discussing custody or visitation.

He could be here to determine just how strong she was.

He could be here to negotiate.

He could be here to bully her...

Or manipulate her.

This wasn't the time for tears, or thinking how plain old sexy he looked. This was the moment she either protected her child from overexposure to everything money could buy, or started a never-ending battle with one of the most powerful families in the United States.

Just when she was ready for the worst, he pulled a

bouquet of flowers from behind his back and handed them to her.

Her heart skipped a beat. Her thoughts scattered.

"These are from Mom. She said to tell you the vase is coming. It's Tiffany something or another. She ordered it hoping it would come to your house before the flowers died."

Her heart plummeted so fast, she wondered if she had any pulse at all. Of all the stupid things to do, jumping to the conclusion that he'd bought her flowers because he loved her, maybe wanted to compromise, was the stupidest, stupidest thing she had ever done.

She took the flowers. "Thank your mother for me." Then she shook her head. "No. Don't. I know my new protocol is to send an appropriate thank-you note."

She made a move to close the door, but he put his foot in it before she could.

She glanced up sharply. That was so not a Jake McCallan thing to do.

"In retrospect, giving you flowers from my mother was pretty dumb. I came here to apologize and ended up looking like a delivery guy."

The way he said that, as if making a mental note never to do it again, almost had her laughing. But she refused to let his charm get to her. Too much was at stake.

"If you want to talk about custody or visitation, save it for a hearing or a meeting with our lawyers. Tell Pete I hired Andi Petrunak as my legal counsel. Too much has passed between us for us to try to negotiate on our own."

He put his foot a little farther in the door. "That's actually why I'm here."

"I thought it was to apologize."

"It was. Then after the apology I was going to tell you that I love you."

Her heart flattened then swelled. "You've never said that before."

"And I'm not sure why. I've loved you since Paris. Knew it in my heart, just wanted to get all our ducks in a row before I said it."

"There's your problem," she said, her voice breaking with raw emotion. She loved this man in a way that encompassed so many things that she couldn't even name them. And he had to have every i dotted and t crossed before he could even hold a decent conversation. "You think too much. You want everything perfect—"

He reached in the door, caught her by the waist and hauled her to him, kissing her fiercely. She wrapped her arms around his neck and let him take her where he would. Not only did she like this side of him, but he needed to be able to live this side of himself freely.

He finally released her. "How's that for not thinking."

"You're getting the hang of it."

She said it so casually that he laughed. "I will figure all this out, you know."

"Don't!" she said, dragging him off her porch and into the small foyer then the empty sitting room. "Don't always do what you think you have to do. Do what you want to do."

"I can't spend my life not planning. It's not how I'm wired. But I did realize that I can't always plan alone."

"I'm listening."

"I knew what you wanted, but I thought that was what you wanted before we started... I think that's how I justified making big sweeping arrangements."

"You never thought to ask?"

He shook his head. "I wanted to surprise you. You

like surprises. I didn't think it through." He winced. "I'm embarrassed to have to admit that."

"You should be."

"Hey, the whole love thing is new to me. Sharing my life is almost scary…except I love you. And when I'm not with you I'm empty."

Tears filled her eyes. He'd been so honest, so courageous, she had to be too. "I was lost without you too."

"So, what do we do?"

She smiled. He hadn't come up with a plan. Hadn't suggested what he wanted first. "You asked."

"I'm learning."

He really was. And her heart almost couldn't take it. "I think we need to be together."

"I do too." He looked around as she took the flowers to the kitchen table. "So, this is where we're going to live?"

Her breath caught and she whipped around to face him. "You're going to live here with me?"

He met her gaze. "I want to be with you. I also want you to be happy. And I think raising a child here would be fun."

"Yes. That's exactly how I see it."

"Except the house is small. It'll be good for a year or two, but if I'm working from home, I'll need a decent-sized office."

She pressed her hand to her chest. "You're working from home?"

"With new technologies, I've found a lot of things can be handled from home. I also trust my employees. I can also fly to New York a few times a week. But when I'm home, I'll need space."

"You can have space."

"We'll sit down with an architect as soon as the baby

is born." He slid out of his jacket and hung it on the newel post. "But first we need dinner. Is there takeout in this town?"

Her heart skipped a beat. "Of course, there's takeout in this town."

"A bed upstairs?"

She winced. "Mattress."

He laughed. "This should be interesting."

She walked over, wrapped her arms around his neck. "That's the point. We are absolutely not going to have a dull life."

He smiled. "No. We're not."

Then he kissed her again, and he knew with absolute certainty that this was what he'd been searching for his entire life. Not surety. Not perfection. But something warm and sweet, hot and sexy, smart and strong, naughty and nice.

Avery.

EPILOGUE

JAKE LEANED AGAINST the window seat in Avery's hospital room, watching his mother cuddle his daughter, her first grandchild. Abigail Maureen McCallan. Apparently, all the women in Avery's mother's family had names that started with *A*, so that took care of naming her after someone in the Novak family. And his mother unashamedly said if she got to pick the middle name she wanted it to be Maureen.

They hadn't waited for the baby's birth to hire an architect and plans for their bigger house were nearly complete. Avery was just about ready to take the Pennsylvania bar exam. And no one seemed to care he wasn't in the office three days a week.

Nestling the baby against her breast, his mom said, "You know, Avery and I saw the cutest wedding dress in Paris." She smiled. "She even tried it on."

"You did?"

"Your mother tricked me into thinking it was an ordinary ball gown. As soon as I put it on, I knew it wasn't." She sighed wistfully. "But it certainly was gorgeous."

Maureen nodded. "Yes, it was." She handed Abigail to Avery's mother. "As soon as Avery can travel, we'll go to Paris together and you can take a look."

Andrea's face fell. "I can't go to Paris."

Maureen batted a hand. "It's not a big deal. We have a plane. And I have a sweet deal with a hotel there. I can get a suite for the three of us for next to nothing."

Andrea brightened.

Jake stifled a gasp. She didn't have a sweet deal. She paid top dollar and was proud of it. But Andrea didn't have to know that.

Sabrina and Seth entered. Sabrina walked directly to Avery and hugged her. Seth carried a huge teddy bear.

Avery laughed. "I don't think the nursery is big enough for that."

Jake shook his head. "I don't think our current house is big enough for that."

Seth slapped him on the back. "Luckily, you're building a new one." He paused. "There is going to be a room for me, right?"

"Two spare bedrooms and a mother-in-law suite," Avery said.

"But don't get too comfortable in the spare bedrooms," Jake put in. "We want to fill them with kids."

"We're thinking of building a bed-and-breakfast in town."

"I'm going to run it," Denny said, pushing away from the wall. "Andrea's going to bake goodies for guests."

Sabrina smiled. "That sounds like a great idea. That way we can visit and not feel like we're intruding." She paused, then gave Jake a narrow-eyed look. "You did that on purpose, didn't you?"

Jake pointed at his temple. "Always thinking."

Andrea shifted to hand the baby to Seth. "Here. Hold her."

He jumped back. "Oh, no. I've never held one of those in my life and don't plan on starting now. I'll hold her when she's two. Or three. Or maybe I'll just introduce myself when she's seven and can play catch."

Avery and her mother laughed. But Maureen frowned and faced Andrea. "See why I despaired of being a grandmother?"

"At least you had a shot. I had a daughter who wanted to save the world and a son who ran into burning buildings."

"Hey, I gave you a grandchild," Avery said with a laugh, but Jake could see her energy was waning.

He rose from the window seat. "I think it might be time for us to let Avery get some rest."

Seth said, "Aw. I just got here."

But Andrea and Maureen were already herding people toward the door.

He'd never seen his mother like this, not just happy but involved.

When everyone was out of the room, he sat on the seat next to the bed and took Avery's hand. "You okay?"

"I'm fine." She winced. "I don't think the drugs have worn off yet."

"Which might explain why you're tired."

"That and ten hours of labor."

He laughed. "That too."

"Little tip. Never tell a woman in labor that you understand her pain." She cut him a look. "You don't."

"Point taken."

"So, you're happy with a girl?"

He laughed. "I'm going to be the most possessive, protective father ever. I've already got plans for upping the security system on the new house."

"Sounds good." She yawned. "Next time, I'm going into labor in the morning instead of eleven o'clock at night."

"Just go to sleep."

The words were barely out of his mouth before her eyes closed. Within seconds, she was out.

He took a breath, rose from the chair beside the bed and walked over to the bassinette.

His little girl was tiny. Only two ounces over five pounds. She had the McCallan trademark black hair and blue eyes but green-eyed Andrea had reminded them that all babies had blue eyes and when she was about a year old they'd know the real color.

He reached down and tucked the mitten over her hand more securely. Any fear he might have had had disappeared. Not because he had planned or prepared for this—but because he was ready for the adventure.

In fact, with Avery, he was looking forward to it.

* * * * *

THE MAVERICK'S
BABY-IN-WAITING

MELISSA SENATE

Dedicated to
Marcia Book Adirim and Susan Litman—
creative geniuses!

Chapter One

"Have you picked out a name for the baby?"

Twenty-six-year-old Mikayla Brown looked from the display of baby photos on the wall of the Rust Creek Falls Clinic, where she was waiting for her ob-gyn appointment, to her friend Amy Wainwright. Names? Oh, yeah, she had names. Mikayla's life might be entirely up in the air at the moment, but names were easy. Late at night, when she lay in bed, unable at this point—seven months along—to get all that comfortable, she'd picture herself sitting in the rocking chair on the farmhouse porch with a baby in her arms and she'd try out all her name ideas on the little one.

Problem was, she had too many possibilities. "I have six if it's a girl," she told Amy. "Seven if it's a boy. And ten or so more I'm thinking of for middle names. Can I give my child four names?"

Amy laughed, putting the *Parenting Now* magazine she'd been flipping through back on the table. "Sure, why not? You're the mama."

Mikayla shivered just slightly. The mama. Her. Mikayla Brown. She barely had her own life together these days, and soon she'd be solely responsible for another life—a tiny, helpless little one with no one to depend on but her. Mikayla had always been a dependable, do-the-right-thing kind of person, and she'd fallen in love with a man she'd thought was cut the same way. Then, boom—her life exploded like a rogue firecracker. One moment, she'd been working happily at a local day care in Cheyenne, Wyoming, and in love with her boyfriend, a good-looking, ambitious lawyer, with her entire future ahead of her. The next moment, she was a single mother-to-be. No engagement. No marriage. No loving father-to-be beside her, just as excited about her prenatal checkup as she was.

But who *was* here today? A good friend. Mikayla was so thankful for Amy Wainwright she could reach over and hug her, and she would if her belly weren't in the way. Her belly was always in the way these days.

Hey, you in there, she directed to her stomach. *Are you a Hazel? A George?* Mikayla loved the idea of honoring her late parents, who'd always been so loving and kind. Or her maternal grandparents, also long gone—Leigh and Clinton, who'd sent birthday and Christmas cards without fail but had moved to Florida when Mikayla was young. Then there was her dear aunt Elizabeth, her mother's sister, who went by Lizzie, and her hilarious uncle Tyler, and their one-of-a-kind son, Brent, Mikayla's cousin. Brent was the one who'd suggested Mikayla move up to Montana—

to Rust Creek Falls—for a fresh start. Which was how Brent's name had ended up on the possibilities list. She owed him big.

Moving to this tiny town in the Montana wilderness had sounded crazy at first. Population five hundred something? More than a half hour's drive from the nearest hospital—when she was now seven months pregnant? No family or friends?

You'll make friends, Brent had assured her. *Sunshine Farm will feel like home*.

Brent had been right. Mikayla had been a little worried that she'd get the side-eye or pity glances from the town's residents. Pregnant and alone. But from the moment she'd arrived at Sunshine Farm three weeks ago and met the owner, Brent's friend Luke Stockton, she'd been invited to Luke and his fiancée's joint bachelor-bachelorette party held that very day. Since the recent wedding, she'd become good friends with Luke's wife, Eva, and Amy, who'd also lived at Sunshine Farm at the time.

Now Amy was engaged, with a gorgeous, sparkling diamond ring on her finger. Mikayla sighed inwardly while ogling the rock. She'd over-fantasized like a bridezilla in training about a ring on her own finger and a fairy-tale wedding. Hell, even a city hall wedding would have been fine. But all that was before she'd caught her baby's father having sex with his paralegal in his law-firm office.

The more Mikayla admired Amy's ring and thought about how her friend had reconnected with her first love, Derek Dalton, the man she'd married and divorced when they'd both been teenagers (long story!), the more Mikayla thought anything was possible. Even for seven-months-pregnant single women far from home and trying to figure out where to go from here.

A door opened, and a woman with a baby bump exited, followed by a man carrying a pamphlet. *Your Second Trimester.* Both their gold wedding rings shone in the room. Or maybe Mikayla's gaze just beelined to rings on fingers these days.

A nurse appeared at the door and smiled at Mikayla. "Mikayla Brown? Dr. Strickland is ready to see you now."

Well, where she was going right now was Exam Room 1. That was all she needed to know at the moment. One step at a time, deep breaths, and she'd be fine.

Mikayla and Amy stood and followed the nurse into the examination room. Mikayla sat on the paper-covered table and Amy on the chair in the corner. The nurse took Mikayla's vitals, handed her a paper gown to change into, then let them know Dr. Strickland would be in shortly.

"You're the absolute best, Amy," Mikayla said, her voice a little clogged with emotion, when the door closed behind the nurse. She quickly shimmied out of her maternity sundress and into the gown, Amy tying the back for her. "Thank you for coming with me today." It meant a lot not to come alone. Her ex had accompanied her to her first appointment back in Cheyenne when she discovered she was pregnant, but he had made it clear he didn't want a baby, wasn't ready for a baby and wasn't sure of anything. He'd added that he was a man of deep principles, a "crusading" attorney (read: litigator for a major corporation), and wouldn't leave Mikayla, "of course." Apparently, he'd been cheating even before she told him she was pregnant. *I have strong feelings for you, Mik, but I am who I am, and I'm not ready for any of this. Sorry.*

Who needed a lying, cheating, no-good rat sitting in the corner chair?

"That is what friends are for, my dear," Amy said, flicking her long auburn hair behind her shoulder. "And honestly? I might have ulterior motives of finding out what goes on at these appointments. One day I hope to be sitting exactly where you are. Okay, maybe no woman loves putting her bare feet into those metal stirrups…"

Mikayla laughed. Amy would make an amazing mother.

And so would she. Mikayla had had to give herself a few too many pep talks over the past several months, that she could do this, that she *would* do this—and well.

There was a gentle knock on the door and a tall, attractive man wearing a white lab coat entered the room with her chart and a warm smile. He introduced himself as Dr. Drew Strickland, an ob-gyn on temporary assignment here from Thunder Canyon, but he let Mikayla know he would absolutely be here through her delivery.

Fifteen minutes later, assured all was progressing as it should with the pregnancy, Mikayla sat up, appreciating the hand squeeze from Amy.

A minute after that, her resolve was blown to bits. The doctor's basic questions were difficult to answer, which made her feel like a moron. He asked if she was staying in Rust Creek Falls long-term, because he could recommend a terrific pediatrician here and a few out in Kalispell if she didn't mind the drive. But Mikayla wasn't too sure of anything.

She felt as though her empty ring finger was glowing neon in the room. No partner. No father for her baby. No family for the little one. Just her. A woman who had no idea what the future held.

"Will the baby's father be present for the labor and delivery?" Dr. Strickland asked.

Were those tears stinging the backs of her eyes? Hadn't she cried enough over that louse? When she first held on to hope that Scott would come around for her and the baby, she'd pictured him in the delivery room—or tried to, anyway. Not that she'd actually been able to imagine Scott Wilton there for the muck *or* the glory. Another reality check—which helped her rally. She and her baby would be just fine. She blinked those dopey tears away and lifted her chin.

"Nope. Just me."

"And me," Amy said with a hand on her shoulder. "Here if you need me. I'll even coach you through Lamaze, not that I'd know what I'm doing."

Mikayla smiled. "Thank God for girlfriends. Thank you, Amy. Honestly, I don't know what I'd do without you." Between Amy and then Eva, her landlady at Sunshine Farm, Mikayla had truly comforting support.

"You know what?" Mikayla added, nodding at the doctor. "I might be on my own, but I have great friends, a very nice doctor, and I'm going to be a great mama to my little one. That's all I need to know right now."

Dr. Strickland beamed back. "I couldn't have said it better myself."

Mikayla smiled. Why did she have a feeling the doc had been waiting for her to come to those conclusions?

"See you in two weeks for the ultrasound," the doctor said. "Call if you have any questions. Even if it's after hours, I'll get back to you right away. That's my promise."

Feeling a lot better about everything than she had an hour ago, Mikayla and Amy left the exam room. Mikayla checked out, and then Amy had a really good idea.

"Of course, we have to go to Daisy's Donuts," Amy said, linking her arm with Mikayla's. "A gooey treat and a fabulous icy decaf something or other. To celebrate an A-OK on the little one," she added, gently patting Mikayla's very pregnant belly.

Mikayla laughed. "Lead the way." She'd been to Daisy's a few too many times since she'd arrived in town, the call of lemon-cream donuts and crumb cake irresistible. It wasn't as if she was going to crave salad, so Mikayla let herself have a decadent treat when she really wanted one.

She was sure the baby appreciated it.

"Jensen Jones, you listen to me! I want you out of that two-bit, Wild West, blip-on-the-map town this instant! You're to fly back to Tulsa immediately. Do you hear me? Immediately! If not sooner!"

Jensen shook his head as his father ranted in his ear via cell phone. Walker Jones the Second was used to his youngest son doing as he was ordered by the big man in the corner office, both at home and at Jones Holdings Inc. But Jensen always drew the line where it needed to be. When his dad was right? Great. When Walker the Second was wrong? Sorry, Dad.

"No can do," Jensen said, glancing around and

wondering if he was headed in the right direction for Daisy's Donuts. Apparently, that was *the* place to get a cup of coffee in Rust Creek Falls. Maybe even the only place. "I've got some business to take care of here. I should be back in Tulsa in a few days. Maybe a week. This negotiation is going a bit slower than I thought it would be." Translation: it wasn't going at all. And Jensen Jones, VP of New Business Development at Jones Holdings, wasn't used to that.

His father let out one of his trademark snorts. "Yeah, because you're in Rusted Falls River or whatever that town is called. Nothing goes right there."

Jensen had to laugh. "Dad, what do you have against Rust Creek Falls? The land out here is amazing." It really was. Jensen was a city guy, born and bred in Tulsa, Oklahoma, and he liked the finer things in life, but out here in the wilds of Montana, a man could think. Breathe. Figure things out. And Jensen had a lot to figure out. He hadn't expected to like this town so much; hell, he'd been as shocked as his father was that three of his four older brothers had found wives in Rust Creek Falls and weren't coming home to Tulsa. *This* was home now for Walker the Third and Hudson. Even jet-setter Autry had come to visit, fallen madly in love with a widowed mother of three little girls and moved the lot of them to Paris to finish a Jones Holdings negotiation. But Autry had made it clear he'd bring his wife and daughters back to Rust Creek Falls when his deals were done.

But just because Jensen liked the wide-open spaces and fresh air didn't mean he'd settle down here. As the youngest of the five Jones brothers, each one a bigger millionaire than the next, he'd always had something to prove. Now three of his brothers had become family men and had given up their workaholic ways. Autry used words like *balance*. Walker the Third wanted to invest in an ergonomically correct toddler-chair company for the day care business he'd added to the Jones Holdings lot. And Hudson knew the middle names of all his nieces and nephews. Middle names! This, from three of the formerly most confirmed bachelors in Tulsa.

"What do I have against Rusted Dried-Up Creek?" his father repeated. "I'll tell you what," he added in one of his famous Jones patriarch bellows. "That town is full of Jones-stealing women! There are sirens there, Jensen. Just like in the Greek myths. You'd better watch out, boy. One is going to sink her claws into you and that'll be the last your mother and I will see of you. Jones Holdings can't operate remotely! I want my sons here in Tulsa where they belong. If not all, then you. You've always been the one I could count on to listen to reason."

His poor father. The man hated not getting what he wanted. And it was rare. His mother said the man-stealing in Rust Creek Falls couldn't be helped, that there was something in the water—literally. Apparently, at a big wedding a couple years ago, some local drunk had spiked the punch with an old-timey potion or something and no man was safe from the feminine wiles of Rust Creek Falls women. Especially the millionaire Jones brothers.

"Dad, I assure you, I'm not about to fall for anyone. The last thing on my mind is marriage. You've got nothing to worry about." He wasn't exaggerating for his father's sake, either. Jensen was done with love. So there would never be a marriage.

"Yeah, I think that's what Autry said right before he proposed to that mother of seven."

Jensen rolled his eyes. "*Three*, Dad. Three lovely little girls. Autry is very happy with Marissa. So is Walker with Lindsay. As is Hudson with Bella."

His father made a noise that sounded like a harrumph. "They were happy running Jones Holdings right here in Tulsa until those women got to them! Just come home now. I'm thinking of buying a major-league baseball team. You can help me decide which one."

"I'll see you in a few days, Dad," Jensen said. "Speaking of buying pricey things—what are you getting Mom for your fortieth anniversary?" Forty years was something to celebrate. Hell, *five* years was something to celebrate.

"That woman will be the death of me!" Walker the Second bellowed. "I— Oh, Jensen, my assistant is signaling me that Nick Bates from Runyon Corporation is on line two. Time for a takeover. Get home quick or I'll come get you myself. And I'm not kidding."

Before Jensen could say a word, a click sounded in his ear.

Now it was Jensen's turn to harrumph. His parents' anniversary was in two weeks and his mom and dad were barely speaking. There had always been rifts among the Jones boys and their parents over the years, but Walker the Second and Patricia Jones had always been such a strong team, bossy and snobby and trying to order around their sons as a united front. Now there were cracks in the forty-year marriage. Lately,

Jensen had heard the strain in their voices, seen it on their faces, and once he'd caught his mother crying when she thought she was alone in the family mansion. Of course, she'd refused to acknowledge those were tears and insisted she was just allergic to their cook's "awful perfume."

As the youngest, Jensen had always fought for his brothers' respect and his parents' attention and had barely been noticed in the big crew. But he was the one who'd watched his brothers grow up one by one and go their own ways, even if that way was the family business. The five Jones brothers might as well be living and working on different continents for how close they were, and that included Walker and Hudson, who lived here in town and worked together, though they had gotten more brotherly, thanks to their wives.

But Jensen was the one who cared about family dinners and holidays and birthday celebrations, insisting, even as a teenager, that his older brothers come home for his big sports games. When he was seventeen, his parents had taken him to a therapist, insisting that Jensen be cured of "caring too much," that it would make him soft when family in the Jones world meant business.

He still cared. And his parents still didn't get it.

But there was one thing his father would get his way on. Jensen *would* be coming home in a few days—once he finally convinced the most stubborn old coot in Montana to sell a perfect hundred acres of land to him for a project very close to his heart. The man, a seventy-six-year-old named Guthrie Barnes, was holding out, despite Jensen upping the price well past what the land was worth. But Jensen was a Jones and a skilled negotiator. He'd get that land. And then he'd go home.

Because no woman, siren or otherwise, could tempt him beyond the bedroom. Adrienne, his ex, had made sure of that. He wasn't even sure if he could count her as an ex, since she'd never really been his; she'd been after his money and had racked up close to a million dollars on various credit cards she'd opened in his name, then fled when he'd confronted her. The worst part? She'd admitted she'd done her research for weeks before setting her sights on him, reading up on him, asking questions, finding out his likes and dislikes, what made him tick. When she'd engineered their meeting, the trap had been set so well he'd fallen right into it. He'd walked away from that relationship in disbelief that he could have been so stupid. She'd walked away with his ability to trust.

The only thing he had, really had, was his family, and hell, he barely had that. If his snobby, imperious, stubborn father and his snobbier, refuses-to-talk-about-her-feelings mother thought they were going to throw away forty years and the family because they were too set in their ways or too stubborn to deal with each other, well, then they didn't know what was coming.

Jensen was coming. Well, more like he was packing a wallop for the Jones patriarch and matriarch. Family was supposed to be there. *Should* always be there. Disagreements, problems, rifts, whatever. You worked it out. So, hell, yeah, he was going to unite the Jones family and save his parents' marriage. They were damned lucky and had no idea, no clue how blessed they were for all they had.

But Jensen knew. He knew because he'd been so

willing to go there, to love, to open up his heart and
life to another person—before Adrienne had destroyed all that. And three of his brothers knew—
they'd surrendered to love and were now truly happy.
And he'd need their new family-men status to help
him work on the parents. That meant Autry flying in
from Paris. He had no doubt the jet-setter would. Because when it came down to it, Jensen could count on
his brothers. And it was time for the whole family to
be able to count on one another.

The bell jangled over his head as he entered the
donut shop, the smell of freshly baked pastries min-
gling with coffee. A large, strong blast of caffeine,
some sugary fortification and he'd be good to go on
his plans.

Except when he looked left, all thought fled from
his head. His brain was operating in slow motion, his
gaze on a woman sitting at a table and biting into a
donut with yellow custard oozing out. She licked her
lips. He licked his, mesmerized.

Was it his imagination or was she *glowing*?

She had big brown eyes and long, silky brown hair
past her shoulders. There was something very…lush
about her. Jensen couldn't take his eyes off her—well,
the half of her that was visible above the table, covered by a red-and-white-checked tablecloth. And he
was aware that he was staring. Luckily, the beauty
in question was more interested in her donut and the
woman sitting beside her than in anything else. She
put down the donut and picked up an iced drink, then
laughed at something her companion said.

He even loved her laugh. Full-bodied. Happy.

Oh, yeah, this was a woman who knew how to have

a good time. If a donut and a joke or whatever her friend had said could elicit that happiness and laughter, then this was someone Jensen would like to whisk off to dinner tonight. Maybe to Kalispell, about forty-five minutes away, to an amazing Italian restaurant his brother Walker had told him about. Kalispell had a nice hotel where they could have a nightcap before spending the night naked in bed, taking a soak together, and then he'd bring her home in the morning and go meet Guthrie Barnes with a better offer on the land to get the man to sell. A great night, a deal and back in Tulsa midweek. Now that was the Jones way. His father would be proud.

A woman behind the counter, her name tag reading Eva, smiled at him. He was pretty sure he'd met her at her and her husband's joint bachelor-bachelorette party a few weeks ago. "May I help you?"

"I'd like to send refills of whatever is making those women so happy," he said, nodding his chin toward the brunette beauty.

Eva slid a glance over and raised an eyebrow. "You sure about that?"

Was that challenge in her voice? Jensen loved a challenge. "I'm a man who knows what he wants."

Eva grinned. "Well, then. I'll just ring you up and then bring over their refills."

"Thank you, ma'am," he said. "You can add a café Americano and a chocolate cider donut for me."

She'd raised another eyebrow after the *ma'am*; she couldn't be more than midtwenties, but he was a gentleman born and bred.

After handing him his much-needed coffee and donut, Eva went over to the women's table with two more donuts and two more coffee drinks. She whispered something, then lifted her chin at him. Two sets of eyes widened, and they looked over.

He locked eyes with his brunette. The most beautiful woman he'd ever seen. The woman he planned on spending the night with. He'd show her an amazing evening, treat her like a princess, give her anything her heart desired, and then they'd go their separate ways, maybe not even knowing each other's last names. They'd each get what they needed—a night of pure fantasy—and then they'd go back to real life.

He froze, mentally slapping his palm to his forehead. He hadn't even checked her ring finger. The auburn-haired woman she was with wore an engagement ring; he could see that a mile away. But now that he was looking at his brunette's hand, he was relieved to see there was no ring.

Which meant she was his. For the night. Maybe for the few days it would take him to convince Guthrie Barnes to sell.

Eva waved him over, and he sidled up. The brunette was staring at him. The auburn-haired friend seemed delighted by the turn of events. "Mikayla Brown, Amy Wainwright, I don't even have to ask this man's name to know he's a Jones brother. I'm right, right?" she said, looking at him.

He laughed. "Was it the diamond-encrusted *J* on my belt buckle that gave me away?"

"That and the fact that everything you're wearing probably cost you more than rent on this place for a few months. And I'm pretty sure I saw you with your brothers at our party at the manor a few weeks ago. We didn't have a chance to meet then—I think the whole town was there. I'm Eva Stockton."

He smiled. "Jensen Jones. And yes, I was there. Great party. Congratulations on your marriage." He bit into the donut on his plate. Chocolate cider, his favorite. "Mmm—this donut is so good you should charge a thousand bucks for just one."

"You'd probably pay that," Eva said, shaking her head with a smile.

"Hey, my family might have done all right in business, but we're not idiots. *Two* thousand."

The three women laughed, and then the bell jangled, so Eva went back to the counter.

"Mikayla," he said, unable to take his eyes off her. "I know this is going to sound crazy. We just met. We don't know a thing about each other. But I'm going to be in town for a few days and would love for you to show me around, show me the sights—if you're free, of course."

His fantasy woman looked positively shocked. Her mouth dropped slightly open, that sexy, pink lower lip so inviting, and she glanced at her friend. Both their eyes widened again, as if his asking her out, politely couched in terms of a sightseeing guide, was so unusual. The woman was beautiful, her lush breasts in that yellow sundress so damned sexy. Surely she was hit on constantly. Maybe not by millionaires, though.

Ah, Jensen thought, disappointment socking him in the gut. That was it. That was what was so unusual about his interest. She probably wasn't used to attention from a man with so many commas in his bank account.

Another gold digger? Oh, hell, what did it matter

if she were? Jensen wasn't going there—never again. His heart wasn't up for grabs. Mikayla Brown was gorgeous, not wearing a ring, and he had a few days to enjoy her company—around town and in bed. He'd wine and dine her, she'd give him her *full* attention and then they'd both go their separate ways, maybe hooking up once or twice a year when he came to Rust Creek Falls to visit his brothers. Perfect.

The more he looked at her, the more he had another thought: *Forget Kalispell. I'm whisking her away to Ibiza or a Greek island for the weekend.* No harm in a decadent no-strings weekend romance if they were both for it, right?

She was staring at him. About to say yes. Of course she was. C'mon.

"Oh, I don't think I'm your type, Mr. Jones," Mikayla said. She took another bite of her donut, a hint of pink tongue catching a flick of errant custard.

He held her gaze, able to feel his desire for her in every cell of his body. "Trust me. You are."

She took a breath, lifted her chin and stood up.

Which was when it became obvious that she was very pregnant.

Chapter Two

Mikayla gave the guy five seconds to run screaming out the door of Daisy's Donuts. Maybe even three.

A wealthy, hot man with a diamond-studded belt buckle, slicked-back movie-star blond hair and intense blue eyes glittering with desire and challenge? Yeah, he'd run as soon as he realized he was coming on to a pregnant woman.

All six feet two inches of muscular millionaire cowboy froze, those gorgeous blue eyes on her seven-months-pregnant belly.

She would have burst out laughing if a tiny part of her wasn't a bit angry. A minute ago she'd been his biggest fantasy—apparently. Now, not so much.

Reality always won.

"Oh," he said. "You're…"

Ding, ding, ding. "Pregnant."

"I…I didn't mean to intrude on your time together," he said quickly, slowly backing away with his coffee and what was left of his donut. "Enjoy your afternoon. It was very nice meeting you both."

So, eight seconds. He was out the door and probably stopped around the corner, catching his breath from actually having been flirting with a pregnant woman.

"Why is every Jones brother better-looking than the last?" Eva asked, coming over with extra napkins.

The man *was* beyond good-looking. He was the kind of gorgeous that was hard to draw your gaze from, and Mikayla had felt a connection, a tiny little spark of chemistry that went beyond just the physical. There had been something sweet under the sizzling in their two-minute conversation—before her belly had introduced itself.

But he was gone. As expected. And as it should be! Mikayla Brown wasn't looking for a man. Or a savior. Or a father for her baby. That wasn't how life worked. If she met someone and they fell in love and he was wonderful and father material, okay, fine.

Now she did burst out laughing. Ha ha ha. Like that would happen.

She'd been burned bad by the father of her baby, which hurt like hell. She'd cried her eyes out, wished until she'd marked every star, and she'd still been abandoned, her baby unwanted by the man who'd helped create him or her. She hated that with every fiber of her being. And she didn't understand it. But that was when that handy word came in again: *reality.* Things were what they were, and she damned well was going to make the best of them. She had a baby to consider, a life to bring forth, a child to raise. She was going to be the best mother she could be.

And anyway, the silver lining? She'd *noticed* Jensen Jones. Could imagine herself kissing Jensen Jones. Which meant that flicker of hope and faith was still alive inside her. Her ex had taken himself out of the equation, but his loss hadn't taken the red-blooded woman out of her. Score one for Mikayla.

Her hundredth pep talk issued, Mikayla took a sip of her decaf iced mocha. "Well, at least he liked the top half of me. Which includes my brain. So that's something." She took another bite of her donut.

"If only he could have seen your feet," Amy said, "And the sparkly blue pedicure I gave you last week. That would have hooked him."

"Jensen Jones doesn't strike me as a man who'd like sparkly blue toenails," Mikayla said. "Did you know that Jackie Kennedy Onassis once said that fingernails should be the color of ballet slippers and toes a classic red? He seems like one to agree. Too highfalutin for me, anyway. I'm an eat-ribs-with-my-fingers and blue-toenail-polish kind of woman."

Amy laughed. "We all should be that woman."

Eva came over with a tray of samples. "Want to try my new red velvet donut holes? Fresh out of the oven."

Mikayla adored Eva, who not only baked for Daisy's, worked the counter when they were understaffed and had recently finished business school, but was letting her stay at Sunshine Farm. "Ooh, of course," Mikayla said, snatching one and popping the heavenly treat into her mouth. This would have to be her last bite or she'd gain a hundred pounds in this final trimester.

Eva sat down. "Mikayla, you were great today, you

know that, right? Standing up like that was hilarious. I've never seen a man stammer without saying a word quite like that."

"Poor guy," Amy said, sipping her iced latte. "Did you see the way he looked at Mik? He was clearly swooning over her."

"What's his deal, anyway?" Mikayla asked. "Not that I care."

Both women smirked at her.

Mikayla smiled. "I definitely would have remembered meeting him at your and Luke's party, Eva, but there was so many people and I left a bit early. He has how many brothers?"

"Four," Amy said. "All rich beyond belief. They're from Tulsa and all work as major bigwigs in the corporation their father started. Hudson and Walker—you know them from town—still work for Jones Holdings. They opened a satellite office here in town. And Autry whisked a widowed mom and her three little girls to Paris for the year, but they're due back. There's another brother, Gideon, who was at the party, too, since he was visiting Hudson and Walker that week, but I didn't meet him. Put the five Jones millionaires in a row at a party and women start swooning. Even if three are taken."

"No one knows much about Jensen," Eva said. "Other than he's rich and I heard he's a workaholic. He's in town working a deal, I think."

"Well, sometimes a gal needs a donut and some eye candy, and I got both, so I'm good for a while," Mikayla said. "I'm not looking for anything. I have great new friends and a great place to live. I'm set."

Eva squeezed Mikayla's hand. "It's so nice having

another woman at Sunshine Farm. I'm so glad you're living in the house with us."

Eva Armstrong Stockton was so kind and generous. She and her husband were thinking about officially starting a guesthouse at the ranch. There wasn't much in terms of places to stay in Rust Creek Falls. There was a boardinghouse and a high-end hotel that was more Jensen Jones's speed. Mikayla knew that the Stocktons hoped to turn the cabins on their property into little guesthouses, the kind of place that people could come to when they needed somewhere to go, somewhere like home. People like Amy, who'd reconnected with her first love in Rust Creek Falls. And people just like Mikayla.

She was temporarily in flux. The Stocktons had told her she was welcome to stay in their ranch house as long as she liked, even when she had her baby, who was sure to wake everyone up a few times a night. She'd have friends and support and community. She knew she was lucky.

So was it wrong that she couldn't stop thinking about that tiny spark of something wonderful that had ignited between her and Jensen Jones? She'd have to fill her nights somehow, so fantasizing about him was really quite smart.

Walker and Hudson were belly-laughing so hard in the lobby of Maverick Manor that Hudson actually had to stand up and catch his breath.

What was so hilarious, apparently, was the idea of their parents coming to Rust Creek Falls for a surprise fortieth anniversary party.

"A *planned* party wouldn't get them here," Walker

said, running a hand through his blond hair. "God, I needed that laugh. Thanks, Jensen."

"They hate this town," Hudson said, sitting back down in his club chair, an expanse of Montana wilderness visible through the floor-to-ceiling window behind him. He picked up his beer and took a drink. "They showed up for our weddings, then turned around and flew home, grumbling all the way about Jones-stealing women and Rust Creek Falls not even being on the map."

"Those Jones-stealing women are their *daughters-in-law*. Jeez," Jensen said, sipping his scotch. "You'd think Mom especially would like some women in the family after five sons."

Walker popped a walnut from the dish on the table into his mouth. "I tried—hard. I talked to Dad about how much I like Rust Creek Falls, that we can easily work from the Jones Holding satellite building we built in town, that we're—wait for it—*happy*, and he just doesn't get it. Or want to hear it."

"Lost cause," Hudson said, shaking his head. "I'm over it. You have to be. It's the only way to move on."

Family couldn't be a lost cause, though. If you gave up, that was it. You accepted defeat. Jensen knew Hudson had always had a hard time dealing with the Jones patriarch; he was the cowboy in the family, the one who'd always gone his own way.

He knew his father had to be proud of the way the Jones brothers had forged their own identities and paths. And to bring this family together, Jensen would do whatever it took.

"Forty years is a big deal," Jensen said. "That has to mean something."

Walker shrugged. "Look, you want to plan some big shindig, I'm in. But I remember you getting disappointed more than a time or two, Jensen. Mom and Dad don't care about anniversaries and family get-togethers. They never will."

"I'm in, too," Hudson said. "And I'm sure Autry will fly in from Paris with his family and that Gideon, who's traveling on company business, will make an appearance. But it will end up being just us celebrating our parents' anniversary. I seriously doubt Mom and Dad will show up."

Jensen grumbled to himself, staring hard at the trees and woodlands out the window. Why was everything he wanted—woman, land, anniversary party— not going his way? Maybe whatever was in the water in Rust Creek Falls had a negative effect just on *him*. "I'll figure something out," Jensen said, taking another sip of his scotch.

Except he couldn't figure anything out right now. Because from the moment he'd left Daisy's Donuts this morning, feeling like the biggest jerk who ever lived, his mind had been a scramble. Why couldn't he stop thinking about Mikayla Brown? Yes, she was lovely to look at and there was some kind of instantaneous chemical reaction between them that rarely happened—to him, at least. But the woman was very, very pregnant! About to have a baby.

And even if Jensen could overlook that one detail— one big detail—there was no way Mikayla was in the market for a casual weekend fling.

Yet he couldn't shake the thought of seeing her for the first time sitting there and biting into that custard donut. The deep brown of her intelligent, kind eyes.

The melodic sound of her laughter. Her calm voice. What the heck was her story? No wedding ring. Unmarried and pregnant in a small town like Rust Creek Falls.

"Since you're so family oriented," Hudson said, shaking him out of his thoughts, "you're invited to the Stockton triplets' party tomorrow afternoon. It's not their birthday, but Auntie Bella can't resist throwing a party for her brother's adorable kids, so we're celebrating the fact that all three triplets are potty trained."

"A potty-trained party?" Jensen couldn't help but laugh. "Should I bring superhero underwear as a gift?"

"Actually, yes," Hudson said. "Two boys and a girl, if you forgot. And Katie is nuts about Wonder Woman," he added with a smile. "Listen, Bella would love to see you and catch up, so I hope you can make it."

Triplets. That had to be a handful. Three handfuls. Made one baby seem not quite as…scary.

Which made him think of Mikayla again. For all he knew she was having quintuplets, though. *So forget her, man*, he told himself. *She's off-limits. She's not looking for a good time. And that's all you can take on these days. A good time. No commitments. No future. No hurt feelings.*

"I'll be there," Jensen said. Which was what he wanted to hear his parents say when he made up some ruse to get them to their own party. Their own surprise party. He wanted to surprise them, wanted them to know their sons cared, even if they themselves had forgotten to show how much they did. And his parents did care, somewhere deep down where their feelings were buried—Jensen was sure.

He glanced at his watch. Guthrie Barnes had agreed to meet with him face-to-face to discuss the land deal. He had to be over there on the outskirts of town in fifteen minutes. He stood up and slapped down a fifty. "Drinks on me. See you tomorrow at the party."

Walker raised an eyebrow. "This is Rust Creek Falls, Jensen. And Maverick Manor may be the most upscale place to get a drink in town, but two good scotches and a beer still won't run you even close to fifty bucks."

"For the till, then, for the owner to stock up," he said, tipping the Stetson he'd bought specifically to make himself look more like a land guy than a businessman to Barnes.

In ten minutes, he'd parked the shiny black pickup he'd rented in front of the Barnes ranch house. He got out and surveyed the land, which stretched as far as he could see. The access road to the highway was two minutes away—perfect. And the location on the outskirts of town would allow convoys through and choppers to land out here without clogging up traffic in the center of town.

These hundred acres would be perfect for the crisis distribution center he was planning on. The man who'd been like a second father to him had died in a flash flood while volunteering not too far from here, and Jensen wanted to honor his memory, as did his brothers, in a way that would help the area and community. Davison Parkwell had been a very close friend of his father's once, but the two had had a falling-out and his father had refused to talk to him, let alone about him, in the past five years. Walker the Second hadn't even gone to Davison's funeral. But Davison had been there for Jensen in ways his father hadn't been, as a Boy Scout leader, a coach of his baseball team, a mentor. His dad had always been too busy, but Davison and his wife, who'd died years before him, hadn't had children and they'd doted on the Jones boys, particularly Jensen and Gideon, the two youngest, in any way they could. Not with money, which they'd all had in truckloads, but with *time*. Whenever Jensen had had a problem, his heart and mind all messed up over a girl or a coach making him feel like dung or because he'd learned that all the Jones money couldn't buy what really mattered in life, he'd sought out Davison Parkwell, who'd listened and comforted and had taught him that riding out in the country could soothe a lot of ailments. He'd been right. Saddling up and taking off always managed to clear Jensen's head.

Maybe he'd go for a ride once he'd squared things away with Barnes. Anything to get his mind off Mikayla Brown, her brown eyes and her very pregnant belly.

But right now, Jensen was going to pay it back and pay it forward—just the way Davison would want. Victims of natural disasters, such as the Great Flood in Rust Creek Falls a few years ago, wouldn't have to wait for supplies and food and fresh water or shelter; they'd have a place to go right here.

Jensen glanced at the run-down farmhouse at the edge of the land. Peeling paint. Rotting posts. A barn that looked like it might collapse any day. What the hell? Why wouldn't Guthrie Barnes, clearly having financial issues, sell the land? Jensen was offering a small fortune. The old-timer had hung up on his assistant twice and told Jensen no on the phone once already.

Two old dogs with graying muzzles ran up to Jensen, and he gave them both a pat, waiting a beat for Barnes to come out. He didn't. Jensen walked up the three porch steps, the middle of which was half-gone, and knocked on the front door. He was surprised he didn't punch a hole right through it.

Barnes opened the door but didn't step out or invite Jensen in. "I had you come out here face-to-face so I could make myself clearer than my previous noes have been. Obviously, you rich city types don't care what people like me have to say. You just keep coming, run roughshod. Well, you're not going to bulldoze me, Jones. My answer is *no*. Now go back to New York or wherever it is you come from."

With that, he slammed the door in Jensen's face. A piece of rotting wood fell off and landed on Jensen's boot.

"Well, guys," he said to the dogs, "that didn't go well." He peered in the window, but the old man shoved the curtains closed. He took another look at the falling-down house and shook his head. Stubborn old coot.

Jensen got back into the truck. This was the perfect land for the crisis distribution center and shelter. The perfect site. And his assistant had made clear to Barnes what Jensen's plans for the land were. The man had not been moved.

Frustrated, Jensen drove back to Walker's house, surprised, as he always was every time he saw the place, how magnificent it was—a luxury log cabin nestled in the woods. *I could live here*, he thought, breathing in the pine and listening to the blissful quiet, broken only by the sound of a wise owl, a coyote or crickets.

His brother and his wife weren't home, and as Jensen walked around, he was drawn to a photo on the gorgeous river-rock mantel over the huge stone fireplace in the living room, a picture of the Jones family at his brother's wedding last year. *I'm gonna get you people together in two weeks for the party whether you like it or not*, he thought, tapping on the frame.

He moved down the mantel, looking at the many pictures. Happy family after happy family: his brother Hudson and his wife, Bella. Bella's brother Jamie Stockton, his wife, Fallon O'Reilly Stockton, and their triplets—the ones having the party tomorrow. His brother Walker and Lindsay. His brother Autry with Marissa and their three little girls in front of the Eiffel Tower. A shot of Gideon with a girlfriend, though they'd probably broken up by now. And then there was a picture of Jensen, alone. As usual, these days.

Something twisted in his gut, and he turned away from the mantel. Sometimes, usually late at night when he couldn't sleep, he'd get the unsettling feeling that life was moving on without him. His brothers were getting married, settling down. Then there was him, the bachelor without the plus-one, since he was afraid that even asking the women he dated to accompany him to events made them think things were more serious than they were. He wasn't interested in serious. Might never be again.

From the time he was knee-high, his parents had drummed it into his head that people would try to take advantage of him because of his money and family name. He'd vowed he would never be fooled. He could remember Davison dismissing that kind of talk with a wave of his hand and saying, "It's better to have loved and lost," and all that. But was it? What the hell did Jensen have to show for loving Adrienne? A million-dollar loss. His trust stolen. His heart broken.

He didn't trust women anymore. Stupid and sad of him, maybe, but it was true.

A beautiful brunette with soulful brown eyes and a very pregnant belly came to mind again. Dammit. Why couldn't he shake the thought of her? He didn't know a thing about Mikayla Brown, what her situation was, if she had the support of family, if she had a significant other. Was she on her own? Why did he even care?

All he knew was that he couldn't get her off his damned mind. Which was why he'd steer clear of town and Mikayla Brown until he got Barnes to agree to the land deal, then hightail it out of Rust Creek Falls.

Chapter Three

Your baby will be soothed to sleep in this must-have bouncer that features gentle vibration and sweet lullabies.

Mikayla's gaze moved from the description on the box to the price tag. Two hundred ninety-nine dollars and ninety-nine cents. Her heart plummeted. Baby Bonanza, a baby-supplies emporium in Kalispell, was supposed to have reasonable prices, but last week, when she'd driven out here to buy a crib, she'd been shocked by the cost and had to start a layaway account. She certainly couldn't afford this bouncer. Unless she took the packs of diapers, pajamas and onesies and the infant car seat and snap-in stroller base out of her cart.

Well, she already had a built-in bouncer that featured vibration and sweet lullabies: herself. There was a rocker right in her room at Sunshine Farm, and she'd hold her baby against her chest, gently rock the little one and sing Brahms's "Lullaby" herself. Who needed a bouncer for three hundred bucks?

I wish I could buy you everything, she said silently to her baby. She didn't have much in savings, and since her job at the day care had ended in June, she'd been unemployed for a couple months. Trying to get a new job when she was seven months pregnant seemed foolhardy, but she really had no choice. Perhaps she could find a job where she could bring her newborn.

Right. Because every workplace wanted a crying baby interrupting things.

You will figure it out, Mikayla. Trust in yourself.

She reached into her purse for the list of baby must-haves that Baby Bonanza had stacked at the front of the shop.

Crib. Bassinet. Bouncer. Play mat. Bottles. Wipes. Wipes warmer. Diaper master...

Apparently, a diaper master was a special little garbage pail in which you threw out diapers. Wouldn't a regular old garbage can with a lid work? For a quarter of the price?

"Ooh, I'm definitely getting that deluxe bouncer, Mom," a very pregnant woman said as she and an older woman walked up behind Mikayla. She was eyeing the model that had given Mikayla sticker shock. "Only the best for my little Arabella," she added while patting her belly. She looked to be around seven or eight months along.

"That one only vibrates and plays music," her mother said, reading the description on the side of the box. She pointed at another box on the shelf above.

"This double-deluxe model says it vibrates *and* gently massages the baby, a must when cranky. It's only fifty dollars more. Worth every penny."

"Oh, definitely that one," the expectant mom said. Her mother lifted the even more expensive model into the cart, which already had a lot of items.

Only fifty dollars more. Jeez. That's two weeks' worth of layaway payments for me.

It was just stuff, she reminded herself. And not what mattered.

An image of her own mother popped into her mind. Widowed when Mikayla was a teenager, Hazel Brown had been a wonderful mother, and Mikayla had lost her just three years ago to a car accident. How she wished her mother was here now, by her side, explaining things, telling her what to expect, telling her everything would be okay. At least she knew her mama was looking down on her, watching over her like a guardian angel.

Chin up, she moved away from the expensive bouncers. The next aisle was filled with baby blankets and crib sheets that were so adorable her heart lifted again. She could afford one package of sheets and a waterproof liner. After all, that was what laundry three times a day was for.

Smiling, she put into her cart a lemon-yellow sheet with tiny pastel animals, along with a waterproof pad, then turned and headed for the checkout, but her gaze was caught by the cradle and crib aisle. Last week she'd put a beautiful white spindle crib on layaway. She stared at the floor model, struck by the fact that in just a couple months, the crib would be in her room at Sunshine Farm, her baby nestled inside on little animal-print sheets. She smiled at the rocking bassinets, one of which she'd also put on layaway, and the toddler beds in the shapes of race cars and butterflies. She couldn't even imagine her baby walking and talking and sleeping in a big-kid bed. That seemed so far down the road.

"Oh, how adorbs!" another expectant mom said—this time to her doting husband, who was pushing their cart with one arm around his wife. Their gold wedding rings gleamed in the dimly lit aisle.

Mikayla glanced over to see what was so "adorbs," and oh, God, it was. A plush baby blanket, hand knit, with little bulldogs on it. Each corner of the blanket had little chewing triangles for when the baby started teething.

"Aw, Oliver, these bulldogs look just like our Humphrey." Into the cart the forty-five-dollar baby blanket went. Mikayla knew the price because she'd ogled the blanket not two minutes ago.

And there she was, the hugely pregnant single woman with no ring, no husband, and not able to buy a quarter of what she wanted for her child.

She sighed and was about to turn toward the checkout when a gorgeous man appeared at the other end of the aisle.

The gorgeous man she'd last seen running out of Daisy's Donuts. This morning he wasn't wearing a suit, as he had been yesterday. Today he was wearing sexy jeans, a navy blue Henley shirt, the zillion-dollar belt buckle and cowboy boots. His thick, silky blond hair was movie-star perfect, even though he probably hadn't done a thing to it.

Then suddenly he froze as he noticed Mikayla at the end of the aisle. "Mikayla?" He grinned. "Well, I guess if I'm going to run into you anywhere, it would be in a baby store."

She knew why she was here. But why was Jensen here? He wasn't a father, was he?

"Buying a little relative a gift?" she asked.

"My brother's nephews and niece," he said. She was momentarily mesmerized by his blue eyes and the slight crinkles at the corners, his strong nose and square jawline. "They're celebrating being potty trained with a party today, but I have no idea what to buy them as a gift."

She was trying to remember back to the bachelor/bachelorette party and the Jones brothers she'd met. "Oh, that's right—Hudson is married to Bella and she's Jamie Stockton's sister," she said. "I remember meeting Jamie and his wife. They have two-year-old triplets. They potty trained three babies at once? That's one heck of an achievement. Definitely partyworthy."

He grinned. "I don't doubt it. So I want to get them something worthy. Any ideas?"

"Hmm," Mikayla said, glancing around. What would be just right for two-year-olds? "I noticed some wonderful educational toys and lots of great electronics in that aisle," she said, pointing. "And those big stuffed animals are so adorable," she added, gesturing at the three-foot-tall giraffe with a little seat built in. "Oh, I love those toddler beds in the shape of a race car and a butterfly."

"Sold," he said as his gorgeous blue eyes lit on the beds.

"What? Really?" She'd noticed the very high price tags when she was here last week. The beds cost a small fortune. Times three? A big fortune. The cost of things clearly didn't faze him. When you were a Jones millionaire, it was probably like buying a cup of coffee at a gas station. Barely a blip on the budget.

She wondered what it would be like not to have a budget. But she truly couldn't imagine.

"Do two-and-a-half-year-olds sleep in those kind of beds, or would they still be in cribs?" he asked.

"They're probably just the age to move into big-kid beds," she said.

"Perfect. I knew you were the woman to ask."

"Ha, I have no idea what a newborn needs, let alone a toddler. I'm seven months along and just learning on the go. There must be a million books written about what to expect when you're pregnant, but until I'm actually holding a newborn and need to do the zillions of things infants require..."

"I suppose you'll hire a baby nurse," he said. "That should make things easier."

She almost laughed. Baby nurse! Was he kidding with that one? As if she could afford another crib sheet in addition to the one in her cart, let alone a living, breathing, experienced baby nurse to care for her infant during the night while Mikayla got eight hours of interrupted sleep.

"Uh, *I'll* be the baby nurse. And nanny. And chief bottle washer."

He smiled. "One-woman operation, huh?"

Her own smile faded. "Yeah. Just the way it is."

Her heart pinching, Mikayla wanted to flee and stay at the same time. That was a weird dichotomy.

"So what are you buying today?" he asked, glancing in her cart.

"Just a crib sheet and some pajamas. I guess I can't

help window-shopping for the nursery I'd love to have, but that's silly when I'm staying at Sunshine Farm and don't know when I'll move into my own place."

He tilted his head and stared at her. "Sunshine Farm? Isn't that Luke and Eva's ranch house?"

She could feel her cheeks turning pink. She was pregnant and didn't even have her own place.

"That property is gorgeous," he said. "I love the big yellow barn. I think I heard my brothers say the Stocktons intend to turn the place into a guest ranch."

Mikayla nodded. "I'm trying to be a very good guest so that I don't ruin their fantasy for them. But when the baby comes…" Her eyes widened and she grinned. "I can't believe they haven't told me to scram before my due date, but they apparently like the idea of a baby in the house."

He winced. Slightly, but he did. She knew what he was thinking: Who'd want to wake up in the middle of the night to a baby wailing? Or change a diaper—ever? Mikayla wondered if he'd feel differently if it were his own baby, but she figured he'd hire a day and night nurse if he ever had a kid of his own.

"Are you planning on staying in Rust Creek Falls permanently?" he asked.

"I really don't know," she said, quite honestly. "I'm kind of…figuring things out right now." Could the floor open up and swallow her and her cart? He'd probably never had to figure out the basics of life—like a place to live and money to buy a crib. *Move along, Mikayla*, she told herself. *There's no sense even making this man's acquaintance. You live on different planets.* "Well," she said with what probably looked like a forced smile. "I'd better get going. Nice to see you again, Jensen."

Too bad pulling her eyes off him was so hard. She could stand here and look at this man all day and night.

"Nice to see you again, too," he said, kind of wistfully, if she wasn't mistaken. Huh. Once again, Mikayla the Amazing Mind Reader had a good idea what he was thinking: *Shame she's pregnant. She could be showing me the sights around town, including lovers' lane, where we could have had some fun.*

Was there even a lovers' lane in Rust Creek Falls? As if Mikayla would know.

"Can I help you?" a store employee asked as she walked over, smiling at Mikayla and Jensen. "Oh, and congratulations, you two. Mommy and Daddy are getting their nursery in order before the big day, I see."

Mikayla turned beet red.

Jensen practically choked.

"Oh, we're not together," Mikayla rushed to say. *Why do I always feel the need to explain?* she wondered. For a second there, she'd been someone's wife, her baby had a father and she was setting up her nursery in advance of the big event. Just the way she'd dreamed.

The sales clerk cringed. "Sorry. I'm always putting my foot in my big mouth. You could have been brother and sister, too."

"We're definitely not," Jensen said. "I'll take three race car beds," he added to the clerk. "And they must be delivered this afternoon by one. Oh, and I'd like the beds personalized with the names across the fronts. Jared, Henry and Katie."

"Did you want the butterfly bed for Katie?" the salesclerk asked, pointing at the pink-and-purple bed.

Jensen shook his head. "Apparently, Katie loves cars just like her brothers, so a race car it is. Her favorite color is orange, so maybe her name can be stenciled in orange."

The manager nodded. After Jensen gave the delivery information, she said, "I'll make sure everything is correct and delivered with bows by 1:00 p.m. to the Stockton residence in Rust Creek Falls."

"Thanks," Jensen said. Then he turned to Mikayla. "And thanks for your help. I never would have thought to buy the beds. They're perfect."

She managed a smile. "Well, 'bye," she said too brightly and practically ran down the aisle to the checkout.

Crazy thing was, the moment she stopped, she missed being around him.

Well, the woman was definitely not trying to find herself a husband—and a rich one, at that, Jensen thought. She couldn't get away from him fast enough.

He wondered why. Most single women flirted with him outright, making no mistake of their interest. Mikayla Brown's interest was less than zero.

As he watched her wheel her cart to the checkout, Jensen stood about fifty feet away, partially blocked from view by a giant stuffed panda he pretended interest in buying. He was trying to come up with some reason to stall her, to talk to her more, maybe offer to take her for coffee—decaf—or an early lunch.

Why, though? he asked himself. *The woman is about*

to have a baby! And the last thing Jensen planned to be was anyone's daddy. Maybe in ten years. Or never. But definitely not in a couple of months.

"I'd like to put twenty-five dollars down on the crib I have on layaway," he heard Mikayla say to the cashier. "And I'd also like to add this car seat and snap-in stroller to my account."

A crib and car seat on layaway. Jesus. He knew not everyone could afford everything they wanted right then and there, and racking up debt on credit cards wasn't a great idea, but these seemed to be necessities for a newborn. It killed him.

When she left the store with her meager purchase of a crib sheet and two pairs of cotton pajamas, grand total $24.52, he walked up to the cashier.

"I'd like to pay off the balance of Mikayla Brown's layaway items," he said. "The woman who just left."

"Oh, she sure is lucky to have a guardian angel," the woman said. She typed in Mikayla's name into the computerized cash register. "Ah, the crib, a bassinet, diapers, wipes, a changing table and pad, and an infant car seat with a snap-in stroller."

Just the basics, Jensen realized. He could do a lot better than that for her. "Does she have a wish list?"

"Oh, yes," the woman said. "Helps our expecting mothers keep track of what they'd like, particularly for registries for baby showers."

"I'll pay off the layaway and also take everything on the wish list," Jensen said.

The woman's mouth dropped open. "Wow, you're like a summertime Santa Claus." She punched in a bunch of keys. "I can have everything delivered to

Ms. Brown's address—Sunshine Farm in Rust Creek Falls—by late this afternoon. We have everything in stock here, and instant delivery is how we keep folks from going to the big-box store outside town."

"Thanks for all your help," Jensen said.

He felt much better as he exited the store into the bright August sunshine. He couldn't have Mikayla Brown, but he could help her out.

He lifted his face as the refreshing breeze ruffled his hair. This was a perfect morning for a long ride. Walker kept horses and had told Jensen to take one out whenever he wanted. A ride would clear his head, hopefully ridding it of Mikayla's beautiful face and her not-so-great life situation. He had to forget her.

So why the hell couldn't he?

"Last place I'd ever expect to see you, Jensen," called out a familiar voice.

Jensen turned to find his brother Walker and Walker's wife, Lindsay, exiting their car in the parking lot of the baby store and heading toward him.

"I came out here to pick up some gifts for the potty party," he said. "Try saying *that* five times fast."

Lindsay laughed, tossing her long brown hair behind her shoulder. "Us, too. Oh, Jensen, I keep meaning to tell you. I've heard through the grapevine that several women in town are *very* interested in meeting you. Everyone keeps asking me, 'Is he single? Seeing anyone? Should I tell my sister to go for it?'"

Walker shook his head with a grin. "I told you, Lindz. They're all wasting their time."

She playfully socked her husband in the arm. "Oh, come on. Until I hear it from the man himself, I won't believe you. Who wouldn't want to meet the love of their life?"

No wonder Lindsay was such a good lawyer. She put it right out there. No escaping the truth.

"I'm open to a dinner out or seeing the sights around the county," Jensen said. "But beyond that—no. I'm not looking for a relationship."

"Every time a Jones man says that, one finds him," Lindsay said. "So beware."

Jensen froze as the image of Mikayla Brown putting two mere packages of baby pajamas on the checkout came to mind.

"Told you," Walker said to his wife. "Look up the word *bachelor* in the dictionary and you'll find a little photo of my kid brother—the ladies' man Jensen Jones."

"Ladies' man?" Jensen said on a laugh. "I haven't taken out one woman since I've been in Rust Creek Falls."

"Yeah, because Dad's been after you to get the hell out of here before some woman gets you to put a ring on her finger."

"Don't you have three stuffed animals to buy or something?" Jensen grumbled at his brother.

Lindsay cracked up. "We most certainly do. Come on, Walker. You've been ragging on your baby brother since he was born."

"I owe you, Lindsay," Jensen said.

He wasn't anti-commitment in general. Just for himself. And maybe even just for now. For the next few years, at least. Maybe when he was forty he'd settle down.

But as he watched his brother and his wife walk

hand in hand into Baby Bonanza, once again he was struck by how alone in the world he was. He'd never really felt that way before, except when Adrienne betrayed him.

What in the hell was going on with him?

Chapter Four

"Mikayla, your fairy godmother is here," Eva called out from downstairs.

Huh? Mikayla got up from her bed, where she'd been making a list of possible jobs she could apply for after the baby was born, and glanced out the window. A huge Baby Bonanza truck was in front of the farmhouse.

She headed downstairs to find Eva standing at the front door, watching two burly guys taking out a giant box marked White Spindle Crib.

That's weird, she thought. *That's the crib I put on layaway.*

"Eva! Did you and Luke buy me that crib?" Mikayla asked, stunned.

Eva shook her head. "Wasn't me. And besides, you told me you planned to keep the baby bedside in a bassinet."

But then who? Amy? Maybe her cousin Brent?

The delivery guys leaned the box on the porch, then went back for another box, this one a deluxe bouncer—the exact one she'd ogled and had on her wish list. Wait—what? The porch was soon full of baby paraphernalia—all items that looked very familiar.

"Um, Eva, this is bizarre. This is everything from either my layaway account or my wish list at Baby Bonanza."

"Rich relative?" Eva asked.

"Not a one," Mikayla said. She knew Brent loved her, but not *this* much, and besides, he could barely keep himself afloat.

The burlier delivery guy held a clipboard and walked over to Mikayla. "I assume you're Mikayla Brown. No offense," he added, gesturing at her huge belly.

She smiled. "Well, I am the likely recipient of all this, but I didn't order any of it. I mean, it's all stuff from my layaway and wish list, but I owe a ton more on layaway and the wish list is exactly that—just wishful thinking. There must be some mistake."

The guy glanced at the order form on his clipboard. "Nope. No mistake. Paid in full, including delivery and our tip. You can thank—" he scanned the sheet "—Jensen Jones."

Eva gasped.

Mikayla's mouth dropped open. *What?*

"Where should we place everything?" the delivery guy asked. "The order includes white-glove assembly."

"Of course it does," Eva said with a grin. "I take back what I said, Mik. You don't have a fairy godmother. You have a fairy god*father*."

Jensen Jones, any kind of father? Ha. Mikayla couldn't see it. Hadn't he run screaming—well, maybe not screaming—out of Daisy's Donuts when he realized the woman he was trying to pick up was pregnant?

But hadn't he also driven all the way to Kalispell to buy presents for his brother's triplet toddler nephews and niece? Granted, there wasn't a dedicated baby shop in Rust Creek Falls, but he could have bought three stuffed animals at Crawford's General Store and called it a day. He hadn't.

She bit her lip and recalled how she'd dashed off to the checkout, needing to put a little distance between them. He must have overheard her paying another week on her layaway, then gone and bought everything for her—including all the stuff she'd added to her wish list, items she'd never spend money on. A wipes warmer? Come on.

"Why would Jensen Jones have bought me all this?" Mikayla said more to the air than to Eva.

"Oh, I have a few ideas why." Eva turned to the delivery guy. "Upstairs, first room on the right."

"Wait a minute," Mikayla said, holding up a hand. "I can't accept this. Any of it." She glanced at the deluxe bouncer that had almost had her in tears in the store. The huge container of wipes and the crazy wipes warmer so the baby's tush wouldn't startle from a chill. The diaper pail. The beautiful white spindle crib on the side of the giant box. The Exersaucer. A play mat. Crib mobile. Bassinet. Changing table with a deluxe pad. The lovely pale yellow baby carriage. The blanket with the bulldogs. And so many onesies and pajamas.

"Look, am I bringing this stuff upstairs or not?" the guy asked, looking at Mikayla.

Mikayla's stomach twisted. "Sorry, but no."

Eva shrugged at the delivery guy, who sighed—hard—and gestured to his coworker to start taking the stuff back to the truck.

"Well, this is a first," the man said, "so I guess we'll hold the order for twenty-four hours until we get it squared away. If you change your mind in the meantime, and the bearer is willing to pay another delivery fee, we'll be back."

Mikayla offered a tight smile, all she could manage. "I apologize for wasting your time and energy," she said, then headed inside, wanting to kick something and cry at the same time. What the ever-loving hell had Jensen Jones done?

Eva was right behind her. She followed Mikayla into the living room, where Mikayla paced the room, hands on hips.

"I'm not a charity case!" Mikayla said. "I mean, I am, sort of. I'm here on your generosity."

"Mikayla Brown, don't you dare. You're here because you need a place to stay and we have a guest ranch that we're slowly pulling together. You, my dear, are our very second guest after Amy. You're helping us learn how to be good proprietors. This is not about charity."

She squeezed Eva's hand. "Thank you, Eva. I love being here."

"How'd he even know what was on your layaway and registry?" Eva asked, sitting down on the sofa and tucking her legs beneath her.

Mikayla stopped pacing and sat down, too. She explained about running into Jensen at Baby Bonanza.

"Wow," Eva said. "He's got it bad for you."

"Oh, come on. He does not. You saw him run out of Daisy's Donuts."

Eva laughed. "Yeah, because he was in shock. That doesn't mean he's not still crazy about you."

"I'm pretty sure that's exactly what it means, Eva."

"Oh, really? Then why did he buy out Baby Bonanza, complete with white-glove assembly?"

"Because he can?" Mikayla suggested. "Because that's what rich people do? Buy what they want? Buy people?"

"He's not buying you. Has he asked you for anything?"

"No. Except my advice on what to buy for the Stockton triplets for their potty-training party."

Eva grinned. "I was at that party this afternoon with Luke. The beds were a big hit. Good pick."

"Well, Mr. Jones and I lead very different lives. And no matter his reasons, buying all that stuff for me was just plain…inappropriate. He doesn't even know me. We've had two conversations, each less than ten minutes."

And despite that, the man had wanted to make her wishes—via her wish list for her child's nursery— come true. No one had ever done anything like that for her before, but granted, no one in her life had that kind of money to throw around. Her ex earned a high salary, but he was frugal, which had seemed sensible to Mikayla. She'd been raised that way out of need.

She recalled the porch filled with all the items, all the things she longed to provide for her baby. For a hot second, she felt like Cinderella. But there was no such thing as Prince Charming outside of lovely fairy tales.

"You should go give him a piece of your mind," Eva said, wiggling her eyebrows.

"Eva Stockton, you are a troublemaker," Mikayla said, but she couldn't help laughing. "I *will* go give him a piece of my mind. In my world, you don't just make decisions for other people. You don't buy out stores for people. Just because you can."

"Just promise me you'll tell me every word that was said. Don't forget anything. Make yourself remember in advance."

"You're terrible," Mikayla said, popping up. "But I love you. I'll see you later."

As Mikayla headed outside to her car, she remembered her cousin Brent telling her that everyone in Rust Creek Falls was warm and friendly, at least the people he'd met when he'd come to visit Luke. Brent was right.

But why did Mikayla have a feeling that *nice* wasn't what was behind Jensen's generosity? Something else was.

And she had no idea what that something was.

When the doorbell rang for the second time since Walker and Lindsay had left for a summer evening stroll in the park, Jensen hoped it wasn't yet another single woman dropping off "just a little something to welcome you to Rust Creek Falls—and I made it my-self. Folks are so surprised that someone who looks like me is such a good cook!" Giggle. Giggle, giggle. Faux blush.

He wasn't exaggerating. That was exactly what the very attractive redhead had said when she'd buzzed the bell a half hour ago. She'd been carrying a foil-wrapped swordfish steak with a side of roasted potatoes.

"I'd be happy to heat it up for you," she'd said, sticking out one shapely skinny-jeans-covered leg.

A little white lie had seemed in order. "I'm expecting a business call any minute. Overseas," he'd added. "But thank you. I appreciate the welcome."

She did not look pleased but gave him a perfumed card with her name and contact information. "I'll expect a call," she'd said. Pushy.

He'd given her a tight smile and closed the door.

The problem was that despite his hunger—for the swordfish and a night with a gorgeous woman with long legs—he only had eyes for and interest in one woman. One completely-wrong-for-him woman with a very big belly. How on earth could he be so taken by a woman seven months pregnant? Yes, Mikayla Brown was pretty. And, despite the pregnancy, very sexy. *That* confused him. He liked her hair—long, silky and brown. And her eyes—also brown and smart and sparkly. She struck him as very down-to-earth, said what was on her mind. No flirting, no nonsense.

Okay, so he liked her. He found her attractive and liked her as a human being. That was all. *No big whoop, Jones.* He felt much better about his bizarre reaction to Mikayla. She was just plain likable, and who wouldn't feel...*something* toward a very pregnant woman? A bit protective, perhaps? It was amazing how much lighter and happier he felt now that his feelings made sense to him; sometimes they didn't and kept him up at night.

The doorbell rang again. He had eaten the redhead's dinner—delicious, by the way—so maybe now it was another attractive woman with a pie or cookies. Was that wrong? To take the swordfish and rosemary potatoes and pie—he was hoping for pecan—when he had no interest in the bearer's ulterior motive of dating a millionaire?

As if he had any doubt why he was on the radar of the single women of Rust Creek Falls. Several years ago, he'd heard through the grapevine that a group of women in Tulsa had rated the five Jones brothers and he'd won best personality. They'd been tied for looks. So at least he knew he had something going for him besides his bank accounts.

He peered through the peephole, a smile forming at the sight of Mikayla Brown on the porch. Here to thank him profusely, he figured. He opened the door, trying not to appear too pleased with himself.

The look on her face was something like *Who the hell do you think you are?*

"Jensen Jones, let me make myself very clear," Mikayla said, lifting her chin and looking directly into his eyes. "I'm not a charity case. I don't need any man, even a rich one, buying out the Baby Bonanza for me."

He frowned. Now wait just a minute. "Mika—"

She held up a hand. "Jensen, I learned in the cruddiest way possible that I can't lean on anyone. That I have to rely on myself. That hard-won wisdom took some really tough weeks to get to. I may not have a lot of money, but I've always taken care of myself, and I will take care of myself and my child. So thank you, but no, thank you."

Huh. That wasn't the speech he expected. At all.

"I don't think of you as a charity case, Mikayla. I think of you as a person I met here in town who did me a favor at the Baby Bonanza—those beds were a huge hit. So, when I heard you at the cashier paying on lay-away, I got the impulse to do you a favor. That's all."

Her expression went from *Who the hell do you think you are?* to *Well, I guess that was thoughtful of you, but.* The early-evening breeze blew her hair toward her face, and he wanted so badly to reach out and move the silky strands, but she beat him to it, tucking her hair behind her ears. "I can't even imagine how much that favor cost, Jensen. You know, if someone wanted to give me a realistic gift—a basic bouncer, a baby mobile—I'd happily accept and say thank you. But my entire layaway, my entire wish list? *That* I can't accept from anyone but myself."

"My father would call that cutting off your nose to spite your face," he said, nonetheless full of admiration for her way of thinking.

"I am who I am," she said with a shrug of her tanned shoulders.

"I yam who I yam," he said in his best Popeye imitation.

She tilted her head and grinned and then made a face at him. "Don't try to charm me into liking you, Jones."

"But I did?" he asked.

"You charmed me into not storming off with a *You can't buy me!* tossed over my shoulder."

"Is that what you think I was trying to do?" he asked, his smile fading.

"Actually, I don't think so. I mean, why would you? What are you getting? A hot tamale?" She waved her hands down her very, very, very pregnant belly. "Hot sex for a night? I can barely turn over in bed. Oh, maybe it's the *after* that you're most interested in—the package deal of a new mother and an infant who'll wake up all night long. Right. Sure." She laughed and shook her head. "I know, like any reasonably intelligent person would, that you're not trying to buy me."

He held her gaze, the smile gone, his tone dead serious. "I'll be very honest here, Mikayla. I think you're incredibly hot."

She gaped at him.

"I know you're seven months pregnant. I know there can't be anything between us. I'm not the marrying kind. Or the daddy kind. I'm a workaholic businessman in town on a land deal that isn't happening, and I'm not leaving till I make it happen."

"You always get what you want?" she asked.

He glanced over at the fields and the Montana wilderness beyond, then back at Mikayla. "No. I don't."

"Huh. Just when I expect you to be all slick and flirty, you hit me with *real*. Stop disarming me, Jones."

God, he liked this woman. His smile returned. "We met under some pretty comical circumstances—if you find that sort of thing funny, being as you're the pregnant one—and we're becoming friends. Right time, right place, and I bought out your wish list for you. There was nothing behind it but the want to do something nice for you. That's it."

"Well, now, I believe that." She extended her hand.

He shook it, the feel of her soft, warm hand in his having more impact on several parts of his anatomy than he expected. One little touch could poke at his chest and his groin?

"I can't accept your generosity, Jensen. But it clearly came from a thoughtful place, and for that, thank you."

She lowered her hand and glanced behind him at the house. "This is some home. A luxury log cabin? It's even grander than Maverick Manor."

He turned and looked at the mansion of a log cabin. Logs. Mansion. Who'd have thought? Walker, that was who. Though Hudson was the brother who'd always been a cowboy at heart, Walker was a man of the land himself. "I think that's what Walker was going for. You should see the fireplace. The spa bathroom's as big as the family room. A Michelin-starred chef's dream kitchen. And all the while you feel like you're in the woods, roughing it."

She gave a little snort laugh. "Well, I wouldn't call a spa bathroom roughing it. But it sure sounds nice."

She smiled and started to walk away toward her car.

No. Come back. Come in. Let me show you that fireplace. You can take a bath in that giant luxe bathroom!

But why? So he could stare at her face and admire her lush breasts and share some decaf coffee? *Nothing* could happen between them. And developing a friendship with Mikayla was out of the question. He was too attracted to her. Why, he had no idea. The pregnancy should have negated the attraction, let alone his startling physical draw to her. There was something between them and he had no idea what it was. But he wasn't looking for a future, a package deal, as she'd called it. He wasn't interested in being a family man or settling down or trying to forget what Adrienne had taught him: that in the end, people really couldn't be trusted with the soft parts of you.

So he let Mikayla walk away.

But he couldn't leave things this way—good and fine and okay between them. He had to screw up their truce so that he could try to distance himself from the way he felt about her. Yes, that made sense. It did, right? He thought of his father, sitting at his massive cherrywood desk in his Jones Holdings corner office, yelling at one of his executive VPs. *Don't let one get you, Jensen!* he heard his father bellow in his head.

Emotional distance. Work. Those were the tenets he lived by now.

As for Rust Creek Falls's Jones-stealing women? Those he had to watch out for.

Just one. Mikayla. The seven-months-pregnant beauty heading for her car.

Whatever was in the water in this town, he'd drunk it. Jeez. He had to break the damned spell.

"Mikayla," he called.

She turned around, her expression so sweet he almost didn't say a word.

But he had to. For his own self-preservation. To stop this. "About the cost of the stuff. It's just money. Seriously, the entire bill affected me as much as buying a double café Americano." For good measure, he rested his hands on his silver-and-gold diamond-encrusted belt buckle.

As expected, her sweet expression turned into momentary shock, then disappointment, then disdain.

Mission accomplished.

She stared at him. Glared at him. "There's no such thing as 'just money' when you have a few hundred to your name, Jensen. But you wouldn't know anything about that, would you?"

"Hell, no," he said unnecessarily flippantly. But it was true.

She slowly shook her head. "I guess we're done

here. I said what I came to say. I take back most of it. The part about not being able to accept your 'generosity,' I don't take back."

Sorry, Mikayla, he thought, his gut twisting. *I wish things could be different.* But how? Would he wish she weren't pregnant? Or that he was a different kind of man?

He didn't know. Twenty-eight years old and he didn't know a damned thing about himself other than signing his name to deals was the only kind of commitment he could handle—and wanted.

She stomped to her car, an ancient two-door sedan with rust on the bottom.

His chest feeling tight and heavy, he watched her drive away until she was out of sight. Had he felt this bad when he discovered Adrienne's betrayal? Not quite.

And that was scary as hell.

Chapter Five

The next morning, Mikayla finished her mint-chocolate-chip ice cream cone—a major craving that she'd had to satisfy as the only way to appease her rotten mood—then reached into her shoulder bag and crumpled up the classified section of the free weekly newspaper.

No, sorry was the refrain of the day from the few businesses in town that were looking for help. One look at her belly and she wasn't even in contention for a job.

Who was she kidding? Who would want to hire her when she'd have to take time off in just a couple months? And when she was ready to go back to work, she wouldn't be able to afford day care—

Day care. The light bulb went off. There was a day care in Rust Creek Falls—she'd heard someone mention it. Just Kids or something like that. She had only a couple years' experience under her belt as a day care aide; in Cheyenne she'd been working at a day care and taking night classes in early-childhood education, but then her pregnancy and the explosion of her relationship with Scott had upended everything.

Mikayla typed *day care* and *Rust Creek Falls* into her phone's search bar. Just Us Kids Day Care Center. Owned and operated by Walker and Hudson Jones.

She frowned. Oh, Lord. Did the Jones brothers own everything in town? They weren't even from here!

Well, at least Jensen "It's Just Money" Jones wasn't involved in the day care. She narrowed her eyes as his too-handsome face and amazing body slid into her mind. She never wanted to see him again. And surely Jensen wouldn't be caught dead in a day care center.

Forget Jensen Jones, she ordered herself. Forget what happened yesterday. Forget how hot he looked in his jeans. The way his thick blond hair fell over his forehead when he glanced down, how he ran his fingers through that sexy mass of movie-star hair. What she should remember? That they had absolutely nothing in common—including, and most important, *values*. Humph. Double humph!

Mikayla closed her eyes for a moment, trying to focus on the fresh morning breeze and the feel of the sun on her face. She didn't need to be upset over some out-of-touch-with-the-real-world Hemsworth; she needed a job. She *needed* to be self-sufficient. And she needed Just Us Kids to hire her, even though at this point, Jensen might put in a bad word for her with his brothers.

Except he wouldn't. She knew that. He might be Mr. Clueless Moneybags, but kindness ran under that hard, sexy chest of his. If she told him she needed a job and had childcare experience, he'd probably fly her across town in his private jet to the day care, interrupt everything and demand she be given a job on the spot. She smiled at the thought, then slapped herself upside the head for letting him charm her in absentia. What the hell was wrong with her?

Now she was reading a man she barely knew? Hadn't he told her exactly who he was with his parting shot last night? *It's just money...*

She would *not* call Jensen Jones. She'd get the job on her own. She had friends who could vouch for her. Eva and Luke and Amy. And she had a decent résumé when it came to working with children. Aside from the day care, she'd always made extra money babysitting kids of all ages.

Perhaps Just Us Kids would allow her to start now and then bring her newborn to work? She doubted she could afford to pay the monthly tuition out of her salary, but perhaps they could work out an arrangement or maybe employees who enrolled their children got discounts? She'd never know if she didn't ask.

To make this fresh start work in Rust Creek Falls, she needed a job. Once she had some paychecks tucked away, she could get her own place and provide a home for her child.

She glanced at her phone again. The day care was just a few blocks from here. Mikayla lifted her chin, took a deep breath, smoothed her not-exactly-professional midi sundress, whipped out her mirrored compact to make sure she didn't have ice cream or cone remnants on her chin or in her teeth and then headed up the street and made a left.

There it was. Just Us Kids. *Go get 'em*, she told herself.

A sign on the front door of the one-story building read Please Press Buzzer and Await Staff Member to Allow Entry. *Couldn't be too careful*, she thought, nodding at the sign. She pressed, noting that a woman sat at a desk in a small lobby area, typing away at a computer.

The woman glanced up; Mikayla recognized her from Luke's bachelor party. It was Bella Stockton Jones, Hudson's wife. Her brother Jamie was the father of the triplets for whom Jensen had bought the toddler beds. Bella smiled and waved and opened the door.

The moment Mikayla stepped inside the inviting space, she felt at home. This environment she knew well. There were beanbags in every primary color. Kid-size tables and chairs. Rows of flowers made out of kids' handprints lining the lobby walls. Floor mats with the alphabet and numbers. And little kids at play, some using kiddie scissors in an origami lesson, others sitting in a group on a plush rug, being read to by a teacher. The familiarity was so comforting that a warmth enveloped Mikayla.

"Mikayla, right?" Bella said.

"Right. And you're Bella Jones."

"Here for a tour of the day care for your little one?" Bella asked with a smile. "I'm the manager at Just Us Kids."

"Well, I'm actually here because I'm hoping for a job. I moved to town a few weeks ago, but in Cheyenne I worked for Happy Kids Day Care for over two years and was taking classes in early-childhood education. I worked in all the rooms—infant, toddler, preschool and with the older kids after school."

Bella shook her head with a strange expression, and Mikayla's heart sank. Another no.

"The universe works in mysterious ways," Bella said. "Look at this." She swiveled her desktop monitor. *Help Wanted: Just Us Kids Day Care Center is looking for an experienced childcare provider for the newborn and baby room...*

Mikayla gasped. The head shaking had been about the coincidence! It wasn't a no! "I have my résumé," Mikayla added, taking the folder from her bag and handing over a sheet of paper.

"Have a seat," Bella said, gesturing at the chair on the other side of her desk. As she scanned the résumé, Mikayla sent a prayer heavenward.

Thirty minutes later, Mikayla Brown had a job offer—contingent on Bella checking her references, which included her former boss from the Cheyenne day care and Eva Stockton. *Yes!* she thought, wanting to do the Snoopy dance right here and now. And aside from the perk of health insurance starting the first of September, day care employees enrolled their children at Just Us Kids *free*. Mikayla wanted to throw her arms around Bella and hug her, but there was that belly issue again.

"Thank you so much!" Mikayla said. "I'm so excited to start at Just Us Kids. I'll see you bright and early a week from Monday at seven o'clock."

Bella smiled and extended her hand. "See you then." The phone rang at the desk. "Mikayla, why don't you take a walk around, peer in the rooms, check out the playground, and then I'll see you out."

As her new boss answered the phone, Mikayla headed deeper inside the large, colorful main room.

She smiled as she watched the group of preschoolers work on their origami. As she passed another large room, a younger group was singing the alphabet song. She headed down a hallway with a beautiful mural of a petting zoo and came to the baby room. This was where she'd spend her time. She popped her head in and waved at the woman very quietly singing a lullaby to a drowsy baby in her arms. Three other infants were fast asleep in cribs.

Mikayla continued down the hall and stopped at a water fountain.

"Look, Jensen, I know this deal means a lot to you, but you can't keep upping the price. Just look elsewhere."

Mikayla froze at the sound of the male voice, which she realized was coming from an office not a foot away marked Walker Jones.

Jensen was here?

"Barnes's land is perfect for the crisis distribution center," she heard Jensen say. "It's near two access roads, which is key. And yet it's far enough from the center of town that it won't affect residents."

"The site is perfect, agreed," another male voice said, and she wondered if it was the other brother, Hudson.

"Davison lost his life fighting for those who needed help, and I'm not letting him down," Jensen said. "He knew having ready supplies and trained volunteers in a crisis was vital—he talked to me about his dream of building a distribution center right here. But Barnes wouldn't sell to him, and then we lost Davison. He loved this town and that land is going unused. I just have to figure out Barnes's angle for not selling. I have a cap—don't worry. And I'm sure I won't need to go that high."

"We all loved Davison," a man said—Mikayla was pretty sure it was Jensen's brother Walker. "But Dad's going to flip out on you about this. You know that, right?"

"Okay, so I haven't exactly mentioned the particulars of the land deal to Dad, just that it's something good for Jones Holdings. Dad will definitely not be pleased that I'm carrying on his late former best friend's volunteer work and pet project. But I also know it's part of the key to cracking dear ole Dad. The two men had a rift years ago, and it needs to be healed if Dad is ever going to find peace—even if Dad has to do that alone."

"Dad isn't going to come to terms with whatever ruined their friendship," Walker said. "And no doubt it was Dad who screwed up. He didn't even go to Davison's funeral."

The other voice chimed in. "Jensen, between this land deal and Mom and Dad's anniversary party, you're really setting yourself up for serious disappointment."

"I have to try, right?" Jensen said. "You don't try, you get zippo."

You are definitely right, Mikayla thought. *An hour ago, I was scarfing down ice cream over not being able to find a job, but here I am, hired.*

Maybe there was more to Jensen Jones and how his mind, heart and wallet worked than Mikayla had thought. Maybe he really was about being generous because he could be, not because he was trying to buy or impress anybody.

"Oh, if anyone needs the plane this afternoon, it's available," Jensen said. "I was scheduled to fly to LA to handle a negotiation for Autry, but I bumped it up to this morning via Skype, so I'm all set."

"Oh, good," Hudson said. "I need to fly to New York tonight. Now I can leave earlier than planned."

"Jensen, did I ever thank you for the pool cue you sent me from Morocco as a thanks for letting you bunk with us?" That voice, as she'd thought, clearly belonged to Walker.

"No, you did not, jerk," Jensen said, then laughed. God, she loved the sound of his laughter.

"Well, thank you. Man, it's a work of art. One of a kind. I used it last night in a round against Lindsay and won by a landslide. Okay, I won by one."

Mikayla smiled, then felt the smile fade. These men lived in a different universe. Private jets? Planning meetings in LA for an hour? Moroccan pool cues?

Bella seemed so down-to-earth. And from what Mikayla had heard, Bella had worked in the day care before the Jones family had bought the business. She probably wasn't all that different from Mikayla, yet she apparently had loads in common with her millionaire husband, Hudson Jones. Walker's wife, Lindsay, was a lawyer and had been very friendly to Mikayla on the two occasions they'd met. So obviously the Jones brothers didn't live in different universes than mere Rust Creek Falls mortals.

What the hell was she doing? Imagining herself getting involved with Jensen? *Puh-leeze!* Never going to happen. She was about to have a baby. And Jensen was leaving town after he settled this land deal of his.

Her fantasies could not include any type of relationship with him, let alone a future.

Hadn't "you can look but not touch" been her motto
since childhood?

She heard Jensen's voice get louder, as though he
was heading toward the closed office door, and she
turned and rushed back to the front desk to say goodbye to Bella. Except Bella wasn't at the desk and Mikayla didn't want to leave without saying goodbye and
thanking her again.

Ugh. She *couldn't* run into Jensen. Because if she
let herself look at him, let herself talk to him, she'd
get all ridiculously weak-kneed by his hotness, he'd
start disarming her again with that way of his and
she wouldn't be able to blame anything on hormones,
since she knew full well it was *him*. How was that fair?

"Do you like my picture, mister?"

Walking through the main room of the day care toward the front door, Jensen glanced down to see a little kid around three or four with a mop of brown hair
suddenly standing in front of him, holding a piece of
blue construction paper. There was a purple sun with
a smiley face, an orange tree and lots of green grass at
the bottom of the paper. There was also a stick figure
and what looked like a pink dog. Or maybe it was a cat.

"Um, sure," Jensen said, glancing around for a
teacher. Anyone. Someone. Unfortunately, the woman
wearing the Ms. Allie, Lead Teacher name tag was
deep in conversation across the room with Bella, his
sister-in-law. He noticed Bella keeping an eye on him,
so he bent down a bit to be less than six foot two. "I
like the dog."

"What dog?" the boy said, looking from Jensen to his paper.

"That one," he said, pointing to the floppy-eared pink mutt with four legs and a long tail.

The little boy scrunched up his face. "It's not a dog! It's a space alien! Why do you think it's pink!" he yelped, then his eyes started filling up.

Oh, God. Bella and Ms. Allie came rushing over.

"That man thought the space alien was a dog," the boy complained to his teacher as he used his palms to wipe away his tears.

Ms. Allie put a hand on the boy's shoulder. "Dylan, the great thing about art is that everyone can see something different in the same thing."

The boy didn't look convinced. He scampered back to his table with his drawing. He said to the girl next to him, "Does this look like a dog or a space alien?"

The girl looked at the picture. "Definitely a space alien."

Happy once again, the boy began coloring a new picture.

"I'm a real hit with kids," Jensen whispered on a sigh to Bella. "You should hire me for birthday parties."

Bella laughed. "Allie, this is my brother-in-law Jensen. Jensen, meet Allie, our lead teacher."

They smiled at each other, and Allie headed over to the table with the drawing kids.

"Sorry about that," he said to Bella. "I'm clueless when it comes to talking to kids."

He really was. A disaster. At the party the other day, he'd had no idea for an entire minute that one of the Stockton triplets had been trying to get his attention to say thank you for the race car bed—at his uncle Hudson's behest. His brother had had to elbow him in the ribs and point down, and there was little Jared, staring up at Jensen.

"My pleasure," he'd said to Jared. "Much health and happiness," Jensen had added, and the little boy had stared blankly at him and toddled away.

"Much health and happiness? Really?" Hudson had said, shaking his head. "Are we toasting someone's retirement from Jones Holdings or are we at a potty party for two-and-a-half-year-olds?"

Jensen had shrugged. "I don't speak toddler."

Hudson had laughed. "Oh, that's clear, brother."

Now Jensen glanced around the colorful main room of the day care, kid after kid doing kid things in kid lingo. He felt really out of place.

"I'm sure you'd be great with kids," Bella said. "You just haven't spent much time around pint-size people."

"The second part of what you said is true. The first part is very iffy."

Bella smiled, then glanced at the lobby area. "Oh, gosh, there's Mikayla waiting for me. See you later, Jensen."

Every cell inside him perked up. Mikayla was here? He glanced toward the lobby, where the room narrowed, and could just make out her gorgeous long brown hair and the crazy wrap-around-the-ankles flat brown sandals she wore. She had on an ankle bracelet and a toe ring.

He figured he'd give them a minute to talk, then he'd sidle up and ask Mikayla to lunch.

"Thank you again, Bella," he heard Mikayla say. "Can't wait to start working here."

"See you a week from Monday," Bella said. "I'll call your references right now and will run a comprehensive background check, but I have no doubt I'll hear great things."

Mikayla's smile could have melted a block of ice. So she'd gotten herself a job here, had she? Good for her.

"New job calls for a celebration lunch, don't you think?" he said to Mikayla as he sauntered over. "Anywhere you want to go. My treat."

He would describe the look on Bella's face as utter shock. And more than a bit of *you do see she's pregnant, right, playboy?*

The look on Mikayla's face was more *I don't think so, Richie Rich. I had enough of you and your "treating" yesterday.*

"That's very kind of you, Jensen, but…"

Was that his heart plummeting toward his stomach? *Give her the out. Be a gentleman. She's still angry at you. As well she should be. And you should be grateful one of you is keeping a distance.* "But you're busy. I understand. Another time."

"Another time," she said and rushed out.

He watched her walk up the sidewalk until she turned the corner.

"I didn't think Mikayla would be your type," Bella said, her eyebrows sky-high.

He turned back to his sister-in-law. "What is my type?" he asked, truly wondering how he appeared to others.

"A good-time girl," she said. "For the short-term."

"Mikayla's not due for two months," he pointed out.

"You're as incorrigible as I thought," she said, shaking her head on a laugh. "I'll tell you, Jensen Jones. Your brothers were like you. Then they got cupid's arrow straight through the heart and settled down.

It's gonna happen to you. Who knows, might have already."

"Meaning Mikayla? She's due in two months!"

Bella laughed so hard she almost fell out of her chair. "Yeah, you *just* told me that, remember? But she *is* single."

He threw a glance at his Rolex. "Ah, almost ten o'clock. I have a business call to make. Overseas," he said, practically running out the door.

He could hear his sister-in-law's laughter following him to his car.

He supposed he deserved the mocking.

But who said anything about "settling down"?

And just what the hell was he going to do about his attraction to this very pregnant person?

Chapter Six

Thirteen business texts—on a Saturday morning, no less.

Ten personal ones from his father. All along the lines of: When will you be back? Do I need to come drag you home, son? I will!

And one from Guthrie Barnes. I've learned how to block you on this fool piece of new technology. Quit bugging me about my land, you hear!

Jensen wanted to slam his phone against his little round table at Daisy's Donuts, but since he liked their coffee best in town, he didn't want to get banned. *Okay, Jones. Focus.* He spent the next ten minutes answering texts and emails related to business, set up two video meetings, responded to his dad that it would be a few more days at most—though he had no idea if that was true—and then tried to figure out how to handle Barnes.

He hated that he was bothering the old man, who'd made it crystal clear he didn't want to hear from Jensen again; in fact, he'd made that clear the first time Jensen had contacted him. But something wasn't quite right here. Jensen couldn't put his finger on it.

Why the heck wouldn't the man sell the land? He'd been widowed for almost a decade and lived alone in the falling-down home. Had no family in town anymore. He was a curmudgeonly recluse, according to Jensen's brothers, and no one knew much about him. Maybe if Jensen wrote him an honest letter, from the heart, about what this project meant to him, what Davison had meant to him, maybe he'd crack the old coot. Hell, Jensen would even handwrite it.

"And here's your double espresso," Eva said with a smile as she set the steaming cup on his table. "Oh, Jensen, I hope you're coming to the barbecue at Sunshine Farm this afternoon. Your brothers will be there. And half the town. Oh, and someone else you know— Mikayla Brown."

Ooh, a homespun party on Mikayla's turf? She'd feel more comfortable and therefore be more open to talking to him. "I'd love to come, and thanks for the invitation," he said. He hadn't seen Mikayla in two days, which had seemed like an eternity given that he didn't know how long he'd have in Rust Creek Falls.

"Special occasion?" he asked, taking a sip of the excellent espresso. Second one of the day, and it hit the spot. Again.

"Luke's sister Dana has come home for her summer break from college, and the Stocktons love a reason to get together, especially when there's barbecue involved. Luke's great on the grill, so come hungry."

He couldn't help picturing Mikayla. Oh, he'd come hungry, all right. He *was* hungry.

"Ah, finally," Eva said, glancing up at the clock on the wall. "It's noon. My shift's over. See you at one at Sunshine Farm."

He smiled. "I'll be there."

He smiled at the woman who came to relieve Eva behind the counter, then drained his espresso and left. Time to pick up something to bring to the barbecue—where and what, he had no clue. Usually he'd bring a great bottle of something or a two-hundred-year-old cheese. He wished he could fly in his favorite potato salad from a great gourmet deli in Tulsa, and he would if there were time.

Since it was so close to 1:00 p.m. by the time he fired off the last of his business emails back at the log mansion, got out of the shower and dressed in jeans, a Western shirt and his more down-to-earth cowboy boots, he swiped a bottle of wine from Walker's collection and left a hundred-dollar bill tucked into the rack.

When he arrived at Sunshine Farm, streams of people were walking around the property. Eva hadn't been kidding; half the town was here. He presented the wine to Eva and got a kiss on the cheek for that, then left to find his lovely Mikayla.

His Mikayla? Had he just thought that? He hadn't seen her for two days and had thought of her constantly.

He looked around everywhere but didn't see her. And let's face it—she was hard to miss.

The Stocktons were standing near the huge grill—Daniel and his wife, Annie. Jamie and his wife, Fallon, and the triplet potty-training champs, and his sister-in-law Bella, happily married to his brother Hudson, who was deep in conversation with Walker over by the stables. Hopefully they weren't talking business on a Saturday at a barbecue, but they probably were. Hadn't Jensen himself been dealing with business all morning? Working for Jones Holdings Inc. was a 24-7 job.

Jensen shook his head. He'd have to do something about that.

Beer in hand, he walked around the property, admiring the big yellow barn and the sturdy farmhouse. He wondered which windows were Mikayla's. Maybe she was inside?

No. She wasn't. She was right there, thanking Luke, on grill duty, for the hamburger he'd just given her. He watched her squirt ketchup and mustard and heap relish and tomatoes on the burger, then add a sour pickle spear.

He headed over for a burger of his own, then quickly caught up to her at the drinks table for a sweet iced tea.

"I get to have a celebratory lunch with you after all," he said with a smile.

She whirled around. "Jensen. I didn't know you were coming."

How did she always look so pretty? She wore a pink tank top and a floaty white cotton skirt down to her calves and those sexy wrap-around-the-ankle sandals. Her silky brown hair cascaded around her sun-kissed shoulders. And if he wasn't mistaken, she looked even more pregnant.

"I make friends wherever I go," he said, adding ice cubes to his drink. *Eyes off the belly*, he ordered himself. "I'm always invited to parties."

She laughed. "Is that true?"

"No. More like I looked so miserable dealing with thirteen business emails at Daisy's on a Saturday morning that Eva felt sorry for me and invited me."

She laughed again, the beautiful sound reaching right inside him.

"And it's a good thing you didn't see me bomb with the preschool set at Just Us Kids the other day," he said. "I actually made a little kid cry."

"Aw, you probably just haven't spent much time with kids. Am I right?"

"You're right. I've never dated anyone with kids. And my brother Autry's girls are in Paris, so I don't get to spend much time with children."

"The key with talking to kids is to just be real," she said.

"I think that's what got me into trouble."

She laughed again, and he loved making her happy. Why, he didn't know. "Oh, those two seats just opened up," she said, upping her chin across the lawn. "Let's grab 'em before someone beats us to them."

His heart pinged. She was actually inviting him to sit with her. That was a good sign. That she didn't hate his guts anymore.

"I thought pregnant women got seats everywhere they went. Isn't that Life 101?" he asked as he followed her, hoping that the constant trail of little kids racing around didn't end with his hamburger or drink toppling over on someone's head.

"Here in Rust Creek Falls? Definitely. Back home in Cheyenne? I stood for a half hour on a very slow, very un-air-conditioned bus to work one ninety-two-degree day when my car conked out."

He hated the thought of Mikayla so uncomfortable.

Relying on a cruddy car. Standing for a half hour on a sweltering bus when no one gave her a seat. "I would have gotten up for you in a heartbeat."

Oh, Lord. He'd said that in a much more serious way than he'd meant to.

She sat down. "I'm sure you would have, Jensen."

He put his cup on the grass in front of his chair and sat beside her, so close he could smell her shampoo. Green apple, he was pretty sure. "So how'd a Cheyenne girl end up in a tiny Montana town? You have family here?"

She took a bite of her loaded burger, and he had the feeling she was happy not to have to answer right away. "I don't have much family anywhere. I have a cousin I love to death—Brent—who's on the rodeo circuit right now. It was his suggestion I move here. Luke used to work on a ranch in Wyoming with Brent, so when I was looking for a fresh start, Brent made a call and voilà, I'm now living at Sunshine Farm."

He watched her face light up as she looked around the property. She clearly liked it here.

"Every night, just looking out my bedroom window at all this open land, all this fresh air, those gorgeous woods in the distance makes me feel so hopeful. Instead of feeling closed in like I did in Cheyenne, these endless fields and stretches of blue sky make me feel like anything can happen. Like the world is full of possibilities." She glanced at him as though she'd forgotten she was actually talking to someone. She bit her lip. "I sound crazy, probably."

He took a drink of his iced tea. "Not at all. I know exactly what you mean. I feel like I can really think here."

She nodded. "Exactly. But you're leaving soon?"

"If I ever get this land deal settled. For the first time ever, I might be licked. By a seventysomething more stubborn than my own father. I never thought I'd meet anyone who could hold a candle to Walker Jones the Second in that regard."

She smiled. "I have a confession. When I was taking a tour of Just Us Kids the other day, I did catch the tail end of a conversation you were having with your brothers. Something about a crisis distribution center you want to build on that land?"

He nodded and told her all about Davison Parkwell and his volunteer work, how much the crisis center would mean to the man who'd been like a second father to him. "I guess if I can't get the land, I'll have to find a new location. I just hope it doesn't come to that. Davison loved this part of Montana, and given how many of my brothers have ties to Rust Creek Falls, the site feels right here," he added, touching the left side of his chest.

She tilted her head and seemed to be taking that in. "What's keeping him from selling?" she asked, taking a bite of her pickle spear.

Damned if he knew. "No idea. The land is going unused, his house is falling apart and he has no family in town. I don't get it. Why doesn't he take the money and run? He could spend his senior days in luxury somewhere warm with a shuffleboard court."

"My grandmother loved Wyoming winters and hated shuffleboard, so you never know," she said. "But *something* is making Barnes stubborn about keeping the land. Find out what and that's your ticket."

"Or just the reason for the door being slammed in my face with every higher offer," he pointed out.

"Yes, but maybe if you knew why, your negotiation would have somewhere to go other than nowhere."

"You sure you don't have an MBA?" he asked. "Because you're absolutely right. I have to find out why he won't sell."

"You could ask around," she said. "Find out what makes him tick."

Guthrie Barnes? Never heard of him. Who? Those had been the usual responses he'd gotten to his queries around town about the man. Barnes had lived in Rust Creek Falls for over fifty years, almost his entire adult life. How could he be so invisible?

Jensen frowned. "I tried that but didn't get very far. But I'll keep digging."

"Never give up—that has to be everybody's motto."

He almost wished she hadn't said that. Because there was no way he was giving up on his attraction to her, which went far beyond the physical. He could sit here and talk to her for hours. He wanted to hear her opinion on everything.

"Have faith," she said, touching his hand, and again, every cell in his body reacted to that small point of contact. He never wanted her to move her hand from his, but she did, unfortunately.

What the hell was happening here?

How could he be so enamored with this woman? She wasn't a no-strings candidate. She was going to have a baby in two months!

That funny feeling came over him, the one that made his head pound and his gut tighten. The one that made him say stupid things to change the subject.

"So is the baby's father in the picture?" he asked before he could stop himself.

He felt her stiffen beside him. She picked up her iced tea and took a long sip, then spent a good half minute putting it down on the grass in front of her chair.

Idiot, he chastised himself with a virtual palm slam to his forehead. Why had he asked that? As if he didn't know why—to squash the too-real conversation they'd been having.

"Can't cath me!" a pint-size guest shouted, taking off toward the pastures with a pie in his hands. It was one of his brother's nephews. Henry or Jared. They looked a lot alike.

"Cath?" Jensen repeated.

"It's toddler for *catch*," Mikayla said, shaking her head. "Duh."

Did she just "duh" him?

She smiled and then elbowed him in the ribs. "Let's go try to catch the little thief before he ends up falling face-first into all that apple goodness."

Jensen jumped up and they ran after the tyke. "Did I mention I was all state on the cross-country team in high school and college?"

"Then why is a two-year-old faster than you are?" she asked with a grin.

"Um, maybe because I'm trying to stay paced with a woman who could have a baby any day?"

"Touché," she said. "But more like any *month*."

He smiled at her. Mikayla Brown, he was learning, would not let him get away with anything. He liked that.

"Oh, no, Henry's heading straight for that tree!" someone shouted.

"I'm on it," Jensen said and pulled ahead, putting his old training days and current running regimen to good use.

"Thought you said no one could catch you, Henry!" he said in as baby friendly a voice as he could manage, passing the boy and then slowly jogging backward in front of him.

"You didn't cath me," Henry said with a look of triumph, making a break to the left.

"Oh, so we're playing tag?" Jensen asked. "Why didn't you say so?"

Jensen pretended not to be able to catch the kid, then finally leaned over, exaggerating being out of breath, and touched his shoulder. "Tag, you're it!"

The boy started laughing. "I'm it!"

Jensen jogged slowly back toward the crowd. "You'll never catch me!" he said, grinning.

"Will too!" Henry shouted, his face full of gleeful concentration.

Just as Henry was in grabbing distance to his father, Jensen slowed enough for the boy to tag him.

"Tag! You're it!" Henry shouted with a huge smile.

"Aw, you got me!" Jensen said. "You were too fast for me. I can't move a muscle."

"I win!" Henry said. "Daddy, I winned the game!"

"Yay!" Jamie Stockton said, high-fiving his son. Jamie's wife, Fallon, took the pie and set it back on the dessert buffet, dragging her arm across her forehead with a "Phew."

"How did he manage not to drop the pie?" Mikayla asked.

"Christmas miracle in August?" Jensen suggested with a shrug.

She laughed. "I thought you said you were terrible with kids and made them cry. Seems like you made Henry's day. And saved the pie!"

Huh. He guessed he hadn't done half-bad this time.

"Must be your influence rubbing off on me," he said.

"You always know what to say, don't you?" She shook her head with a smile and they headed back to their seats.

"Hardly," he said, taking the last two bites of his cheeseburger. "Or I wouldn't have awkwardly asked you about the father of your baby." He let his head drop backward with a sigh. "Or just reminded you of that fact."

She smiled and took a bite of her own burger. "Nothing wrong with asking. I always like dealing with the elephant in the room—or however that saying goes. You know?"

He nodded. "Except it's none of my business."

She reached up and placed her hand on the side of his face, then kissed him—right on the lips. And not a friendly kiss. A *kiss* kiss. A romantic kiss. An invitation-to-something kiss.

But what, exactly?

Whoa. One moment Mikayla was finishing her burger, craving another pickle spear, and the next she was planting a kiss on Jensen's soft, warm, inviting mouth.

Had she really done that? She had. The look of half shock, half very pleased on his handsome face told her so. What the hell had she been thinking? He'd exasperated her just minutes ago! Then he'd gone and gently and sweetly caught little Henry Stockton, saving the day and the pie in an adorable way.

Why couldn't he be as bad with kids as he'd said he was? At least then she could cross him off her list of potential love interests. There was only one name on that list, a name that shouldn't be there, anyway.

No worries, she assured herself. His interest in her wasn't real. He found her attractive, probably because, like Eva and Amy had said, she was one of those annoying pregnant women who only carried the added weight in her belly. But two months from now when she was nine months pregnant and as big as his family's mansion in Tulsa, he'd be flying back in a heartbeat. If not way before. Come on. She was clearly some kind of a challenge for him. How many pregnant women had he tried to pick up and romance for a fling? Probably none before her.

Independence had to be her goal. Men were simply not a good bet for a woman in her condition. And Jensen Jones had to be in some serious denial. The minute she went into labor, he'd run for the door the way he had in Daisy's Donuts.

But instead of telling him she should go mingle and running for the hills herself, she'd kissed him.

She dared a glance at him. "Uh, I don't know why I did that."

"I do," he said.

She looked at him, eyes narrowed. "Why?"

"You find me incredibly attractive and that, combined with our undeniable chemistry, made you unable to resist me." He was dead serious. No flirtation or megawatt smile accompanied that bit of overconfident male nerve.

She raised an eyebrow. "Oh, is that why?" Yes, actually, it was exactly why.

"Give me one other reason, Mikayla."

"I'm hormonal," she said, hoping he'd believe it. She *was* hormonal.

"You could have kissed that guy," he said, pointing at a tall cowboy. "Or him," he added, gesturing at a blond surfer type. "Instead, you kissed *me*."

"Well, it's not like I'm going to do it again!" she whispered, praying no one saw or was listening to this crazy conversation.

"I hope you do," he said. Too seriously. While looking her right in the eyes.

"Why? To what end, Jensen Jones? What is the point in us kissing or getting to know each other?"

"For one, we like each other. You have to admit you like me, even though I'm filthy rich and enjoy throwing my money around."

"Okay, fine. I like you. Even though you're rich and make it obvious."

He grinned. "And then there's the chemistry."

"I guess," she said, wishing it weren't true.

"And finally, we're both single. We should be enjoying each other's company. Whatever that may mean."

"What *does* it mean?" she asked. Although she had a pretty good idea.

"In two months, you're going to be too busy to give me a passing thought. And I'm going to be back in Tulsa anyway. Right now, though, we're both available. We like each other. We want to kiss each other.

So let's *do* it. God, Mikayla, I just want to spoil you rotten. Let me."

Was he completely insane? "You're talking about an agreed-upon fling. With a very pregnant woman. Seriously?"

"Serious as a hurricane." He tilted his head and a sly smile curved those lips. "Aha. You're thinking about it."

Lord. Was she? She was. Maybe? Could it hurt? Her last hurrah before giving her time and attention to motherhood?

"I'm thinking about it," she said, mentally shaking her head. Was she nuts? "I need to sleep on it." She glanced toward the yellow barn, where bunches of people were heading to say goodbye to Luke and Eva. "Looks like the party is winding down."

"Guess it's time for me to go," he said, standing up and collecting their paper plates and cups, which surprised her. Why couldn't he act all entitled so she'd lean toward no on his crazy proposal? "I'll drop by tomorrow morning for your answer."

"What if I'm not sure tomorrow morning?" she asked.

Again, his gorgeous blue eyes were intense on her. "I think you will be, either way."

"What if my answer is '*no* way'?"

"Then like the song says, I'll have to bow out gracefully."

Huh. She had no idea what song he was talking about, but she hadn't expected him to agree to bow out. To walk away. To leave her alone. *Did* she want that? "Okay. I'll see you tomorrow morning, then."

She watched him take their plates and cups to the

garbage can, then head over to where Luke and Eva stood with Luke's sister. He shook their hands, then looked back at her and held up a hand in farewell, and she wanted to run to him and just be held by him and never let him go.

Which meant that tomorrow morning, her answer had to be no. Right?

Chapter Seven

At nine fifteen that night, Jensen and his brothers were finishing up a late dinner at Maverick Manor. They'd covered business, including some potential investment properties in Montana, and had figured out the basics for their parents' surprise anniversary party.

"The real surprise," Hudson said, taking the last bite of his pasta, "is whether Mom and Dad will show."

Jensen finished his beer. "I've got that covered. They'll show."

Walker shook his head. "You're overestimating them, li'l bro."

"Nah," Jensen said, in full confidence. He ate the last of his risotto. "God, this is good. This place should have a Michelin star."

"Jensen, seriously," Hudson said. "We're talking about *Mom* and *Dad*. Walker the Second and Patricia

Jones. You think they're going to come to Rust Creek Falls on some pretext? They barely showed up for our weddings."

Jensen almost snorted at that one. "They'll show. Trust me."

"How are you so sure?" Walker asked, leaning back and sipping his scotch.

"Because the night before the surprise party, I'm going to call Dad and tell him I decided to move to Rust Creek Falls, that I've fallen head over heels in love with a local woman and, sorry, I'm following in my brothers' footsteps. They'll be on their private plane so fast the earth will move."

Hudson smiled. "I have to hand it to you, Jensen. Brilliant."

"And so simple, yet scarily effective," Walker added. He tipped his scotch at Jensen.

It would definitely work. Jensen knew his parents. Particularly his father. "It's too bad I have to resort to that, but hey, we're getting Mom and Dad here, we're celebrating forty years, Autry and Gideon have both agreed to fly in, and you can guys can show them what a great town this is and change their minds about Rust Creek Falls."

Hudson raised an eyebrow. "Since when are you a champion of Rust Creek Falls, Jensen?"

"Since he started kissing pregnant women at barbecues," Walker suggested.

Hudson frowned. "You're going to scare Mom and Dad into jetting here by telling them you've fallen for a single woman who's seven months pregnant? That'll work for sure, but I don't like the idea of using Mikayla that way."

Now it was Jensen's turn to frown. "Whoa—hold up. Who said anything about Mikayla? I'm just telling them I fell for someone. Not mentioning names."

"So you *did* fall for someone?" Walker asked, challenge in his intense eyes.

Jensen felt his cheeks burn. "It's a *ruse*. And the ruse has nothing to do with Mikayla Brown. So lay off."

Hudson leaned forward. "But you did kiss her—the very pregnant woman—at Luke and Eva's barbecue?"

"We got caught up in a moment, that's all," Jensen said, slugging his beer. Did older brothers ever get less annoying? These two were like a freight train barreling toward him at 150 miles per hour.

"Well, don't try to turn *a* moment into two moments. Or five minutes. Or a week," Hudson said. "Mikayla's been hired at Just Us Kids, and she's starting next Monday. She's an employee now, and that makes her part of the Jones business family. So back off."

Jensen rolled his eyes. "Mikayla and I are *friends*. That's it. And I happen to like her. She happens to be gorgeous and ridiculously sexy despite—"

Walker and Hudson shook their heads slowly and in unison. "Don't even think about it, Jensen," Walker said. "She's about to have a baby. You did notice that, right?"

"I think that's quite evident," Jensen said.

And yes, that made things a bit more complicated than if she were not expecting. Nothing about the situation was standard operating procedure. Including why he was so drawn to her. *That* he couldn't quite figure out.

"So take a giant step back," Hudson said. "You have to, Jensen."

Walker nodded. "Listen to your elders."

Huh. His brothers were just looking out for him. Getting ensnared in the life of a heavily pregnant single woman was crazy for a guy like Jensen. His brothers knew it, and hell, he was actually kind of touched.

"Because let's face it, Jensen," Walker said. "You're not the stuff dads are made of."

"Jensen, someone's father," Hudson said on a snort. "Nope, can't see it. Ever."

Wait. They wanted him to back off from Mikayla because they didn't think he was up to the task of being her man? Of being a father figure? Of being a father, period?

Walker sipped his scotch and looked over the dessert menu. "If Mikayla Brown needs a man, she needs a stand-up guy who'll see her through these last weeks of her pregnancy, be her Lamaze coach and marry her. He'll be her husband and the father of her child."

Hudson nodded. "The *last* thing she needs is a jet-setting playboy out for a weeklong challenge or a first—sleeping with a hot pregnant woman and then walking away."

Jensen sat back, his gut twisting. What the hell? Who did Walker and Hudson think they were? Know-it-all jerks.

Though he *was* well-known in Oklahoma for his long list of ex-lovers, high turnover rate and refusal to commit. And he'd never opened up to these jackals known as his brothers about Adrienne and how she'd changed him—and then changed him back and for the worse. He'd been willing to commit. He'd *wanted* to.

Until she reminded him what his parents had instilled in him since birth. People would always say yes to him because of his name and money. Most of them— ninety-eight percent, his mother had said often— couldn't care less about him.

He thought of Adrienne and her gorgeous long blond hair and how he'd buried his face in those silky strands during sex, her nails raking down his back, whispering one untrue bittersweet nothing after the next. Those big, angelic blue eyes, hiding a lying, conniving, greedy gold digger who'd stolen so much from him, and he wasn't talking about the almost million dollars.

Actually, he should thank his brothers for reminding him who he was. Who he had to be. He *wasn't* daddy material. He wasn't even husband material. And women couldn't be trusted. Come on. He knew that. Mikayla was a sweet, smart, beautiful woman with her own mind and her own thing going on. She hadn't slapped him across the face for suggesting a short no-strings affair. She was sleeping on it.

Thinking about it right now, most likely. In bed. Naked.

Did pregnant women sleep naked? He had no idea. Why would he?

Based on what he knew about her, she seemed to want to take care of herself; she wasn't looking for a white knight. Then again, how different could she be? Especially in her…condition. She *needed*.

Yeah, it was a damned good thing his brothers had unwittingly knocked some sense into him. For a minute there, maybe he'd been getting a little soft in the heart area where Mikayla was concerned. He'd romance her.

He'd treat her like a queen. He'd give her everything she wanted, everything her baby needed, and then he'd fly home.

A brief affair really was perfect for them both. He was sure Mikayla was coming to that conclusion right this minute. His attraction to her was very likely just about forbidden fruit. That was all. How could it be anything more?

Meanwhile, she'd get a rich boyfriend for the next two weeks—he'd leave right after the anniversary party. Hell, maybe through the end of August if it took that long to convince Barnes to sell or for Jensen to find a new site for the distribution center.

And what would Jensen get? To look at her beautiful face and hear her laughter and interesting take on things. And hopefully to get her in bed every night until he left. He'd work her out of his system and he'd leave town, his heart intact.

Win-win for both.

Toss. Turn. Toss. Turn.

As if Mikayla could get comfortable when she *hadn't* been up all night contemplating whether to have a red-hot fling with a gorgeous, sexy millionaire.

She sat up, fluffed her top pillow for the tenth time and glanced at the bedside clock—5:47 a.m. Maybe what she needed was a mind-clearing cup of herbal tea and a bracing walk in the fields. A quick shower helped wake her up, and she headed downstairs to the kitchen, surprised to hear voices.

Eva and Amy Wainwright were sitting at the table, both in workout clothes, sipping coffee and talking quietly.

So as not to wake her, she figured. And Luke, who was likely still in bed, the way they all should be.

"Morning," Mikayla whispered, and they whipped their heads to her.

"You're up early," Amy said. "Feeling okay?"

"Absolutely fine. Just couldn't sleep. But why are you two so wide-awake?"

"Sunrise yoga at six fifteen in the park," Eva explained. "It supposedly helps usher in a day of equilibrium."

"Equil-*what*-brium?" Luke asked with a smile as he came in and poured himself a mug of coffee, his hair cutely mussed.

"It's a term we use in the childcare business, too," Mikayla said, making herself a cup of chamomile tea. "Like when three-year-olds want to push their plate of vegetables off the table but know they shouldn't and often do it anyway. Forces competing in your mind and body for balance."

"Wow, Bella Jones is sure going to be glad she hired you at Just Us Kids," Amy said, clinking Mikayla's teacup with her coffee mug. "You know your stuff."

"Oh, trust me, I'm having some issues with competing forces myself," she said, adding cream to her cup.

"See you ladies later," Luke said with a nod and a kiss on his wife's cheek. "Hope you find that equil-what-brium," he added with a devilish smile before leaving through the side door.

"I'll bet it has something to do with the hot kiss I saw at the barbecue yesterday," Eva said, wiggling her eyebrows. "Am I right?"

"Wait—what? What hot kiss?" Amy asked, whipping her head from Eva to Mikayla.

Yikes, who else had seen that kiss? Was she the talk of the town? God, she hoped not.

Mikayla sighed, sat down at the table and took a sip of her tea. No mind clearing yet. "Well, there I'd been, thinking the usual about Jensen Jones—world-class millionaire flirt—and then little Henry Stockton ran off with the pie and Jensen saved the day in such a sweet, touching way that I saw him differently. In those moments, instead of a too-confident, too-smooth, too-diamond-encrusted gorgeous millionaire used to getting what he wants when he wants it, I saw a good, kind man. A gorgeous, sexy, good, kind man. And we were talking for real about this and that, and I just leaned right over and kissed him." She shook her head. "I still can't believe I did it."

Amy broke into a grin and clapped. "Love it! Bet he did, too."

Mikayla thought of Jensen's expression when she'd pulled her face away from his, the surprise and delight in his blue eyes. The *desire*. "I think he did. To the point that he asked me to have a wild no-strings affair until he leaves town."

"An affair?" Eva repeated, eyes wide. "Like a no-holds-barred hot, temporary romance?"

"Exactly that," Mikayla said. "Crazy, right? I'm seven months pregnant!"

Amy raised her mug. "Exactly why you should go for it. If you don't, two months from now, you'll kick yourself. You won't have a minute to yourself to pee, let alone to do anything you're used to doing. But a week or two of being wined and dined by a single and available Jones? Do it, do it, do it," she added on a chant.

Eva laughed. "Sorry, Mik, but I agree with Amy. Motherhood will completely change your life. Sleepless nights. Sole responsibility for someone else. So yes, grab this crazy chance to be Cinderella for a few weeks."

Amy glanced at her phone on the table. "Oh, gosh, it's after six already. We'd better hit the road to get our equil-what-briums back," she added, popping up with a grin.

Eva put their mugs in the sink and the two headed to the door with their orange yoga mats slung across their torsos.

"Wait," Mikayla said, "you guys can't leave until you give me the flip side. Why any sane single pregnant woman *wouldn't* have a whirlwind no-strings affair with Jensen."

"Sorry, hon," Eva said. "But there is no flip side. You and Jensen are so different that it's highly unlikely you'll get attached to him, right?"

Amy nodded. "He's hot and rich with one hell of a smile. Enjoy yourself. Then he leaves and you both go back to your lives with some great memories."

"Got it," Mikayla said. "No flip side. Okay, go bend your bodies into positions I haven't been able to do in months."

They laughed and headed out.

As Mikayla sat there, she realized that they might not be right about the no-flip-side thing. She was already a little attached to Jensen. More than a little. Last night wasn't the first time she'd tossed and turned because of him, and not because of her giant belly getting in the way of comfort. And now she really did like him as a person. Too much. There was a lot more to Jensen Jones than his bank balance.

She had way too much going on to fall in love. So she'd never go so far as to have her heart involved. A little piece of it, sure. But like Eva said, she and Jensen were very different, from two polar-opposite worlds. He wasn't going to fall in love with her and she wasn't going to fall for him.

So why *not* be treated like a princess for the first time in her life for a week or two before her universe became changing diapers and waking up every couple of hours and worrying every two minutes that she was doing this motherhood thing wrong? A send-off. Yes. That was what a hot, brief affair with Jensen would be. A send-off, a last hurrah.

By the time she heard his pickup truck pull up, Mikayla was one thousand percent sure of her decision.

Chapter Eight

"Um, Jensen, when you said you wanted to take me out to breakfast, I thought you meant to Daisy's Donuts."

Jensen smiled at his new paramour and held open the door to Kalispell's four-star hotel, which, according to Walker, had the best breakfast chef in the state. "We're celebrating," he said. "And besides, you can go to Daisy's any day."

She smiled and glanced around the opulent lobby with its marble floors and ornate chandeliers. "So this is what it's like to be a Jones woman—temporary woman," she quickly added. "I like it."

Temporary Jones woman. That sounded weird. Even to him. But the wonder and delight in Mikayla's eyes as they entered the restaurant and followed the hostess through the elegant space to the outdoor patio had him quickly forgetting anything but her happiness.

They were seated in front of a long patch of wild-flowers. In moments, Mikayla had been served her decaf, which she described as heavenly.

"I'm getting the pregnant-lady special," she said, scanning the menu. "Otherwise known as eggs, bacon *and* pancakes."

Jensen grinned. "Walker says the pancakes here melt on the tongue."

And Walker turned out to know what he was talking about. Breakfast was delicious. Coffees were topped off before they could even think of going lukewarm. And Mikayla made sounds of utter happiness with most bites. Jensen forked a bite of his Western omelet and held it up to Mikayla's mouth.

"Don't mind if I do," she said, slipping those pink lips around the fork. He could stare at her all day. And night.

As she took a sip of her decaf, though, her expression changed. Then a second later, it was back to a pleasant smile.

"Mik? You okay?" he asked.

She glanced away for a moment, then looked straight at him. "We've been a temporary no-strings couple for all of an hour and a half, and every five minutes or so, I rethink the whole idea."

Temporary no-strings couple sounded a lot better than temporary Jones woman. "Because you keep forgetting that we each get what we need?" he asked, sipping his orange juice. Ah, fresh squeezed, of course.

"What if what we want changes, though?" she asked.

How could it possibly? Nothing would change. They each had their own lives to go back to—well, for Mikayla a life just starting. "Like what? We've been honest with each other, right? You know I'm incapable of anything more than this. And I know you deserve the world. So I'm going to give you the world as far as I can."

"I'm still not clear on what you're getting out of this arrangement, Jensen. Hot pregnancy sex?" She snorted.

He smiled. "Your *company*, Mikayla. Whatever that encompasses. Picnics, the opera, a weekend in Paris, strolls to Daisy's Donuts for the Boston cream."

She shook her head, but a grin was forming. "You're crazy."

"Crazy hot, right?" he asked, wiggling his eyebrows.

"That, too," she said, giving him a playful punch on the arm. "But, seriously," she added, sliding a look at him. "What if you got more emotionally involved than you expected?"

"What if you did?" he countered.

"I guess we'd cross that bridge if we came to it."

"Exactly. But, Mikayla, I should explicitly state right now that I'm going home in two weeks tops. You're having a baby. We're on separate paths. There's no future intersection."

She took a long sip of her decaf, then nodded. "Except we're sitting here together. Our paths have crossed to the point that we're a temporary couple."

Yes, a *temporary* couple. "So what are you saying?"

She put down her cup and seemed to struggle to put into words what she was thinking. "I don't know. That something about all this feels…wrong? I'm not looking for a white knight. I think I've made that clear. But I'm letting you wine and dine me."

"You're letting me be me," Jensen said. "This is who I am."

She laughed. "So you're saying I'm doing you a favor? I'm letting you do you?"

He grinned. "Exactly."

She shook her head. "You *are* crazy."

"Crazy right, though," he said.

She gave him another playful sock on the arm. "I guess," she conceded as they stood up and made their way out of the restaurant.

By a huge potted fruit tree outside, Mikayla stopped and kissed Jensen on the cheek.

"Thank you, again, for that feast. Hit every one of my cravings."

"Good. That's the plan." He linked arms with her and turned left, loving the feel of her even slightly connected to his body. "For the next two weeks, we fulfill each other's cravings."

She stopped, glanced down at her belly and waved a hand, in royal fashion, down the front of her. "You do see this, though, right? You do know I'm pregnant?"

"Mikayla, anyone could spot that belly two miles away."

He got a harder punch on the arm for that.

"Clearly, you're very pregnant and about to have a baby. I know that. And you're beautiful and glowing and fun to be with. We're both single. We both find ourselves with some free time, I might add. So let's enjoy ourselves."

She nodded. "You know, when you put it like that, it makes sense again."

With all that settled, they started walking, past people looking into windows of shops. Downtown Kalispell was busy as usual with pedestrians, joggers, dog walkers and a bit of traffic. Their conversation was, thankfully, halted by a man coming toward them with a leash in each hand, one connected to a majestic Great Dane and the other to a waddling little pug. Mikayla fussed over both of them and had to know their names and how old they were, and as he saw the joy in her eyes, Jensen wished he could give her a houseful of dogs. He would, too, if she had a house. And if she wasn't about to have a baby.

As they moved down the sidewalk, they stopped to watch a young street performer play a cello bigger than he was and did some window-shopping of their own, but Mikayla didn't want to go into any of the stores. "Just looking," she'd say when he'd encourage her to go in any store she wanted. It finally dawned on him that she didn't want him buying her everything she expressed the slightest interest in.

As they headed past another shop, he heard a slight gasp and glanced at Mikayla; she'd stopped dead, staring at the window display. Baby stuff, Jensen realized. He glanced up at the sign—Littlest Memories. Next door was a lingerie boutique that he hoped would catch her interest. He could see her in the little lacy black number on the mannequin.

But there was something off again about Mikayla's expression as she looked at the display in Littlest Memories. She seemed almost lost in thought, her gaze on what looked like a small yellow boat.

"It's a baby cradle in the shape of a canoe," Mikayla said, her voice so wistful and whispery that he moved closer. "When he was alive, my dad loved to go canoeing. He took me fishing every Sunday and then we'd canoe down the river. I can't believe my child won't get to meet such a wonderful man." She sniffled and turned away.

Jensen reached for her hand and held it. "In spirit, maybe he or she can. You can take your little one canoeing down the river every Sunday and tell him or her stories about Granddad Brown and how special he was. That would probably mean the world to your son or daughter, hearing all about the grandfather he or she didn't get the chance to know."

Mikayla turned to Jensen, her expression happier. "You're absolutely right, Jensen. Thank you. Did you spend a lot of time doing dad-son stuff with your father? Canoeing and fishing and camping and all that?"

Now it was Jensen's turn to frown. "With my dad? Ha. Walker Jones the Second is only interested in business, not family."

"He did have five kids," Mikayla said. "He must have liked children."

"Nah. He was only in it for the 'heirs and spares' aspect."

"Ouch. Did it bother you as a kid not getting to spend time with him?"

He nodded. "It did. My brothers tried to make me feel better about it, and when they were around, they'd toss around a football or take me to the movies. But the older my brothers got, the more my father could relate to them. I was always the youngest and told to 'listen and learn.'"

"I guess having all the money in the world doesn't buy everything, does it?" she said.

"No. Definitely not." Still holding hands, they began walking again. "The man I was telling you about, Davison, my mentor, used to take me fishing at least once a month. He loved doing all that stuff. He had no kids and enjoyed teaching someone the ropes."

"I'm glad you had him," she said.

"Me, too. Did I tell you I'm planning a surprise fortieth anniversary party for my folks in a couple weeks? I have to come up with some crazy lie to get them here for it. Inviting them for a visit would only result in excuses about them being too busy. But Davison used to take his wife to a different country every year to celebrate their anniversary. The anniversary before she died, she'd discovered a late love of sushi, so he took her to Japan for the best in the country. My dad doesn't even know what my mom's favorite food *is*."

"What is it?"

"A salad, of course, balsamic on the side." He grinned. "My dad would guess filet mignon when my mother hasn't eaten meat in years." He shook his head.

"So how did a guy raised by him get to be so in tune with what *I* want?" she said, raising her eyebrows. "You should be completely clueless."

"Told you. Because I'm hot for you. Very hot for you, Mikayla."

"Nut!" she said, laughing.

He grinned back. How weird was it that he could talk to her about anything? His parents. Davison. Business. His off-the-charts attraction to her.

"So…" she began, biting her lip and looking away for a moment.

"So…what? And please don't say buttons."

"Huh?" she asked.

"My family's housekeeper had a thing with this

expression. Anytime one of us would say 'So,' she'd say, 'Sew buttons.'"

"You know, Jensen, you might have grown up in a mansion with cooks and housekeepers, and your belt buckle probably cost more than a car, but sometimes I don't think we're all that different. Like when you talk about Davison and what the distribution center means to you. Or when you talk about your parents and the party you're planning. None of that really has anything to do with wealth. It's just about here," she said, tapping her heart with her palm.

"Are you accusing me of being a nice guy?"

She grinned. "Sometimes, yes, you are."

He laughed. "What were you really going to say before? The 'so...'"

"Oh," she said, her cheeks turning pink. "I guess I thought you'd booked a room at the fancy hotel."

He stared at her. In a split second, he was picturing her naked on a bed. "Did you *want* me to have booked a room?"

Now the cheeks were red. "No! I mean, I don't know. I don't know how this hot no-strings affair is supposed to go. I've never had one of these before."

"I guess we just do what we want," he said. "I'd be more than happy—okay, ecstatic—to book a room and carry you into our suite and lay you on the bed and ravish you."

"As if you could *lift* me," she said with a grin.

"Oh, trust me. I could." Before she could say a word, he slid a hand underneath her and one around her and had her in his arms. "Told you."

"Get a room!" someone called out from across the street.

Mikayla giggled, glancing at the pack of young women smiling at them. "Weren't we just talking about exactly that?"

He smiled. "Shall we, then?" He started back toward the direction of the hotel, Mikayla in his arms.

"Well, actually, I'm not sure I'm ready for bright-light-of-day sex, Jensen. Some romance, some buildup, the sun long set, and that's a different story."

"Sounds good to me. And I'm not necessarily talking about tonight. I'm not interested in rushing you into bed, Mikayla. When you're ready, you'll make it clear."

She kissed him on the cheek, so tenderly that it went straight to his heart and affected his knees to the point he had to set her down on her feet.

He wasn't sure what all this off-balance stuff was about. Maybe he just felt extra protective of Mikayla. That had to be it.

"Mikayla!" Eva called from downstairs. "Delivery!" she added in a singsong voice. "Hurry. I'm dying to see what else he could possibly have gotten you."

Mikayla felt her cheeks burn. Jensen Jones was a gift buyer—three days in his company had made that clear. If he passed a store and saw something his brothers might like, he bought it. Without asking the price. A few days ago, after their amazing breakfast in Kalispell to celebrate their new status as a no-strings couple—which, honestly, Mikayla wasn't sure was something to celebrate—they'd passed a gift shop and Jensen had said, "Hey, check out those cute chairs in the shapes of animals. I'd bet Just Us Kids would love those." He'd called his sister-in-law to ask how many preschoolers were enrolled, then ordered that many to be delivered to the day care, plus a few extra for good measure. He did stuff like that all the time.

Take yesterday. Mikayla and Jensen had been on a picnic and she'd taken off her sandals, since her feet had been kind of achy and swollen. Not only had Jensen taken her feet in his hands and massaged them until she purred, but the next day, he'd booked her the "supreme" pedicure with a half-hour foot massage at the hotel spa in Kalispell. She'd never experienced anything like it.

After the massage, when she'd mentioned she was craving so many ice cream flavors she couldn't figure out which one would soothe the itch, she'd arrived home to find a note on the freezer from Luke: "M: Twelve pints of Max's Creamery ice cream in every flavor imaginable were delivered for you this afternoon. Eva and I are invited for sundaes tonight, right?" Max's was a famed ice cream shop in Los Angeles with celebrities constantly being photographed going in and out. Now Mikayla had twelve pints in her freezer.

Earlier today, when she'd already been thinking the man had gone *way* overboard and needed a talking-to, he'd gone and done something extra wonderful that didn't involve his wallet. As they'd been leaving Daisy's Donuts with their coffee drinks, a boy, maybe seven or eight, had been trying to get his foam airplane to fly in the adjacent grassy area, but he kept crashing it. Jensen had shown him how to angle it and flick his wrist so that the plane would soar upward. It had taken the boy three tries and Jensen showing him again and again, but finally the plane had soared. The look of happiness on that little boy's face had made Mikayla's knees wobble.

"You just did for that boy what Davison did for you," she'd said. "Even just one time. He'll never forget it."

Jensen had waved it off, but she could see he was touched by her comment. The man had a good heart. He was just operating in his own universe. And those very different universes would make it a lot easier to walk away when it was time for Jensen to go.

Mikayla and Eva watched as the delivery guy walked up to the house carrying a long box with a red ribbon around it. "Mikayla Brown?"

"That's me," she said, signing the receipt. What on earth could it be? she wondered. Too wide to be long-stemmed roses. Too narrow to be much of anything else.

"What is it?" Eva asked as she closed the door behind Mikayla and followed her into the living room.

"I can't imagine." With Eva's help, they tore open the box, and what was inside, under packing paper and foam, made Mikayla gasp.

The yellow canoe cradle she'd almost sobbed over in Kalispell.

"That man," Mikayla said, shaking her head as tears poked her eyes.

"This is the cutest cradle I've ever seen. You can take your baby boating his first day on earth."

Mikayla laughed. She recalled what he'd said about her father always being there in spirit when she would take her own baby canoeing. Jensen wouldn't be around, of course, but his kindness and generosity *would* be, in the form of the cradle that her infant would lie in.

Sometimes, this thing with Jensen gave her the warm fuzzies and she felt totally deserving of the moniker Eva had given her: Her Royal Highness, Princess Mikayla of Rust Creek Falls. Or for short, Lucky Beyotch. Then other times, her chest tightened and she could hear her mother giving her a warning from above. *Are you crazy? That man is going to break your heart. Walk away now and focus on what's coming— not what's leaving.*

He couldn't break her heart if she didn't fall in love with him. And yes, she knew you couldn't decide to love or not love someone; that happened with or without your permission. But you could make a choice to put yourself in the position to fall. Which was what Mikayla was doing. So was her mama right? Should she tell him they'd had some fun, some amazing kisses, but she needed to keep her head level and not in the clouds?

She couldn't imagine walking away from him just yet. Or before she had to.

Which meant that like it or not, she was falling for him.

Jensen sure had his work cut out for him the next day. Mikayla had insisted on a wallet-free twenty-four hours. They could not participate in a single thing that cost money. Not even a cup of coffee from Daisy's or the local newspaper. No ordering, no delivery, no family jets. He'd heard the challenge in her voice, as if he couldn't handle such a thing. Ha. The woman had no idea. Jensen could spend a day locked in a utility closet with Mikayla and have the time of his life.

Knowing Mikayla liked picnics, he suggested a

little feast in Rust Creek Falls Park. He scavenged from his brother's well-stocked fridge and pantry, then met Mikayla at the park's entrance.

"I like this no-money thing," he said, setting down the blanket she'd brought and then laying out fried chicken and potato salad. "I didn't think it was possible to go an hour without spending a few hundred bucks."

She grinned and grabbed a chicken wing. "All we need is this beautiful day, this lovely park and our good conversation. And this incredible fried chicken. Mmm."

He smiled and took a drumstick and a heap of potato salad. They *did* have good conversations. Too good. Mikayla was so easy to talk to. There was never an awkward silence.

Until the tail end of their lunch. Mikayla had been telling him about Cheyenne and that her favorite park there, which had been right on her way to work, had a fenced dog run. "I could barely drag myself away some days. I could watch dogs play and run for hours. But then—" She stopped talking.

He paused in reaching for his bottle of soda. "But then?" he prompted.

Her expression tightened and she glanced away. He thought she was going to say, "Eh, it's nothing," and change the subject.

"But then," she said, reaching for her ginger ale, "I started seeing Scott and his new girlfriend there with her dog. One of those little white yippy types."

"Scott?" he repeated, then realized she had to be talking about her ex-boyfriend.

Her baby's father.

"You know what? I feel like going home," she said,

shifting to her knees to collect their containers and plates and cups.

He put a gentle hand on her waist. "Mik, you can talk to me about anything. Including your ex."

She frowned, the sadness in her eyes making him want to hold her. "Talking about him will just remind me that I can't trust anyone, Jensen. Including you." She quickly stuffed everything back in the picnic basket, then stood. "Thank you for lunch. Everything was del—" She gave a tight smile and then started walking toward town.

He jumped up, collected the blanket and stuffed it into the basket with a little too much force. He hated her rat bastard of an ex with all the passion of a thousand burning suns. Damn the jerk for hurting Mikayla. For making her close herself off from what she needed. People. Him.

Love.

He froze, taking a breath and shifting the picnic basket in his other hand. Love in *general*, he amended. He wouldn't want hurt and anger and bitterness to keep her from opening up to a relationship. To having a good man love her. Not that he wanted any other man near her heart, mind, soul or delectable body.

And like he was one to talk? He was still bitter over *his* ex.

He quickly caught up with Mikayla in the parking lot. "My last girlfriend did me in. I know I told you a little about it. But I don't talk about it for the same reason you don't. So I get it, believe me."

"Oh, I know you get it," she said, turning to him. "You proposed this temporary no-strings affair because you don't believe in love anymore."

I want to, he thought out of nowhere. Whoa there! Where had that come from? He *wanted* to? Since when?

Since the first moment he saw Mikayla sitting down in Daisy's Donuts, eating a custard cruller.

They drove to Sunshine Farm in silence. The big yellow barn came into view, and he felt Mikayla physically relax beside him now that she was almost home. As they arrived at the farmhouse, he couldn't bear the idea of leaving her.

Stop being selfish. Mikayla's had enough of selfish to last her a lifetime. Think of her needs, not yours. "I'll just bring this in for you," he said, gesturing at the heavyweight picnic blanket. "And then I'll let you get some rest."

She nodded and opened the door. He put the blanket in a big basket near the door and turned to go, wishing he could stay, wishing he could just sit on the sofa with her and talk. Or not talk. Just be.

"Scott is a class-A jerk," she said, staring at the floor.

He held his tongue, knowing if he didn't blurt out something stupid, she'd go on. Open up, even if just a little.

She took his hand and led him upstairs to her bedroom and closed the door behind them. "The jerk knew I loved that dog park even though I didn't have a dog. He knew I stopped there every single day and that it was a real highlight for me—especially given how distant he'd been since I told him I was pregnant. But the day after—" she hesitated and expelled a long breath "—the day after I walked in on him and his paralegal going at it on his desk…" She paused, shaking her head. "The very next day, Scott and the paralegal were at the dog park with her little yippy pup. They were holding hands and smiling as they watched the dogs play."

Jensen winced. She'd walked in on him having sex with his paralegal? On his *desk*? Oh, Mikayla. His heart ached for her. The woman was pregnant! With the rat bastard's child! "He sounds pretty damned cold."

She sat down on the bed and stared out the window. "I used to think he was just focused and busy with his work. He had a lot of clients, a lot of balls in the air. And the pregnancy was unexpected and he'd made it clear he wasn't ready for a child. But now that I know what I know, *cold* is the right word."

Just what Mikayla's baby needed—a cold father. Jensen had one of those and didn't wish it on anyone.

"I can't even imagine how hard, how awful it was walking in on him." Jensen shook his head. "Makes me see red."

"Me, too. Or it did. Now that I've been here awhile, I feel stronger and more myself. I don't feel so lost and alone."

He sat down beside her and squeezed her hand. "Good." He never wanted her to feel that way.

"You know what else?" Mikayla asked. "The jerk hasn't even tried to contact me since I left. He doesn't care about his own child at all."

I do, he thought. Then froze.

What?

Calm down, he told himself. He cared about Mikayla and her situation—that was all he meant. He hated the idea of anyone treating her with less than total respect.

"I'm so impressed by you, Mikayla. You're strong. Independent. Focused. You moved out here on your own for a fresh start, and after less than a month you have good friends and a job lined up. You rock."

Her expression changed from sad to surprised. "I used to give myself pep talks when I got scared about the future. It's kinda nice to have someone else take over. And even if I feel more like 'I pebble' than 'I rock,' I'll take the compliment. I am *trying*. Every day, I try."

"I know. And that's one of the reasons I find you so incredibly irresistible."

She grinned and reached out to caress his cheek. "Told you it wasn't the sexy belly. Wait till you see my stretch marks."

Before he could think about what the hell he was doing, he placed a hand on her huge tummy. "You're going to be fine, Mikayla Brown. I have no doubt about it."

She grabbed him and laid one on him, a hot kiss that he felt in every cell of his body. Ooh, yes! He wanted her so bad. With his hands entwined in her silky hair, he deepened the kiss, pulling her as close as she could get.

Very gently he lay her down on the bed, carefully hovering over her as he kissed her neck, his hands exploring her creamy shoulders. He wanted to touch every bit of her, but he wasn't sure how far they could go.

"I want you, Jensen Jones," she said, her brown eyes smoldering. "And yes, I'm sure. And yes, right now."

He grinned. "Is it safe?" he asked, his hand on her belly.

"It's safe. My doctor assured me it was. I never thought I'd follow up on the okay, though."

"I never thought I'd have a first time again," he said. "But sex with a pregnant woman? A first."

She laughed and pulled him close. "I want to do this. We have this time together, Jensen. That's it."

"Then why are we still dressed?" he asked, tracing a finger down her tank top, across the visible curves of her lush, creamy breasts.

He ripped off his shirt and then took off hers. He kissed his way across her chest to her neck and shoulders as he took off her white bra. A deep groan came from his throat at the sight of her lush breasts, her hair pooled on the pillow, her expression full of desire and anticipation.

Finally, completely naked and unable to wait a moment longer, Jensen Jones made love to Mikayla. It was everything he'd fantasized about since he laid eyes on her in Daisy's Donuts.

When they were both sated and breathing hard, smiling and holding hands, she lay against his side, his arms around her, and he was shocked that he didn't want to leave, hadn't made an excuse. He wanted to stay right where he was.

"That was amazing," he said. "Who knew?"

She grinned. "Not me. Well, now I do."

He tightened his grip on her and kissed her shoulder, then relaxed, his eyes closed. He'd experienced the strangest sensation while they'd been having sex. An *emotional* sensation. Jensen had been continually aware of her belly and pregnancy, though he'd loosened up about being careful when she'd made it clear she didn't want him to be *too* gentle. But the sensation had been ever present in his head, adding a texture to the way he made love to her that he'd never felt before. Maybe it had something to do with feeling—for the first time—that they were one? He'd thought he'd loved his ex, but he'd never really experienced that the way he had just now.

He caressed her shoulders, his hands falling to her breasts and sweeping over her belly. "Mik? Who's in there? A little guy or a girl?"

She turned to face him, wonder lighting her eyes. "I don't know. I want it to be a surprise."

"Maybe you're having twins, one of each."

"Uh, nope. Just one. And that's enough, trust me." She put her hand over his. On her belly.

"Whoa," he said, bolting upright. "I just felt something. The baby moved!"

Mikayla laughed. "He or she is quite the little kicker."

Huh. Of course—babies did that in the womb. Everyone knew that. But Jensen had never felt a baby kick before. Till now.

"You're having a baby." He put his other hand on her belly, wanting to double his chances of feeling another kick.

"I know. I think everyone knows."

"No, I mean, you're having a *baby*. A brand-new person is about to come into the world." Wow, he thought, getting it for the first time. Mikayla wasn't a gorgeous, sexy woman who *happened to be* pregnant— which was how he'd always looked at the situation. She was a gorgeous, sexy *pregnant* woman—period. One who would have a baby in a month or two.

Her life was going to change completely. He wouldn't be a part of it, of course, but he realized expensive ice cream and hand-crafted cradles and fancy breakfasts weren't cutting it. He wanted to do something big for Mikayla, something special before they parted. Before she had a little one to take care of round the clock.

"I want to treat you to a real night out," he said. "Someplace really fun. A real last hurrah for you before the baby comes."

He'd been about to add, *And a real last hurrah for us,* but he caught himself, which made him kind of uncomfortable. They *would* go their separate ways very soon. They both knew that. So why hold back from stating the obvious?

Because you just made love for the first time. Because you don't have to bring up certain truths in tender moments.

Because if you don't state the obvious, you might forget it entirely. Forget that you're leaving, going home...when Rust Creek Falls and this woman feel more like home than Tulsa ever has.

"Kalispell has a terrific steak house," Mikayla said. "I've been craving steak like crazy lately."

Kalispell was great, but he was thinking bigger. Farther away. More...festive. Ah, yes. He knew exactly where he wanted to take Mikayla. "How about Vegas instead? One of my favorite hotels there has the best steak house on the Strip. We can fly out Saturday afternoon and return Sunday. We'll be back early enough for you to get a good night's sleep for your first day at Just Us Kids."

She grinned and caressed his cheek. "A weekend

away before I start my job. That sounds great. And I've never been to Las Vegas. I wonder if it's okay for me to fly. I'll check with Dr. Strickland. I think I once read that most airlines ban flying after thirty-six weeks, but I'm barely at thirty-one weeks."

"Definitely check with your doctor. But the usual rules won't apply anyway, since we won't be flying commercial. We'll take the family jet."

"Well, la-di-da," she said with a wiggle of her eyebrows. "A second first for me."

"I think many more of those are coming our way," he said, pulling her closer into his arms, breathing in the warm, flowery scent of her.

She tilted her head as though she was about to ask, *Like what?* But she didn't. She just curled up against him, her head on his chest. He kissed the top of her head, his hand in her silky hair.

He was glad she didn't ask, because he had no idea what he'd meant. His mouth seemed to have a mind of its own lately, words flying out before he had a chance to censor them. Was that a good thing or a bad thing?

Jensen didn't like not being sure of the answer to that question.

Chapter Nine

Okay, how did I get here? Mikayla wondered, looking around the luxury hotel's glamorous lobby. A couple of weeks ago, she'd been counting dollar bills in her head to figure out when she'd pay off her baby's crib from layaway. Now she was flying in private jets and staying in fancy hotels with a millionaire. A millionaire she'd slept with! If anyone had told her back in early August that this would be her life, she would have burst out laughing and said, *Good one.* But this *was* her life. She wasn't having an extended dream. She was really here. Doing this. With Jensen Jones.

All because I was craving a donut one summer day, she thought with a smile, recalling the morning she met Jensen for the first time. *The universe really does work in mysterious ways.*

Their room turned out to be a corner suite, of course. She should have known. The view of the Las Vegas

Strip from the fifty-first floor, the sparkling lights, the constant thrum of activity took her breath away.

"So what's on our agenda?" she asked, turning to face him.

"I thought we'd start with a bubble bath. Together," he said. "Then we'll dress for dinner and spend some time in the casino. I'm not much of a gambler, but it's fun to play a little."

Dress for dinner. Mikayla frowned. She'd brought the only dress she fit into, a stretchy knee-length tank dress and her flat sandals. Now she realized she didn't have the clothes or accessories for a fancy place like this.

"What's wrong?" he asked, and she realized he was watching her with concern.

"My overnight bag contains a ten-dollar dress I bought in a thrift shop back in Cheyenne, one that would grow with me over the months of my pregnancy. It's black, at least, but it's hardly elegant. Or fancy. I didn't really know what to expect, I guess."

"Mikayla, I'm being dead serious when I tell you that you would make a burlap sack look beautiful and elegant. I'm sure you'll be absolutely lovely in your grow-with-you dress."

When she'd first met Jensen, she would have taken that as a line, nothing more. But Jensen was always sincere, and his kindness, his thoughtfulness, moved her so much that for a moment she couldn't speak. Until she remembered something about the thrift shop dress. Her frown was back. "It stopped growing with me two months ago. But it'll do in a pinch."

He squeezed her hand and gave her the dazzling smile that also tended to render her speechless. "Tell you what," he said. "Why don't you go start our bubble bath and I'll order up some herbal tea and something sweet. We'll have the most Zen bath ever."

Jensen naked and all hers in a bath, feeding her something sweet. Something with whipped cream would be an added bonus. "I hope the sex isn't all that Zen," she said like a nymphomaniac. "I want crazed and wild."

She couldn't help but think of her last relationship, how Scott had been so turned off by the pregnancy— and the impending baby—that he hadn't touched her from the moment she'd told him the big news. Their sex life hadn't been so great before that, either, but Mikayla hadn't had many relationships or partners, and though she'd known something was off about their chemistry, she hadn't really had much to compare it to.

Now she did.

And wow. When she and Jensen had made love, he'd looked into her eyes, his hands on her face, and whispered that she was *so beautiful*, that she smelled like summer flowers, that she was amazing in bed, that he couldn't get enough of her. Had any man ever made her feel that way?

And she was close to eight months pregnant.

He grinned. "Your wish is my command, Ms. Brown."

At his bow, she laughed and headed into the bathroom—then gasped. What the *h-e*-double-chopsticks was this place? The bathroom was bigger than her room at Sunshine Farm. The spa bath was bigger than her bed. Everything was marble and polished gold, and there was a set of fluffy white his-and-hers robes on hooks and matching slippers in the corner.

She turned the water on in the Jacuzzi, careful not to make it too hot, per her pregnancy guidebook. The bubbles were mesmerizing. Ooh, boy, could she take a bath in this? she thought, adding a packet of lavender bubble bath. She breathed in the fragrant bubbles. She couldn't wait to get in. With Jensen.

She set the robes closer to the tub, then twisted her hair up into a topknot and eased into the water. *Ooh, ah, yes*, she thought, leaning her head against the bath pillow. Heavenly. She was so relaxed she almost fell asleep.

"Room for me?" Jensen asked, walking into the bathroom completely naked and carrying a platter containing a tea set and a bowl of strawberries and whipped cream. The man had read her mind.

She sucked in a breath at the sight of him. She'd seen him naked, of course. Just yesterday. And had hardly forgotten one iota of his incredible body. But whoa, he was sexy. So tall and muscular and a magnificent specimen of manhood. *Oh, and that, too*, she thought with a smile, trying to stop herself from laughing. She was enjoying this insanity a little too much—naked millionaires and hotel suites that probably cost more than six months' salary at her old job.

Jensen set the tray on the sliding metal platform next to the tub, then slid into the water behind her, wrapping his arms around her shoulders and pulling her back against his chest. "Ah, I could stay here forever."

"Except not forever," she said without thinking.

Why had she brought real life into this dream? This was fantasy. She knew it. "Forget I said that."

He gently squeezed her, nuzzling her neck. "Nope. Can't do that. Everything gets said between us, Mik. That's how I want it. And you, too, apparently."

"I figure the less I say about how things really are, the less I'll think about those things."

"What things? That we're temporary?"

At the word, a lump formed in her throat. Jeez. Now she was getting all teary over this?

She let out a sigh. She might as well be honest. "Maybe I just never want this fantasy to end."

"It does feel like a fantasy, doesn't it?" he asked, rubbing her shoulders. "I'd sworn off relationships, and here I am, in a bubble bath with a pregnant woman."

She smiled. "Ditto me, except with a naked millionaire. I feel like I get the better deal."

"Nope. You're a better person than I am, Mikayla. I'm honored to know you and to be with you. Even for a short time."

Dammit. Why did he have to be so earnest about how highly he thought of her? Why couldn't he just be flirtatious and glib?

If he were, she wouldn't be falling in love with him.

"Well, we both know this beautiful fantasy will come to an end. I'm leaving and that will be that." He sat up a bit and pulled over the sliding arm of the tray and poured her tea, adding a splash of cream just the way she liked.

She took a sip of the chamomile brew, which did help soothe her a little. "And that will be that," she seconded. She just had to remember it. He was leaving.

And she was having a baby. Their lives would take very different paths.

"And in the short time we have together, you must be fed strawberries with fresh whipped cream while luxuriating in a bubble bath," he said, swiping a fat red strawberry through the cream and holding it to her lips.

"With a sexy millionaire," she added, trying very hard to remember their deal. She was being treated like a princess, temporarily, until he went back home. That was it. She bit into the strawberry and worked to shake off her sad thoughts, but when she felt him lay his head against hers, holding her closer, she wanted to cry.

Because she loved him.

Trying to avoid it had been ridiculous. Who wouldn't fall in love with Jensen Jones? He was everything she'd ever wanted—and a few things she'd never put much stock in, like how big his bank account was. If Jensen was dirt-poor, she'd be just as in love. Because she'd take a picnic with him in Rust Creek Falls Park over this hotel any day. Yeah, this was nice. Very nice. But this wasn't her. Mikayla was all about going on picnics and wiping runny noses at day care centers, and doing laundry and craving donuts, which were affordable.

Jensen's generosity was just a crazy bonus. Maybe it would help keep her grounded, too. The more he flung his money around, the more she remembered they were from different worlds and would never, ever have a future together.

So why did she believe in her heart, mind and soul that he *did* have feelings for her beyond the physical?

She knew why: Jensen wouldn't be here otherwise.

He wasn't in love, that she was sure of. Because she figured this passionate man would move heaven and earth to be with the woman he loved. Even if it meant staying in a tiny Montana town like Rust Creek Falls. But he had strong feelings for her. That she knew in her bones and cells. Given what he'd told her about his own ex, even having strong feelings was a lot for Jensen. He very likely hadn't planned on feeling anything for a woman for quite a while.

The water was getting a bit cool, so they reluctantly stepped out of the tub, Jensen drying her with a soft, thick towel before wrapping her robe around her.

There was a knock on the suite door. Jensen tightened his own robe and went to answer it. She stuck her head out of the bathroom and saw a man wearing a name tag that read Bart Wintowski, Assistant Concierge, carrying in three garment bags and a bunch of boxes. Jensen had him lay everything on the bed.

"What's all this?" Mikayla asked when the man left with the fat tip Jensen had handed him.

"You can toss that ten-dollar dress that doesn't fit," Jensen said. "I asked one of the hotel boutiques to send up a few things you might like for tonight. Whichever pieces you don't choose, we can send back."

She gasped. "You're kidding."

"Nope. Go see."

She unzipped the first bag and fell in love. A sparkly midnight blue gown in a floaty jersey with an empire waist and a slit to the thigh. Sexy, schmexy. Beside it was a box containing high-heeled silver sandals and a silver evening bag. The next garment bag held a sleeveless red dress, tea length, with beautiful embroidery around the neckline and hem. In the box near it, black stilettos and a black evening bag. And the third bag contained a silver dress with a plunging neckline. It also had an accompanying box of shoes and bag. Above the bags was a velvet box containing jewelry pieces.

All three dresses would accommodate her belly, too. Whodathunk this fancy hotel would have boutiques with maternity evening wear?

She stared at the gorgeous dresses on the bed, then turned to her prince. "Jensen, you shouldn't have. But oh, hell, I'm glad you did. I feel like Cinderella."

"Surprise me with your choice," he said, kissing her on the cheek and disappearing into the second bedroom.

The midnight blue with the slit up to there was her fantasy dress, the kind she always wished she'd had an occasion to wear. During her time with he-who-would-not-be-named-anymore, they hadn't attended any functions or parties. Sometimes, Mikayla had wondered if her ex hadn't thought her good enough to hobnob with his lawyer colleagues. Now she knew it was he who wasn't good enough. *Good riddance to you*, she thought, slipping the dress—thankfully zipper-free—over her head. It floated over her breasts and belly and down to her ankles, the thigh slit making her smile. She tried on the silver shoes. High but very comfortable. Then she transferred her phone, wallet, compact and lip gloss into her fancy new evening bag.

In the bathroom she added a bit of makeup, a little more than she usually wore. The dress called for it. On the vanity was a basket of small appliances—a hair dryer, curling iron and straightening iron—and loads of travel-size styling products. She dried her hair and used the curling iron to add a few beachy waves. A slick of her red lip gloss, a tiny dab of her favorite perfume and she was ready.

When she came back into the main room, she heard a wolf whistle.

"Holy wow," Jensen said, looking her up and down and back again. "You look exquisite."

And so did he in his dark suit, sans tie. He looked like a combination of a movie star, a secret agent and a cowboy in one.

"Thank you for all this." This being her last hurrah. And she was going to do it up. Until she came to Rust Creek Falls, no one had ever just handed her anything. Suddenly, she was being treated like royalty.

And it was so magical and such a fantasy that it truly did keep her head where it needed to be. Remembering that Jensen wasn't hers. That he would be leaving and that she had to accept it. Fantasy wasn't real life. And nothing about this day and night was remotely close to real life. Unless you were a Jones.

If only Mikayla was one of those women who took a long time to get ready. Or if Jensen had forgotten his wallet and needed to run back to the suite to get it. But no. The universe had timed it perfectly so that they would arrive at the elevator bank on their floor at the exact time that a couple a few suites down did.

"Aw! You're about to pop, aren't you, sweetie?" the young woman said to Mikayla. She, too, wore a slinky dress with a slit up to the thigh. But her stomach was flatter than the pancakes Mikayla had had for breakfast that morning.

"Guess it's all over for you, eh?" her husband said to Jensen. Or at least Mikayla assumed he was her husband based on the wedding rings they wore. "But you had your fun or she wouldn't be in this condition." The couple burst out laughing as though that was hilarious. Or original.

Jensen smiled tightly and stared at the glowing floor numbers over the elevator. He looked so uncomfortable that Mikayla felt like she had to correct the guy.

"He's not the father," she said with an equally tight smile. *But thanks for playing.*

"Aw!" the woman said for the second time. "You're not the father and you're here in Vegas for a quickie wedding to make her an honorable woman!" She stared at Mikayla's left hand, empty of a ring. "Aren't you wonderful!"

"We're not here to get married," Mikayla said.

The couple stared at her, waiting for the elaboration.

"We're having a torrid affair," Jensen said. "That's why we're here." He pulled Mikayla to him and gave her a kiss that almost made her knees buckle.

The woman gasped. "Seriously? Ew. Does your husband know?"

"I don't have a husband," Mikayla said.

The couple inched away from them until they were standing by the other elevator bank. Mikayla suppressed a giggle when the elevator she and Jensen stood in front of dinged and opened, and the couple didn't get on with them. No doubt they didn't want to catch their cheater cooties.

"Served them right," Mikayla said as the door closed.

Jensen pressed the floor marked Casino. "Figures they assumed I was the baby's father."

Well, most people would, considering that they were together in a hotel and she was very pregnant.

"Does that bother you?" she asked, glancing from him to the numbers panel doing down, down, down.

"More that it just feels…strange. I mean, I'm *not* the baby's father. Correcting people feels equally strange."

"Guess this part isn't a fantasy for you," she said, trying to inject some lightness in her tone. "I mean, here I am in my dream dress, in this luxe hotel, with a gorgeous, sexy millionaire, and for tonight, all my fantasies are real." *Including that you are the father of my child. That you love me. That we are here for our last big night out before the baby comes. Our baby. That we're married and will spend forever together…*

Good God.

"Fantasy?" he repeated. "What do you mean?"

She coughed. "Well, I get to play house a little while we're here. You know what I mean?"

"No." His expression was half neutral, half tense.

Oh, yikes. How the hell had the conversation veered to this? "Jensen, do you remember when you said that we should be able to talk about anything?"

"Of course. And I meant it."

She bit her lip, then just went for it. "Well, put yourself in my shoes for a moment. For the past several months, I've been getting more and more pregnant and less and less married. I walk around without a ring on my finger. Everyone knows I'm single and pregnant. Poor Mikayla."

"But that couple assumed we were together. Married," he added, with such disdain in his voice that she knew the word was hard for him to say.

"You know that woman figured I had to take off my ring from pregnancy bloat."

He scrunched up his handsome face. She was talking about pregnancy bloat? Some fantasy. *Get this conversation back on track, Mikayla.* If that was even possible.

"I just mean that the assumptions are…nice, Jensen. For me."

He stared at her, understanding coming into his blue eyes. Then disappointment.

"You know what?" she said. "Forget it. Forget all that. Let's ignore everyone else and their assumptions and be who we are and have a good time. Isn't that why we're here?"

Back to her self–pep talk. But inside she felt anything but spirited. She wanted to run back upstairs and dive into that Jacuzzi and stay there—alone—until her fingers and toes were prunes.

Jensen Jones's fantasy was about sex and romance and having a very good time—until he got on that plane back to Tulsa. Why did she keep forgetting that?

When the elevator door pinged open, Jensen took her hand and held it to his lips. "Mikayla, we *are* who we are. Being mistaken for a dad isn't who I am. Who I'd ever want to be. I don't even own a pair of dad jeans." He smiled and tipped up her chin with his finger. The attempt at a light joke didn't do anything to make her feel less alone in the world.

Here she was, the opposite of alone, and she couldn't have felt lonelier at the moment.

But Jensen was right. He was who he was and she had to stop trying to make him someone else. Trying to change him and their deal.

He wasn't her baby's father.

He wasn't her husband.

She forced a big smile. "Let's go have fun. I have a gorgeous dress to show off."

He looked her up and down. "And I have a gorgeous woman to show off. Let's go spend an hour in the casino and then we'll head to that steak house I promised you."

The moment they entered the casino, a sharp-dressed waiter immediately appeared with a tray of drinks, all alcoholic. Jensen flagged down a waitress carrying soft drinks and took two glasses of sparkling water.

Mikayla was amazed at how much free stuff there was. Waiter after waiter carried through trays of appetizers and drinks. The casino was crowded, everyone dressed up. She sure was glad she hadn't had to stuff herself into her grow-with-me dress.

A hand that did not belong to Mikayla or Jensen reached out and patted Mikayla's tummy as they stopped at the blackjack table. For heaven's sake, Mikayla thought, why did total strangers think that was okay?

"Oh, what are you, eight months along?" the middle-aged woman asked, her hazel eyes glassy as she shifted her wineglass into her other hand. Someone had clearly been drinking for hours. The woman didn't wait for a response. "Here's my prediction. If it's a girl, the baby will get your brown hair and eyes, and if it's a boy, he'll get your husband's blond hair and blue eyes," she added, pointing her glass at Jensen. "The good genes are always wasted on the boys!" A burst of cigarette-tinged hoarse laughter followed. Thankfully, the woman moved on.

Jensen raised an eyebrow and mock shivered. "It will never cease to amaze me when someone, even someone falling down drunk, mistakes me for a husband and father-to-be. I feel like I have a blinking neon sign over my head that reads Bachelor Dude."

Mikayla bit her lip. Guess he wasn't going to play along with her fantasy. For a minute there, she figured he'd bend over backward, as usual, to make her happy, and pretend he was her husband and the baby's father—just for tonight.

As if he could bear that, she realized. Why was she so thickheaded sometimes? Of course he couldn't play that game. Play house. It was everything he didn't want. And she had no right to force that role on him.

Leave the poor rich guy alone, she ordered herself. *Just have the good time you're here to have.*

For the next hour, as they played a few tables, they were asked four times when their little one was due, if Jensen was a first-time father and if he was ready to kiss his freedom goodbye—in a good way, chuckle, chuckle (which made Mikayla want to pummel that guy).

"Know if you're having a boy or a girl?" a very pretty twentysomething in a slinky dress asked at the roulette table, her thigh slit much higher than Mikayla's. The question was directed to Mikayla, but the redhead immediately shifted her attention to Jensen—with a look of pure desire.

"It'll be a surprise," Mikayla said, her attention on the dealer. *Get your expertly made-up eyes off my man*, she wanted to screech at the woman.

"*Trying* to have your last bit of fun before the baby comes, huh?" the redhead purred, sliding a glance at Mikayla's belly before turning her smoldering gaze back on Jensen. "I'm in room 2104, here on boring business," she whispered to him. But Mikayla had heard her loud and clear.

Oh, no, you didn't! Mikayla thought, staring down the woman. "He's not interested in your room number."

The redhead gave Mikayla a *we'll see about that later* look.

Jensen lost the bet, stood up and didn't acknowledge the redhead or her come-on as he led Mikayla from the table. He did not look happy. He did not look like a man having his last bit of fun or his last hurrah.

"*Dude,*" a middle-aged man in loud plaid Bermuda shorts and carrying a huge belly himself said to Jensen as he passed by. "They never get their bodies back. Sad but true." He shook his head.

Mikayla caught Jensen making a fist, his eyes narrowed. If he were a cartoon bull, steam would be coming out of his ears and he'd charge right for the guy. Uh-oh.

She ushered him away from the jerk and out of the casino.

What was with all the comments? *Mind your own business*, she wanted to scream at the room. *Eyes on your own paper! Get a life!*

Then again, she was a heavily pregnant woman in a casino. And the only one. She stood out for the crazies.

As they walked to the restaurant, Jensen put his hands around his mouth like a megaphone and said, "It's not my baby. Jeez!" He shook his head. "Is this what it's like for you all the time? People touching you and asking you nosy questions?"

Mikayla felt her heart actually sink.

It's not my baby. Jeez. It. Is. Not. My. Baby.

No kidding, Jensen. *This is definitely not your baby.*

"Well, not in Rust Creek Falls," she said when she forced an instant recovery. "But it happened in Cheyenne before I moved. People are just interested, I guess. A few people were sweet about it, like the woman who almost cried and said her youngest was turning eighteen next week and she wished she could go back to being pregnant all over again. They don't realize they're being a little invasive."

"A little? I'd say three-quarters of the comments and questions were downright rude. And that last jerka-zoid? I almost flattened him. Who do these nutjobs think they are? And you're damned right I wasn't in-terested in that lady's hotel room number. She thought you were my pregnant wife and yet she was coming on to me?" He rolled his eyes, disgust marring his gorgeous features. "As if I'd ditch you and run for the elevator?"

She had to admit she was enjoying his takedown of the snake. But she'd never seen him so angry; Mi-kayla was usually the rager in this duo. Maybe she should interject a little levity, calm him down. "Well, they do say what happens in Vegas stays in Vegas. Anything goes here."

"Still, people should mind their own business. What gives anyone the right to comment on your body? Your pregnancy? Or how I might feel about being a father?" He shook his head.

"For one thing," he continued, "I'm *not* the father of anyone's baby. I hate assumptions, you know? Don't assume things about me, people!"

More head shaking. More ear steam.

Well, if Mikayla had had any shred of hope that Jensen might fall madly in love with her and want to be in her and her baby's life, it stayed behind in the lobby as they entered the steak house.

As if Mikayla had an appetite.

Being mistaken for her baby's daddy had made him lose his mind.

Mikayla let out a sigh, and Jensen was so involved in his own head that he didn't even hear. She was surprised he didn't continue his rant with "And another thing…"

The man had made himself clear from the get-go. Had he not run screaming out of Daisy's Donuts eight seconds after discovering the woman he was trying to pick up was pregnant? Had he not proposed this no-strings temporary affair? Had he not said mere hours ago that he would be leaving Rust Creek Falls?

As they were seated in the heavenly smelling restaurant, Mikayla said, "Jensen, let's change the subject and enjoy our dinner."

"Good idea," he said.

Except as they looked over the menu, she could tell he was still out of sorts and so was she. But by the time their entrées arrived, their small talk had elevated their moods and they actually laughed as they reminisced about the Stocktons' party at Sunshine Farm and little Henry Stockton running off with the pie. Her filet mignon and roasted potatoes were the most amazing she'd ever had, and she tried to focus on the flavor and the elegance of the restaurant and the other diners. A trio of jazz musicians played on a short stage by a grand window, adding to the absolutely lovely ambience. When else would she experience this? *Just let it all go*, she told herself.

Except she couldn't. She was a woman in love. And as they headed to their suite after dinner, she called herself all kinds of a fool. What business did she have falling for Jensen Jones? Why hadn't she listened to her mama's advice, which was always playing in her head and heart, even if her mom wasn't here anymore?

Up on the fifty-first floor, Jensen slipped the key card in the door of their suite. "Home sweet home, for the night, anyway. Phew, I feel completely better now. Between that excellent dinner and the *lack* of conversation about marriage and fatherhood, I started feeling like myself again. And now," he said, slipping his arms around her, "I can romance my woman without the peanut gallery making comments."

My woman. Ha.

But she wished. She let out another sigh, and this one he caught.

"You okay?" he asked, bringing a hand to her cheek.

She nodded and stepped inside the suite. The moment the door closed, she found herself unexpectedly relaxing. Maybe because now they were alone, all those nutjobs were shut away, their comments going, going, gone from her spinning head, which was now much clearer.

Still, Mikayla wasn't much in the mood for romance right now. But when she glanced over at Jensen, standing in front of the minibar and taking out the lemon-infused water he'd ordered especially for her, her heart opened back up again. The fridge and little freezer were full of specially ordered things Mikayla craved. Like Cajun-coated peanuts. And a pint of Max's chocolate-chocolate chip. He poured her a glass of the lemon water, took out the rest of the strawberries and cream and a beer for himself, and set them on the table near the sliding glass doors.

Oh, hell. This man she loved would be leaving in a week. And that would be that. *Enjoy him for the here and now,* she told herself for the thirtieth time since they'd struck their bargain.

You knew the deal when you kissed on it. Grow up, Mikayla. You have to when the baby comes. Might as well start now. He's not going to propose. He's not going to ask to be your baby's father. He's who he is. And you're an independent woman who's going to make it just fine on your own.

She'd take this Cinderella treatment for the duration of their affair and then it was back to reality.

"Strawberry?" he asked, holding one up to her, no trace of his earlier discomfort in his tone.

Apparently, he'd gotten over those stupid comments and the people mistaking him for her baby daddy or her husband. He wasn't either of those things, so who really cared, right? That was obviously what had calmed Jensen down.

The man wasn't in love with her. She was the only fool who'd fallen. And that wasn't part of their deal.

No one was supposed to fall in love. No one was supposed to get hurt.

So that stabbing feeling in the region of her heart? Not pregnancy-related heartburn. Heart*ache*. Heart*break*.

Tomorrow, when they got home, she'd tell him it was over, that this wasn't working for her anymore. How could it when it was starting to hurt?

Chapter Ten

Jensen considered himself a smart guy. But when it came to Mikayla, he could be a real dummy. For instance, instead of saying, "Ooh, yes, I'll have some of everything," to his offer of the hotel's amazing buffet breakfast with their famed omelet bar, Mikayla had said she just wanted a muffin to go and a decaf latte. He'd taken that at face value.

On the plane back to Rust Creek Falls, she'd said she was feeling tired and closed her eyes the entire trip home. He'd stayed silent to let her rest, taking the free time to respond to business emails, read a couple of industry magazines and scour online maps for possible other locations for the crisis distribution center, since Guthrie Barnes had shut him down. And when the plane was preparing for landing and she'd turned to look out the window, claiming her tummy was a "bit queasy," and said the same during the drive back to Rust Creek Falls, he'd stopped at a convenience store for a ginger ale, which of course she didn't drink.

Because she hadn't been hungry for a corn muffin or tired or queasy. She'd been avoiding him—avoiding looking at him, talking to him, *being* with him.

The big clue in? When they'd finally arrived at Sunshine Farm and she'd insisted on carrying her own bag inside with a quick "Thank you for a wonderful trip, Jensen" before hurrying in.

Something was wrong. And three hours after dropping her off, when he figured he'd given her the space she obviously needed from him, he'd texted her. No response. He'd called her. Straight to voice mail.

She was pulling away. But why? Hadn't they had an amazing trip to Vegas—minus some of the people they'd been trapped with in close quarters? Last night they'd taken yet another bubble bath and made love afterward, falling asleep in each other's arms. Then this morning, the wall went up—without him even realizing it.

Enough of this, he told himself, checking his phone to see if she'd responded. No. He even checked the battery level to make sure his phone hadn't died. Eighty-seven percent. The woman was avoiding him!

He got in his car and drove back over to Sunshine Farm. Eva answered the door, giving him one of those tight smiles that said she was about to tell him a little white lie.

"Sorry, Jensen, but Mikayla's resting," Eva said.

I'm sure she's not practicing yoga or out jogging, but she's not resting, Jensen thought, frowning. "Could you let her know I'm here? That I really want to talk to her?"

Eva gave him something of a hopeful shrug and disappeared. She was back in three seconds. "She's sleeping, actually. I'll let her know you stopped by."

He supposed that was possible. Oh, hell, maybe she *had* just been tired and queasy all day. Like he knew what it was like to be eight months pregnant?

He mentally kicked himself. Why was he such a self-absorbed bastard sometimes? He cared about this woman. "Is she okay?"

Eva smiled. "She's fine. I think the big trip just caught up with her."

Or something else did. Self-absorbed or not, Jensen had a feeling he wasn't entirely wrong. Mikayla was pulling away, and he didn't like it.

"Okay, well, you'll let her know I stopped by?" he asked.

"I sure will, Jensen."

He let out a hard sigh on the way back to his car. He could do one thing, at least. He could make Mikayla more comfortable—physically if not emotionally. He sat down in the driver's seat, pulled out his phone and ordered her the best adjustable bed on the market, with massage features. Delivery for tomorrow cost a mint, but Mikayla was worth every penny. He most definitely wouldn't ever have any idea what it felt like to be pregnant, but he wanted Mikayla to be able to rest and sleep well.

He drove back to Walker's house, hoping his phone would light up with a text or a call from Mikayla, but it didn't.

It didn't for the next few hours.

That night, he wanted to talk to her so badly he almost drove over to Sunshine Farm again, prepared to storm the place—not that he'd want to go up against Luke Stockton. But if she wasn't responding, he had to respect that, right? He had to leave her alone—for the time being, at least. She obviously needed some space from him.

He lay down on the bed in the guest room at Walker's log palace, edgy and jumping out of his skin. He grabbed his phone and sent her one last text, one that didn't require a response. But he couldn't go to sleep without telling her.

Have a great first day of work tomorrow.

By morning, still no response. Another strange sensation gripped him—in his chest, his stomach, his throat. He couldn't quite place it; it felt almost more emotional than physical. What the hell was it?

Heartache, you idiot, a growly voice hissed at him from somewhere deep within. *This is what heartache feels like when* you're *the cause of it.*

Okay, where the hell had that come from?

Something about it felt very true. But how did it make any sense? He was the cause of his own heartache? Huh? His heart wasn't even involved. Or an eighth was, since he liked Mikayla so much. The two of them had shaken on an agreement. A fun couple of weeks. No one was supposed to be heartbroken here.

He flipped onto his belly, then flipped back, practically tearing off his T-shirt, since he was suddenly so hot. Steamed. He didn't like being on the outs with Mikayla. Not one damned bit.

So what was going to happen now? He couldn't keep calling and texting and showing up when she'd made herself clear. But he couldn't just let things end like this. He didn't know what had happened, why she'd pulled away, what he'd done wrong.

He just wanted things to go back to the way they were. *Fixing problems is your specialty, Jones*, he reminded himself. *So figure it out. And fix it.*

Mikayla almost couldn't believe this was work, that she was getting paid to do this. She sat in a padded rocking chair in the baby room of Just Us Kids Day Care Center, a four-month-old girl with wispy brown curls nestled in her arms. It was just after ten o'clock, and she'd been here since seven, which worked out well, since Mikayla had always been an early riser. She and Bella, her boss, had agreed on a part-time schedule until her baby was born. Then she'd take three months off before coming back full-time, with her little one as an enrollee. She felt so lucky.

And that gratitude was helping her keep her mind off a certain gorgeous, sexy, six-foot-two-inch man. She shouldn't have let all his calls and texts go unanswered, but she'd been a little annoyed that he'd come barging over yesterday despite her lack of response. The man was clearly used to getting what he wanted. Well, she hadn't been ready to talk to him. She supposed she could have texted that, that she was just getting her head together. But all the texts she'd started hadn't sounded right.

She knew why, too. Because it was really hard to break your own heart by telling the man you were in love with that you were done with him, that you couldn't continue your relationship. Mikayla had cried herself to sleep last night. At least babies didn't mind puffy eyes.

This is what I should be focusing on, she told herself, staring at the tiny, beautiful creature in her arms. *This is my future. I'm going to have a baby, and this job, which I'm so lucky and grateful to have, is training for my life.*

What the hell had she even been doing in Las Vegas in some bought-for-her slinky dress? That wasn't real life. That wasn't her life. *This* was.

But it was Jensen's life. And another reminder that they were from very different worlds and had very different futures.

She sure had missed him last night, though. The feel of his arms around her, making her feel so safe and protected, as though she didn't have a care.

Adorable Jolie Windham, the baby she was feeding, was all done with her bottle and ready to be burped. Mikayla shifted, sitting forward, carefully bringing the baby up to her chest and gently patting her back. She smelled so delicious, and Mikayla loved everything about babies and this job. Jolie gave a big burp for such a little human, and Mikayla rocked her for a while until her eyes began to close. Then she transferred her into her crib. Of course, the moment she put her down, the baby began fussing and then full-out wailing.

"Oh, no, you don't, little one," Mikayla whispered, picking up the baby and rocking her a bit more. "You can't wake up the whole room." The baby quieted, her eyes closing again, and Mikayla waited until she was fully asleep this time, then put her in the crib.

"You're a natural," Bella said, smiling, from where she stood at the changing table with seven-month-old Eric Wexler.

Mikayla beamed. The praise felt good. Being here felt good. When she got her first paycheck, she was sending her cousin Brent a little gift, maybe something very Montana, to thank him for suggesting she start fresh by moving to Rust Creek Falls and for finding her a place to stay. Brent had changed her life, and she owed him big.

Her last hour passed quickly, and then it was time to go. Mikayla wanted to help out a bit, so she took out the whites laundry from the dryer and folded the burp cloths neatly, then said goodbye to her colleagues and boss and headed out.

She checked her phone in her car. Just one text from Jensen today: Thinking about you.

I'm thinking about you, too. Too much. Once she got home, she'd call him and tell him their time together was over.

Last night, he'd texted to wish her good luck on her first day. Thoughtful jerk. Well, okay, he wasn't a jerk. He was just…who he was. A confirmed bachelor who had no interest in settling down and being a husband and father. Someday, Mikayla would want to find love and a father for her baby. If she could ever fall out of love with Jensen. Forgetting him would take a long, long time.

She headed home, the sight of the farmhouse always making her feel comforted. She waved at Eva, who was painting a piece of furniture in the barn, then walked inside the house, the smell of chocolate-chip cookies filling the air. Nice to live with a baker.

She'd take a little nap, then come down for lunch and Eva's cookies. But when she sat down on her bed, she popped right back up. Which wasn't easy when you were eight months pregnant.

What the heckeroo?

This wasn't her bed. *Her* bed was perfectly serviceable, comfortable, but nothing like what her butt had just sunk into.

She stared at the very plush-looking queen-size bed where her old full-size had been. This one had to be adjustable, because the head was raised. And there was a remote control on her bedside table.

Massage. Vibrate. Bluetooth. There were controls for just about anything you'd want to do in bed.

And at the foot of the bed was a package containing thousand-thread-count blue gingham sheets and a gorgeous blue-and-white quilt with matching shams, plus four down pillows and one long body pillow.

This had Jensen Jones written all over it.

She lay down on the bed. *Oh. My. God.* This was beyond heavenly. She played with the remote control, testing all the features, the massager working her lower back while she raised her feet a bit.

She'd give herself five minutes to enjoy everything about this bed, and then she was calling Jensen to let him know they had to end things between them and that he had to take the bed back.

Even if she loved this darn bed. Even if she loved the man.

She forced herself out of the amazing bed and picked up her phone and called him. He answered on the first ring. She had to admit, the guy never played games.

"Mikayla, I'm so glad you finally called. I've missed you like crazy. And you're clearly avoiding me, so let's talk this out. I can pick you up and we'll go to the park or take a long drive—"

"Jensen, I'm sorry, but I can't do this anymore. I should have talked to you about it yesterday or answered your calls or texts, but I was overwhelmed and just needed some time to think."

"And what you think is that we should stop spending time together? Mikayla, we only have another week together. We *want* to be together. So let's be together."

How could she tell him what was bothering her? She wasn't about to tell him she loved him and that it was starting to hurt too much that he didn't love her back and would be walking out of her life.

"It's over, Jensen. Please just accept it."

"I can't. Unless you can tell me why. Maybe then I'll be able to understand why you're pushing me away."

Because I'm in love with you, you idiot! she wanted to scream. *Because it's too painful. Because you're leaving me.*

She couldn't say that, and her head and heart were too muddled for her to come up with something else, so she said nothing.

"I'm coming over. See you in a few." *Click.*

Great. The sight of him always tended to weaken her resolve. Now what?

She paced her room, ignoring her fabulous new bed. Boy, she could use a massage right now.

She heard the approach of a car and looked out the window. There was the big, shiny black pickup he'd rented. She watched him get out of the truck. Of course, he wore a navy blue T-shirt and faded jeans and his cowboy boots, looking more like a regular guy and less like the high-rolling millionaire he was. Well, except for the diamond-encrusted *J* of his belt buckle glinting in the sun.

She headed downstairs to let him in. Maybe she should lead him to the family room and they could talk there. Anywhere but her bedroom.

He knocked and she opened the door, and as always, the very Jensenness of him did her in. She lost her breath. Her speech. Her focus. All she could see and think about was him.

"Please don't push me away, Mik."

Straight to the point, no muss, no fuss, no song and dance.

She stepped back for him to enter and forced herself to walk to the family room. He trailed her. She poked her head in to make sure the room was empty, but it turned out Luke and some men were having a meeting in there. Dang. They could go for a walk, but it was crazy hot today and she didn't think she could get very far.

Her bedroom, it was.

She led the way upstairs. Once inside, she closed the door behind him. Part of her wanted to push him against the door and kiss him senseless. The other part knew she had to say her piece and move on with her life, which wouldn't include him.

"Jensen, I'm going to be very honest with you. I've foolishly gone and developed feelings for you, but it's clear that we're not on the same page there, so I need to say goodbye."

"Of course I have feelings for you, Mikayla. You know I do."

"I don't mean that I like you and enjoy sex with you, Jensen. I'm talking way beyond that."

"Ah." He bit his lip slightly and turned, the truth dawning in his blue eyes. "You're talking about Vegas. How I reacted about those crazies thinking I was your baby's father. Or your husband." He looked so miserable that she almost felt bad for him. Almost.

"Well, your reaction certainly hit me over the head with the truth I've been ignoring. You told me all that, Jensen. From the beginning, you were honest. But still, yes, your reaction made me realize I've been clinging to the hope that you'd change your mind."

"Mikayla, I can't—"

"I know you can't." *Or won't.* "It's ironic, really, that I want the one thing you can't give me."

He let out a hard sigh and sat in the rocking chair, running a hand through his movie-star blond hair. But he didn't say anything. He didn't correct her or give her the one thing she wanted.

Him. His heart. His future.

"Jensen, I could keep dating you until it's time for you to fly away, but I'm only going to get hurt worse that way."

He glanced at her, and she could practically see his mind working, looking for his in, how to make this work for her and him.

"I love the bed," she said, pointing at it. "I gave it a try for five minutes. But I can't keep it."

"It's a gift. I want you to have it."

"I can't be bought, Jensen," she said, anger tingeing her voice. "Maybe other women you've been with were happy to have you shower them with gifts, but I'm not. That's not what I want from you."

"What do you want?" he asked. "Specifically."

You. All of you. But maybe she'd start slow—take baby steps so as not to scare him. "The only thing I know for sure is that you're not looking for a commitment. I am."

"Maybe someday, though," he said, something different in his tone. As though he was testing out the words on his tongue, in his head, in his heart. "I mean, these are extraordinary circumstances we're in. More you than me."

"Right. Which is why I don't have the luxury of time. In a few weeks, I'm going to be a mother. The baby will change everything and need all the love I have to give."

"But we have one final week together, Mik. Why take that from each other?"

She shook her head. Why didn't he understand? She'd felt so close to him before Vegas; she just assumed he'd get it, know how she felt without her having to say it. But he obviously didn't. "Because I've already been rejected by my child's father. I refuse to set myself up for more of that." She tried to take a deep breath, but she could barely get any air. "Just go, Jensen."

"But, Mik—"

She waited for him to say something that would change her mind. She waited for him to say, *I love you, too. I want a commitment with you, too.*

But he said nothing.

"Just go," she said again. "It's over between us.

We had some fun, but it's only fun till someone gets hurt, right?"

The look he gave her almost undid her. "I'm sorry, Mikayla. I wish I could be the man you need."

With that, he turned and walked out.

A sudden pain gripped Mikayla's abdomen. She bent over, a strangled scream coming from her throat.

"Jensen!" she called, hoping he'd hear. "Jensen!"

He rushed back into the room. "Mikayla, what's wrong?"

"I don't know," she said on a moan, doubling over in pain again. "My belly feels like it's tightening. Ow!" she yelped. What was this?

She felt his arms around her, walking her toward the door, then he scooped her up in his arms like she weighed next to nothing and carried her down the stairs and out the door.

As he settled her in the passenger side of his truck, she closed her eyes against the pain and said, "Please, God, please, please, please. Don't let anything be wrong with my baby."

"That goes double for me, God," he said, lifting his eyes toward the roof of the truck.

The pain was so intense that she gripped both the center console and the door handle.

"Hold on, Mik. I'll take you to the clinic and I'll call your doctor and have him or her meet us there."

"Drew Strickland," she said, handing him her phone, her eyes squeezed shut. "He's in my contacts."

She barely heard him make the call. The pain was so severe that her entire abdomen felt like it was twisting in some kind of charley horse. She was sure she'd pass out.

She tried to remember what she'd read about pre-term labor. She was barely thirty-two weeks along. This couldn't be labor. But the pains were so intense and felt like the descriptions that had scared her half to death. Contractions. Tightening. The worst cramps you'd ever feel.

I can't be in labor! It's too early!

She tried to breathe hard, forcibly expelling air out, and it helped a bit. She was aware of Jensen talking on the phone, then placing it in the console holder.

"Okay, you're all set, Mik. Dr. Strickland will meet us at the clinic. He said if need be, he'll have an ambulance transport you to the hospital in Kalispell."

That was the last thing she heard before her moans of pain drowned out anything else he said.

Chapter Eleven

"Braxton-Hicks contractions," Dr. Strickland said. "The baby is fine. You're fine. You're not in labor. But the contractions get pretty intense and mimic labor."

Relief overwhelmed Mikayla to the point that she felt woozy. In a moment, it passed, and gratitude replaced every emotion. Her baby was okay. That meant *everything* was okay.

"Whoa, so it's gonna be that painful," Mikayla said with a grimace. "The real thing, I mean."

Dr. Strickland smiled. "Sorry, but yes." He spent some time talking to Mikayla about what to expect when she was in actual labor and how to know when to come to the clinic. "Is Mr. Jones your birth partner?" he asked.

Jensen's eyes practically bugged out of his head. "Her what?"

"Birth partner," Dr. Strickland repeated. "Coaching her along through the delivery process, reminding her to breathe, having a hand that gets squeezed very hard."

Poor Jensen looked like he might pass out before he even got to the labor and delivery room.

"Jensen and I are just friends," Mikayla said as lightly as she could. Though she'd bet he'd make a great birth partner.

Besides, Amy had generously offered to be her Lamaze coach. Then again, even though they were good friends and Amy made her feel like she'd do anything for her, being her birth partner was going a step too far and would be taking advantage of her friend's kindness and generosity.

Would she give birth alone, though? Just her and the doctor and a nurse?

Yes, idiot, she chastised herself. *And you'll be fine. Just fine. You're going to be a single mother. You might as well start by giving birth alone.*

I'll be fine, she silently said to herself again.

Once Dr. Strickland left, Mikayla turned to Jensen, who was sitting beside her, clutching her hand. He looked white as a ghost.

He hadn't left her side since they'd arrived. When they'd come in, Jensen carrying her, a staffer had rushed over with a wheelchair and Jensen had gotten a break. She couldn't be easy to carry and run with, and he'd done it twice. Then he'd sat beside her, holding her hand while a nurse took her vitals and they waited for the doctor to examine her.

Damn, it felt good to have him there. A prebirth partner. It felt *so* good, in fact, that Mikayla knew, without a shred of doubt, that she couldn't accept less from a man she loved than the full monty. Full love in return. Not fancy trips and beds that did everything but feed her a midnight snack. If she was going to let a man into her life, he would have to be available, emotionally and mentally, for the long haul.

That wasn't Jensen Jones.

It really was time to say goodbye. She appreciated him and everything he'd done today—but it was wrong. He wasn't her boyfriend. He wasn't part of her future. He wasn't going to stick around, and he had to stop making her think he cared when he didn't.

Cared in the long-haul sense.

Heck, if Amy or Eva or Luke had been with her when she'd doubled over, they'd have been here instead of Jensen. He was really just her friend. With temporary benefits.

But no more.

She sucked in a breath and sat up, slapping her hands on her thighs. It was also time to tell Jensen how she felt. The truth. "I'd appreciate a ride home, but then, as I've been saying, it's time for us to go our separate ways, Jensen."

"Mik—"

She held up a hand. "Getting the behoosus scared out of me made me realize that if I'm going to have a man I'm sleeping with beside me at such a time, he'd better be fully invested in our relationship. Otherwise, it just makes no sense. And it's really kind of sad."

"I make you sad?" he asked, frowning, his expression a mix of confusion and hurt.

"What's *not* happening between us makes me sad,

Jensen. The possibilities. But you've told me all along you're here temporarily. That I'm your temporary lady. And now I know for sure, surer than I was in Vegas, that the end has come. A bit earlier than you wanted, maybe. But for my sake, I can't see you anymore."

He dropped his head back, staring up at the ceiling for a moment. "I just want to be clear on something, Mikayla. I *do* care. A lot. So much so that I'm not walking away from you today—sorry. Probably not for the next few days. I won't lay a finger on you, except to carry you if need be. I won't tell you how beautiful you are, how sexy, how much I want you. I won't do anything I really want. But I do care, and I'm going to make sure you're okay for the next few days."

Oh, hell. Now what? "I'm a grown woman, Jensen." She got off the examination table, clutching the open back of her goofy cotton clinic gown. "I know you've already seen me completely naked, but…"

He stood. "I'll give you your privacy," he said, heading toward the door. "And I know you're a grown woman, Mik. But you just had a scare and could use someone with time on his hands to be around just in case. So you're stuck with me. Sorry. I'll be waiting right outside."

She narrowed her eyes at him. "A little too used to getting your way, Jones."

And she was a little too used to his showing her, time and again, how much he really did care. Why couldn't he understand how the dichotomy, the discrepancy, between what was clearly in his heart and the old tapes on repeat in his head didn't serve him? Or *them*.

"Look, Luke and his hands are out working the ranch. Eva has her job at Daisy's. If you need help, Mikayla, someone should be close at hand. Someone just visiting their brothers."

"Like you," she said. He was right, though. She had a cell phone, of course, and could call for help if need be, but having someone there for her, literally and figuratively, did allay some residual anxiety from today. "Oh, fine, since you're so annoyingly honest all the time, I'll be, too. I'm kind of relieved you're sticking around—but in a strictly *platonic* sense. *That* I can deal with. Nothing confusing going on. We're just friends."

"Friends," he said, extending his hand.

She could see very clearly in his eyes that friendship was just the first layer of what he wanted from her. There was desire there, an aching desire. And she knew he was battling with himself about walking away when it was time for him to go back to Tulsa. But these days, Mikayla could barely hold in her pee. Jensen had to flip his heart on his own. She couldn't do it for him. And she wasn't going to hold her breath, either.

He opened the door to leave so she could get dressed.

"Jensen, just one question. I want you to answer it honestly. Do you want to leave me? Not this minute, I mean. When it's time for you to return to Tulsa."

He stared at her. "What? That's not—"

"It is. It's the entire point of our conversation. Do you want to leave me and go back to Tulsa and live your life with me as part of your past?"

He let out a sigh. "Mikayla, that's pretty darn complicated a question."

"Is it?"

"I was always planning on going home. We both know that. That was never up for discussion."

"Then this is over, Jensen. I know what I need to know, right?"

He closed his eyes for a second but didn't respond and left the room, closing the door gently behind him.

Tears poked her eyes, but she blinked them back. *Perspective, Mik. Repeat your mantra five times fast. Your baby is okay and that means everything is okay.*

"It's you and me, kid," she whispered to her belly as she pulled on her maternity sundress and slipped her feet into her sandals.

But we always knew that.

The trip back to Sunshine Farm was quiet. Dead silent, really. Jensen almost wanted to make a wrong turn and prolong bringing her home, but the ranch wasn't all that far from the clinic, and even a new-comer to town couldn't get lost in Rust Creek Falls.

I know what I need to know, right? Her words echoed in his head.

No, Mikayla, You don't. You don't know the half of it. It isn't as simple, as black-and-white, as you make it seem. Davison's favorite phrase had been "Things aren't always what they seem." Surely Mikayla knew he'd stay if he could, if he was cut out for commitment and parenthood. He wasn't.

There, he'd just proved her point. That was what she needed to know—that he wasn't husband and fa-ther material. He wasn't even birth partner material.

When her doctor had rubbed that weird jelly stuff

on her belly for the ultrasound and the image of Mikayla's baby appeared on the monitor, Jensen's knees had almost buckled—and he'd been sitting down. He'd had to grip the side of his chair. It had been one thing to feel the baby kick and understand that there was actually a little human growing inside her. It was another to see the baby on the screen. Hear its heartbeat.

That amazing baby deserved the world. And he'd never be the kind of father a child deserved. Business first. Work first. The office first. Deals first. He'd been raised that way. And getting his heart handed to him by Adrienne, that betrayal, had told him if it happened once, it would happen again.

There would not be a next time.

He almost chuckled bitterly as he recalled Dr. Strickland asking if he was Mikayla's birth partner. First total strangers in Vegas mistook him for an impending dad. Then the doctor had pegged him for a birth partner. How weird was that? That night in Las Vegas, he'd tried to imagine himself answering those nosey parkers with *Yes, we're expecting a boy.* Or, *Freedom? I've had my freedom. I can't wait to give it up for the baby my wife and I will raise with love and joy.*

For a minute, after he'd gotten a little scotch in him, Jensen Jones had wanted to be that guy. That family man. But he wasn't that guy; he'd never be that guy. That was just the way it was.

So let her go, Jensen. Do the right thing.

"We're still friends, though, right?" he asked as he pulled up in front of the farmhouse. The catch in his voice annoyed him. Black-and-white, he reminded himself. No gray. No voice catching, no wanting more but not much more. "The 'we' discussion is over, like you said, but the friendship still stands. Right? Because I can't let you get out of this car until you say yes."

She smiled. That was good.

"The friendship stands."

Phew. "Very glad to hear you say that. Oh, and since it does, tough noogies on the bed. You're keeping it. Friends help friends, and given what you've been through today, you need that bed. So that's final."

She held out her arm. "No twisting required. I love that bed. That *bed* is a friend."

He laughed. "Well, let's get you upstairs and in it. Did you know you can listen to music via Bluetooth on the remote?"

"I wouldn't be surprised if that bed made smoothies and pancakes," she said. "Did I say thank you, by the way? It might be the most thoughtful gift anyone's ever given me. Well, besides the little yellow canoe cradle." Her expression changed for a moment, and because he knew her well now, he could read the shift in her features—bittersweet longing for what wasn't, what she wished could be.

Dammit.

He wanted so badly to reach out and hug her. But he stayed put and restricted himself to a quick hand squeeze. "That's my job. Being thoughtful where you're concerned. Friends do that. I just happen to be a friend with money."

"Understatement of the year," she said with a grin as he came around to help her out.

"Shall I carry you?" he asked, positioning himself to pick her up.

"I can walk. But it was nice to be carried. I think that was a first, too."

"Lots of firsts with us," he said, his voice cracking a bit again. Why did that have to keep happening?

She nodded and led the way into the house and up the stairs. She closed her bedroom door and sent him a smile. "I'll just change and be right out."

She disappeared into the bathroom, then came back in striped pink-and-red yoga pants and a long white T-shirt that read Baby on Board. "Ahh," she said, getting into the bed. "Heavenly." She picked up the remote and pressed some buttons. "Ahhh. Ahhhhh."

Jensen watched her enjoy the bed's massage features, his own smile at her happiness and comfort warring with something else pushing at him, some heavyhearted feeling he didn't want to allow in. He sat down in the rocking chair by the window. "I'll just stay until you fall asleep," he said.

Unfortunately, she fell asleep way too soon. Now he had no reason to stay. Unless she woke up and needed something. But he heard Eva come in downstairs. If anything happened, he knew Mikayla would be in good hands.

And he needed to think. He felt like he was being yanked in five directions. He needed air and space.

He wanted to kiss her goodbye, even on her forehead, and whisper "Sweet dreams," but when he got up, he went straight for the door and left, the evening breeze just what he needed.

In his truck, he turned the ignition but then left

the gear in Park, pulled out his phone and texted her: Going back to Walker's for the night. If you need anything, text or call and I'll be right over.

Then he added, Let me know how you're feeling when you wake up so I won't worry all night.

He wanted to also add *I miss you already*. But friends didn't get that gushy.

Gushy. If he felt gushy in the first place, did that mean he felt more than he was willing to admit to himself?

En route to Walker's house, his phone rang, thankfully distracting himself from his thoughts. He answered via the Bluetooth system.

Ugh. His father.

"Hey, Dad."

"I expected you home by now, Jensen. Just what in hell is keeping you in that town? And don't say it's a woman."

All the fight went out of Jensen, and the truth came tumbling out of his mouth. "It's a woman. She's eight months pregnant and I'm crazy about her, but things are complicated."

Silence.

"Dad?" he prompted. "Still there?"

More silence. Walker Jones the Second was rarely at a loss for words.

His father cleared his throat. "Well, that does sound complicated. Anyhoo," he said, using one of his favorite subject shifters, "the real reason I called is that your mother and I are planning a trip to visit you, Hudson and Walker this weekend. We plan to arrive around five on Saturday. I suppose we'll stay at Walker's log cabin."

Only Walker Jones the Second would refer to Walker's mansion as a cabin.

And wait—*what?* His parents were coming this weekend—on their anniversary? How had Jensen pulled this off without even trying? His mood perked up considerably. He hadn't even had to resort to the ruse he'd planned.

Unless they were coming to tell their sons in person they were getting a divorce. Was Jensen that cynical? Maybe. Would his folks bother flying out to a town they hated, a town they believed had robbed them of their sons, just to tell them they were splitting up after forty years? Doubtful.

Stop overthinking. Just be happy. They'll have no idea they're walking right into your tender trap of a surprise anniversary party.

"That's great, Dad. We'll you see then."

Now he had something else to overthink. The fact that he wanted Mikayla to be his date for the party. And to meet his parents. And his other brothers. His last girlfriend hadn't met any of his family, and it hadn't been all that important to him. But he wanted Mikayla to meet them. He wanted them to meet *her*.

Why, though? Was this part of the *gush?*

Just what the hell was going on with him?

"You do realize you're acting like a mother hen?" Mikayla said to who else—Jensen.

After a nap in that amazing bed, she'd woken up feeling rested and calm. She'd texted Jensen back that she felt great and to thank him again for being there for her, and he texted back that he had the makings for his world-famous spaghetti and meatballs and garlic bread, if she was up for him coming over and cooking for her.

A gorgeous, sexy man cooking one of her favorite meals for her? Hell, yes. And then she remembered her tender hold on her resolve to keep Jensen at arm's length during the tenure of their "friendship."

As friends, he'd texted back, reading her mind, as usual.

Which was why he was now hovering over her in the kitchen, holding her elbow as she carried the tray of garlic bread from the oven to the counter. "You heard Dr. Strickland. I'm fine. The baby is fine. I'm not on bed rest."

"Yes, but you should probably take it easy. For a few days, at least. Today was pretty crazy."

"I am taking it easy. I'm carrying a loaf of garlic bread, which weighs about two ounces. It's not going to send me crashing to the floor."

"Maybe not," he said, grating fresh Parmesan cheese onto the spaghetti. She had no idea where he'd gotten that delicious-looking hunk of cheese in Rust Creek Falls. He'd probably had it flown in by private jet from Italy. Seriously, she wouldn't be surprised. "Yes, but you can't be too careful, Mik."

Eva was working at Daisy's and Luke had a rancher's association meeting, so they had the house to themselves for the next couple of hours. Jensen had arrived with a brand of spaghetti she'd never heard of before in some fancy pouch, the ingredients for fresh marinara sauce, already-cooked little meatballs that just needed warming, a bunch of spices and the makings for garlic bread, which she'd had no idea she'd been craving until he mentioned it.

She shook her head and inhaled the aroma of the garlic bread, which smelled amazing. "I'm going to eat this entire loaf myself, sorry."

"Oh, then I'd better steal a piece now," he said, smiling.

As she crossed the kitchen to get a knife, he hovered again. "Jensen, I'm not going to break."

He held up both hands in surrender. "I just never want to see you in pain again."

Aw, foo. Stop caring so much about me, mister. You're going to keep me in love with you and that's the last thing we both need, trust me.

She managed a smile and put her hands on his shoulders for emphasis, then realized she was touching him when, by her own edict, that was out of bounds. She pulled her hands away. "Didn't you hear Dr. Strickland? I'm going to be in *a lot* of pain very soon. Goes with the territory," she added, patting her huge stomach.

Her smile faded fast. *Duh, Mikayla. Jensen won't be here for that. He'll probably be leaving early next week.*

She didn't buy that, though. There was really nothing keeping Jensen in town anymore. The land deal with Guthrie Barnes hadn't happened, and he'd already scouted out two other locations that he could live with. He'd told Mikayla he'd planned on crunching the numbers once he was back home and reconfiguring his ideas for those sites. Maybe that meant he'd be coming to Rust Creek Falls in the future once the deal was made and construction began. Or maybe not. The man was an executive. She doubted he'd ever worn a hard hat in his life.

He sure had a hard heart, though. But not really, she amended. He had a *big* heart, and there was nothing hard about it. He was just a man who knew what he didn't want. A wife. A baby. Commitment.

But Jensen Jones did have very strong feelings for her; he'd said so himself. And those strong feelings felt a lot like love to her. Jensen could *say* he wasn't in love all he wanted, though he hadn't in so many words. He acted like a man in love. Everything he did indicated his heart belonged to Mikayla. And didn't her mother always tell her to pay more attention to what people did rather than what they said? *Actions speak louder than words* was a favorite old adage of hers.

But how did you get someone to completely change his way of thinking?

As they brought their serving bowls and platters to the dining room and sat down, Jensen did make sure to swipe one good-size piece of the garlic bread, making Mikayla laugh.

"Oh, by the way," he said, twirling spaghetti around his fork, "my parents are coming to town on Saturday night, and my brothers and I are throwing them a surprise fortieth anniversary party, just family. Will you come? Please?"

Mikayla stared at him, her own meatball-stabbed fork paused in midair. Just family. For God's sake, did the man hear himself? He wanted her to meet his *family*. At a *family-only* anniversary party.

Oh, yeah, he loved her.

She grinned, her heart soaring. *He loves me*, she said silently to her belly, which she was talking to more and more like a trusted confidant these days. *He may not know it yet, but he does. And your mama is going to help him realize it before he gets on that plane back to Tulsa. Because Jensen* is *home.*

Sounded right to her. Or was it all just wishful thinking and late-stage pregnancy hormones?

Chapter Twelve

When Bella had heard about Mikayla's "scare," she'd insisted Mikayla take a few days off and come in to Just Us Kids on Friday if she was up to it. She was up to it and ready to get back to work. Her hours were just part-time, and changing infants' diapers and singing lullabies was exactly how she wanted to spend her mornings.

"Hudson will be glad to hear that," Bella said, grinning as she and Mikayla headed to the baby room. "He filled in for you yesterday and Lee Pearson peed all over Hudson's favorite shirt. How many times have I told that man to make sure the male babies can't aim for him?"

Mikayla laughed. "Not that that's funny," she added quickly.

"Oh, it most certainly is," Bella said on a chuckle.

In the baby room, she scooped up eight-month-old Haley Lotts from her crib. "Someone's ready for tummy time," she whispered to the baby, giving her a nuzzle.

A cry split the quiet of the room. Uh-oh, Mikayla had better go calm down the crier before the other five sleeping babies were woken up.

"I'll go see why CJ is fussing up a storm," Mikayla said. She hurried across the room and picked up the little guy, whose face was all scrunched up. He calmed down for a second, then let out the wail of all wails. "Ah, I think I know what's ailing you, my little friend." She brought the baby over to the changing table, took care of business, dusted some cornstarch on CJ's bottom and put a fresh diaper on him. "There you go. Good as new."

She loved the way CJ was staring up at her with wonder and happiness. Babies were so sweet and trusting. "How about a lullaby and then we'll see if you'll continue your nap?" She brought the baby over to a rocker in the far corner, away from the row of cribs, and settled him in her arms. She sang two songs and CJ's eyes began to droop. "Yup," she whispered, "it's back to the crib."

As the hours passed, Mikayla changed more diapers, read a few board books to some crawlers in the gated area, walked up and down the length of the room with a crier until she finally quieted and then fed lunch to the solid-fooders, with the pureed peas, applesauce and sweet potatoes on her shirt to prove it.

When her workday ended, Mikayla didn't want to leave. And not even because when she was here and focused on the little ones, she tended not to think about

Jensen and their crazy relationship. *Friendship*, she amended. Not being able to think too much about her personal life was a bonus of being busy at work.

She didn't want to leave, because she loved her job. And she loved how much experience she was getting with all the stages of babyhood. By the time her baby was born, she'd know the deal for each month of infancy.

On her way down the hall, she stopped in Hudson Jones's office to hand in her amended time card, since she'd ended up working only two days this week. Hudson sat at his desk, going through some paperwork.

"Thank God you're back, Mikayla," he said with a grin.

She smiled. "I hear I owe you a new shirt."

He laughed, and for a second she was startled by the resemblance to Jensen. The Jones brothers didn't look identical, but they all had those amazing blue eyes. She'd done such a good job of not thinking of Jensen today, but chatting with his brother threw that out the window.

"And *I* hear you're coming to our parents' anniversary party," Hudson said, stamping an invoice. "I should warn you. Patricia and Walker the Second aren't for the faint of heart. They're going to assume you're the reason Jensen is still here—and that he might never leave. Like Walker and me."

"Ha. I'll be the first to tell them they have nothing to worry about. Jensen isn't the settling-down kind."

Hudson raised an eyebrow. "I'm pretty sure my brother and I—and Autry, who now has three girls—said the same thing."

Well, Mikayla was sure now that Jensen would be

getting on a plane with his parents on Sunday morning. So much for all her hope and optimism at dinner last night, about getting him to realize how strongly he felt about her—and what that really meant.

Because his good-night text to her had read I'm so happy you're coming to the anniversary party Sat. night. A special way to spend our final night together.

Her heart had plummeted with such a thud she was surprised Eva hadn't come running into her room. She'd been the one to tell Jensen they were through as a temporary couple. She was just a friend now, like any number of people he'd met in town. Their relationship wasn't special. Of course he was going home. That had always been the plan.

She tried to force some levity into her voice when she felt like crying. "He's leaving on Sunday morning with your parents. There's no reason for him to stay in town any longer."

Hudson stopped stamping and looked at her. "You're here."

The lump in her throat grew. "We're just friends, Hudson. I have to accept it," she added on a whisper, surprising herself.

He held her gaze for a moment, then leaned forward. "Don't give up on Jensen. He had his heart smashed a few years ago and it did a number on him. He's just guarded."

She shook her head. "And resolute. He's told me in no uncertain terms that he's going home. He doesn't want to be a husband and father. And I'm about to become a mother."

"Well, all I know for sure is that I've seen a change in Jensen since he met you." Hudson bit his lip as though deciding whether to say more. "He's fighting his feelings—I know, because I've been there myself. We didn't exactly have the best role models when it came to love and relationships."

Mikayla was surprised to hear that. She didn't know much about the Jones parents, just that the patriarch was very…patriarchal. "But your parents have been married for forty years!"

"They love each other—I do believe that. But they're both so tough. Our dad is authoritarian and devoted to his job—work always comes first. Before his wife and before his kids. He expects his sons to operate the same way, and so far, three of us have found balance, a word our father has never heard of."

He's fighting his feelings… "So you're saying there's a chance Jensen might not leave Sunday morning with your parents?" she asked.

"Well, if I know my parents, and I do, they're going to try to forcibly drag him to the plane. But Jensen has always been his own man. And sometimes being told what to do can help someone realize what he really *wants* to do. You know what I mean?"

"He won't stay in Rust Creek Falls just to spite bossy parents, though," she said.

"No, Jensen doesn't do things for spite. He'd stay for *you*."

I wish. "I don't think so, Hudson. He's made his feelings crystal clear. And I've been here before. With a man who's told me what he doesn't want. I need to move on and accept that Jensen and I will never have a future."

"Well, I'm a firm believer in the wisdom of 'you

never know.' I've been surprised before. I'm sure you have, too."

Jensen constantly surprised her. But she had no doubt he was leaving Sunday.

With her heart.

On Saturday morning, Amy and Eva were riffling through Mikayla's closet, trying to figure out what she could wear to Jensen's parents' anniversary party that night.

"How about this?" Amy said, holding up the black grow-with-me tank dress.

"Ooh, it would be perfect with this pretty cardigan over it," Eva said, taking out a lightweight silver pointelle sweater.

"I guess I could squeeze myself into that one last time," Mikayla said, smiling at the thought of the concierge's assistant bringing in the three fancy dresses. The one she wore in Las Vegas would be a little much for tonight. Unless the Jones family wore gowns and tuxedos for family parties and get-togethers. She wouldn't be surprised.

"Oh, guess what!" Eva said, shoving her blond hair behind her shoulders. "I almost forgot to tell you, Mikayla. We're getting a new tenant at Sunshine Farm. And it's thanks to Amy."

Mikayla grinned. "That's great, Eva. So it's a friend of yours, Amy?"

"I don't even know her!" Amy said. "Apparently, a journalist wrote a piece about me reconnecting with my ex-husband while I was staying here at Sunshine Farm. She dubbed the place the Lonelyhearts Ranch.

And this woman, Josselyn, read the article and emailed Eva about coming to stay for a while."

Lonelyhearts Ranch, Mikayla thought. Sounded pretty on the money to her. "How did a journalist hear about you and Derek?"

Amy shrugged and reached behind her to tighten her ponytail. "I have no idea! I'm just glad it brought another person Eva and Luke's way—someone who needs Sunshine Farm like I did."

"And like I *do*," Mikayla said. "This place saved me, Eva."

Eva and Amy gave Mikayla "aw" faces and hugged her.

"I'm so glad, Mikayla. This is exactly what I wanted Sunshine Farm to be," Eva said.

"So when is the new tenant arriving?" Mikayla asked. She loved the idea of having a new friend right here in the house.

"Any day now," Eva said. "Josselyn's going to be the new librarian at the elementary school at the end of August. We're getting a cabin ready for her. Our very first guest cabin! I'm ridiculously excited about this."

Mikayla smiled. "That's great, Eva. You and Luke are so generous."

"Speaking of generous," Amy said, "what's the latest on your hot romance with the giver of this amazing bed that I totally want for my own?"

Mikayla tried not to let her sadness show on her face, but who was she kidding? She was an open book. She let out a heavy sigh and dropped down on the edge of her bed, the dress on its hanger pooling in her lap. "We're just friends now."

"Uh-oh," Eva said, sitting down beside Mikayla and

putting an arm around her shoulders. "Last I knew, you guys came back from Vegas, Jensen came to see you here and you had me tell him you were resting." She grimaced. "I should have known there was trouble in paradise."

Amy sat down on the other side of Mikayla. "You two ended things?"

"*Things* only ever added up to a temporary no-strings romance while he's in town," Mikayla reminded her girlfriends. "Not much to end, but I had to."

"Why?" Amy asked.

"Because one of us fell in love," Mikayla said. "And it wasn't the six-foot-two blond millionaire Adonis."

Eva frowned. "Oh, crud. I'm sorry."

"Me, too," Amy said. "I thought for sure you two would be jetting off into the sunset."

For a few seconds here and there over the past couple of weeks, Mikayla had allowed herself to believe it was possible. Now she knew it wasn't. "Nope. We're just friends now." She forced her gaze off Amy's engagement ring and Eva's wedding ring and onto her grow-with-me dress. She had to change the subject before she started bawling. "I hope this thing stretches over this giant belly of mine," she said way too brightly, holding up the dress on its hanger. "I'm sure a Jones family anniversary party is on the dressy side."

Eva narrowed her eyes. "Do *friends* invite *friends* to a family-only anniversary party? I think not! That is a completely dateworthy event. So, it's a date."

"I have to agree," Amy said. "Mik, sounds like you and Jensen *are* serious—no matter what you two call it."

"A serious friendship and a serious relationship are

two very different things, though," Mikayla pointed out. "Take Thursday night. He made me the most delicious comfort-food dinner ever—spaghetti and meatballs and garlic bread. Then he cleaned everything up himself. As he left, he gave me a kiss—on the cheek. That's serious *friendship*."

"Huh," Eva said, frowning. "I guess so. But what man does all that for a woman he's not in love with?"

"I asked myself the same thing that night," Mikayla said. "I really thought there was hope, that he just had to come to this big realization that he loved me, too—and would."

Amy scrunched up her face. "What dashed it? I'm almost afraid to ask."

"A text when he got home from making me that serious-friendship dinner. How he was so happy I said yes to going to the party because it'll be a special way to spend our last night together." She sighed. "I have to face facts. He's leaving tomorrow morning. There's no us."

She almost couldn't believe it. After tonight, Cinderella would lose her Prince. No more Jensen. That megawatt smile—gone. Those gorgeous blue eyes— gone. His friendship, which she'd always had, even when they were a temporary couple—gone. *That* she'd miss most of all. His sweetness. His kindness. The way he loved her, whether he knew that was what he was doing or not.

She knew.

And she'd miss him like hell.

Saturday afternoon, Jensen drove out to Guthrie Barnes's property, sure of what he had to do. It certainly wasn't what he'd come to town expecting to do, but neither was getting involved with a very pregnant woman.

It wasn't as if Jensen had planned on giving his father the signed land deal for the crisis distribution center for an anniversary present, but he'd had a strong hunch that a tribute to his old friend would have brought peace to Walker the Second's heart. Whatever had come between the two men didn't matter anymore; Davison was gone. And they'd never be able to make things right between them face-to-face. But in memory, his father could finally come to terms with his feelings. Jensen truly believed that doing so would change his father—that the armor he'd put on an already hard shell would break off, that he'd love more deeply. His wife. His children. Even his work, which he'd always approached with his head, not his heart.

But there was no signed land deal, not on this trip. He had the two alternate locations chosen, had his assistant gathering information and crunching numbers, and once he was back home in Tulsa, he'd put together an offer for one of the sites. He wasn't going to try for Guthrie Barnes's property one last time. Because he'd learned something important over the past few weeks. That he had to honor someone's feelings instead of trying to turn that person to his way of thinking. The way he'd done with Mikayla. Guthrie Barnes had made it clear as water that he wanted nothing to do with selling his land, and Jensen would honor that.

But first he wanted to apologize to Barnes, to shake the man's hand and let him know he wouldn't be bothering him anymore, and that whatever kept the man from selling, he admired his hold on his principles. Money had never swayed Guthrie Barnes.

Now he stood on the rickety old top step to Barnes's ramshackle house and knocked on the wooden door, which looked like it might fall off one hinge any second.

The screen door opened. Barnes appeared, his wiry gray hair sprouting in every direction. "Oh, hell, it's you. Didn't I—"

Jensen held up a hand. "I'm only here to apologize for not honoring your refusal to sell, which you couldn't have made more clear. I'm sorry I kept at you, Mr. Barnes. That wasn't right or fair."

The man harrumphed. But before Barnes could slam the door in Jensen's face, Jensen took a check out of his shirt pocket and held it up. "I'd like you to have this, regardless, as an apology for having to deal with me breathing down your neck." The amount would cover some basic upkeep around the place. "No amount of money would sway you, so I figure you've got a good reason not to sell. I won't be bothering you anymore, Mr. Barnes."

The man opened the door and took the check and stared at it. Jensen figured he'd rip it up and throw the confetti at him. He turned to go; he had a party to get ready for and didn't want random bits of check on him.

"My little girl died on that land," Barnes said.

Jensen gasped and turned around. "Your little girl?" Nothing in the information he'd gathered on Barnes even mentioned a child.

The old man stared out the screen door at the land. "It was fifty-one years ago. My wife and I had just moved to Rust Creek Falls and were showing Lynnie the fish in the creek at the far end of our property.

There was a flash flood and—" The man reached up a hand to his eyes. "Lynnie was just two years old."

Oh, God. Tears burned the backs of Jensen's eyes. "I am so sorry, Mr. Barnes. I can't begin to imagine the heartbreak."

The man began weeping, and Jensen opened the screen door and ushered him out to the weathered bench along the outside windows. He sat Barnes down and sat beside him, an arm around the man's shoulders, which shook with his sobs.

"Mr. Barnes, I'm going to open the crisis distribution center and have two other locations scouted out. If you'll allow it, I'd like to name the center after Lynnie." Davison would want that. Jensen knew that without a doubt.

The man looked at Jensen. "You'd name it after Lynnie?"

"As I've mentioned, my mentor—Davison Parkwell—died in a flash flood, too," Jensen said. "Last year, he was volunteering on the outskirts of town and helping to rescue two people when he got pulled in. Remember back in 2013 when another flood practically destroyed Rust Creek Falls? A crisis distribution center is exactly what this area needs."

Barnes nodded and swiped under his eyes. "My wife passed on over ten years ago, but I stayed here because it's all I have left of Lynnie. I stay away from the creek when it rains, of course, but I go down there at least once a day to just remember before—" He clamped his mouth tightly together.

Jensen sat there, his arm around Guthrie Barnes's shoulders, and the two of them just looked out at the land, the majestic trees in the distance, the clear blue sky.

"I'll accept your original offer, Jones," Guthrie said. "If you'll really name the center after my Lynnie. Lynnie Barnes."

Jensen blinked back the sting of tears. "Only if you accept my last offer, which was triple the original bid. And I'll build you a new house at the edge of the property, near the creek. You have my word on the name. The Lynnie Barnes Crisis Distribution Center."

Barnes sucked in a breath and extended his hand. Jensen shook it.

And they continued to sit there for a good while.

Tonight would be his last hours with Mikayla, the woman of his dreams. Had he just thought that? The woman of his dreams? Yes, she absolutely was, he realized. She was everything he'd ever wanted in a woman, including things he had no idea he even liked. Such as those crazy wrap-around-the-ankle sandals. Or the way she called him out on anything he deserved to be called out on.

This made no sense, but he could sit here with Guthrie Barnes forever, as lost in thought as the older man was. The more he prolonged getting ready and heading over to the party, the longer he didn't have to really focus on the fact that when he saw Mikayla tonight, it would be for the last time for a long time. In fact, the woman had him so tied up in knots that maybe he wouldn't come back to Rust Creek Falls at all. He could work on the distribution center remotely. He could video chat with his brothers. He didn't need to send himself off a cliff by running to the woman who challenged him in the one area he couldn't abide.

His heart. Commitment. A future.

He wasn't going there ever again. So tonight would be goodbye.

Which was why he stayed put on Guthrie's bench, listening—truly listening—to the man open up about his little girl, how cute she'd been, that she'd wanted pigtails every day, that she hated the color pink but would only wear dresses.

It was only after he'd finally left and was sitting in his truck that he realized little Lynnie Barnes had crept inside his heart just like Mikayla had. Man, this town had changed him.

Which was why he had to leave.

Chapter Thirteen

Everything was set for the surprise party. Jensen was picking up his parents from the airport at five. His brother Walker had already picked up Autry and his family and Gideon, who'd flown in a couple of hours ago. Hudson was en route to the caterers' for the buffet Jensen had ordered. And Mikayla would be driving over to Walker's for the party at six.

At the airport, Jensen spotted his parents quickly. They tended to stand out in any crowd. His father was six foot three and looked like he owned wherever he was, and his mother never dressed down, not even for travel. Patricia Jones's blond bob was perfect, her red lipstick never leaving a mark on a cheek, since she paid well for that nontransference feature. She wore a bright white pantsuit and heels and so much jewelry on her neck that Jensen was surprised she didn't topple over. His father was, of course, in a suit.

After slightly awkward hugs, Walker the Second clapped his hands and said, "Okay. Our flight leaves in an hour. We might as well have a light dinner at that burger joint over there. It's ridiculous how I love a good fifty-dollar steak *and* a six-dollar airport burger." He chuckled and his wife smiled.

"What do you mean, our flight leaves in an hour?" Jensen asked, looking from his father to his mother and back.

"We came to get you, Jensen," his father said. "Here you are. So let's head home to Tulsa."

Jensen stopped dead in his tracks. His father had to be pulling a fast one. Even Walker the Second couldn't be this devious. "You said you were coming to visit your sons. Walker and Hudson aren't here. And I doubt you intend for them to meet us here for a burger."

"We just saw your brothers at Autry's wedding in that dive bar," his dad said, grimacing. "With the poker name."

"Ace in the Hole," Jensen said on a sigh. "Look, we went to a lot of trouble for your visit, and the two of you are coming to Walker's whether you want to or not."

"Don't you speak to your mother in that tone, young man!" Walker said, jabbing a finger at Jensen.

"Oh, put that away, Walker," Patricia Jones said, pushing her husband's finger aside. "Now, Jensen, what is this about an eight-months-pregnant woman?"

Ah. How could he be so stupid? *That* was why his parents had come. To drag him back home—alone. They were afraid he'd stay in Rust Creek Falls and marry Mikayla.

He mentally shook his head. He'd been planning on

using a fib about falling for a woman to trick his parents into rushing to Montana to save him, but then, in a rare moment when he'd been all heartsick, he'd blurted out the truth to his dad without even realizing it.

"We can talk about everything at Walker's," Jensen said. "Let's go pick up your luggage."

"Oh, we don't have luggage, dear," his mother said. "Since we didn't intend on staying the night." She patted the small overnight bag on his father's shoulder. "Of course, we never travel without a change of clothes and our toiletries, since mishaps can occur. One bump from turbulence or a clumsy passerby and you end up with your gin and tonic all over yourself."

Was he completely out of his mind or did his mother just wink at him slightly? Patricia Jones had softened up a bit about losing her sons to Rust Creek Falls with the third such marriage—Autry's last year—but her husband had not. Clearly, his mother had expected to stay the night at Walker's, even if his father thought they were flying in, dragging Jensen back to their private plane and turning right around and flying home.

I always knew you had it in you, Mom, he thought, smiling at her.

She smiled back.

"Fine, fine," his father grumbled, unaware as usual. "I could use a scotch."

His mother nodded at Jensen and off they went to Jensen's pickup. In a half hour they were at Walker's house. When he parked, Jensen quickly texted Walker a We're here to alert him that everyone should go into surprise mode.

As the three of them walked to the front door of the log mansion, Jensen actually felt excited again.

The party had to have some kind of effect on his father. As would the distribution center. Even though it wouldn't be named for Davison, the man was the driving force behind it. Jensen was sure his father would come around. Ninety percent sure, he amended as he rang the doorbell.

Walker pulled open the front door. "Mom, Dad, glad to see you. Come in."

As Walker opened the door wide, the huge Happy 40th Anniversary banner was in full view and everyone inside the grand entryway shouted, "Surprise! Happy fortieth anniversary!"

"What on earth?" Patricia said, her mouth dropping open. Tears glistened in her eyes.

One parent down, one to go.

"Oh my God, is that Autry?" his mother said, rushing over to give each of her sons a hug. "And Gideon!" she practically screamed. "All my boys are here!"

"Happy anniversary," Jensen said.

"Well, if you made your mother happy, I'm glad," Walker the Second said.

Jensen poured his dad a scotch. "Forty years is something to celebrate, Dad."

"So is getting you home to Tulsa where you belong." His father looked around the grand living room, and Jensen realized he was looking for "the pregnant woman."

Mikayla wouldn't be here for fifteen minutes. Jensen had figured it would be better to let his parents get acclimated to the surprise party, mellow a bit and then meet Mikayla. Though now that he thought about it, did it really matter? It wasn't as if he was staying in town to be with Mikayla. He was going home with his parents tomorrow.

Jensen spent the next few minutes chatting with the two brothers he hadn't seen in a while. Autry lived in Paris with his wife and three little girls for the time being. And Gideon, the closet to Jensen in age, was always traveling for the business.

The doorbell rang. Mikayla.

He turned just as Bella opened the door to reveal Mikayla in a black dress. She looked so beautiful. Her long brown hair was loose past her shoulders, and she was glowing, as usual.

"If you think my son is going to marry you, you've got another think coming, young lady," he heard his father bellow.

Oh, God. Oh, no. His father did not just say that.

There was a chorus of "Dad!" and apologies on his behalf from his brothers.

Walker the Second's cheeks were red, but Jensen knew his father well enough to know it wasn't from embarrassment at his outburst; the man was simply furious. "I mean it. Enough of this! I want Jensen back in Tulsa where he belongs."

Mikayla stood like a deer in headlights until Bella led her toward the buffet.

"Dad, if I want to marry Mikayla and stay in Rust Creek Falls, I damn well will!" Jensen said between gritted teeth.

He glanced at Mikayla, who looked like she wanted to bolt. He wasn't sure if she'd heard what he'd said.

"Over my dead body!" Walker the Second whispered in Jensen's ear as he took him by the arm and pulled him over by the bar. "Listen here, Jensen. That woman is in trouble, obviously. Alone and about to have a baby. Poor, given what she's wearing. She's got her hooks in you and you've always been too tenderhearted. Don't ruin your life by falling for it." He glanced around. "The party was nice. Thank you. But we can go home now. I'll call Stewart and have him get the plane ready."

Jensen forced himself to mentally count to five. Slugging his own father, particularly at his parents' fortieth anniversary party, wasn't how Jensen wanted this night to be remembered. *One. Two. Three. Four. Five*, he counted again until he felt himself calming down. "Dad, enough." This time it was Jensen who pulled his dad away—into the study. He closed the door behind them.

"Yes, it *is* enough," his father said. "That pregnant woman has you so distracted and discombobulated that you didn't even accomplish what you came to Rust Creek Falls to do—get that land you wanted. This is how you want to live your life? By throwing away all your hard-earned experience at making deals?"

"Actually, Dad, I did make that deal. My lawyer is drawing up the papers as we speak. I got it done because I channeled Davison and I put people before business."

His father narrowed his eyes. "What does the deal have to do with Davison?"

Jensen explained everything. The raw memory of losing his lifelong mentor to the flash flood. Davison's commitment to volunteering in the area to rescue and help rebuild during natural disasters. Jensen's dedication to building a resource center as tribute to Davison. "But then the old man who kept turning me down for the land explained why he wouldn't sell. Because he'd lost his two-year-old daughter to a flood by the creek at the edge of his property. He wanted the land to stand forever."

"So how'd you get him to sell?" his father asked, taking a sip of his scotch.

"I didn't try to get him to do anything. In fact, I told him that when I decided on a new location for the center, I'd like to name it after his little girl. And then he told me I could have his land if I truly would name the center after his daughter. We shook hands and that was that."

His father took another long sip of his drink and glanced out the window. He was quiet for a moment, then said, "That does sound like something Davison would have done. He always put people before business. Old fool." Anger etched into the lines on his face, his father seemed lost in thought, but then his expression softened into what Jensen was pretty sure was sorrow.

Here it was. The opening Jensen had been waiting for for years now. "Dad, what happened between you and Davison?"

His father sat down in a wing chair by the window with a heavy sigh. "He told me how to live my life and I told him where he could shove it."

"What was his advice?"

Walker the Second lifted his chin. "Some nonsense about putting my kids first or I'd lose them all."

Ah. Now Jensen was beginning to understand. The prophecy had stung because it both felt possible *and* had come true.

"He kept at it and I got sick of hearing it," his father said, his voice tinged with anger. "We had one hell of an argument, the kind where you say things you can't take back." He got a faraway look in his eyes and turned his attention toward the window again. "I told him to leave me the hell alone and stormed off. That was the last time I spoke to him."

"Oh, Dad. You must have been heartsick."

His father stared at Jensen, the famous pointer finger jabbing in his direction once again. "No one tells me how to live or raise my boys." He glanced at Jensen, and if Jensen wasn't mistaken, his eyes were glistening. "But he was right, wasn't he? I've lost my sons one by one. Now you. I'm sure Gideon is next."

Jensen walked over to his father's chair and knelt beside it. "Dad, you haven't lost any of us. We've all been trying so hard to make you understand that Walker, Hudson and Autry are happy. They've settled down, found their life's partners. They're *happy*, Dad. That should be all you need to know."

"And you?" he asked. "You don't seem happy to me. Maybe this pregnant woman isn't the one."

"No one is," Jensen said, standing up and crossing his arms against his chest. "I'm not meant to settle down. No wife, no kids. I make deals. That's what I do."

"So you don't love this Mikayla woman?"

"Doesn't matter," Jensen said. "I'm not cut out for parenthood. She's about to have a baby."

"Who told you you weren't cut out for parenthood?" his dad asked.

"I just know I'm not." *Because I'm your son. You raised me this way. And I've taken the reins and run with them.*

"Well, Jensen, you're dead wrong. I think you'd make a great father."

Jensen whirled around. "What?"

"You're one of the best men I know," he added. "Like I said, you've got a tenderness in you—kids like that. You're kindhearted. Patient. You tell good jokes. You're smart. And you're loyal and give a thousand percent of yourself to whatever you do. Sounds like the makings of a good father to me."

Jensen thought his legs might give out—that was how surprised he was.

"I'd like to help out with the crisis distribution center," Walker the Second said. "Maybe I can donate funding for a certain aspect. And perhaps we can commemorate a bridge to Davison."

A bridge. Yes. Davison would love that. And so would Jensen.

His father stood up. "You do whatever feels right to you about Mikayla, Jensen. If you love that woman, go get her. If not, then I'll see you on the plane tomorrow morning. But I'm sorry I've been so controlling. I'm going to apologize to your brothers now. And their wives. And then I'm going to give your mother her anniversary present."

Jensen might have passed out from shock if he wasn't so interested in knowing what his father had bought his mother. "What is it?"

"A gold heart locket with five tiny picture frames that flip open. She can put photos of her boys in there. I know she'd like that. I have you to thank for making me realize I should buy her something. If you hadn't asked what I'd gotten her on the phone a few weeks back, I probably wouldn't have bought anything." He shook his head. "I'm a real piece of work, aren't I?"

Jensen wrapped his dad in a bear hug. "Were. Sounds like you're on your way to being a great husband and the dad we always wanted. Happy anniversary."

His father hugged back him—hard—and then Jensen watched him leave the room and go up to Walker, taking him aside. He saw the shock on his brother's face when their father hugged him. Jensen smiled as his dad went to Hudson next.

He glanced around the room until his gaze landed on Mikayla. She was sitting on the sofa, talking to his mom, Bella, Lindsay and Autry's wife, Marissa. She was wearing her grow-with-me dress, he realized, remembering it from Las Vegas.

Sounds like the makings of a good father to me. He recalled his father's words.

That was the thing. Jensen had known all along that he would probably be a great dad, because if he had a kid, being a good dad would be very important to him. His child would come first. He'd love that boy or girl with all his heart.

And that was *really* the issue, Jensen knew now. Love. He didn't want to do it. Didn't want to feel it. Didn't want it in his life. Because love meant losing. Heartache. And if he lost Mikayla, as he probably would to the usual troubles that split couples apart, he would lose everything. He'd never recover. And if anything happened to his child? That would be the end of him. Like Barnes out there in his falling-down house.

But even Guthrie Barnes had come out of seclusion. Before Jensen had left him, the old man had said he was going to pay the pastor at his old church a visit, even though he complained that the pastor was young enough to be his grandson. He thought a talk and maybe one Sunday service would be an okay way to spend tomorrow afternoon, and Jensen had agreed, his heavy heart feeling a lot lighter for the old man's prospects. He had a good hunch that Barnes would find a new lease on life.

But Jensen had constant new leases—and that was how he liked it. New deals, sending him all over Oklahoma. Constant change, never requiring a long commitment of his time or energy. That was Jensen Jones.

He'd planned on leaving tomorrow morning with his folks, and now that decision felt ironclad. He had accomplished what he'd set out to do. He'd given his parents an anniversary party. He'd had a heart-to-heart with his dad that had ended up bringing the entire family closer, including his parents. His dad had cracked wide-open when Jensen had only been expecting a jagged line.

His heart had gone back to feeling all heavy and sludge-like, but he smiled at the thought of how things had worked out, particularly where Davison Parkwell was concerned. He knew the man was grinning down on him, giving him one of his famous pats on the shoulder.

Now all that was left was spending a few more hours with Mikayla and then saying goodbye.

"Your dad apologized for what he said," Mikayla told him a half hour later as she topped a cracker with a chunk of sharp cheddar at the buffet in Walker's living room. "He told me he came to a lot of realizations tonight."

Jensen was so struck by Mikayla's beauty, by how happy he was that she was standing just inches away from him, that he just drank her in for a moment. "We had one hell of a talk. I guess people *can* surprise you. I never would have seen that one coming, though."

"It's funny—your brother Hudson used exactly that phrase the other day."

"I'm sure no one's more shocked at my father's turnaround than Hudson. Well, actually, that honor would go to my mother. She burst into tears when my dad presented her with her gift."

"I saw that. So sweet. And that locket was beautiful. I hope to buy something just like that and put a picture of my baby in it."

Jensen squeezed her hand. "You're going to be such a great mom. Your baby is lucky to have you. I'd put my hand on your tummy, but after seeing all those strangers do that to you in Vegas, I'll keep my hands to myself."

"Please don't," she whispered, taking both his hands and putting them on her belly. "You're not a stranger. You're my best friend."

He swallowed, so touched that he couldn't speak for a second. "Your best friend?" That was certainly how he felt about her, but he was too choked up to say so.

"Aren't you? Best friend I've ever had."

He pulled Mikayla into a hug. "You, too, Mik. My best friend."

"I sure am going to miss you after tomorrow."

Now he really couldn't speak. He waited a beat to catch his breath and get back his equilibrium. "I'm going to miss you, too."

His brothers and their wives wandered over then,

heaping plates with the incredible buffet selections. Gideon and his parents were deep in conversation by the bar. Gideon didn't know how lucky he was; an evolved father would be a hell of a lot easier to deal with.

Because this was his final night with Mikayla, Jensen wanted her all to himself, but just when he was about to scoot over and sneak her into the library for some privacy, his sisters-in-law grabbed her away again.

"You're really leaving tomorrow?" Walker asked when it was just the two of them standing by the window.

Jensen took a swig of his beer. "I am. My work here is done."

"Your work, yes. What about Mikayla?"

"Mikayla and I are just friends," he said. *Best friends.*

But there was nothing *just* about it. And Jensen knew it. Still, he'd be on that plane tomorrow, going back where he belonged.

Chapter Fourteen

The next morning, Jensen pulled up in front of Sunshine Farm. He was going to miss coming over here. He loved that yellow barn and seeing Luke and his hands working on the property and Eva staring up at the house and thinking out loud about renovation plans. And he loved seeing Mikayla so happy here, so at peace, among good friends. He knew she was safe and settled in here, even if Sunshine Farm wouldn't be a permanent home.

The day was going to be a scorcher even by late August's standards, but heat and humidity couldn't keep him in his air-conditioned car and away from seeing Mikayla for another second.

He grabbed the gift bag from the passenger seat, put the little box in his pocket and got out, the sun shining hot on his head and shoulders. He glanced up at Mikayla's second-story bedroom window and could see her standing there, watching him. She wasn't smiling.

She held up a hand and waved, and he waved back, gripped by sadness. How could this be the last time he'd see her? Sure, he'd be back in town every now and then to check on the progress of the distribution center and to see his brothers. But every now and then wasn't every day. Or every morning and night. *You're just getting sentimental*, he told himself. *Like Mikayla said—you're best friends. Of course you're going to miss her.*

He forced those thoughts away and sat on the porch steps, knowing Mikayla would come meet him outside. In a moment, the door opened and she came out, looking beautiful and glowing in her favorite sundress, the pale yellow one with the tiny blue bulldogs dotting the neckline and hem. She wore those crazy brown sandals that wrapped around her ankles. He'd miss those, too.

"How are you feeling this morning?" he asked, his gaze on her belly, which looked even bigger today.

"Like my best friend is flying far away," she said, trying to sit down beside him. She stopped halfway in her attempt, pushed off the top step and got herself up. "As if I can just plop down on a step anymore. Who am I kidding?"

He smiled and wrapped his arm around hers, reaching into his pocket and pulling out the gift box. "This is for you."

"What is it?" she asked.

"Only one way to find out."

She took off the lid, her eyes shining. "Oh, Jensen. It's a heart locket."

He took it out of the little box and opened it. "With

a tiny frame for a photo. You said you liked the one my dad gave my mom last night, so I wanted to get you one for your baby."

She put her arm around him and squeezed. "I will absolutely treasure this, Jensen. Thank you."

"You're welcome."

Mikayla unclasped it and put it around her neck. She touched the heart against her chest. "Where on earth did you find this in Rust Creek Falls on a Sunday morning?"

"I called a jewelry shop in Kalispell and bribed the owner to open before ten. I said it was an emergency."

She smiled and shook her head. "Of course you did."

He could sit here forever, Mikayla beside him. He didn't want to get up, didn't want to drive away, didn't want to leave her. But sitting here in this moment, in this world that wasn't his, was *easy*. There were no worries here. No commitments. No ties. Of course he felt like he could sit here forever. This wasn't real.

Time to go, Jones. "So I guess this is goodbye," he said.

She lifted her chin and looked out at the pastures. "I guess it is."

"Oh, and one more thing. I might have called your bank and made a deposit into your account just so you'd have some security financially. As your best friend, I don't expect you to give me a hard time about it. It's a drop in the bucket to me, so just accept it. Got it?"

He could see tears glistening in her eyes. "Got it."

"Oh, and I might have called Baby Bonanza and

arranged for them to redeliver all the items from your layaway and wish list on Monday morning. I insist."

Her face crumpled, and tears dripped down her cheeks. "If you insist," she whispered.

He pulled her into a hug, breathing in the sunshine-and-flowers scent of her. He wished he could be the man Mikayla deserved, but Jensen was too far gone, too shut down. He was a man who could make deals, buy things, make things happen—but he couldn't make himself into something he wasn't. Someone willing to love.

As he turned to go, he took one last look at Mikayla, then felt tears poking his own eyes.

Why did he feel like he was breaking his own heart here?

Was it supposed to work like that?

"I can't believe he really left," Eva said, shaking her head before she used the power drill in her hands to fasten the curtain rod hardware into the wall of the guest cabin.

Amy moved the low bookshelf between the windows more to the left, then more to the right. "Me, either. I know you said you were just friends. But clearly you were—are—much more."

"He never lied about his intentions," Mikayla said, picking up the package containing the shower curtain Eva had bought. She couldn't do much to help get the cabin ready for Josselyn, the new tenant, but she could hang up a shower curtain.

As she slipped the little silver hangers through the holes, she found herself daydreaming that she was decorating her own home—hers and Jensen's, that he'd come through the door any minute and start making them another delicious comfort-food dinner, hiding a piece of garlic bread for himself because she was known for devouring entire loaves.

Tears stung her eyes again, as they had all morning, and she blinked them back. He was gone, it was over, and she had to get over it. *Focus on the baby*, she told herself. *Tomorrow you'll be back at work and busy and each day will get a little easier.*

Eva and Amy appeared in the doorway of the bathroom. "You know what," Eva said, "let's finish decorating later. I think a little sugar therapy is in order. Let's go to Daisy's and—"

A pain, an intense tightening sensation, gripped her belly, and Mikayla grabbed her abdomen with one hand and clutched the towel rack with the other, grateful it was so well bolted into the wall. Another pain came fast and furious.

Oh, God, that hurt. She tried to breathe over it.

"Mikayla?" Eva said, alarm in her voice. "Are you okay?"

Amy was staring down at the floor by Mikayla's feet. "Oh, boy."

They all stared down—at the little puddle.

"My water must have broken!" Mikayla said just as another pain gripped her. "But I'm only thirty-two weeks!"

"Let's get you to the clinic. I'll call Dr. Strickland," Amy said.

Amy and Eva got on either side of Mikayla and ushered her to the door. As Amy helped Mikayla into the car, Eva rushed to the house to get their purses and the bag Mikayla had packed and ready for this moment.

Eva came flying out of the house, jumped in the car and peeled out. "Clinic, here we come. Hold on, Mikayla!"

"Ow, ow, ow," Mikayla said, breathing out the way she'd learned in the online video she'd watched on Lamaze. She'd been planning on starting Lamaze this week after work.

Too late.

Jensen's bags were packed. The family jet was fueled up for the trip. He'd said all his goodbyes around town. The only thing left to do was leave.

His chest tight, he loaded the car with his luggage and his parents' overnight bag, then they headed to the airport.

"I'll tell you, Jensen, you always manage to surprise me," his father said.

Jensen looked in the rearview mirror and his eyes almost popped out of his head. Was his father holding hands with his mother? In a car? Anywhere?

Holy Oklahoma, he was. His father and mother were holding hands.

Would wonders never cease?

He was about to say the very same to his dad, but it wouldn't be really true; his dad had never surprised him before yesterday. And now. Walker the Second was becoming the person Jensen thought he could be. A man who thought about others.

"How did I surprise you?" Jensen asked. "Do you mean the party?"

"I mean the pregnant woman. Mikayla," his father said. "I thought for sure you'd be on one knee in front

of her at the party, your family looking on as you proposed marriage."

On one knee? Proposing marriage? In front of his
family? The words kept repeating in his head as if he
couldn't understand their meaning. "Marriage? Why
would you think I'd propose?"

"She was there, wasn't she?" his dad said. "Why
else would you have invited her to a family-only party?
Because she's family."

She did *feel* like family.

"We're just very good friends," Jensen said, trying
to focus on the road and not Mikayla.

"If you say so, dear," his mother said. "At least we're
getting our Jensen back, Walker. But I do wonder at
what cost," she added on a sigh.

"What do you mean?" Jensen asked, glancing at
her in the rearview mirror.

"You'll be home, sure, but miserable. You know
what you're like when you're miserable. Stomping
around, unable to concentrate. Forget sleeping. Or
eating."

Actually, Jensen had no doubt all that was true. But
that was because he'd miss Mikayla. They'd spent a
lot of time together. They'd made love. They were…
best friends.

His heart squeezed. *Jensen, let me tell you the only
thing you need to know about women*, Davison had
said a few years before he'd died. *The only piece of
advice you'll ever need. Date any type of woman you
want. But marry your best friend.*

Who was talking about getting married? he thought,
his stomach churning. He wasn't *in* love. This wasn't
love. This was caring. This was friendship.

"Suddenly you want me to propose marriage to a Rust Creek Falls woman?" he asked, peering at his dad.

Oh, God. His parents were kissing!

His mother had just giggled!

"Of course we want you home in Tulsa, Jensen," his mother said as she freshened her lipstick. "But you're in love with Mikayla and she lives here, and so we figured you'd be staying. And she's going to have a baby in a few weeks, so naturally we assumed you'd be taking over as the baby's father."

In love with Mikayla...

Taking over as the baby's father...

"Mikayla and I are—"

"Just friends," his dad finished. "We know." Walker the Second shook his head.

Luckily, the conversation was over, because they'd arrived at the airport. Within minutes they were on board. This was it. No turning back now. He was going home, as he should be.

The moment the plane began taxiing, Jensen wanted to run for the exit door and jump off and go back to Mikayla. But he knew that was because he *couldn't*. The doors were closed. The plane was headed for the runway. In half a minute they'd be in the air.

And Mikayla would be lost to him. A memory.

He closed his eyes, trying to stop the constant thoughts of her, images of her, memories of her, but they wouldn't stop.

His phone buzzed with a text. From Hudson.

Mikayla's in labor! Eva's taking her to the clinic.

Every cell in his body froze. Then adrenaline flooded him. "Stop the plane!" Jensen shouted.

"What on earth?" his father bellowed.

"Mikayla's having her baby. She's in labor!" Jensen said, bolting up.

Jensen glanced out the window. The pilot had indeed turned the plane around and was heading back to their gate. Sometimes a private plane really did come in handy.

His mother smiled. "Mikayla is lovely, Jensen. You'll make a wonderful father."

He thought of Henry Stockton, running off with the pie. The little kid at Just Us Kids and his pink space alien. The boy trying to fly his foam airplane outside Daisy's Donuts. He thought of himself as a kid. And he tried to think of himself as a father, holding an infant against his chest, loving the baby so much, so intensely that he'd spontaneously combust.

No, no, no. Jensen was a solo practitioner.

So why are you rushing off the plane to be with her as she gives birth? Huh? Why?

"Mom, I'm not her boyfriend. I'm not going to be anyone's father. I just…care. I want to be there for her." Yes, that made sense. That was why. Phew. Okay.

"Men are always the last to know," his father said, sharing a grin with his wife.

"Know what?" Jensen asked, looking from his father to his mother.

"You'd better hurry and get to the hospital," his dad said. "Your mother was in labor with Gideon for hours, but you took no time at all. You just never know."

You never did, Jensen thought. Wonders really would never cease with this family. His father was talking about his wife's labor experiences the way he used to talk about mergers and acquisitions.

He hugged his parents and grabbed his bags, and the moment the plane stopped at the private gate, he raced back to the rental car window.

He had to get back to Rust Creek Falls pronto.

Chapter Fifteen

When Jensen came rushing into the Rust Creek Falls Clinic like a bat out of hell, Amy, Eva, Bella and Hudson were standing by the nurses' station, Amy asking for information.

"Is she okay? Is the baby okay?" Jensen shouted, panic exploding in his gut.

"She's in preterm labor but stabilized right now," Amy said. "The nurse won't let us go into her room." She leaned forward and whispered to Jensen, "She's filling in from the hospital in Kalispell—she doesn't know any of us, so we're getting the stranger treatment."

Over my dead body, Jensen thought. He had to be with Mikayla now. He *had* to be.

Because he did care—yes.

Because he did want to be there for her—yes.

But also because...he *loved* her. He loved her more than anything else in this world. There was no denying it anymore. He didn't want to, either.

He needed her.

And she needed him.

"Excuse me," Jensen said to the nurse. "I need to be with Mikayla Brown right away."

"Are you a family member?" the woman asked.

"Yes, I'm the baby's father," he said before he even realized what had come out of his mouth.

Many sets of eyes were staring at him. He felt his brother clapping him on the shoulder. He heard Amy and Eva gasp simultaneously.

"You heard the man," Bella said. "He's the baby's father. He has to get back there!"

The nursed bolted up. "Right this way!" She tapped on a door marked Labor and Delivery and entered. "Ms. Brown, the baby's father is here."

"What?" he heard Mikayla say. "But—"

Jensen plowed into the room and rushed to Mikayla's bed.

This time it was Mikayla who gasped. "But you're in the air. You're flying to Tulsa. You left."

He drew up a chair as close to the bed as possible, wishing the side rails weren't in his way. He took her hands and kissed them. "How could I leave you? I'm your baby's father. And I'm yours. And you're mine."

He realized the nurse was staring at them with confusion on her face. The woman checked Mikayla's IV, then left the room.

"You're mine?" she repeated.

He nodded. "I'm yours. And if you'll have me, I

want to be the baby's father. I *am* the baby's father. I feel like I am in every way possible."

"Oh, Jensen. I will have you. The baby will have you." She laughed and drew him close against her, and he buried his face in the scratchy white blanket covering her chest.

Another strange sensation came over him, a feeling of…completeness. Jeez, he really must love this woman. Because he'd sure never felt anything like that before. As if nothing was missing anymore.

And now that he finally got it, Mikayla's baby—their baby—might come way too prematurely. That could mean complications. He closed his eyes for a moment and shook his head to clear it. He needed to be strong for Mikayla.

"How can you be in labor?" he asked. "You're only thirty-two weeks along!"

"I know. But Dr. Strickland says this time I am definitely in preterm labor. It's too soon for the baby to come. If I deliver now, the baby could face complications."

Oh, God, exactly the word that had been echoing in his head a minute ago. *Complications. Complications. Complications.*

Tears filled her eyes.

"Mikayla, we'll face whatever those are together." He took her hands and held them and kissed her on the forehead. "We're in this together. You and me."

"We are?"

"We always were. Well, since the day we met. It just took me longer than you to realize it. I love you. I love this baby. And I'll move heaven and earth to protect you both."

Tears shone in her beautiful brown eyes. "I have absolutely no doubt of that last one."

"But you don't doubt my love for you, do you?"

"Hell, no," she said. "I knew you loved me days ago."

"Oh, did you now," he said with a grin.

What had his dad said? *Men are always the last to know.* How true.

"We're having a baby, Mik. We're having a *baby*! I hope that doesn't sound like I think I've been doing any of the work."

The laughter he loved listening to filled the room. "I love the sound of *we*," she said.

"Now and forever, Mikayla Brown."

A tap came on the door and Dr. Strickland entered the room. "Ah, so you *are* her birth partner." The doctor extended his hand.

Jensen shook it. "I am. For life."

Dr. Strickland smiled. "Good. Because you're going to be here for a while today. I'm going to hold off delivery as long as I can. But I don't know how long that will be. Mikayla, you might be having this baby today."

"Oh my gosh. I might be a mother today!" she said, the joy on her face clouded by worry. "Everything has to be okay. It just has to be."

Jensen squeezed her hand and nodded.

The doctor scanned her chart and hung it back on the far side of her bed. "Your condition is stabilized right now, so if you want to see friends, that's fine, just a bit at a time."

"I'll go let them know," Jensen said. "Mik, you're okay for thirty seconds?"

"As long as I know you're coming back."

"Always. Every day. Forever."

"Then go get the cavalry."

He smiled and left the room, Dr. Strickland following.

"Jensen," the doctor said, gesturing him aside.

"Everything is going to be okay, right?" Jensen said, fear churning in his stomach.

"Listen, I understand how you're feeling. I do. I can't guarantee you that everything will be okay. I just don't know that right now. She's early at thirty-two weeks."

"Oh, God," Jensen whispered.

"There can be complications, Jensen. I will have to prepare Mikayla for that—mentally and physically. I sure am glad you're there for her emotionally."

"I am. Whatever she needs."

"Good." For a moment, a look crossed the doctor's face that made Jensen think Drew Strickland was remembering something from his own past. "But I promise you this. I will do my absolute best by Mikayla."

Jensen nodded. *Me, too.*

Hazel Leigh Brown came into the world at 11:23 p.m., four pounds, two ounces, and tiny—but perfectly formed and healthy. She had a headful of silky brown wisps and slate-blue eyes. She looked exactly like her mother.

Jensen couldn't stop staring at his daughter—*his* daughter—in the little bassinet beside Mikayla's bed in the clinic. Mikayla was fast asleep, having given birth just over an hour ago, and though the labor was intensive and rough going at times, both mother and baby had come through beautifully.

Jensen had surprised himself by being one hell of a birth partner. At no time had he been in danger of passing out or running from the room. He was in this for the guts and the glory, the good times and bad, sickness and health—all that.

Dr. Strickland had said little Hazel's prognosis was excellent, but the preemie would be staying at the clinic under the staff's care for several weeks.

"I love you, Hazel Brown," he whispered to his little girl. "And if I have my way, your name is soon going to be Hazel Brown Jones. If your mother will consent to be my wife."

"Oh, I will," a groggy voice said.

Jensen jumped up from his chair in the corner and went over to Mikayla's bed. "I love Hazel so much, so fiercely, and I just met her," he said. "How is that possible?"

"Because you loved her all along. And besides, it's very, very easy to love a baby. Plus, look at her. She's the most beautiful baby I've ever seen."

"Like mother, like daughter."

"Like husband and father," she added.

He smiled. "You've changed my life, Mik. Completely. I don't know how I got so lucky, but I'll take it."

"When I'm sprung, maybe we can go celebrate where it all began—at Daisy's Donuts."

He reached over and smoothed back a lock of her hair, then kissed her tenderly on the mouth.

"Let's plan the wedding for when Hazel can attend," Jensen said. "She has to be part of it."

"Definitely," Mikayla said. "In the meantime, I'll stay at Sunshine Farm until Hazel is ready to leave the clinic for good."

"And I'll be scouring Rust Creek Falls for just the right house for our family of three. A family that will likely expand with kids and pets and lots of visiting relatives. Because you can bet my parents are going to rush back here to see their grandchild."

Mikayla beamed. "I love you, Jensen Jones."

"I love you, Mikayla Brown. And I love our daughter."

"So are your parents locking your brother Gideon in a tower, never to be seen by a Rust Creek Falls woman?" Mikayla asked.

"Honestly, they've done such a turnaround that I wouldn't be surprised if they sent Gideon to Rust Creek Falls under false pretenses—so that he'll be happy like his four brothers."

Mikayla laughed. "Wow, I just realized that Hazel will have four uncles—and three aunts so far. As an only child, I'm thrilled for her!"

"You think I like to buy gifts?" he said. "Just wait until they hear you had your baby. *Our* baby. Sunshine Farm isn't big enough to hold the truckload of baby gifts coming your way."

Mikayla smiled, her eyes drooping again. As he let the love of his life drift off, he thought about Mikayla telling him about a journalist dubbing Sunshine Farm the Lonelyhearts Ranch in an article because of the first guest's lovelorn status when she'd arrived. Then the second guest, Mikayla, had been a lonelyheart until he finally realized what she'd known all along.

That two was better than one.

And baby made three.

* * * * *

COMING SOON!

We really hope you enjoyed reading this book. If you're looking for more romance, be sure to head to the shops when new books are available on

Thursday
9th August